The PAKANA *Voice*

Tales of a War Correspondent from Lutruwita (Tasmania) 1814–1856

DR IAN BROINOWSKI

WITH CULTURAL ADVISOR
JIM EVERETT-PURALIA MEENAMATTA

Timbruna, Sunamena and Muntena the three Pakana people on the cover speak to us through time. They are our present, as their eyes peer into our souls and are no longer silent. Each one wishing to tell their story which is in part revealed within these covers. Consider for yourselves what they were feeling, thinking and wondering when the rytia, John Glover sat before them in 1832, observing, then looking down to scribble with his writing stick and paper before peeping again until he had finished.

The images he leaves us are both haunting and discomforting. They are of course seen from a Western perspective, unlikeness evident and in keeping with the tenor of this book. While reading the pages before you please keep these faces in the forefront of your mind to remind you of who the Pakana people are.

Sketchbook No. 43, 1805, 1831-1832 / John Glover; 1805, 1831-1832; CALL Dixon Library, State Library of New South Wales NUMBER DGA 47

*To those who practise the
noble art of journalism*

Contents

Foreword

Readers will be transported back to the colonial years of
Tasmania when W.C., a young British journalist arrives in
Van Diemen's Land. He sees first-hand the madness going
on in what could then be called chaos and lawlessness against the
Pakana and he decides to report from the victim's point of view. This
is the hidden story, the facts of history unleashed. Yet many white
Tasmanians today reside in their own form of denial, refusing to
believe that their ancestors committed atrocities against the Pakana
(Tasmanian Aborigines).

In cases of more recent immigrants who have been conditioned
to believe the massacres and other atrocities didn't happen, there is
an air of apathy towards Lutruwita's (Tasmania's) terrible history. Dr
Ian Broinowski has written this story by researching Van Diemen's
Land newspapers of the early 1800s and introducing W.C. as a witness
of the goings-on reported in newspapers at the time. W.C. not only

reports from the Aboriginal perspective, his journey sees him in love with a Tasmanian Aboriginal woman and he spends time with her and her families.

His adventure with Lowana and her clan is a story that could have been, for even after so much killing had gone on, killings from both black and white, Aborigines were still able to be friendly with some of the colonists. Broinowski, through W.C., has looked at the British colonists and how the world appeared to them over 200 years ago. Yet, from a Tasmanian Aboriginal perspective, these early years from when Lt John Bowen raised the Union Jack at Risdon Cove and events thereafter, there is a feeling of dread. We see the British colonists as savages, well experienced in colonising native peoples, taking what they wanted, killing natives freely in places around the world. The British had learned from the invasions of America, Canada, Africa, India, New Zealand and Australia was a killing ground without morals of any kind. *The Pakana Voice* with W.C.'s honesty and efforts to report injustices, exposes the savagery of British might, of no reasoning or good will and clever tricks to take it all at any price.

There is a satire to this story shown in how W.C. reports, not an attacking response to biased colonial reporters, nor letters to the editor from the *'Landed Gentry'* and farmers and their workers, not to exclude convicts, mostly calling for blood. Eventually there exists no harsher voice than those calling for genocide, as if the original owners of what was then called Van Diemen's Land were only animals roaming the land. All the while the killing by the colonists continued and letters to the editor were either seeking to save the Tasmanian Aborigines who had survived, or removing them all from existence as if they were pests. These are my people, my clans and families who had been here for over 42,000 years, so many killed and our people, the Pakana, we all still carry a living memory of the atrocities against our ancestors. Take for instance, the view expressed in *The Colonial Times and Tasmanian Advertiser* on Friday 6th July 1827, which was certainly persuasive:

> *We are thunderstruck when we consider these murders, at the supiness of the Government, in not instantly removing the blacks. We repeat what we have said ten times before, there never will be an end of such transactions till the natives are removed - removed, REMOVED."*

Obviously the blacks were the problem, fundamentally because they were there and used the land in a much different way to the British. W.C. joined a family of blacks, his Aboriginal friend in Rialim took him in and he met Lowana there and fell deeply in love. He became brutally aware of the British taking as they wished, killing because they could and he could see how much this was doing to the Aborigines while he camped out bush with them, hunting, moving camp, ever on the look out for whites who would hunt blacks for sport, he could feel the emotions and fears of the hunted. W.C. knew of course that the colonisers were from the British Empire, a world power of its time and he knew that justice would be unlikely to be done. He knew too that the very idea that a nation could simply take at will by force, knowing full well that natives had no guns, or other devices to protect themselves and that they could exploit new lands without being accountable.

The British came with guns and a foreign law to monopolise and legitimise their ill-conceived intentions. Raising the British flag, the *Butcher's Apron* to the Irish, gave them a self-indulgent legitimate right under their law to treat Van Diemen's Land as British soil. They brought a hierarchy with them that was entirely unheard of in Pakana society, with a pecking order from the very poor to the very rich and the power of richness. Nevertheless, W.C. cannot leave these events being reported in the newspapers unchallenged. He is careful in how he reports on events already in the newspapers and he reports about losses of life, Pakana emotions and injustice by the British from the Pakana point of view. You, the reader, will learn that Tasmania has a Black history, hardly told in its day, but now this unravelling of hidden stories exposes the lies and injustices of ongoing colonial governance. The Pakana now believe that the hidden stories of the past are why today the Tasmania Government continues to dominate Pakana rights on our own land, seas and waterways.

There is much to learn here in *The Pakana Voice*, Broinowski is a writer of much more than history, or of stories about people of the past, he has an amazing ability to see into the emotions of the period, black and white. The research here is exposed in what the colonial newspapers published and through the hand of Dr Ian Broinowski, we learn from W.C. about the emotions and feelings in the Pakana as they seek their survival from this holocaust that came under British sails.

Will we all learn to share, to have a peace based on the good of contemporary Lutruwita (Tasmanian) society, will we ever see this island state being proud of its achievements to reconcile our differences and create a better future for generations to come? This is the continuing story, you will find it yourself, but only inside yourself for there is no other place for it to exist. By reading *The Pakana Voice* one might hope that you, the reader, will come to understand whatever you didn't before and see that the wrongs depicted in this book are the spine of injustice against Pakana today. This is a must read story, written for leisurely reading, a no rush story that will keep bringing you back to it. Enjoy, there are few books that resonate so much in this way with the unknown in history and perhaps a wisp of how we can all make a change.

Jim Everett-puralia meenamatta
Cape Barren Island, Tasmania.

· ·

JIM EVERETT-PURALIA MEENAMATTA *was born on Flinders Island in 1942, Jim Everett left primary school at 14 to start work. His diverse lifestyle includes fifteen years at sea, three years in the Australian Army, and fifty years formal involvement in the Aboriginal Struggle. His written works include plays, political papers and short stories, and writings published in ten major anthologies. Jim's other work includes television documentary and theatre production. He now lives on Cape Barren Island, often working away from home with various cultural arts programs including developing projects with Aboriginal community artists, as a Writer-in-Residence in Albany WA (2015), and in Wollongong (2015), and finishing a novel for editing. Most recently Jim has initiated the We're Here project in collaboration with Contemporary Art Tasmania, exhibited in Salamanca Arts Centre's 2017 major exhibition Proof of Life, joined the Board of GASP!, and was an associate producer on the Nightingale film production.*

Preamble

As I leaf through the yellowing, faded parchment of W.C.'s scribbled text, on every page a cacophony of voices scramble for attention. His writing is elegant, long easy strokes depicting a character of passion and lover of the written word. Each voice is vying for attention and wanting to be heard. The authors may have lived two centuries ago, but still they appear very much alive and exude vitality and passion for the topic of their attention.

Their articles and letters to the editor, along with proclamations by the governor, are all there for us to read and immerse ourselves in their world. The arrival of the British and their early years in Tasmania are complete with triumphs of extraordinary human survival and achievement in an isolated settlement with its nearest neighbour many days away across treacherous seas. But for the Aboriginal inhabitants, the Pakana people, the years from 1803 to the 1850s were devastating and the brutal reality of their story is only now really being fully revealed and critiqued.

This book examines the way the British viewed these events through the newspapers of the day. Written only from their perspective, it provides a fascinating insight into the thinking of the day and is also an interesting case study of the power of the press. The similarities with today's world are remarkable. Reading some of the editorials and letters from the time of British colonisation of Tasmania, you could be forgiven for thinking that what you were reading had been written by contemporary reporters, commentators and writers of letters to the editor. Substitute asylum seekers, Muslims, Aboriginal affairs or just about any currently highly charged topic and all the key players are still there - racists, libertarians, those with vested interests, land grant holders, the military, business and government. Choose almost any of the letters in W.C.'s book and compare the underlying values, tone and writing style with today's media commentary.

W.C. also looks at the question of whether the press reports the news or makes it. During the 1827–32 'Black War', it is hard to argue the reports are in any way impartial. Most of the written accounts are palpably charged with emotional arguments as they extol their own point of view. Just as today, it is hard to imagine the public and government were not influenced by the power of these words and sentiments. For instance, take the view of the *Colonial Times and Tasmanian Advertiser* Friday 1 December 1826, page 2 which was certainly persuasive:

We make no pompous display of Philanthropy — we say unequivocally, SELF DEFENCE IS THE FIRST LAW OF NATURE. THE GOVERNMENT MUST REMOVE THE NATIVES — IF NOT, THEY WILL BE HUNTED DOWN LIKE WILD BEASTS and DESTROYED!

It was this view that eventually prevailed: the Pakana were taken to Wybalenna on Flinders Island. Does this tirade sound familiar? Just think about the role of contemporary media in relation to off-shore processing of asylum seekers and the islands used for detention.

Who were these people so willingly and avidly expressing their views in the tiny, remote community of Tasmania? Well, they were white of course. As W.C. continually points out, the shadowy absence of news from the Pakana is conspicuous. The writers were all British, even those born on the island, who in their hearts and minds remained citizens of the Mother Country.

Their gender was male with the exception of a lone female poet, Mary Leman Grimstone, but her voice was not heard until the late 1840s, although I suspect she wrote *The Natives Lament* anonymously in 1826. Keep in mind also that there were very few women in the Colony during the early years and most of those were convicts who probably had little time or inclination for such esoteric niceties as writing to newspapers, even if they had been able to read and write.

Obviously, the contributors and readers were literate and hence a minority in the mainly convict population who were by and large illiterate.

British society at this time was uncompromisingly class-ridden, with rigid rules relating to social status and acceptability. The Tasmanian majority, being convicts on the lowest rung, would have had little opportunity to express their views on paper although there were exceptions, most notably Andrew Bent, ex-convict, who became a publisher and advocate for press freedom and a mentor to W.C.

The government was run along military lines with stringently enforced tiers of authority from the top down and it seems unlikely that those within the lower ranks would have had much freedom to express their views in the local rag. Ex-military officers though, appear to have had no such reluctance and are often featured in either newspaper reports or in letters and articles penned in their own hand.

'Respectable society' was certainly small and cloistered from much of the surrounding disagreeableness and mainly fed its self-perpetuating beliefs from within. Shades of today, where clusters on social media devour their own particular fantasies about all kinds of issues and ideas, with no thought of looking beyond the narrow bounds of their assemblage. Although, it should be said that the newspapers of the period did provide a wide variety of news from overseas as well as science, poetry and other interesting topics which are not the focus of this book. Remember too, newspapers were quite expensive and bought mainly through subscription. It was not until much later that the advent of the rolling presses made newspapers available to the masses.

The authors were most likely to have been Protestant: Church of England, Presbyterian, Church of Ireland, Calvinist, Baptist, Episcopalian, Congregationalist and so on. Most Catholics at this time were convicts, often Irish, who'd emanated from situations of dire poverty and would most likely have lacked the necessary literacy skills. Nor would their views have been appreciated, especially as Ireland remained in a state of permanent civil unrest. Many Irish rebels were amongst the convict population.

To sum up: The Press of Van Diemen's Land was fashioned solely by a minority of a small population who were British, white, male, Protestant, literate, of high social standing and generally living comfortably by the standards of the day. In other words, a swarm of macho WASPs [White Anglo-Saxon Protestant]. This cohort was heavily influential in the events of the day and that included the policy and actions related to the Pakana people.

What then were the values and beliefs which drove these people in their everyday lives? Clearly there was some diversity of thought which is reflected so eloquently in the newspapers. However, it is possible to offer generalised perspectives to which most adhered.

First and foremost, they were British. That meant they belonged not only to the most powerful nation on earth, at that time, but were part of the ruling elite. Many had fought against Napoleon or in other theatres of war throughout the Empire and believed they had an inherent right to rule over all other nations and cultures they encountered. This meant of course the land they were now standing on was in principle as British as Hyde Park and they had every right to occupy it and to use it as they pleased. They were both legally and morally entitled to take possession of the Island.

Coupled with this, their status as white males provided an unequivocal sense of superiority which was itself supported by their cultural norms. White supremacy was a given and unquestioned.

They knew their social standing well and relegated the majority of humanity to positions beneath them. This is how nature and God had intended it to be and in their minds this belief was unchallengeable. Such was their unassailable conviction of the righteousness of the social to assign others to lower rank and status. Women, the lower classes, convicts and, of course, Aborigines, were subject to the constraints of this social order.

The tenets of Protestant Christianity were also unimpeded and absolute. Their God and the teachings of the Bible were the only road to salvation; nothing else could be countenanced as a way of understanding the Universe and life beyond. Their version of Christianity dictated and reinforced the preordained pecking order, where everyone and everything had its place, reinforcing their own position of pre-eminence. Seen in a prudential light this was quite a useful proposition.

I am not questioning or judging these people or their set of values and beliefs. That is not what this book is about, but rather it is trying to explain the perspective of the people who wrote so fulsomely and had such a profound impact on the lives of others, namely the Pakana people, in the events which shaped the early British Colony of Van Diemen's Land.

What is extraordinary is the number of newspapers which appeared during W.C.'s working career as a special correspondent. Each had their own point of view, beliefs and doctrines which they espoused unashamedly, making for fascinating reading. Below is the most accurate list I could find although undoubtably there are more to be found:

NEWSPAPERS IN VDL

* *Van Diemen's Land Gazette and General Advertiser 1810–1814, George Clarke*
* *Derwent Star and Van Diemen's Land Intelligencer, Hobart, 1810-1812*
* *Van Diemen's Land Gazette, 21 May 1814*
* *The Hobart Town Gazette and Southern Reporter, 1 June 1816-13 Jan 1821 Andrew Bent*
* *Hobart Town Gazette and Van Diemen's Land Advertiser. 20 Jan 1821- 12 Aug 1825*
* *Hobart Town Gazette 1828 James Ross and George Terry*
* *Colonial Times and Tasmanian Advertiser, Hobart 1825–1827 Andrew Bent and RL Murray. Later Henry Melville*
* *Tasmanian and Port Dalrymple Advertiser Launceston, 1825*
* *Herald of Tasmania, Hobart 1827-1839*
* *Hobart Town Courier 1827–1859 (Break in 1839)*

* *Colonial Advocate and Tasmanian Monthly Review and Register, Hobart 1828*
* *Colonial Times, 1828-1857 Andrew Bent, R L Murray*
* *Launceston Advertiser, 1828 JP Fawkner Hobart 1837-1840*
* *Austral-Asiatic Review (bimonthly), 1828 R L Murray*
* *Launceston Advertiser, Launceston, 1829-1846*
* *Cornwall Press and Commercial Advertiser, 1829*
* *Independent, Launceston, 1831-1835*
* *Colonist and the Van Diemen's Land Commercial and Agricultural Advertiser, Hobart 1832-1834*
* *Trumpeter, Hobart 1833-1850*
* *True Colonist: Van Diemen's Land Political Dispatch and Agricultural and Commercial Advertiser, Hobart 1834-1844, Gilbert Robertson*
* *People's Horn Boy, Hobart 1834*
* *Cornwall Chronicle Launceston, 1835-1880*
* *Van Diemen's Land Monthly Magazine, Hobart 1835*
* *Horton Herald, Hobart 1835-1838*
* *Independent and Cornwall Chronicle, 1835-1818, WL Goodwin*
* *Bent's News and Tasmanian Three-Penny Register, Hobart 1836-1837*
* *Tasmanian Weekly Dispatch 1839-1841*
* *Hobart Town Courier and Van Diemen's Land Gazette, Hobart 1839-1840*
* *Hobart Town Advertiser, Hobart 1839-1861*
* *Tasmanian Weekly Dictator, Hobart 1839*
* *Courier, Hobart 1840-1843*
* *Colonial Morning Advertiser and Colonial Maritime Journal, 1841-?*
* *Van Diemen's Land Chronicle, Hobart 1841*
* *Launceston Examiner, 1842*
* *Launceston Examiner: Commercial and Agricultural Advertiser, Launceston 1842-1899*

* *South Briton and Tasmanian Literary Journal, Hobart 1843*
* *Teetotal Advocate, Hobart 1843*
* *True Catholic. Tasmanian Evangelical Miscellany, Hobart 1843-?*
* *True Colonist, Gilbert Robertson*
* *The Tasmanian and Austral-Asiatic Review, Hobart 1844-1845*
* *Spectator and V.D.L. Gazette, Hobart 1844-1847*
* *Hobart Town Herald, Hobart 1845-1846*
* *Evening Star, Hobart 1845-1846*
* *Hobart Town Herald and Total Abstinence Advocate, Hobart 1846-1847*
* *Hobart Town Herald, or, Southern Reporter, 1846*
* *Britannia and Trades Advocate, Hobart 1846-1851*
* *The Tasmanian and Southern Literary and Political Review*
* *Hobarton Guardian or True Friend of Tasmania 1847-1854*
* *Guardian, or, True Friend of Tasmania, Hobart 1847-1854*
* *Irish Exile and Freedom Advocate, Hobart 1850-1851*
* *Standard of Tasmania, Hobart 1851*
* *Hobarton Mercury, Hobart 1854-1857, George A. Jones and John Davies (became The Mercury)*

I hope this sets the stage for the theatre about to unfold through the voices still living from the past and set out so eminently in W.C.'s dusty and crumpling folios. Let us not pretend that this is easy to read: It is not. The pages are filled with heartache, human loss and trauma on both sides. Should you read it? Maybe, maybe not, but only you will know when you are ready. I hope you find it revealing and that it adds just a little to your understanding of humanity in all its wondrous paradoxes.

Ian Broinowski

IAN BROINOWSKI, *PhD, MEd, BA(Soc Wk), BEc, Dip Teach, worked as an advanced skills teacher in children's services at TAFE Tasmania in Hobart, Australia for many years. Ian has a background in Economics, Social Work and Education. He has taught in a wide range of subjects in aged care, disability services, children's services, community and youth work. He worked for a period as a house parent in Bristol, England and Northern Ireland. He has also held positions as a child welfare officer in Tasmania and NSW. He taught with Curtin University and UTAS and is a member of the Health and Medical Ethics Committee with the University of Tasmania. Ian's publications include Child Care Social Policy and Economics, (1994) Creative Childcare Practice: Program design in early childhood, (2002) and Managing Children's Services 2004. In 2013 he presented a paper at the Future of Education Conference in Florence Italy on the 'Use of Humour in Online Teaching'.*

ADVICE TO READERS

If you are the sort of person who likes to know where fact and fiction begin and end before commencing a book may I suggest you read 'Author's Notes' at this point. They are located at the end of the book.

If on the other hand you have a whimsical nature and are happy to mesh the two in your cognisance, then read the notes at a later time.

Chapter One

Inconsequential Jottings

I am a war correspondent and have spent much of my adult life covering the war in Lutruwita, between the Pakana people and the British Empire. Beyond the bounds of this small Island, few people know of the events which occurred there soon after the British arrived in 1803. The island I am talking about was named Van Diemen's Land by Abel Janszoon Tasman, the first European to accidently 'discover' the land in 1642 and who named it 'Anthoonij van Diemenslandt' after his boss in the Dutch East India Company. Colloquially, it was called Tasmania by the early colonialists. Ironically Tasman never actually set foot on the island of his namesake.

I am in what is euphemistically called my twilight years and, like so many others, have time to reflect about my life, my successes, failures and regrets. Most of all, it allows me time to reflect upon what I wrote and felt about this war which so dominated my life. I am alone now, except for my scruffy old dog Bent, whose loyalty and empathy attuned to my every unpredictable sentiment is well beyond anything another human being could offer. He is named after one of my few heroes and friends Andrew Bent, whose fight for freedom of the press in the 1820s is legendary. Although he succeeded in his cause, he died a pauper many years later.

My work, my quest for the next story and the thrill of the chase has, I fear, proven an impediment to creating any long-lasting human companionship. That is not to say there have not been times of love, lost and broken hearts as well and a few intimacies and fleshly pleasures over the years; even, dare I admit it, the occasional visit to establishments of dubious reputation. Now all that is left is a hint of a smile when my thoughts roam into those far recesses of my memory.

The pseudonym I adopted was W.C., not to be confused with Water Closet, as some of my close friends and detractors suggest! My true name and identity I shall not reveal. The reason is simple and contradictory. My professional writing is for all to read, but I am an innately private person. Who I am is of little consequence, but what I have reported on and written about is. The paradox is I wish to know all about others while reticent to reveal myself. Maintaining anonymity leaves you, the reader, with only what I write, the words and thoughts which are there for all to digest, critique and if they feel so inclined, to use as dunny paper or burn as kindling to keep warm. At least that way it will be of some use to humanity.

I now spend my days with Bent in thought and my nights in dread. We two sit together in my attic room, surrounded by books, a small fire for company, while I sip a delightful malt Whisky into the early hours and try to evade sleep. I wish so much to dodge the nightmares, the faces, the people, the children and blood which invade my consciousness as I close my eyes in the vain hope of finding some peace. My life's work has been to report on the things I have witnessed:

not only battles but the results of war and the human misery it dishes out so readily. I see the agony of people crying, the dying and the dead, both black and white. I relive the sight of the many spears protruding from white corpses; the battered skulls of victims beaten down with waddies: white men, girls and mothers as well as animals. I see the blood from gun shots and the black men and women, mothers with their children, fallen or crumple to the ground.

My dilemma is how best to relate this saga without affecting the self-afflicted pomposity of men of my age whose opinions are irrelevant and meaningful only to those of similar ilk. However, I do possess stacks of twined old newspaper cuttings, letters and articles, all relating to the events of this time. After a long conversation with Bent, whose contribution was to turn over on his back to gain more heat from the fire, we agreed my best approach was to offer an account as reported by the newspapers of the day. This is my domain. I am well acquainted with the quirks, fragilities and extraordinary strengths of newspapers. I have grappled with difficult issues such as: do they simply record the news or create it? Can editors mould public opinion and hence sway decision-makers to their point of view? In this book I have recorded many of the events, ideas, recriminations and pontifications expressed in print from the first accounts in 1814 in the *Van Diemen's Land Gazette and General Advertiser* to the present day *Hobarton Mercury* in 1855 when the European name Van Diemen's Land changed to Tasmania. Although I indulge in some artistic licence by adding background information, or, at times presenting a different perspective on events as they revealed themselves in the magic of print.

This is my life now. I live with the moral guilt of one whose senses were once awash with terror: I saw, smelt, touched, heard and tasted death and suffering, whilst, to my shame, standing aside, disengaged.[i] For I was there to tell the story and pass on the news of what was happening both to others of the time and for generations to come. My weapons in this endeavour were parchment, ink, quill pens and a penchant for languages; such simple things and yet so incredibly influential.

I wonder at times how I survived at all. So many friends who lived close to home safely with family and loved ones have left this earth through illness or accident while danger and serious risk were so much part of my life and yet here I still am. I was fashioned with a tall, spindly physique and with an apparently reverential countenance, the latter of which always struck me as ironic, considering my intense aversion to religion and Christianity especially. Perhaps my lankiness was a form of protection in the bush as I was seen as little threat to natives or whites alike. (Also, I carried no gun, an instrument I never learned to use nor have the desire to.) My demeanour is unimposing and I am capable of listening quietly. For the Aborigines, I was their story teller when no others were willing to present their side in the Colonial newspapers of the day. This they valued, wanting their story to be heard for evermore.

One way to confront my demons is to do what I do best: write. This account is my confession, my healing and my legacy. Perhaps it is a result of pure egoism and has little to do with anything as noble as writing history books or penning an autobiography, but with these musings, I blunder towards death in the hope that someday, perhaps in a century or two, someone will find my scribbles and use them wisely. Once completed they will lie dormant in a nondescript trunk in my attic until I decide their destiny.

Where to begin? Perhaps a little about me to help you to visualise the context and the world into which I was born and reveal how I came to be so captivated with the terrible events which were to unfold before my eyes in Lutruwita.

My life and tastes are modest, although I appreciate quality in both company and Whisky. I was born on the Ides of March, 1795 with a minimal amount of fuss and bother to my parents. They seemed to regard children as a mere distraction, easily observed with an orbiting peripheral vision while ensconced in their reading matter of the moment. Any further exertion was construed as an imposition. Although I sometimes wondered if such a prodigious birthdate engendered my pervasive sense of foreboding.

So it was that my dear younger sister Sophia and I grew up in an all too quiet and reserved family in Martock, a small, quintessential English village in Somerset, South West England. Our house, "The Manse", resonated with age and a sense of permanence. It overlooked the square and was comfortably situated beside the church, All Saints, our twelfth century place of worship.

The front part of the house, with thick walls for summer coolness, was built in 1540, whilst the back with its large, flag-stone kitchen and a fireplace I could stand in until I was ten years old, was erected in 1640. The side house was a more recent addition, dating from 1740.

At the very top of the old house, up two flights of stairs and an erratic ladder of sorts, was my room, known as the 'Bridge' from days of longing to be a sea captain. With its attic profile, small fireplace and a paned window overlooking the village, I could immerse myself into whatever fantasy or book I chose. Even today it remains my retreat from a world which I view with an ever-increasing sense of despair.

Attached to the window sill is a precarious-looking flag pole pointing at an angle from the house. Inculcated with the patriotism of youth from my school and despite my parents' displeasure, I took on a daily dedication to raising the flag of Empire at dawn and lowering it at dusk. I would even salute! The pole is now bereft of adornment and purpose other than as a resting place for our family of wood pigeons. My passion for our glorious civilization has waned somewhat during the intervening years.

While not poor, neither could we be called prosperous. My father's fluency in both ancient Greek (specialising in the "Koine" dialect) and Armenian, provided few prospects for returning an income. He ran a small bookstore called Rare Books of Antiquity and Assorted Curios on the High Street and, while he seemed to spend an inordinate amount of time there, the actual demand for his wares was modest. However, he did retain a steady stream of Latin students whom he regarded as nuisances who took up too much of his precious reading time. To this day I fail to understand how they managed to keep our maid and cook for so many years, but our home would have been in a shambles and we would most certainly have starved without them. The ramifications of my mother stepping into the kitchen does not bear thinking about.

Both my parents were rich in mind and purchasing books took priority over mere basics such as food or coal for the fire. I remember once we ate oatmeal and cabbage for three weeks after my mother spent all our food money on a classical Greek version of Homer's *Iliad*. No one questioned this or thought twice about such priorities in our family. Each lived in their own world of literature and quest for knowledge. On one occasion I tentatively hinted they might like to read Jane Austen's latest work. She was little-known at the time, but her works were well received. Without so much as a glance from the book she was reading on the numerical symbols in ancient Hebrew my mother disdainfully commented that she had no interest in light romantic fiction filled with young women who thought only of marriage. I caught a conspiratorial look from my sister and we silently agreed it would be politic to read our treasured *Pride and Prejudice* in the privacy of our room. Little wonder I inherited such desires and passions for all things intellectual while acquiring few essential skills for living.

I went to a typical boys' public school that offered little other than luke-warm scholarship, rugger and ways to dispense one's talents with minimal effort. One useful trait I did acquire was the art of blending into the background and remaining as unobtrusive as possible, thus relieving me of being called out or chastised for inactivity. Perhaps this is where I learned to observe and study the quirks and quandaries of human nature.

Luckily my home countered this bleakness with light and learning. As a result, after leaving school I managed to gain work as a Printer's Devil or in other words a general dog's body with the *Royal Cornwall Gazette*, our local newspaper. Predictably my inept dexterity resulted in scattering the completed forme holding all the carefully prepared typesetting for page two of the next day's paper at the feet of Mr. Stanley Press, Master Printer, whose pugnacious disposition led him to bellow, with accompanying invectives, that I had the finesse of a water hog and to leave his printing room forthwith! I concluded from his remarks that perhaps I should leave printing to others and apply my energies to writing. I left to indulge my appetite for scribing books about love and betrayal, sacrifice and heroism and other assorted passions of youth, but with little success.

Then I discovered and became enthralled with the writings of Henry Robinson, Special Correspondent for the *Times*. He wrote from the Napoleonic battle fronts in Galicia, Spain and the Peninsula War.[ii] As a young man I found his writing inspirational and exciting. It set my career into its inevitable orbit. Might I have gone in this direction had I known the sacrifices I would have to endure? No room for love or family and ending in the terrible state of mind I find myself in today.

The answer is yes; our destiny is designed by our personal disposition and the world in which we find ourselves. Mine was one of quest, inquisitiveness and seeking adventure. I pushed myself to extremes both physically and emotionally, endowed with the unfortunate attribute of seeking and writing the truth, which, of course, is problematic. As I was to find out early in my career truth is a matter of perception and while the facts may be absolute, interpretation is not. To illustrate the point, take the article from the *Tasmanian* published on Christmas Eve, 1830 which reported: "The ABORIGINES – Two of Mr Allardyec's shepherds were last Sunday attacked and speared by these *savages*, at the Lagoon of Islands." It could have been written "… were last Sunday attacked and speared by Aborigines, at the Lagoon of Islands." Different intimation entirely.

This became my mantra: to try my best to stick to the facts and, in some cases, to deliberately present an alternative explanation to encourage my readers to question their own prejudices and consciences. So began my journey. It was launched with the small amount of money I had saved and a tiny inheritance of thirty six pounds, fifteen shillings and three pence from a distrait Aunt whom I vaguely remember as having squinty hazel eyes and smoking foul smelling Turkish cigarettes. I know it's a cliché in most nineteenth century novels that all young men partaking in an adventure inherit from their Aunt, but in my case it's true and I was very grateful. Still, I needed to work sometimes for my passage, doing anything from scribing for the officers, to scrubbing floors and dishes and sending off articles to newspapers in the vain hope they would publish them and, more importantly, pay!

I left Gravesend, London on the *Princess Charlotte* on a warm summer's day on 30th June 1816. I remember seeing my parents together on the docks, my mother with handkerchief and father clutching a copy of Lord Byron's *Hebrew Melodies*, one finger holding his place, while my little sister visibly sniffed back tears, defiantly holding her head high. She was on the cusp of womanhood. I wondered what I would encounter upon my return and how our lives would unfold for us in the years to come.

My interest in the plight of Aboriginal island populations subjected to British invasions flickered into being when I landed in Colombo, Ceylon a few weeks later on my way to Australia. The Väddas are the original inhabitants and forest dwellers of the Island of Ceylon and their lives, culture and very existence became embroiled in intense battles and conflict with their new rulers. The English newspapers were full of harrowing stories of white settlers being robbed, wounded or killed and of property destroyed by these 'savages'. My restless and unforgiving inquisitiveness sought to find out more, but what I really wanted to learn about was the other side of the story. What had the Väddas to say? What were their perspectives, beliefs and desires in this conflict? I spent much time with the tribes, learning a little of their language, culture and views on the British incursion of their lands. Their spears, bow and arrows were little match for European guns and military obduracy. In 1817, a year after I arrived, they rebelled against the British with predictable consequences. I was blooded in this war; it was where I learned my trade. I learned to watch, remain objective and, hardest of all, to stay detached and be an observer, a recorder of events as they occurred and a scribe for a newspaper that readers might devour briefly over their eggs and toast in London.

Mr. Charles Stevens meets some Veddas and conciliates them. [The Graphic, November 26, 1887.]

GOOD
INN

HOPE INN

Chapter Two

First Visit to Lutruwita,
October 1818 – January 1820

My arrival in October 1818 from Port Jackson on the brig *Jupiter* was of little consequence, as I had no friends or family in Nipaluna, or in Hobart Town, as the British liked to called it. It was especially quiet being a Sunday and after my fellow passengers Mrs. G. F Read and Mr. Edgar Luttrell parted from me I was left alone to explore the town.

There are many descriptions of the colony at this time which are far better than I can offer. I will not bore you with my idle thoughts and impressions other than to say the port appeared small, although fiercely focussed, associated with a village with some fine buildings already standing strong and others in the process of being built. The town presented an air of permanence and some sense of planning. These people were evidently here to stay!

After my first night in modest accommodation above the Hope and Anchor Hotel near the wharf in Macquarie Street, I set off early on a blustery cold morning to locate the newspaper rooms. Leaving the tavern, I took a little time to gain my bearings. In front of me was a tributary flowing leftward past the Bond Store buildings to the waters of the Derwent. Beyond these a small island lay connected by a muddy spit with convicts labouring to bring goods and passengers to the dry land. Ships were scattered in all directions with small boats busily unloading all manner of stores for the small colony.

Turning and looking upward I was struck by the majesty of light and colour emanating from a wide, particularly blue sky and reflecting from the power of the mountain in purple, deeply inviting shades of blue and black. I was in awe of this place. Never had I experienced such a feeling of openness, exhilaration and apprehension all at the same time.

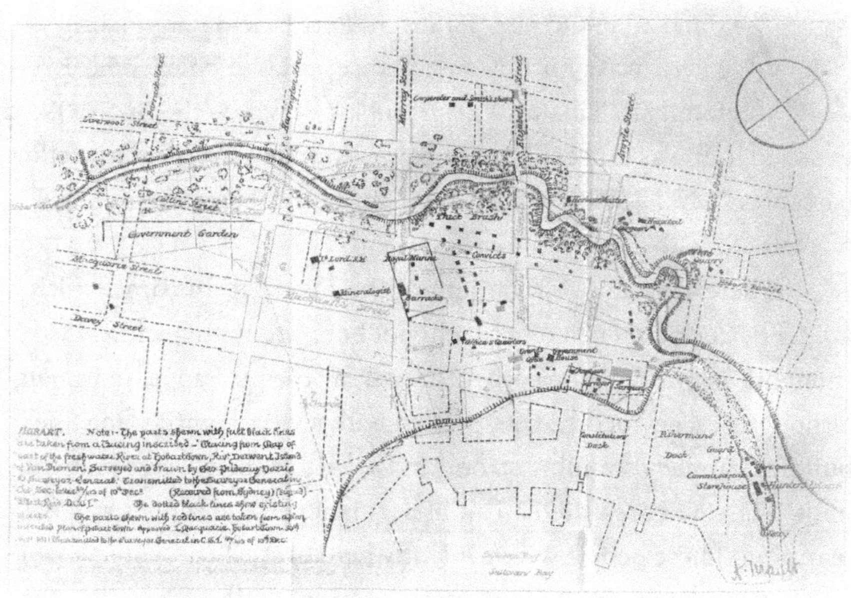

Map From: Walker, James Backhouse (1889) The founding of Hobart by Lieutenant Governor Collins. Tasmanian Library

As I stepped around puddles from last evening's rain and assorted dung and other foul-smelling muck, I noticed with interest several Aboriginal people about the town largely being left alone by the local residents. I wondered what was in their hearts and minds as they walked in this alien world. The paper at this time had the uninspiring name of *The Hobart Town Gazette and Southern Reporter*, perhaps because it was essentially a voice for the government and had most likely been named by a colourless public official.

Its premises were situated not far from my place of residence in a rough-cut timber structure and cottage with a wood slate roof. It was here I was to meet Andrew Bent, the erstwhile convict printer and now editor and printer.

Tentatively, I knocked on the open door. When I received no response I ventured further in until seeing a man a few years older than myself, whom I assumed to be Bent, deep in concentration. I waited with patience and silence watching him at work. The familiar aroma of ink, paper and smudged printers was reminiscent of my less than favourable experiences as a Printer's Devil with the truculent Mr Press. Bent held in his left hand a composing stick, an oblong frame about eight inches long by two in height. It had sides of about half an inch along the bottom and right-hand side. To the left was a sliding mount. He was standing in front of a cabinet with an upper tray consisting of small compartments holding movable type for each letter in capitals. A similar tray for lower case letters was stationed just below. I was surprised at the rag tag collection of type set he had and incredulous that he could even manage to arrange a newspaper with such limited equipment. It was a far cry from even the vast array of choices at the *Royal Cornwall Gazette*!

To his right was a layout of the two-page newspaper in handwriting. Bent was selecting each letter individually and carefully constructing the words and a line of text. He then moved to another table where the half-completed forme lay and inserted the newly created sentence. Watching him at work and with my scant experience of printing I knew this man to be a master at his trade and deserving of his reputation. I also knew he would be working long into the night to finish just this page but even so I could not help marvelling at the miracle of the printing press.

At this point Andrew turned his attention to me and was welcoming and generous in his accommodation of my need to gain as much information as I could when I enquired about what had been occurring on the island with regard to the Pakana people. He showed me where the back copies were stored and so, ensconced between stacks of costly, poor quality rice and bamboo paper recently arrived from China, I carefully surveyed the room.

It was located at the back of the room beside a fireplace containing a still smouldering log from the night before and radiating little enough heat to warm a rather large, well fed ginger cat reposing comfortably on an oft used chair. Stirring ever so slightly he gave me an unequivocal feline stare making it very clear he was not to be disturbed. Taking the hint, I perched myself on the nearest wooden box and began to read.

Occasionally I would look up to see Andrew hard at work and allow my gaze to drift across to the printing press, now still and waiting for all to see it work its wonders. Once the forme had been lowered into place and secured tightly with ink dabbed onto the surface, individual sheets of costly paper would be laid and the long arm pulled to one side with all the strength a man could muster, only to be released and allow the paper to reappear dressed in words, ideas and the joy of written language.

After some time, a young woman appeared with dark complexion, long flowing brown hair and chatting incessantly in a broad Irish accent. Carrying a very young infant in her arms and followed by a convict servant with a tray with cups, tea and freshly cooked bread. She bustled across to me smiling and introduced herself as Mrs Bent, known to all as Mary. Without waiting for comment, she turned to my contented companion saying:

"Will you look at you Daniel, sleeping all the while with our visitor is sitting on a box!"

At which point Andrew arrived, swooped the indignant cat into his arms, sinking into what was clearly his chair and allowing Daniel to settle once again on his lap. Apparently, he was named after Daniel O'Connell the famous Irish Freedom fighter.

He and Mary were clearly in love, demonstrated with an abundance of affection a sight unfamiliar and a little unsettling to me. Recently married and with baby Elizabeth they soon made me feel part of the family. A short time later Mary extricated herself from perching on the armrest of Andrew's chair, still holding her bundle, gave a quick but decisive poke of the fire and left, leaving us alone to become more acquainted.

Although it would seem we were diametrically opposite in character, talents and disposition our friendship was immediate and long lasting. He was detailed, meticulous in his craft, sure of his own beliefs and determined to succeed. I on the other hand was rather hap hazard, disorganised, allowed my life to unfold and uncertain about almost everything. The saying that our greatest virtues are also our greatest enemy is indeed apt in both our cases.

Our journeys here could not have been more different. After some time Andrew told me how he was orphaned as a child, worked also as a Printer's Devil but was caught selling stolen goods at a market resulting in a sentence of death. Commuted to Life he arrived here in 1812 on the *Ruby*. The voyage was a nightmare, secured below for weeks at a time with stinking companions and uneatable food and only memories of home for company. He was luckier than most though, with his skills and recognition Andrew was now a free man and as I could see matrimony really was blissful. I shared a little of myself although he seemed unfazed to hear of my privileged life. Even then Andrew spoke with vigour and passion about his beloved newspapers and especially the need for them to be untethered by government. It surprised me that he would share such intimacies with a stranger such as me but such revelations frequently come my way. Perhaps its my temperament but it is certainly a benefit in my line of work.

What we had in common was a sense of naïve idealism and belief in ourselves. He as a printer and newspaper publisher, me as a writer and thinker.

Oh, how our lives were about to change!

An example of wooden printing press form this era.
Photographer: Jon Augier. Museums Victoria.

When leaving he noticed me looking at the old, small, wooden printing press, clearly well used and still in working order. Andrew gave it a touch of fondness and revealed it to be the one Collins had purchased second hand in London from printer William Bensley and brought to the settlement in 1804. It still remained the only one in VDL.

I have included below some of the articles, letters and commentary I encountered in my wandering through the delicate and thin pages of the papers published in the colony between 1813 and my arrival in 1818.

Many of the articles and letters are self-evident in their meaning and need no comment, while others required some background to place them in context or add to the story. There are those which I simply could not resist placing my rather unique and cryptic interpretation on. If you disagree with my ideas and perspectives, don't bother to write to me because I will most probably be long gone by the time you read this – but of course feel free to challenge anything I say. After all, intellectual debate was my life blood.

It is easy to see why the struggle that took place on this island so rapidly and inevitably began to grow emotionally and physically as two incredibly different races met on the same soil. It is difficult to imagine two more diverse human cultures being thrown together with regard to their ways of life, spiritual beliefs, food and eating habits, weaponry, colour of skin, shelter, land use and in just about every other way imaginable. All humans share elementary commonalities such as the importance of family, sensuous desires, the basic necessities of life and the need for a place to live, but beyond that anything can change.

It seemed to me that in the early stages some desire to live compatibly with the Pakana People existed although this did not last for long. Take a look at this first article in August 1813 which was reprinted many years later as a reminiscence piece in 1855.

1813

TASMANIAN DAILY NEWS (HOBART TOWN, TAS: 1855 - 1858), SATURDAY 25 AUGUST 1855, PAGE 3

CURIOSITIES OF THE EARLY DAYS OF TASMANIA, 1813.

Proclamation: of Governor Davey in regard to the aborigines, in which he states that it is not without extreme concern he has learnt that the resentment of these poor uncivilized beings has, been justly excited, by a most barbarous and inhuman mode of proceeding acted upon towards them, viz., the robbery of their children! Had he not the most positive proofs of such barbarous crimes having been committed, he could not have believed that a British subject would have so ignominiously stained the honour of his country and of himself ; but the facts are too clear and it there fore becomes the indispensable and bounden duty of the Lieutenant-Governor thus publicly to express his utter indignation and abhorrence thereof.

A person named — since dead has killed a native, in his attempt to protect his wife; and he cut off the dead man's head and obliged the native woman, to go with him, carrying her husband's head, suspended-: round her neck. The aborigines were sacrificed, in many instances, to momentary caprice or anger, as if the life of a savage had been unworthy of the slightest consideration; and they sustained the most unjustifiable treatment in defending themselves against outrages, which it was not to be expected that any race of men should, submit to without resistance. In this year the natives used to come into the "camp" for food, in large bodies. 1814.

The aborigines, as many as twenty at a time, were fed by the Rev. R. Knopwood as paupers. In this year races took place at New Town. 1815.

Governor Davey proclaimed martial law to be in force in the colony. Bread was 10d a pound; beef and mutton, 9d; tea. 12s; sugar, 1s.
There were 964 acres in Wheat.

1814

VAN DIEMEN'S LAND GAZETTE AND GENERAL ADVERTISER (HOBART, TAS: 1814), AUGUST 20 1814

Sitting Magistrate for this week. FRANCIS WILLIAMS, Esq.
For the Ensuing week. JAMES GORDON, Esq.

We mentioned from time ago of feveral Natives being brought to town from the woods at South Arm, after receiving feveral articles of clothing from His Honour the Lieut. Governor and other humane Gentlemen of this fettlement, they were conducted through the Streets by A. Campbell. (a prifoner) Their curiosity which had been never before gratified with fuch a fight, prompted them to examine everything with wonder and amazement, without bestowing their attention longer than a moment on any single object.[iii]

The Lieut. Governor having expressed a desire to see the remainder of the Natives left at South Arm, Campbell accompanied with two other Persons again returned to that place, the party spent 3 days in fruitless search after them, when they discovered two natives who informed them that the rest were on Betsey's Island.

Next morning Campbell and party went in a Boat to that Island, accompanied by a native woman of one of the neighbouring Islands and who has lived with Campbell for some years; this woman has been of considerable service to the party, by representing the humane treatment she received from the white People. On landing they saw a number of natives setting round a fire and on the perceiving the children cloathed, they were greatly astonished and felt their dresses; when the natives informed them of their reception in town, they all expressed a wish by Campbell's woman to see Hobart and it was with difficulty the party prevented the Boat from sinking, so eager were they to get in. Campbell brought 13 to town who received every kindness and humanity from the Lieut. Governor, who likewise cloathed them. They were afterwards landed on the Island of Le Bruin, at their own request.

We trust the exertions of Campbell and his party will be a prelude to more intercourse with the native tribes and by the means of such humane treatment, endeavour to reclaim them from a savage life.

A few days ago upwards of 100 Natives, surrounded a house at South Arm and knocked at the door; on the person within opening it and perceiving the natives, he was in great terror and after shutting the door endeavoured to escape by a back window, but seeing it in vain, he again opened the door, when several natives came in, to whom he offered victuals, but they refused to eat. After they had surveyed the premises, an elderly man led the person by the arm, who lived in the house, nearly half a mile into the woods and placed him in the middle of them; and at the moment the natives were about to throw their spears at the unfortunate victim, a native man whom A. Campbell had brought to Hobart some time ago, addressed them, when they all walked away, leaving the person to return to his own residence.

Thus by the humanity already shown to these natives, the life of a fellow creature has been preserved.

The reality was about to change as white people began to expand and settle deeper and deeper into the island. With them came livestock which encroached upon the Pakana hunting grounds and land used for cultivation of crops. Notice in the next report how the driving away of cattle at Tea Tree is rated of less importance than the nocturnal activities of the Banditti of Felons.

1816

HOBART TOWN GAZETTE AND SOUTHERN REPORTER (TAS. : 1816 - 1821), SATURDAY 27 JULY 1816, PAGE 1

HOBART TOWN.
SITTING MAGISTRATE. - A. W. H. HUMPHREY, Esq.

Yesterday fe'night, the Banditti of Felons we mentioned in our Paper of the 13th Instant, as having broke out of the Prison Room attacked the Premises of MR. JOHN BEAMONT, Settler, at the Tea Tree Brush and robbed the House of every moveable article, excepting an Iron-pot. They afterwards went to the residence of Mr. PITT, Settler and robbed him of all his dogs, two muskets and some gunpowder.

A Party of Natives has lately driven seventeen head of horned Cattle from the herd of Mr. J. Beamont, at the Tea-tree Brush and have not been since heard of.

Hobart Town Gazette and Southern Reporter (Tas. : 1816 - 1821), Saturday 27 July 1816, page 1

The Black Natives of this Colony have for the last few weeks manifested a stronger Hostility towards the Up-country Settlers and in killing and driving away their Cattle than has been witnessed since the Settling of this Colony: And since their visit at New Norfolk, they have been at the herd of Mr. Thomas M'Neelance near Jerico and killed two beautiful Cows.

1817

THE HOBART TOWN GAZETTE, and

SOUTHERN REPORTER

PUBLISHED BY AUTHORITY.

Volume the Second.] SATURDAY, JANUARY 11, 1817. [NUMBER 39

His Honor the Lieutenant Governor has thought proper to direct, that all Public Communications which may appear in the HOBART TOWN GAZETTE, and SOUTHERN REPORTER, signed with any Official Signature, are to be considered as Official Communications made to those Persons to whom they may relate.

The relationships were becoming increasingly tense and uncertain as Mr Brumby and Robert Rosne were soon to realise.

HOBART TOWN GAZETTE AND SOUTHERN REPORTER (TAS. : 1816 - 1821), SATURDAY 1 FEBRUARY 1817, PAGE 2

On Monday the 20th ultimo, Mr Brumby, a respectable settler at Port Dalrymple, being in quest of convenient pasturage for his own flock at the lower end of Elizabeth River, fell in with a small party of Natives. Mr. B prudently disdaining all such conduct to these unenlightened savages, after taking a child and loading it with provisions, conducted him back to the Natives, who were apparently highly pleased - a full proof that charity and humanity are the surest paths for conducting these much-lamented Heathens to that light to which they are present strangers to.

HOBART TOWN GAZETTE AND SOUTHERN REPORTER
(TAS. : 1816 - 1821), SATURDAY 24 MAY 1817, PAGE 2

On Saturday last, whilst Robert Rosne, overseer to Capt. Jeffrey's, was searching for sheep strayed from his flock, he promiscuously came upon about fifteen native women and children assembled around a fire, on the Sweet Water Hills. Considering them to be an inoffensive tribe and his mind dwelling on his pursuit, he carelessly approached them to light his pipe, pleased with his reception; but on leaving this peaceable group, he met with a number of savage native men, whose ferocity had nearly been his death.

One of these untutored beings hove a stone at him, which struck him violently on the mouth and staggered him: but little time was given him to recover from this blow, when an ill-fated volley of stones dislocated his shoulder and by repeated hostility severely bruised him. Fortunately, however, he was suffered to leave them alive. In admiring His HONOUR the LIEUTENANT GOVERNOR'S lenient disposition, in respect to the aborigines, it is wise to remark the old adage, that "charity begins at home."

I found this report interesting on several counts. The first that the 'black natives' now had British names. Deleting a person's name is a way of taking their identity. Prisoners are given numbers, orphans other names and so on. The second aspect is the fact that they were charged under British law for crimes they committed and yet there was a dearth of charges laid against white people for stealing Aboriginal children.

The PAKANA *Voice*

1818

THE HOBART TOWN GAZETTE, AND SOUTHERN REPORTER:
PUBLISHED BY AUTHORITY.
[Volume the Third.]   SATURDAY, MAY 16, 1818.   [NUMBER 10...
His Honor the Lieutenant Governor has thought proper to direct, that all Public Communications which may appear in the HOBART TOWN GAZETTE, and SOUTHERN REPORTER, signed with any Official Signature, are to be confided as Official Communications made to those Persons to whom they may relate.

This report I found to be somewhat puzzling but speaks volumes about how differently the British viewed the world and the Pakana people. Apparently, a native who had lived his entire live in the 'woods' was to be punished for being in his native land and unable to show any 'visible' means of obtaining a livelihood. Amused, I read this out loud in the tavern that evening only to be faced with stony silent, incredulous expressions and after a few moments they went on talking as though nothing had been said. I drank alone for the rest of the evening.

HOBART TOWN GAZETTE AND SOUTHERN REPORTER
(TAS. : 1816 - 1821), SATURDAY 7 FEBRUARY 1818, PAGE 2

MONTHLY SESSIONS

The Monthly Sittings of the Court House in Liverpool-street before the Deputy Judge Advocate and the Magistrate for the County of Buckinghamshire took place this morning, for the trial of such offences as were brought before it.

George, a black native, Francis Sullivan and Thomas Antoine, charged with wandering in the woods without any visible means of obtaining a livelihood and putting His Majesty's subjects in bodily fear, were sentenced to labor in the gaol gang for the period of 12 months; and, at the expiration of the said sentence, to find sureties for their good behaviour for 12 months; themselves in £30 each and two sureties of £20 each.

HOBART TOWN GAZETTE AND SOUTHERN REPORTER
(TAS: 1816 - 1821), SATURDAY 14 NOVEMBER 1818, PAGE 1

Two black natives, who have been long among the inhabitants, named James Tedbury and George Frederick, were charged with robbing Roger Gavin of several articles and James Goodwin of a musket, at the Coal River; after which they escaped to the woods and were there apprehended, both armed. They were each sentenced to be transported to such part of this Territory as his Honour the LIEUTENANT GOVERNOR may be pleased to direct, for the term of three years.

The letter below requires no further comment. Cowper expresses himself well and presents a scene of extraordinary ferocity where Pakana are pitched against each other in pitiless and clearly fatal fighting for the sole gratification of rytia (White Man) and one would surmise induced by gambling. His indignation is most certainly understandable and presents an image of his own unprincipled culture.

HOBART TOWN GAZETTE AND SOUTHERN REPORTER
(TAS: 1816 - 1821), SATURDAY 26 DECEMBER 1818, PAGE 1

"THESE, THEREFORE, I CAN PITY." – COWPER.

On the perusal of the last week's Gazette, I was glad to find that someone among us, was not only possessed of humanity and fellow feeling, but that he also dared to be singular, in publicly espousing the cause of a race of beings so much despised and abused, by the generality of those who think themselves to be creatures of superior endowments, while, in truth, they are neither so peaceable nor so just in their demeanour, as the poor aborigines whom they wish to degrade below the brute. That most shameful, cruel and barbarous custom of encouraging the Black people to murder or mangle one another for the sport of the learned, the polite and the refined Europeans for the amusement and gratification of those who are denominated Christians, has, for some time, required a more effectual prohibition than the Letter of the Law.

Last Sunday afternoon, on my way from Church home-wards, I was much grieved and distressed, to hear and to see that the public peace of the Town and the holy rest of the Sabbath, were most impiously violated by the blows and cries of the Blacks, excited to uproar and outrage by the Whites, who take pleasure in the sufferings of their fellow men and, who will propose and give a reward, that the unoffending may be slain, or injured, merely to gratify or indulge the diabolical passions of a base mind, yea " their feet are swift to shed" or to cause to be shed, the "innocent blood !"

Instead of taking delight in the destruction of the harmless Natives, would it not be more honourable and praise-worthy to endeavour to rescue them from misery and to raise them from their low condition? Instead of sinking them in the scale of existence, by defrauding them of their rights and giving them intoxicating liquors, to kill or to hurt one another, would it not be more to the credit of such as are favoured with the benefits of civil Society to try, by every means, to ennoble their minds and to recommend to them sobriety, order and industry ?--" If thou forbear to deliver them, that are ready to be slain :--If thou say, behold, we knew it not ; doth not he that pondereth the heart con-sider it? And he that keepeth thy soul, doth not he know it ? And shall not he render to every man according to his works ?"-- "Woe unto him, that giveth his neighbour drink, to make him drunken, that he may look upon his nakedness!"

Do not those persons, who manifest such a spirit of savage insensibility towards the wretched New Hollanders, know, that their ancestors, a few generations ago, were in a similar state of barbarism ? Consider whence ye are: what a kind Providence has done for you and behave yourselves wisely in a perfect way. Were the Almighty, by an audible voice from Heaven to call upon every one, abetting or visiting those scenes of cruelty, saying, "Where is thy brother?-The voice of thy brother's blood crieth unto me from the ground." What could he answer ? Say not, there is no relation between us ; for has not the Creator made of one blood, all nations of men, for to dwell on all the face of the earth ?-" Why then," O man, "wilt thou despise thy brother ; or, why wilt thou set at nought thy brother ? For, who maketh thee to differ from another? And, what hast thou that thou didst not receive? Now, if thou didst receive it, why dost thou glory, has if thou hadst not received it?" May the reader, with the Poet devoutly say,

"Teach me to feel another's woe," T' amend " the fault I see;

" That mercy I to other's shew, "That mercy shew to me I"

In the conclusion of this paragraph, I hope I may be indulged with the liberty of inserting a remark, which the subject in question, by a train of thoughts suggested as not inapplicable to the present day and not Unworthy of republication: that most accurate observer of men and manners, Dr. Moore in his View of the Causes and Progress of the French Revolution, says, " New and unaccustomed dignities often inspire weak minds with a disposition to display supercilious airs and a ridiculous deportment toward those whom they consider as their inferiors and from whom , they are jealous of a want of respect because of their late equality-" How do this temper and this conduct accord with what Christianity enjoins? "Let your moderation be known unto all men." -"Let nothing be done through strife or vain glory; but in lowliness of mind, let each esteem others better than themselves Wherefore know thyself, O man . Remember, what thou waste and be humble.

** I would not enter on my list of friends," "(Tho' grac'd with polish'd manners and fine sense", Yet wanting sensibility the man, "Who needlessly sets foot upon a worm!"*

MONITOR "THESE, THEREFORE, I CAN PITY."

— COWPER.

The PAKANA *Voice*

1819

THE **HOBART TOWN** GAZETTE, AND
SOUTHERN REPORTER:
PUBLISHED BY AUTHORITY.

[VOLUME the FOURTH.]   SATURDAY, JANUARY 2, 1819.   [NUMBER 130

HONOR the LIEUTENANT GOVERNOR has thought proper to direct, that all Public Communications which may appear in the HOBART TOWN GAZETTE, and SOUTHERN REPORTER, figned with any Official Signature, are to be confidered as Official communications made to thofe Perfons to whom they may relate.
(By COMMAND OF HIS HONOR).   H. E. ROBINSON, Secretary.

**HOBART TOWN GAZETTE AND SOUTHERN REPORTER
(TAS: 1816 - 1821), SATURDAY 2 JANUARY 1819, PAGE 2**

Mr. Florence arrived from Macquarie Harbour on Wednesday, having coasted round in a whale boat. Mr. Florence has had an opportunity of surveying Port Davey as well as Macquarie Harbour; and has been a very consider-able distance up the Rivers which run into both. The Natives, of whom he saw several tribes, were very friendly. We hope to be enabled to give more particulars in a future Paper.

**HOBART TOWN GAZETTE AND SOUTHERN REPORTER
(TAS: 1816 - 1821), SATURDAY 24 APRIL 1819, PAGE 1**

Our statement last week, respecting the affray between the stock-keepers and natives at Mr. Stocker's hut, was erroneous in one part. No stock-keeper was killed, but two were severely speared; and the natives were extremely resolute and ferocious : their Chief was certainly killed.— No farther particulars are yet known ; but are hope to learn them in a few days.

**HOBART TOWN GAZETTE AND SOUTHERN REPORTER
(TAS. : 1816 - 1821), SATURDAY 3 JULY 1819, PAGE 1**

On Tuesday died in the Colonial Hospital, the native woman usually called Black Mary, particularly known as having been at one time the partner of Michael Howe, and subsequently a guide to the parties of troops which were employed successfully in subduing the gang of bush-rangers; in which her knowledge of the country and of their haunts, and especially her instinctive quickness in tracking foot-steps, rendered her a main instrument of the success which attended their exertions. She had been victualled from His Majesty's Store, and had received other indulgences in clothing, &c.; but a complication of disorders, which had been long gaining ground upon her, terminating at last in pulmonic affection, put an end to her life.

This was simply too good a story to leave out even though it has nothing to do with the theme of this book other than taking yet another stance at identity both perceived and real – although I am beginning to wonder what real means anymore.

VAN DIEMEN'S LAND GAZETTE AND GENERAL ADVERTISER (HOBART, TAS: 1814), SATURDAY 30 JULY 1814, PAGE 2 CONTINUED

Sitting Magistrate for this week. FRANCIS WILLIAMS, Esq.

An American Seaman taken in the American Schooner REVENGE, by the Belle Poulle, 36, on finding he was to go to Mill Prison, dis-covered himself to be a woman and that she had worn men's cloaths these three years. She was examined and sent to the Hospital to be clothed. The account she gives of herself, is as follows:— Going coast ways with her Master, Mistress and Family, about three years since, the vessel was wrecked and all on board perished except herself. She was naked and finding the dead body of one of the seamen lying on the land, she conceived the idea of dressing herself in man's apparel and begged her way as a ship wrecked seaman to the nearest sea-port.

She got relieved and also got employment as a lands-man on board a vessel and from thence in the Revenge Schooner. She says her share of prize-money and wages is about 200 dollars. She wishes to be sent home to her native country, which, it is hoped will be granted her. She has a comely face, sun burnt, as well as her hands; and appeared while in men's clothes, a decent, well-looking young Man.

While there were many influences affecting the Pakana people at this time one critical factor were conflicts between nations thousands of miles from the shores of Lutruwita.

At least two major wars in the Americas and Europe were to have extraordinary repercussions for those living quietly in Lutruwita. The first was the American War of Independence two decades before the British arrived. It had caused some consternation amongst the British ruling classes, not the least being where to send their recalcitrants now that convicts could no longer be shipped across the Atlantic. Luckily, Captain James Cook had dropped anchor on a plot of land in Botany Bay, a safe distance from Britain and fortuitously he and Joseph Banks mentioned it to a few people on his return to England.

In my more frivolous moments, I imagine crusty old gentlemen seated pompously in leather backed armchairs chatting over brandy and cigars at their London Club, pondering on what to do with their swarms of the Great Unwashed after the ungrateful Americans had shut the door on British convicts, choosing slavery instead. It must have been a Eureka moment when it was suggested sending them 12,000 miles away from their home was not a bad idea. Not only that, but their Navy was in desperate need of tall timbers to replace masts and warships to go on fighting the dastardly Bonaparte which could easily be found in the Antipodes.

The Napoleonic War being fought across Europe at the time also had a direct effect on the people of Lutruwita. The British became increasingly anxious that the dreaded French were about to settle in Van Diemen's Land. With some cause, I should add, as French scientific expeditions had already occurred, with a team staying there for some months in 1792-93. Importantly Nicolas Baudin had been sent south by Napoleon in 1800 for France's glory and to bring a few plants back for Josephine's garden. The French even mapped Australia in 1802 to 1803. This lead directly to Governor King dispatching Lt Bowen with a few soldiers and convicts to establish a British presence at Risdon Cove in September 1803, marking the beginning of white occupation of Lutruwita.

These critical events between European Nations were to have such a profound impact on the people and nations of Lutruwita in the years to come.

Chapter Three

The Adventure Begins

After reading all I could and talking to people who had some knowledge or experiences with the Aborigines, I decided the only way to really learn was to meet and spend time with one of the tribal clans. Leaving most of my meagre belongings with Bent and with very little planning and brimming overconfidence in my own fortitude and good fortune, I set out to find a group who would accept an intruder and share their lives with a complete stranger. I can say with some sureness I have a natural ability to learn languages quickly and so I made it my goal to learn and master one nation's language. I gained as much as I could before setting out on my foolhardy enterprise, which according to practically every white person I met in Nipaluna (Hobart Town), led me to believe I would be returned impaled on spears, with a bludgeoned skull and dead as a door post! However, youth has little sense of mortality and the desire for adventure supersedes any such fear.

It was not as hard as I first imagined. I crossed Timtumili Minanya or, as the English had named it, Derwent River and ventured into the lands of the Paredarerme (Oyster Cove Nation). My preference was to walk, slow as that made my journey. I thought a horse would present a threat and besides, horses were beyond the meagre contents of my purse. I also had plenty of time to appreciate the forests, wildlife and scenery as I stumbled my way deeper and deeper into Paredarerme territory. Eventually, of course, they found me. One morning I woke to find myself looking straight into a very intimidating face, with its penetrating, interrogative lepena (eyes). A spear pointing menacingly in my direction.

The warrior, much older than I, wore lemmook (kangaroo) skins, had red ochre on his face and animal fat smeared over his body for warmth. His chest and arms held deep scars which I learned much later were from scarification at puberty. The marks were very pronounced and easy to identify so they may also have indicated his clan. His hair was matted, thick and cropped to just below his ears and he had a small, greying moustache and a beard running beneath his chin. His levelled eyebrows suggesting a character of strength and gave an appearance of untempered pride.

Luckily my limited language skills saved the day. At length he lowered his weapon and sat with me in silence as I prepared breakfast and made tea. Soon with gentle enticing I began to point at objects while he supplied a word for each: lonah = rock, nghearetta = Wattle Tree, puggunyenna = bird, mina = me, rytia (white man) and pugganna (black man).

Thus my language lessons began. In time I became quite proficient which I realised belatedly was a rare occurrence. Although many Aborigines seemed to have learned English, as frequently reported in the newspapers of the day, few of the British reciprocated.

Mr. Hackett, for example, expressed his regret at a public meeting some years later, that so few efforts had been made by the whites to learn the language of the blacks and to go among them and explain the really benevolent intentions which we have to them. He did not think there were 5 persons in the island who could converse with or make themselves understood by them. (Courier 23rd Sept 1830.)

Wondering what to do next I packed up and began to tabelty (walk) and all the while he remained at my side. I am not a natural bushman so that evening when I tried in vain to light a patarola (fire) my companion watched on with wry humour. He was soon enveloped with laughter at my ineptness. I too joined in until he took over and in no time at all, using flints and grass, had healthy lopatins (flames) blazing away between us.

Decades later, well after most of their culture had been obliterated, that James Backhouse, a gossip writer, originated the myth that patarola making was beyond the abilities of Aborigines. Perhaps it was a classic need to blame the victim for the cruelties which have been bestowed upon them.

LAUNCESTON EXAMINER (TAS: 1842 - 1899),
SATURDAY 8 FEBRUARY 1845, PAGE 7

A Narrative of a Visit to the Australian Colonies by JAMES BACKHOUSE. London: Hamilton Adams, & Co., 1844.

I learned that the aborigines of V. D. Land had no artificial method of obtaining fire before their acquaintance with Europeans; they say they obtained it first from the sky, probably meaning by lightning. They preserved fire by carrying ignited sticks or bark with them and if these went out, they looked for the smoke of the fire of some other party, or of one of the fires that they had left, as these often continued to burn for several days. The arithmetic of the aborigines is very limited, amounting only to one, two, plenty. As they cannot state in numbers the amount of persons present on any occasion, they give their names.

Each tribe of the aborigines is divided into several families and each family, consisting of a few individuals, occupies its own fire. Though they rarely remain two days in a place, they seldom travel far at a time. Each tribe keeps much to its own district, a circumstance that may in some measure account for the variety of dialect. The practice of burning the dead, is said to have extended to the natives of Bruny Island; but those of the east coast put the deceased into hollow trees and fenced them in with bushes, they do not consider a person completely dead till the sun goes down!

Duterrau, Benjamin. (1930). A Wild Native Taking a Kangaroo, His Dog Having Caught It, He Runs to Kill It with His Waddy, 1836, Printed 1930/Benjamin Duterrau. Dixon Library, State Library of New South Wales FL872816

The following evening the fellow disappeared and I began to wonder if our time together had come to an end. Just when despair was beginning to take hold he returned with a speared *lukangana* (wallaby) and soon started the process of preparing our food. He adeptly skinned the animal with a stone tool, setting the skin in a tree to dry. It would to be used later for water carrying, cloths &c. He was decidedly in command of the situation, instructing me to find *moonara* (wood) and put it on the fire. We ate well that night and began to share stories.

He told me it now took so long for him to find food because the *rytia* had killed many of the tribe's animals and the strange beasts the *rytia* had brought in were devouring the land of grass and feed. Sometimes in need of food his people would kill the sheep, but then the white invaders would come and murder them.

HOBART TOWN GAZETTE AND SOUTHERN REPORTER (TAS. : 1816 - 1821), SATURDAY 18 DECEMBER 1819, PAGE 2

An inhabitant in this town has had the good fortune within these few days to re-cover upwards of 270 fine sheep which had been some time ago driven away from his flock at the Coal River ; but we regret to state, that two other persons have not been so fortunate as the individual before mentioned ; for on Tuesday last, 300 sheep, be-longing to Mr. James Triffitt, son. of New Norfolk, were found dead on his pasture ground at Stony-hut Plains.

It appears that the natives, who had made their appearance at that place, committed this great slaughter during the momentary absence of the flock-keepers, which will be a serious loss to an industrious individual, most of them being fine ewes ; and this misfortune is the more distressing when it is considered that out of a thousand sheep the owner can only find two hundred alive, of which number many were much disfigured by some of their eyes being taken out and others with their backs broken. It is evident that

> *the remainder must have been driven farther into the interior by the hostile disposition of the natives : and within these few days, Mr. James Austin, settler in the district of Glenorchy, has met with the serious loss of nearly 300 sheep being stolen out of his flock by some persons unknown.*

The number of animals were now very low because so many had been killed and his people were now hungry as well. In fact, some of his people endured the humiliation of having to go to the white people's village and beg for food. These were desperate times for him and he feared for his children.

Decades later the newspapers would blithely reminisce on this;

Sketchbook No. 98, 1831-1832 / John Glover. (1831). NSW 31. [Number of fallen logs];Dixon Library, State Library of New South Wales FL436459

1814

PEOPLE'S ADVOCATE OR TRUE FRIEND OF TASMANIA (LAUNCESTON, TAS. : 1855 - 1856), MONDAY 11 AUGUST 1856, PAGE 2

Prices at New Town established. Aborigines fed as paupers by Reverend R. Knopwood. Price of Wheat taken into store, 10s, a bushel-Exportation of Grain prohibited.

This was my modest contribution;

The PAKANA *Voice*
BY W.C. SPECIAL CORRESPONDENT—*LUTRUWITA*
25TH AUGUST 1814

Widespread food shortages are being reported in some parts of the Oyster Cove Nation. These are particularly critical for the Moomairremener clan whose land is continually being taken by the British.

Clan leaders say that it is increasingly hard to find food as the British kill the animals which are a vital food source. Older people and young children are especially vulnerable and many are becoming sick due to the lack of food.

The main cause is the British bringing in new animals which are unsuited to the land and eat vegetation normally consumed by native animals and destroying their cultivated crops. Coupled with this that clansmen are cautious to use their hunting grounds or take these new animals for food for fear of being shot.

It has now come to pass that the British holy man, Knopwood is giving out food to people which is reported to be quite unpalatable.

Many of his clan and others were now fighting back against things they simply could not understand. Why do *rytia* kill so many animals and leaving skins or carcasses to rot on the ground, or take only the skin and other parts of the body? It simply made no sense and worst of all it left him and his clan to starve. I read this account in the newspaper which seems to vindicate my friend's apprehensions;

HOBART TOWN GAZETTE AND SOUTHERN REPORTER
(TAS. : 1816 - 1821), SATURDAY 31 AUGUST 1816, PAGE 1

A few days ago a party of about twenty Black Natives pursued three of the Government Stock-keepers near New Norfolk and began throwing their Spears at them, when the men turned about and began firing, but at which they not regarding still kept on throwing their spears: this made the Stock-keepers resolved to kill some of them, which they soon accomplished by leaving three dead in the field and taking one prisoner and which soon made the Natives quit their military array and disband themselves

In the engagement they threw upwards of 40 Spears, which was very surprising that not one of them hit the men.

HOBART TOWN GAZETTE AND SOUTHERN REPORTER
(TAS. : 1816 - 1821), SATURDAY 28 NOVEMBER 1818, PAGE 1

Sitting Magistrate — Thomas Archer, Esq. Assize of Bread — Wheaten 8d. Household 7d.

SAVAGE MURDER

We regret we are called again to record another and not a new act of savage barbarity.

On the 25th of October last a party of five persons, consisting of James Foley, John Sherberd, Zachariah Chaffey, William Garth and John Kemp, all young men residing at this Settlement, proceeded in an open boat belonging to Mr. T. W. Birch to Oyster Bay, distant from our harbour about 150 miles N.E. in order to procure swan feathers and kangaroo, seal and swan skins. Their labours were attended with more than usual success ; having at this place procured 300lbs. of swan feathers, 60 swan skins 100 kangaroo skins and 34 live swans ; and at Big Swan Port (commonly called the White Rock), which lies nearly contiguous, they got 150 seal skins. Their labours being thus successfully terminated, they were inclined to return home; and in order to arrange for that purpose, on the 13th instant they put into Grindstone Bay 31 miles distant from Oyster Bay, where from contrary winds they were detained three days.

During their stay at this place, they went a second time to Big Swan Port, for the purpose of increasing their number of seal skins, leaving behind John Kemp in care of the live swans, 4 kangaroo dogs, 3 muskets, some ammunition, sealing knives and the various skins, &c. they had procured. After having obtained more seal skins, they returned the same day to Grindstone Bay ; and when near the shore, the first object which attracted their sight was the corpse of their unfortunate companion Kemp lying at the water's edge, cut and mangled in a manner too shocking to relate. Foley instantly jumped out of the boat and had only time to perceive that the greater part of the articles left with the deceased were destroyed or taken away, when the natives, who were in ambuscade, suddenly appeared on the beach, armed with spears. He made all speed to return and with the help of Chaffey with the greatest difficulty got the body in the boat ; immediately after which, they moved off and fortunately got out of the reach of the natives. On the approach of the boat, two of the dogs that were at some distance on a rising ground set up a terrible howl, ran to the water and swam to the boat ; one was also found dead by the body of Kemp and the other, from the blood and foot-marks on the sand, is conjectured to have been killed by the native's spears. A native girl, who had been some time among those at present walking about the streets of Hobart Town, accompanied this group, which consisted of nearly 20. She often in an apparent friendly, but artful manner entreated the party to return, which *they very prudently declined and instantly made sail from the awful scene. Owing to unfavourable winds for four days and the putrid state of the body, they were reluctantly compelled to put into East Bay, where they performed the last offices of humanity to their unfortunate fellow creature. It may be regretted that the muskets and ammunition are now in the possession of these natives, as their natural fear of fire-arms maybe in some degree removed by the native girl before noticed. We have only to hope, that this unhappy circumstance will put persons, who are in the habit of frequenting the woods and islands, on their guard in future not to lose sight for a moment of their arms, or to go any distance with-out them, which would probably in all cases pre-vent disasters of this description and the necessity of proceeding to extremities on either side, so much to be desired. We are credibly informed by a person who has often visited Oyster Bay, that it is a favourite resort of the natives, no less than 500 having been seen assembled there at once.*

IMPACT OF LAISSEZ-FAIRE ON THE PEOPLE OF LUTRUWITA

The Pakana people were in fact up against a far greater force than a few young men on a killing spree. Little could they have imagined a judicious Scotsman seated in a small, dark, candle-lit room located up narrow winding stone stairs in his sober Edinburgh room carefully and methodically devising the theory of capitalism which would ultimately have such a devastating effect on lives so very far away. Adam Smith published *An Inquiry into the Nature and Causes of the Wealth of Nations* in 1776, which espoused the ideas of supply and demand, free markets and minimal government involvement that are generally known by the term *laissez-faire*.

This is exactly the doctrine that was followed in the new colony and hence the implicit outrage at the ferocity of the natives expressed by the newspaper editor. The animals were a resource which were there to be exploited and those enterprising enough to do so, should be rewarded with profits and enabled to feed their families and improve their lifestyles.

The contrast could not be starker between the two economies. The Pakana people also viewed animals as a way to feed their families but only took what they needed and no more. Theirs was a collective, communal society with no sense of individual wealth let alone the idea of hunting to the point of extinction, which rapidly became a consequence of capitalism and free enterprise economies. Within a few decades Lutruwita was to lose the emu, tiger and many other species.

Returning to my little adventure... After a few days living in this way, trust gradually grew between us and we began to call each other by name: his was Rialim. We slept peacefully with the knowledge that dawn would see us wake and eat together. We walked for miles and I had no idea where he was taking me. Rialim though clearly knew every square inch of his domain and seemed to hold a roadmap in his head of his surrounds from trees, hills, rocky outcrops and far off hills and mountains. On the fourth day we saw smoke coming from a cluster of trees and I was beckoned to follow until we came across a small cluster of shelters, families, fires, food, dogs and children. This was his clan, the Moomairremener. He was welcomed by a gaggle of *cuckana ludawinna* and *lowana keetana*, (little boys and girls), his wife and extended family.

Rialim was clearly well respected and loved by all around him. While he became inextricably enmeshed in the convolutions of domesticity, I was greeted with an entrancing smile by a young woman about my age, confident with a gracious posture and a welcoming presence. She had very short, cropped helical black *cethana* (hair) with sharp, slightly S-shaped eyebrows and exquisitely enticing lips. Her *towrick* (ears), with one ever so slightly above the other, stood out from her short hair and subtly enhanced her appeal. Around her neck were strung beautifully fashioned *kanalaritja* (shell necklaces) sitting easily between her agreeably asymmetrical *wagley* (breasts). The rest of her body was muscular and strong and partially covered with *lyenna* skins. She was striking in every respect. She spoke in a soft melodious voice revealing a faltering smile and much gesticulating;

"Nena...Mina",

I interpreted to mean something like; did I understand her language?

I stood open-mouthed, feeling decidedly ridiculous as is the case when you have learned a few words of another's language only to be confronted with a natural speaker who rattles off a sentence that flies way over your head. Her *pinina* (laughter) was delightful and to my great surprise and relief I found she spoke remarkably good English, spattered with a healthy mix of expletives, with 'bloody' featuring frequently as she talked rapidly and without hesitation. I was spellbound. Her eyes were the deepest, darkest black I had ever seen, so enticing, so mesmerising; I could almost sense her primordial ancestors drawing me into their being.[1]

---

1   EDITOR'S NOTE: *It should be remembered that W.C. was a hopeless romantic with a vivid imagination which is unsurprising given his early years were filled endless tales of fantasy and Greek mythology. It is easy to see how faced with someone as beautiful and enticing as Lowana his thoughts would burst easily into make believe and so visions of primordial ancestors should be seen as just that: the imaginings of a love-struck young man. It has no bearing on Aboriginal culture and certainly there is no intent to offend.*

Tanleboueyer / A native of the district of Oyster Bay & the Wife to Manalargerna / was attach'd to the mission in 1830, printed 1835 / Benjamin Duterrau, 1767-1851; Dixon Library, State Library of New South Wales CALL NUMBER DL Pe 20 ; FL8791849 was her name.

Transfixed I was jolted back by her voice when she said, 'Mina Lowana. *Nena (you)...*' pointing to me.

"W.C.",

I said sheepishly. Using my nickname made me feel like a school boy all over again with all the associated emotions. It took me a long time to realise that *lowana* actually meant 'girl' in her language. I had assumed it was her name. Lowana knew she had played a trick on me and every time I called her name there would be an ever so subtle ripple of amusement from the others. I never managed to procure her name, which may have been payback for me not revealing mine. Poignantly, Lowana told me much later the first thing she saw were my bright blue eyes, the first she had ever seen; so frightening and yet irresistible.

I later learned she had spent some time with a gang of bushrangers which may explain her grasp of some rather colourful language. I could not ascertain whether her admission had been by choice, inducement or brutal force. Mingling of outlaws and Aboriginal girls seemed to occur in different parts of the land and at times was mentioned in newspapers.

HOBART TOWN GAZETTE AND SOUTHERN REPORTER
(TAS. : 1816 - 1821), SATURDAY 30 NOVEMBER 1816, PAGE 1

The following are the names of the Banditti who committed that depredation:— Michael Howe, head and leader of the gang, a convict; Peter Septon, a convict; Richard Collyer, ditto;George Jones, ditto; Matthew Keegan, ditto; John Brown, ditto; John Parker, ditto; John Chapman, ditto; Thomas Coyne, ditto; and James Geary, private 73d. regt.; Thomas McCaig, a free man, also; **Two Black Native Girls, armed as well as the men.**

The Adventure Begins

Reports from the country state, that the condition of the land and the forwardness of cultivation in the different districts are highly satisfactory. We are happy to perceive that sowing of wheat is proceeding with great spirit and that the plough has entirely superseded the hoe.

On Thursday returned to Town a small party of Capt. NAIRN'S Company of the 46th Regt. who were lately sent in quest of the Bush Rangers; the following particulars of their pursuit we lay before our Readers:—

*After a diligent search in the woods the party at Jericho perceived Michael Howe, **accompanied with a Native Black Girl, named Mary Cockerill, with whom Howe cohabited.** On the approach of the party Howe darted into a thicket and effected his escape, after firing at the native girl, who, from fatigue, was unable to keep pace with him in his flight and was taken. Howe being so closely pursued, threw away his blunderbuss and knapsack. The native girl then led the party to the Shannon River, a distance of 11 miles from Jericho, where they found four huts, which they burnt. While thus employed, they perceived three of the bushrangers (Howe, Septon, & Geary) at the side of a high hill, contiguous to the river.*

On the appearance of the party, they were not in the least alarmed, for being in an advantageous position on the other side of the river, they by their gesticulations put them at defiance and afterwards made off. The party then forded the river and for two days, continued eagerly their pursuit, accompanied by their native guide, till all traces of them were lost; still their exertions were not in vain, for she led them to the discovery of 56 sheep, the property of different individuals which had been driven into the woods by the runaways. From the severe hardships endured by the party in this arduous pursuit, their provisions being all expended, they were compelled to kill two of the sheep for their present substinence, & the remainder with difficulty they brought with them to town; part of which have been since claimed by the owners.

> *The native girl has since been repeatedly examined; and we have no doubt,*
> *some important information may be derived regarding the numerous*
> *depredations of the bush-rangers.*
>
> *HOBART TOWN; PRINTED BY ANDREW BENT*

I know it sounds clichéd, but I was smitten; I could barely speak and foolishly scuffled my way through the rest of the encounter. Lowana had no such reservations and took control of the situation, leading me like a puppy to meet her family and friends. All were accepting, warm and welcoming, which I found ironic after the reserved reception I had received from my own countrymen when I'd arrived in Hobart a few weeks earlier.

Lowana and I spent much time together over the next few days and weeks. I loved being in her company; she was strong, clever and had a mischievous sense of humour. After a while we both realised this was becoming something more than mere acquaintance. I was somewhat hapless in such matters. A life of cerebral pleasures and a boys' school had left me in baffling blissful ignorance of anything remotely related to the female sex. Other than my mother and sister, I had known few women in my life and any talk of bodily functioning had been answered in the context of Greek Mythology or some equally mystifying response. I was an untried youth, although I must say not an unwilling partaker of the ensuing, most intimate and pleasing assignation.

I settled into life with Lowana, Rialim and their clan. Most of the people were related in some way or had married into the tribe. I soon discovered there were strict social conventions related to marriage and punishments for adultery, unsuitable marriages and other infringements of tribal laws. Each had grown up living in a family group including Rialim's parents who married in their teens and would stay together for life as was their custom. They often talked of other clans, also made up of families they knew or were related to and on occasions met up with for social and practical reasons. At first, I thought only the girls would live with their husband's clan although much later I learned that men also moved to their wife's clan. Wymurick from Robbins Island off the North West coast joined his wife's clan and later became their leader while Manalargenna lived with his first wife's clan at Ben Lomond.

There were times as I rested in my shelter that I would hear the melodious and yet harmonious sound of a singer, sometimes alone, sometimes joined by several of the tribe. I was reminded of tunes sung by Arabs from Asia Minor whom I had met on my journey eastward. Dancing too was enjoyed by all with imitations associated with many of the animals and nature which were part of their everyday lives, including the emu dance and thunder and lightning, in which they moved their feet rapidly, stamping noisily on the ground, accompanied by loud shouting and a good deal of dust.

In years to come, dances began to incorporate European animals such as horses. Actors formed a string, moving in a circle half stooping, holding each other's loins with one man posing as if to hold the reins and a woman as driver. Over time the dances also reflected battle scenes with the British.

Families in any society need the companionship of others for a whole range of reasons including finding a partner, mutual benefits from hunting and protection against hostility.

Lowana's brothers and sisters, grandparents and other relatives all lived together, eating, telling stories, sharing, fighting and laughing just as groups of humans have done for ever - making babies, giving birth, caring for their sick and elderly and making their homes warm and comforting.

Their clan had a leader, or chief, older and well regarded for his fighting and physical skills, intelligence and ability to lead.

It took me a while to understand that the whole collection of clans made up a nation and there were several nations in Lutruwita, each with its different language, custom and social norms.

Lowana's clan was part of the Paredarerme Nation which stretched across to the coast and was bordered by the Nuenonne (South East), Lairmairrener (Big River), Tyerremotepanner (Northern Midlands), Plangermaireener (Ben Lomond) and Pyemmairre (North East) Nations.[iv] Like any human society there were disputes between nations and clans but generally they worked together for mutual benefits. There were well established routes covering the island allowing people to cross the territory of others in search of food and to trade.

Each clan had a recognizable name and its own identity. The Moomairremener clan, I found out, were one of many in the Oyster Bay Nation. Others included Leetermairremener – St Patricks Head; Linetemairrener –North Moulting Lagoon; Loontitetermairrelehoinner – North Oyster Bay; Toorernomairremener – Schouten Island; Poredareme – Little Swanport; Laremairremener – Grindstone Bay; Tyreddeme – Maria Island; Portmairremener – Prosser River and Pydairrerme – Forestier and Tasman Peninsular.

Although there were nine nations in Lutruwita, Lowana's clan may have been aware only of those closest to their country. Each nation lived in its own territory and appear to be bound by obvious land marks such as rivers, mountain ranges &c. I wondered if national boundaries could be understood by studying the topography of Tasmania.

Clans and nations also had control of the richness of their plains and eucalyptus woodlands which contained an abundance of kangaroo and other animals.

Lowana and her community slept in bark huts, often with substantial foundations, built for warmth and protection using mud or clay to cover gaps, depending on the season. Her clan moved with the seasons from inland to the coast, which, when you think about it, was very sensible and not unlike the British going to Brighton for the summer holidays!

I was simply fascinated and mystified by just how adept and attuned Lowana and her family were to living within their natural surrounds. As with many human societies, tasks and duties were often gender-defined. For example, women made necklaces, reed baskets, collected berries or caught possums and wombats while men hunted with wooden spears and *waddies* with incredible skill and accuracy. Everything they did or made had a purpose and an immediate practical use. Nothing was wasted and the bush simply regrew after they left. I was intrigued to watch the *luna* making baskets, deftly weaving grass fibres in and out, around the base and sides. For someone who finds doing up his shoelaces a daily challenge, this was truly a sight to behold. I sat for hours trying to figure out how it was done but to no avail. The end products were pleasing to the eye, sturdy and useful. When living near the coast some baskets were made from bull kelp and were used for carrying water.

Making *kanalaritja* (shell necklace) was also a big part of life for the *luna*. Lowana and her friends would set out in the early morning to scour the beaches for special shells for their craft. Once I hinted, I would like to come too but was told in no uncertain terms that this was for women only. They made more than were needed and used the rest for trading with other clans or nations.

The *kanalaritja* were prized and worn by both sexes. The work was fine, intricate and delicate and resulted in exceptionally beautiful pieces. On one occasion I noticed an older woman working on a piece which ran out at a length before her into the pinkish sand. It must have been eight feet and others were even longer. Lowana saw me looking at her work and deftly wrapped a completed necklace several times around her neck and shoulders. The result was mesmerising!

Sometimes Lowana wore a fur around her neck whilst Rialim used leather bands or intricately woven bones to enhance his dress. Once he saw me looking at the bone pendant and told me it was his grandfather's jaw bone. I have to admit my sensitivities were awash with a mix of revulsion, inquisitiveness and fascination. This memory and sentiment resurfaced many years later when visiting some of the churches in Italy and France with an assortment of gruesome human bones of Saints on display with worshipers kneeling before them. When I was in Ceylon there seemed to be numerous bones of Buddha adorned with gold and in receipt of multitudes of prayers and blessing. Was Rialim's respect and love for his ancestor so different?

One of my greatest pleasures was to watch Lowana; her movements were refined and agile with grace and power and, when necessary, extraordinary speed. She reminded me of the veracity and independence of the girls from ancient Sparta I had read so much about as a child.

Thomas Bock (1790–1855) Trukanini (Truganini, Trugernana) 1831 later copy portraits labelled in error "Wortabowigee" Fanny Watercolour 13.4 x 13.5 (image) 29.4 x 22.3 (sheet) Presented by the Tasmanian Government, 1889

I once saw her chase a *lurgu* (female kangaroo) and swiftly pitch a *rugga* (spear) into the leaping animal bringing it swiftly to the ground with a final blow from a *waddy*.

As she walked back with the animal across her back, I thought it may be prudent not to upset her too much.

Seeing Lowana *wanga* (kill), skin and cook our meal made me wonder about male supremacy and how everything I had been brought up to believe in made no sense in this setting. Being white and male offered few attributes pertinent to being able to navigate most of the situations I was presented with in this environment. Of course, some of the men were stronger than Lowana, but she could match any of them in skill, physical and mental.

Talking of bodies, the time had to come when all had to be revealed. I was living, eating, laughing and sleeping with people who were either completely naked or partially covered with animal skins. Little notice was taken of different body parts. There I sat in thick, woollen, bulky and uncomfortable clothes trying to assimilate as best as I could.

Neill, Robert. (1828). Savages of Van Diemen's Land Hunting, 1828 NSW Library Dixon Library, State Library of New South Wales V163

Then one morning Lowana got up and left the hut to help with the food and returned to see me beginning the laborious process of dressing. Looking directly at me, with an ever so subtle grin and finger running down the crest of my *rowick* (nose), she whispered, *'parra garah'* (no) and left.

So that was it. I was naked. Trying to stand, I realised that it's one thing to live all your life with bare feet running and walking across bushland and everything that prickles, cuts and bites, but it's quite another to step out with feet as soft as mush-paper which had only ever touched the floor briefly before going to bed. Feeling the brisk air engulfing my nakedness I opened the fur flap of our hut. You can imagine the reaction when this tall, lanky, pale white man stepped out with nothing on except boots. There was such mirth and amusement I nearly had to retreat, but then I too joined in the laughter.

*Neill, Robert. (1828). Savages of Van Diemen's Land Reposing,
1828 Dixon Library, State Library of New South Wales V164*

My white body seemed to be the main point of interest with children playing tag to see how close they could get to touch my *lathanama* (leg) without me spotting them first. Soon I felt at ease and relished the sense of freedom. I was free from the burdens of my cultural demands. Rialim gave me some skins to wear, but even so one evening I began to shiver and watched as the others helped rub animal fat onto each other's skin for warmth. Without warning I felt fingers on my skin as Lowana began to gently rub the fat onto my shoulder and then gradually moved down and across my body. It was the most sensuous, entrancing, all-consuming experience I have ever had. I could sense her breath, smell her aroma and hear her whispers as I closed my eyes to take in every ounce of pleasure. The problem was of course my body began to respond in a predictable way which required a great deal of self-control and a firm grasp over the rather inadequate coverage below. Lowana was aware exactly of what was occurring and, I fear, so were those around us, evidenced by their stifled mirth. I thought it best to keep my eyes closed and hands well and truly in place until the process was concluded.

A few days later I woke up with toothache. Naturally I panicked with little chance of getting to Hobart to see a doctor although such a thought only served to increase my distress. Lowana seeing my anguish disappeared for some time and returned with a paste of sort nestled on a piece of bark. Its aroma was strong and made me sneeze. Without a word she beckoned me to open my mouth and began to rub the paste into the gum around the culprit. It was spicy, sharp and very hot but amazingly it worked. Why did I doubt? Cultural pride, the leveller pain can bring or simple cowardliness? Either way, after that I accepted with gratitude the remedies, I was offered for an endless stream of minor ailments from ant bites, mild fever and even a cracked bone in my arm which was held with a splint and healed with natural remedies.

I had many fears during that time but my greatest were from snakes, spiders and a particularly fiendish ant characterised by its black body, red nippers and rapacious temperament. They clearly took a liking to my soft whiteness and jumping some distance to lodge their fangs deep into my skin and rendering an agonisingly painful bite. Luckily on one occasion an elderly *luna* took pity on me gave over a bracken fern to rub on my sore providing almost immediate relief. I had so much to learn!

Once we were camped near the ocean when to my delight, I saw Lowana walk calmly into the sea, glide effortlessly under the waves, remaining submerged for an inordinate, nerve wracking amount of time and resurface with a sizable *nunnya* (crayfish) flapping inside her basket. I sat with the coarseness of granite sand settling within my bare buttocks and relishing the freshness and freedom of the beach which seemed to stretch forever in one direction while meshing into a rocky cliff near to us. Experiencing the surf, dark green ocean, expansive cloud clustered sky I just wanted this moment to last forever.

I should mention here to my consternation that I cannot swim at all and water is certainly not an element I am comfortable with. You have to understand that the only exercise my parents undertook was on the occasions they had to climb the ladder in the library in order to claim a rare book from the top shelf. Outdoors activities were

Outdoors activities were restricted to having tea in the orchard on the odd, warm summer evening. Naturally I modelled their lifestyle so you can imagine my incredulity on seeing this person I loved using her body in ways I could never have imagined.

Without a word, Lowana began to make a fire and cook the crayfish. A little later she dived off a cliff and came up with a collection of mussels and abalone. Soon the other women the clan began to arrive each bringing with them an assortment of native currants, cherries, kangaroo apple and other foods. I watched as one *luna* ground wattle seed and grasstree, yamina, to make flour for damper.

Two women carefully untied what looked like a bundle of large kelp to reveal two abalone shells cupped together and when opened small, red embers glowed from within as a tiny waft of smoke floated away. I later learned they contained Banksia pods which smoulder for many hours within their shell like cocoon. The women then adeptly lit a fire in preparation for cooking the vast array of food being brought for us to eat.

Others arrived later from one of the islands sliding their boats onto the beach with a seal and mutton birds to add to our repast. I learned from Lowana that *luna* were the best at hunting seals. Much to my amusement she showed me how they could imitate seals by scratching themselves and rolling around on the ground until the seals became used to their presence and they were then unceremoniously clubbed to death. It seemed to me *luna* did most of the work necessary for the clan to survive which I reflected was not too dissimilar to my culture.

I noticed earlier just how adept the men were at hunting. They could deliver a spear with great accuracy for over sixty yards and spin a waddy through the air to bring down possums or birds. Women and men employed many different and clever trapping methods to capture wallabies, kangaroo, birds and other prey. Then, as I watched, the

animals were thrown directly into the fire allowing fur or feathers
to be burnt after which the entrails were scraped out and the carcass
returned to the flames for roasting.

By this time several clans were settling in to share their food.
I realised too that family was Lutruwita. Everything was centred
around family with everyone closely united by their bond to each
other. I was rarely alone with Lowana, enmeshed by a constant
mingling, comings and goings with children everywhere, elders
sitting, respected by their very presence and all those in between.

Ever attuned to language my ears soon picked up unfamiliar
words and phrases. Also, I noticed unalike gestures, ways of eating
and more particularly the differences in the men's scarification.
Rialim told me we were now close to Pyemmairre land and the
Leenethmairrener clan had joined them for trade, to organise
marriages and for music and food. While there had been times of
conflict between the two nations today their wariness of each other
was put aside for mutual benefits.

As I ate my senses were
awash with unusual tastes,
smells and texture. Much
of the food was delicious
although there were a few
occasions when even my
most practiced persona
could not disguise the truth
often to the amusement of
those around me. I became
practiced at eating oysters
and other shell fish and
throwing the shells over my

*F.25 The entrance to Port Arthur. No.22 Pencil
heightened with white; In Sketches etc., 1836-
ca. 1912 / by Thos. Jas. Lempriere A. C. G. Van
Diemens Land; Dixon Library, State Library
of New South Wales CALL NUMBER DGA
64/vols.1-2 ; FL513709*

shoulder into the midden behind. All along the coast were vast piles of shells cast aside by hundreds and hundreds of generations of people. My innermost bleakness lead me to cogitate on how much longer this could last.

The next day we walked along the coast to find a group making both a *ninga* (canoe made of tea tree bark) and another *tuylini* (canoe made from stringy bark). I watched, fascinated and in awe for hours while men and children gathered quantities of eucalyptus bark and dry reeds or rushes, delivering them to those skilled in boat building and who made long bundles which were in turn tied together ensuring the ends were upturned at stem and stern allowing the middle to shape into a hollow. I noticed one as long as the whale boats I had seen in Hobart and it could carry several people, their dogs and spears. Some even had a clay base for fire and cooking. Rialim told me of the Needwonnee clans living in the south of Lutruwita who took dangerous journeys to an island group the rytji call Maatsuyker which was most treacherous but they were a brave seafaring people.

These they used to sail across to the various islands close by, although some of their journeys would take them some distance from land, often with whole families aboard. Their boats were both sturdy and robust and easily manipulated in the water with *praywi* (paddles), *lurana* (legs) and *nguwana* (arms).

I saw two British sailing ships making their way around the coast towards Storm Bay and *Timtumili Minanya* (Derwent River). As they drew closer one of the women spotted a glint of light from the ship and pointed it out to me. It was a spyglass and abruptly I knew my private world had been violated, invaded and I felt both irritated and ashamed of my own people to think they had such a right.

Soon they would spew out hundreds of stench-ridden convicts and fortune seekers, compounding the ever-increasing tension between the races. I could only wonder what the future had in store for the Pakana people I had grown to love and admire so much.

I didn't have to wait for long. A few days later I was awoken by screams, yells and cries from outside our hut. I rushed out to see Lowana holding her mother who was inconsolable and barely able to stand. Tears flooded her cheeks. Others too were either crying or standing immobile, staring directionless and without seeing, unable to move. I had never seen nor since then witnessed such an expression of human despair and grief. I waited a long time until Lowana came to me, eyes now dry but face pained and anguished. While she held me and sobbed a little more, I realised for just a moment that I was no longer seen as a *rytia* but as me, a person and a human being just like her.

They had just learned that there had been a terrible battle between stockmen and a clan from the Northern Midland Nation. It was Lowana's sister's clan. Her *nowantareena* (sister) had been taken and repeatedly raped by the men, but had escaped. Her husband, their chief, had been killed and their children were missing. I could say nothing to soothe her, only attend to her sobs and breaking heart. Holding her close I could feel her body gradually ease until silence ensured. Her body stiffened for a few seconds until eventually Lowana moved away with her arms outstretched, holding my shoulders in a vice-like grip. Her black eyes searched mine, seeking I know not what. I felt a chill and a sensation beyond description as I felt her imperceptibly slip away. It would be years later before I could make sense of what had just occurred.

HOBART TOWN GAZETTE AND SOUTHERN REPORTER
(TAS. 1816 - 1821), SATURDAY 17 APRIL 1819, PAGE 2

HOBART TOWN.

Two encounters have lately occurred between the stock-keepers and the natives, near the Macquarie River. The one at the grazing ground occupied by the stock of James Gordon, Esq. and Mr. E. Miller; in which the natives are stated to have been found spearing sheep, but retreated upon the approach of Mr, Miller and a servant unarmed ; a native woman accompanied them to the hut and took the food which was offered to her; but soon escaped and no violence took place. The other at the grazing ground of Mr. Stocker; where a very serious affray occurred, of which different accounts have been received and of which until we can obtain farther information, we shall merely give the outline:

One account says that the natives attacked the flock and, after being opposed by the stock-keepers, they came on in very large numbers ; that of the three stockmen, one was killed and one wounded ; that one native man [The Chief] was also killed ; and that the hut was burned down. The other account says that a native woman, supposed to be the wife of a Chief, had been maltreated by two of the stock-keepers; that she escaped after much illusage ; and that the tribes returned and attacked, as above described, the people and the stock. From the peculiarly ferocious manner in which they appear to have acted in this instance, so very different from the one before mentioned, there seems much reason to believe that some immediate and great cause had existed. We hope that more may be known before our next publication.

On Tuesday se'nnight, as two children, sons of Mr. Davis, settler at Humphrey's Rivulet, were playing near where their father was at work, one of them, a lad about nine years of age, took up a tomahawk which very incautiously was left near him and with one blow severed the three fore-fingers off the right hand of his brother, a boy of four years old. The child is in a mending way.

This reminded me of a *luna* whom I had seen some weeks before sitting by the fire for hours, cross legged, monotonously rocking as if in a trance, her face expressionless but desperate. I discretely enquired what was ailing her so much. Her precious child, they told me, was taken by rytia to raise as a servant and to learn their ways. This practice I soon realised was of such concern to the Governor he issued this proclamation:

HOBART TOWN GAZETTE AND SOUTHERN REPORTER
(TAS: 1816 - 1821), SATURDAY 13 MARCH 1819, PAGE 1

GOVT. AND GENERAL ORDERS.
Government House, Hobart Town. 13th March, 1819

*FROM Information received by HIS HONOUR the LIEUTENANT GOVERNOR, there seems Reason to apprehend that Outrages have been recently perpetrated against some of the Native People in the Remote Country adjoining the River Plenty, though the Result of the Inquiries instituted upon these Reports has not established the Facts alleged, farther than that two Native Children have remained in **the Hands of a Person resident above the Falls:**- Upon this subject, which the Lieutenant Governor considers of the highest importance as well to Humanity as to the Peace and Security of the Settlement, His HONOUR cannot omit addressing the Settlers.*

The LIEUTENANT GOVERNOR is aware that many of the Settlers and Stock-keepers consider the Natives as a Hostile People, seeking, without Provocation, Opportunities to Destroy them and their Stock; and towards whom any attempts at Forbearance or Conciliation would be useless, It is, however, most certain that if the Natives were intent upon destruction of this Kind and if they were incessantly to Watch for Opportunities of effecting it, the mischief done by them to the Owners of Cattle or Sheep which are now dispersed for grazing over so great a part of the Interior Country, would be increased a Hundred Fold. But so far from any systematic plan for destroying the Stock or People, being pursued by the Native Tribes, their Meetings with the Herdsmen appear generally to be incidental; and it is the Opinion of the best informed Persons who have been longest in the Settlement, that the former are seldom the Assailants and that when they are, they act under the impression of recent Injuries done to some of them by White People.

It is undeniable that in many former instances, Cruelties have been perpetrated repugnant to Humanity and disgraceful to the British Character while few attempts can he traced on the part of the Colonists to conciliate the Native People, or to make them sensible that Peace and Forbearance are the Objects desired. The Impressions remaining from earlier injuries are kept up by the occasional Outrages of Miscreants whose Scene of Crime is so remote as to render detection difficult; and who sometimes wantonly fire at and kill the Men and at others pursue the Women for the purpose of compelling them to abandon their Children.- This last Outrage is perhaps the most certain of all to excite in the Sufferers a strong thirst for revenge against all White Men and to incite the Natives to take Vengeance indiscriminately according to the general Practice of an uncivilized People, wherever in their Migrations they fall in with the Herds and Stockmen. It's not only those who perpetrate such Enormities against a People comparatively Defenceless that Suffer; all the Owners of Stock and the Stock-keepers are involved in the Consequences brought on by the wanton and criminal Acts of a few.

From the Conduct of the Native People, when free from any feeling of Injury, towards those who have fought Intercourse with them, there is a strong reason to hope that they might be conciliated.- On the North East Coast, where, Boats occasionally touch and at Macquarie Harbour, where the Native have, been lately seen, they have been found Unsuspicious and Peaceable ; manifesting no Disposition to injure; and they are known to be equally, Inoffensive in other Places where the Stock keepers treat them with mildness and forbearance.

GOVT. AND GENERAL ORDERS.

A careful Avoidance, on the Part of the Settlers and Stockmen, of Conduct tending to excite suspicion of intended Injury and a strict Forbearance from all Acts or Appearances of Hostility, except when rendered indispensable for positive Self-defence, or the Preservation of the Stock, may yet remove from the Minds of the Native People the Impressions left by past Cruelties, so that the Meetings between them and the Colonists which the extension of the Grazing Grounds and progressive Occupation of the Country, must render yearly more frequent, may be Injurious to neither; and that those mischiefs, which a Perseverance in Cruelty and Aggression must lead to and which must involve the Stock in perpetual Danger and the Stockmen in responsibility for the Lives that many be lost, may be prevented.

To effect this object, is no less the Interest than the Duty of the Settlers and Stockmen; to bring to condign punishment anyone who shall be open to Proof of having Destroyed or maltreated any of the Native People (not strictly in Self' defence) will be the Duty and is the Determination of the LIEUTENANT GOVERNOR; supported by the Magistracy and by the assistance of all the just and the well-disposed Settlers.

With a View to prevent a Continuance of the cruelty before mentioned, of depriving the Natives of their Children ; It is hereby Ordered, that the Resident Magistrate at the District of Pitt Water end Coal River and the District Constables in all the other Districts, do forth-with take an Account of all the Native Youths and Children which are Resident with any of the Settlers or Stock-keepers; stating from whom and in what Manner they were obtained.

The same Magistrates and the District Constables are in future to take an Account of any Native Person or Child, which shall come or be brought into their District, or Country adjoining; together with the Circumstances attending it - These Reports to be transmitted to the Secretary's Office, Hobart Town.

No person whatever will be allowed to retain possession of a Native Youth or Child, unless it shall be, clearly proved that the Consent of the Parents had been given; or that the Child had been found in a state to demand Shelter and Protection, to which Case the Person into whose Hands it may fall is immediately to report the Circumstance to the nearest Magistrate or Constable.

All Native Youths and Children, who shall be known to be with any of the Settlers or Stock-keepers, unless so accounted for, will be removed to Hobart Town, where they will be supported and instructed at the Charge and under the Direction of Government.

By Command of His Honour
The Lieutenant Governor
H.E. Robinson, Secretary.

It would appear that not everyone grasped what was really happening to the Pakana people.

HOBART TOWN GAZETTE AND SOUTHERN REPORTER (TAS: 1816 - 1821), SATURDAY 25 APRIL 1818, PAGE 2

The weather in this settlement we believe was never more favourable to agriculture than it has been this season, having been warm, with occasional rains. Our reports from different districts stating that ploughing and sowing proceed briskly; and that in several places wheat, got in this month, has made its appearance. It is gratifying to hear that the settlers are so very forward this year in the pursuits of husbandry.

Notwithstanding the hostility which has so long prevailed in the breasts of the Natives of this Island towards Europeans, we now perceive with heartfelt satisfaction that hatred in some measure gradually subsiding. Several of them are to be seen about this town and its environs, who obtain subsistence from the charitable and well-disposed.

The more we contemplate the peculiar situation of this people, the more deeply we are impressed with the great arrearage of justice which is due them. What parent would be deemed other than barbarous, who surrounded by particular branches of his family, all of them happy, should feel no concern, or if he felt it, make no efforts to extend similar happiness to other branches, the sadness of whose conditions would be enough to make cruelty weep? And are not the Aborigines of this Colony the children of our Government? Are we not all happy but they? And are not they miserable?

Can they raise themselves from this sad condition? Or do they not claim our assistance? And shall that assistance be denied? Those who fancy that "God did not make of one blood all the nations upon the earth" must be convinced that the Natives of whatever matter formed, can be civilized, nay, can be Christianized, The moral Governor of the world will hold us accountable. The Aborigines demand our protection. They are the most helpless members ; and, being such, have a peculiar claim upon us All, to extend every Aid in our power, as well in relation to their necessities, as to those enlightening means which shall at last introduce them from the chilling rigours of the forest, into the same delightful temperature which we enjoy.

Even now after so many years I think of Lowana, recall our time together; the thirst for each other, its intensity and love. When we touched *rri* (hands), the first time she leant forward *pikina* (to kiss) and when we lay together for *trukra* (to have sex). We lived every minute with the intensity only perilous love can endure because we both knew, though never spoke, that there was no future for us. At season's end she would follow her clan to their winter camp closer to the sea while I would return to my world of words, buildings and social constraints.

We were also cognizant that her and her family's fate would soon be played out to an uncertain destiny. Forces way beyond either of us were contriving to determine their fate: the English were unstoppable, their numbers now far greater than her Pakana people and their desire for land insatiable. I had read enough of human history to know of the power and lust associated with relentless empires. I had read about Alexander the Great, his conquests across Persia and beyond. The decimation of the Etruscans by Rome, the sacking of Rome by the Gauls and the voracious desire for gold and riches in the Americas by Spain and Portugal. In more recent times the Dutch, French and now the English are rising in fortune and supremacy. Common to all was the desire for riches, power over others and an unquestioned sense of pre-eminence. It would have been naïve indeed to imagine that the British Empire would behave differently from any other. Was I the only one to see this?

The clan prepared to move once more and this time it would be without me. Lowana and I were at our most intimate on that last night and lay together until the *palana* (stars) and *wiggetena* (moon) inevitably lulled us to sleep. That time remains with me as fresh in my mind as if it were yesterday and still invokes a tear whenever I allow my thoughts to roam.

Aborigines making & straightening spears, 1835 / Benjamin Duterrau, 1767-1851; Dixon Library, State Library of New South Wales
CALL NUMBER DL Pd 64 ; FL8801906

Lowana was up before me so with a heavy heart I once again covered my naked body, according to the constraints of my world. I stepped out to where every member of the clan stood in silence, with their belongings, ready to leave. I looked upon the people whose generosity of spirit had so inspired me. I turned, letting my gaze sit lightly on its children, grandparents and families until it settled on Lowana as our eyes met for the last time. We knew we would never meet again. I must have seemed like an apparition. I was no longer W.C. their friend, brother, or lover of Lowana. I was, once again, *rytia*, their feared, hated, invader and now and forever I would be apart from them and no longer a part of their lives. My clothes were a barrier ripping through our threads of humanity and love for each other.

With expressions impossible to read each turned and began to walk away until only two remained: Rialim and Lowana. The people who had had such an indelible impact on my life in the last few weeks and months remain with me as I write these words so many years later.

He is there, close, facing me, my eyes captive to his; deep, deep dark peering far into the crevices my very soul just as he had on the morning of our first meeting. Rialim, the one who had taken me in hand without so much as knowing my name. This trust was absolute, taking me to his home, sharing the lives of his family, children and way of life. He was the one who by his actions and few words, taught me the etiquette and mores of his people even down to shaving with a flint and other discretions associated with bodily functioning. But he was much more than this and became like a father to me. As you know mine was not one to engage with children in any real sense. I remember the occasional nod of approval as he read my exam results and once, I recall an ever so slight smile at something I said. He loved me of course but his thoughts were elsewhere and obtuse for most of my childhood.

Rialim on the other hand spent time with me trying in vain to teach the essentials of living in his world. Could you imagine me trying to throw a spear, cut open a wallaby or dancing barefooted around a campfire? My aptitude for translating ancient Hebrew or conversing in Latin proved of little consequence in the wilds of Lutruwita. I did however learn his language and became quite proficient within a very short time something I think he appreciated.

I feared though as time went on something began to change between us. I cannot pinpoint it but there were occasions I knew he was watching me with Lowana. His eyes and sensitivity were tuned into his entire environment including not only the bush, its dangers and opportunities but the people around him as well. All the while he maintained his demeanour, talked with me and allowed me to walk with him as he hunted or delved further into the forests and hills within his sphere.

I knew instinctively that all was not right. At times he would abruptly walk away, not laugh so much or turn his head as we spoke. Perhaps he was anxious for Lowana, or me or both. There could have been annoyance, worriment or fear for the future lurking in his mind. He was my age before he ever set eyes on a rytia and in truth I was his enemy. My people were relentlessly taking land, food and killing his people. Either way I will never know truly what he was thinking or feeling during that time and to be honest I was so besotted and in love my energies were directed to only one person. Perhaps I should have been more aware and thoughtful but I wasn't and now I can never change what was to be.

There we stood, he with spear in one hand, wallaby skins wrapped around his sinewy, powerful body wearing an unfathomable expression under streaks of red ochre, a well-trimmed moustache, beard and knotted hair. Not a glimmer of movement, no smile, grimace or any other language of the body could I read. What was he seeing I wonder? A rytia pretending to be Pakana or perhaps a boy desperate to be a man. My eyes began to water just a fraction, I squeezed them shut and opened to emptiness. He was gone, vanished silently from my life just as he had arrived although to this day he remains in my heart and an enigma. I still have no notion of what he thought or felt about me nor my relationship with Lowana. I can only surmise but perhaps better not to think too hard about something I will surely never resolve.

Lowana and I were alone with only the crackle of smouldering fires and the gentle rustle of the trees around us for company. Although at times, as with Rialim, the language of her body had been unfamiliar to me and mine to her. Now her intent was clear and unequivocal. I could read every sensitive nuance reflected in her movements and subtleties of expression as if we had known each other all our lives. We stood apart until she came close, silently locking her captivating black eyes to mine and ever so gently, slowly traced her finger down one side of my face. When eventually we parted it was without a word. Our fingers slipped apart as we took our own pathways to our separate destinies: hers as a warrior to fight and kill and die, mine a quest for I know not what.

Then she was gone, leaving only an eerie silence, the sounds of the forest and smell of dying fires, I felt desolate, drained of emotion and being. I watched as a large black snake slide silently through the camp leaving in its wake an indent in the sand which I could never cross. I knew, within my heart, I would never love again.

I had left the Moomairremener people to return to 'civilization' and eventually made it back to Hobart Town.

Over the next few years I heard rumours of conflicts with natives involving a feared female fighter. It was said she had spent time with notorious bushrangers and had learned how white men fought their battles. She became proficient in firing guns, determined the white man's vulnerability lay when they needed to reload between firing and understood their modus operandi in warfare. Such knowledge was invaluable in her ensuing battles. Unsurprisingly, her knowledge of firearms did not rate a mention in the newspapers which were at this time little more than an instrument of government propaganda.

HOBART TOWN GAZETTE AND SOUTHERN REPORTER
(TAS. : 1816 - 1821), SATURDAY 20 MARCH 1819, PAGE 2

A man returned from Oyster Bay, on Monday, who had been speared by the Natives supposed to be the same by whom John Kemp was killed some time ago. The tribe which frequents Oyster Bay should be particularly guarded against, as they seem to have such a strong and rooted animosity towards the white people. It is well known that some time before Kemp was killed, a native man was shot in the woods by some of the stockmen to the Eastward and that the women have been also deprived of their children in that quarter.

The feared and revered female fighter was of course Lowana, who gained a formidable reputation as a warrior willing to fight ruthlessly for her people. I realise now, looking back to when I held her after tragedy befell her sister's family, that it was the beginning of her metamorphosis from the young captivating woman I loved to fearsome warrior. When she stiffened in my arms, her emotions were taking hold and determining her future. Hatred, revenge and bitterness are indeed powerful contributors to the human spirit.

Lowana eventually gathered around her similarly minded men and women from different clans and led them into battle against the invaders. They speared stockmen, used fire, killed sheep, cattle and bullocks and caused fear and havoc amongst the colonists. I could hardly reconcile my memories of her with what she was to become. It is reported she once said, 'She liked a *luta tawin* (white man) as she did a black snake'. I wondered if I too had become a black snake in her eyes: my hope is that a glimmer of her love for me would remain forever, but then I am an insufferable romantic.

It was some years later while posted in Anuradhapura, Ceylon, that I woke in the night with a jolt. An icy chill seared my spine and I knew she was no longer alive. I waited all that day for her spirit to leave with the setting of the sun. For me she will always remain within my soul and being.

It was not until I received post from Andrew Bent with a collection of newspapers that I learned what had happened. Early on 9th December 1826 while Lowana, her family and their clan were sleeping, the *rytia* surrounded and pitilessly attacked for no apparent reason. Fourteen of her people were killed and Kickerterpoller, their leader and ten others were captured. Lowana died fighting to her last breath. Her beautiful body no match for the shots that ripped it mercilessly apart. She was barely one score and ten. Even today she talks to me, although only in her own language—now vanished forever. Regardless of the emotional toll this took on me it was still my job to report on it and you can see my article listed around this date.

On occasions, alone in my attic retreat, I say 'Lowana' out loud and no one hears me except perhaps my dear old sleepy dog, Bent, whose tail gives ever so slight a wag when I mutter her name.

I wonder now if my writing had been compromised as a result of my personal life and was biased in favour of the Aborigines. I hope not. Remember too, I had seen the terrible injuries inflicted on white people from bloody spears deep in their bodies and seen people beaten beyond recognition by the brutal blows of *waddies*. I had witnessed the tormented faces of loved ones whose lives were forever torn apart by such violence. These images were also reflected in my reports although perhaps I was more willing than my colleagues in the local press to report both sides of the story.

I returned to Moomairremener country some years later to find the entire clan had vanished. I stood alone in the spot where their village had been and could only sense a faint breeze and the *tangara* (weeping) of spirits. To this day I dare not think about their destiny although the look in Rialim's fatalistic eyes in our last glimpse of each other returns to haunt my nocturnal turbulence.

My return to Nipaluna (Hobart Town) was far from triumphant. Polite society looked at me askance and most respectable citizens thought I was either a traitor or had lost my mind and should, at the very least, be locked up or sent Home to England. Rumours had been swirling around for weeks after Lieutenant Norton of the *Baring* had reported sighting a rather tall lanky white man naked with a group of natives on the coast a few weeks before. It didn't help that I smelt of animal fat for several weeks although I also became acutely aware of the stench around me. My senses were alert and on edge after so long living in the wild with scents of flowers, eucalypts and the freshness of the wind. Now to be with people who literally stank, smelling the quagmire of the once pristine water ways running through the town with sewage and carcasses of dead animals nor being able to drink clean water, generated a mix of revulsion and desolation.

I also found there was a dearth of intellectual thought or compatibility in such a confined, stifling and isolated community. Largely populated by convicts and cerebrally barren military officers and self-important administrators, I could find little solace or joy.

The saving grace for me came in the form of Governor Sorell who, with his drinking buddy Reverend Knopwood, took me out on several of their entertaining, liquor-charged evenings. They seemed genuinely interested in what I had found and gleaned from my experiences.

HOBART TOWN GAZETTE AND SOUTHERN REPORTER
(TAS. : 1816 - 1821), SATURDAY 24 MAY 1817, PAGE 1

PROCLAMATION, By WILLIAM SORELL, Esquire
Lieutenant Governor of the Settlements in Van Diemen's Land &c, &c, &c.

WHEREAS it has been represented to His HONOUR the Lieutenant GOVERNOR that several Settlers and others are in the habit of maliciously and wantonly firing at and destroying, the defenceless NATIVES or ABORIGINES of this Island; and whereas it has been commanded by His Majesty's Government and has been strictly enjoined by His Excellency the Governor in Chief, that the Natives of New South Wales and its Dependencies should be considered as under the British Government and Protection ;

These Instructions render it no less His Honour the Lieutenant Governor's Duty than it is his disposition to forbid and prevent and when perpetrated to punish, any ill-treatment of the Native People of this Island and to Support and Encourage all Measures which may tend to conciliate and civilise them:

His Honour the Lieutenant Governor thus publicly declares his determination, that if, after the promulgation of this Publication, any Person or Persons shall be charged with killing, firing at, or committing any Act of Outrage or Aggression on the Native People, the Offender or Offenders shall be sent to Port Jackson to take their Trial before the Criminal Court.

And all Magistrates and Peace Officers and others His Majesty's Subjects in these Settlements, are enjoined to enforce the provisions

Of this Proclamation.
GIVEN under my Hand, at Government House,
Hobart Town, this Nineteenth Day of May, One thousand eight hundred
and seventeen.

"WILLIAM SORELL."
GOD SAVE THE KING!
ACTING ASSISTANT COMMISSARY GENERAL'S OFFICE,

Sorell, I gathered had unaffectedly tried to work towards some resolution or compromise with the Aborigines and did his best to protect them. I began to realise I was becoming an outcast in a very small town and providentially I secured a post as Special Correspondent for the *Times of London* to cover the Vaddas insurrection which apparently had more 'appeal' to the readers back home.

On the 4th of January 1820 I boarded the *Regalia*, under the command of Captain Dixon and sailed to Ceylon. It would be some years before I was to return to Tasmania. As we sailed beyond its shores I felt a deep sense of foreboding settle upon my being.

Chapter Four

Correspondence from a Friend
Ceylon 1821 - 1827

During my time as Special Correspondent in Ceylon for the *Times* my dear friend Andrew Bent kindly favoured me with a constant stream of articles, letters and information about the state of the Aborigines in Lutruwita.

I include herewith a selection, which show a little of what was happening and how the newspapers were responding. How I wish I had been there during that time, but my need to earn a living meant I must go where my editor sent me.

It would be nearly six years before I could return to Tasmania, one of my favourite although increasingly dark and tragic places on Earth.

1820

HOBART TOWN GAZETTE, and

SOUTHERN REPORTER:

PUBLISHED BY AUTHORITY.

Vol. V.]   SATURDAY, JANUARY 22, 1820.   [No. 192.

His Honor the LIEUTENANT GOVERNOR has thought proper to direct, that all Public Communications which may appear in the

HOBART TOWN GAZETTE AND SOUTHERN REPORTER
(TAS: 1816 - 1821), SATURDAY 22 APRIL 1820, PAGE 2

We are sorry to learn, that before The Governor Macquarie proceeded to sea one of her seamen was severely wounded in a whale-boat, which was lying about 50 yards off the land, by a native with a spear, which went through his wrist and entered his body; he is, however, in a fair way of recovering. The brig had constant very bad weather during the whole of the time she lay at Port Davey.

1821

Hobart Town Gazette, and

VAN DIEMEN's LAND ADVERTISER.

PUBLISHED BY AUTHORITY.

Vol. VI.]   SATURDAY, JANUARY 27, 1821.   [No. 240.

Honor the LIEUTENANT GOVERNOR has thought proper to direct, that all Public Communications which may appear in the *Hobart Town Gazette*, and Diemen's Land Advertiser, figned with any Official Signature, are to be confidered as Official Communications made to thofe Perfons to whom they may relate.

(By Command of His Honor)

H. E. ROBINSON, Secretary.

HOBART TOWN GAZETTE AND VAN DIEMEN'S LAND ADVERTISER
(TAS: 1821 - 1825), SATURDAY 22 SEPTEMBER 1821,

The Native Boy, who was found in the woods, near the River Plenty, about two years and a half ago and has been since under the protection of the Lieutenant Governor and who was christened by the name of George Van Diemen, went to England in the Mary, in the care of William Kermode, Esq.

He is supposed to be almost 9 years old. It is hoped, that this favourable opportunity of ascertaining the capacity and disposition of the Native of this Island, may afford ground for placing them higher amongst the human species than the impressions hitherto assumed of this race of people have appeared to warrant.

This was my contribution to the story of a young boy's adventure.

The PAKANA Voice

BY W.C. SPECIAL CORRESPONDENT—*LUTRUWITA*

A young child was taken by the British Governor for his 'protection' after being found in his natural bush habitation. His real name was changed to George Vandiemen. A white man, William Kermode took it upon himself to remove the boy from his home without any attempt to locate his parents or clan and transport him to England. He spent some years at a school in Lancashshire, to be educated in the British way of thinking far away from his home.

According to the Hobart Town Gazette this was an attempt to see if 'the natives of this island, may afford ground for placing them higher amongst the human species than the impressions hitherto assumed of this race of people have appeared to warrant.' Apparently George's success at school did not place the race in any higher standing in the eyes of the British settlers!

George died a few years after returning to lutruwita. It is unknown if he ever saw his family again.

1823

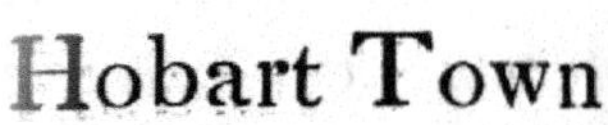

Eighth Volume.]   SATURDAY, JANUARY 4, 1823.   [Number 348.

The imagery of this next article is magical!

HOBART TOWN GAZETTE AND VAN DIEMEN'S LAND ADVERTISER
(TAS: 1821 - 1825), SATURDAY 23 AUGUST 1823, PAGE 2

A singular and unprecedented circumstance occurred a few days ago in the Macquarie district. - A fine horse, worth 100 guineas, the property of a Gentleman residing in that district, had been missing for several days; when, to the astonishment of many who saw it, the animal was rode at a full gallop down a valley in view of Allenvale-house by a black native girl, with a long tether rope round the horse's neck.

A servant was immediately sent on horseback in pursuit of the fair Tasmania jockey (the first of her race who has perhaps ever be-fore been seen on a horse at full speed); but, owing to her riding the animal so wonderfully fast, the man could not come up with her, after a pursuit of four days. -The proprietor, Mr. J. Riseley, has requested us to say, that he will give £5 reward for the recovery of his animal.

1824

HOBART TOWN GAZETTE AND VAN DIEMEN'S LAND ADVERTISER
(TAS: 1821 - 1825), FRIDAY 26 MARCH 1824, PAGE 2

Sit. Magistrate—Rev. R. Knopwood, M. A.

We are sorry to state, that the natives continue the same mischievous conduct which we reported some time ago to have taken place; very recently they have destroyed a hut belonging to Mrs. Collins, at the Blue Hills and killed James Doyle, one of the stock-keepers.

HOBART TOWN GAZETTE AND VAN DIEMEN'S LAND ADVERTISER
(TAS: 1821 - 1825), FRIDAY 2 APRIL 1824, PAGE 2

We are sorry to learn, that another stock-keeper has been speared by the Natives and that the poor man's life is despaired of; his name is James Taylor, servant to Mr. John Cassidy, of the Old Beach. It does not appear that Musquito or Blackjack were seen with this party, though there is reason to believe they must have been near the spot, from the circumstance of the Natives having been, with one or two instances only excepted, entirely harmless, until these two Blacks have lately appeared among them.

HOBART TOWN GAZETTE AND VAN DIEMEN'S LAND ADVERTISER
(TAS: 1821 - 1825), FRIDAY 28 MAY 1824, PAGE 2

TRIALS

William Tibbs, the first prisoner who has been tried before this tribunal of justice, was put to the bar on an indictment charging him with shooting at a black man, na-med John Jackson, on the 17th of January last, whereby the unfortunate man lost his life.

After the evidence had been gone through and the prisoner had made his defence, The learned CHIEF JUSTICE, in summing up the evidence, observed, that there were but two questions for the consideration of the Jury ; the first was whether the prisoner at the bar was the person who fired the pistol and if he was, how far he was justified in so doing.

The Jury in a few minutes returned a verdict of -- Guilty.

Tibbs has been only a few months in the Colony and was well recommended on his arrival.

I could not discover what sentence he was given, although this was the only trial I could find of a white man charged with the murder of a Pakana person. It would appear we are not quite all equal under the Law of Great Britain although sometimes a skerrick of humanity breaks through judicial consciousness.

HOBART TOWN GAZETTE AND VAN DIEMEN'S LAND ADVERTISER
(TAS: 1821 - 1825), FRIDAY 11 JUNE 1824, PAGE 2

A poor black native boy, named Troy, was then arraigned for house-breaking, but no witness appeared to support the prosecution and he was, of course, discharged.

His HONOUR very kindly requested Mr. Bisdee, the Gaoler, to protect the youth, until something could be done for him.

HOBART TOWN GAZETTE AND VAN DIEMEN'S LAND ADVERTISER
(TAS: 1821 - 1825), SATURDAY 24 JULY 1824, PAGE 2

To the Editor, of the Hobart Town Gazette.

Sir,-The liberal, bold and judicious manner in which you have written of the Black Natives is generally acknowledged ; but as ideas may strike " an old Settler," which may not enter the mind of a new one, (and allow me to state, my dear Sir, that there are now many young ones in the Colony,) I do hope I may be allowed to make a few suggestions on the subject of civilizing those poor creatures.

In the first place, I would beg the European hunters of kangaroo in this Colony to remember the fable of the boys and the frogs; and hence to infer that what proves their amusement, is the cause of starvation to the Natives. For it cannot admit of doubt, that to the flesh of the kangaroo and opossum, the Aborigines naturally look for support ; and if that support be abstracted for the thought-less recreation or superfluous profit of intrusive Europeans,-what, Sir, can result, but desperation, degeneracy, extinction, or recriminative robbery ?

In the next place, I would contend that such a result should be humanely expected and so far as possible averted by us in a just spirit of brotherly con-ciliation. We ought to feel that we have invaded a domain from which our invasion has expelled those who were born, bred and providentially supplied in it; that we have driven by our usurpation, families from their birth-place and then completed our cruelty by destroying in sport and consuming for profit, the principal means of their subsistence.

In the last place, Sir, on a conviction of the unprovoked aggressions we have perpetrated, we ought to devise some way of compensation ; and, for my own part, I will say that nothing would more readily effect the desired good than serving out by public subscription, with the humane concurrence of Government, bread and meat in adequate quantities to maintain the existence of those who, because black, have for our sakes been bereaved of their original possession and goaded by attendant hunger to acts of sanguinary retaliation. For, unless we do something of this sort, their existence will from necessity be soon extinct, as their natural sup-ply of nutriment becomes through our means daily scarcer; and-by doing it, we should acquire their good-will, through which an opening would be speedily given for the introduction of that knowledge which not only regards temporalities, but also " maketh wise unto salvation."

Indulging an earnest hope "that these few rough hints may receive from your Readers, that serious attention which, the forlorn and broken-hearted object of them merit,

I am, Sir,
Your most respectful Servant,
And constant Subscriber,

Zeno.

I think Zeno is someone I would have easily get along with. I know as a reporter I should not show my biases but since I am writing long after the events portrayed here, I consider it permissible. Zeno would not have been popular in the British Colony, but clearly, he had social standing as well as the strength of intellect and character to say what he thought. That is, hunting for sport is robbing the Aborigines of food.

Secondly he admits openly that 'we have invaded a domain from which our invasion has expelled those who were born, bred and providentially supplied in it; that we have driven by our usurpation, families from their birth-place and then completed our cruelty by destroying in sport and consuming for profit, the principal means of their subsistence.'

Brave words indeed! Not only that, but he goes on to talk about 'the unprovoked aggressions we have perpetrated' on the people of this land. I take my hat off to Zeno and salute him with a nip of malt; as if I needed an excuse!

You may have noticed the papers refer to the Pakana people as 'Black Natives'. I understand this was to distinguish them from British subjects who were born in the Colony and referred to themselves as 'natives'.

Then the stories of murder and mayhem began in earnest. I do not doubt the horror experienced by the British settlers at this time or during the following few years, but I ask you to search for the negative spaces in these stories. Certainly, there is some artistic licence here which as a journalist I condone. We all have to 'sell' our stories and entice readers into our web of intrigue and mystery. That is what sells papers and keeps food on our table. The ethics of such practice are another thing altogether. Perhaps my ethics became frayed a long time ago.

The heart of the dilemma is whether newspapers report the news or create it? War and war stories sell papers; we all know and play to our readers appetites which is part of the 'game,' so the negative spaces one needs to look for are those things that are not being reported. Ask oneself: are there experiences, pain and tragedies not being reported?

Biased reporting readily influences public opinion and ultimately affects the decisions made by those in positions of power. Keeping in mind that newspapers are generally read by people who agree with the views they espouse and they buy it because they will read what they want to hear and reaffirm their encrusted opinions. Which is exactly what the VDL newspapers were doing. In order to sell they probably worked on the adage cranky old editors knew very well: 'If it bleeds, it leads'. Is it any wonder I became an irredeemable cynic?

Sitting Magistrate - Rev. R. Knopwood, M.A.

The following proposition is respect-fully submitted to our mathematical Readers for solution:- To divide a rectangular parallelogram into two equal parts, one of which parts shall be similar to the whole parallelogram.

It will be recollected by our Readers, that a few weeks ago we, briefly noticed the death of Mr. Matthew Osborne, a stock-owner, residing in the district of Bath, about four miles beyond Jericho. We are now, by his afflicted widow, furnished with the following particulars of that deplorable and horrid event, to which we feel ourselves duteously urged to invite public attention:

It appears that for some days previously to his death, Mr. Osborne had been in town, whence he returned home, late in the evening of Wednesday, June 9th. About an hour after his return, an assigned servant to a settler named Beagent, at the Tea- tree Brush, called to offer Mrs. Osborne a kangaroo, which she agreed to pay for, in tobacco. After some conversation on the subject, Mr. Osborne made a remark, on hearing which, as he had not been seen, the man startled and in a very embarrassed manner, said "O! Mr. Osborne, is it you? I thought you were in camp; I have called at the request of two poor blacks, who are in great want; and I hope you will send them some provision!" — "What could you mean by bringing them about the place," cried Mrs. Osborne, " did you mean them to murder me?" — "Be under no apprehension," answered he, "they are quite tame and I have been sitting at their fire in yonder glen, for the last two hours." — 'They would not have come if they had thought any man was on the premises, for fear of being shot."—

At this moment a black man was seen within a short distance and on being recognized as Black Tom, the notorious companion of Musquito, the de-ceased observed to Beagent's man, that "he must be a very bad fellow to consort with such a murderer, especially as he knew how many acts of barbarity had lately been ascribed to him"

HOBART TOWN GAZETTE AND VAN DIEMEN'S LAND ADVERTISER (TAS: 1821 - 1825), FRIDAY 16 JULY 1824, PAGE 2

— "I don't care," was the reply; "I would not betray him for three free pardons and £50 besides." The deceased was of course alarmed and he gave a dish-full of potatoes to him, on which he joined Black Tom and immediately disappeared. Nothing further occurred until the following morning; when, as Mrs. Osborne was churning in the dairy, her husband rushed in and cried, "O! Mary, Mary, the hill is covered with sav-ages!" She of course was agonized with dreadful fears of being murdered and was proceeding to run away, when the deceased exclaimed, "Don't be frightened, my dear, but go into the house and I'll stand sentry before it." In a few minutes the blacks had arrived within 50 yards of the door, Black Tom being their apparent leader; when Mr. Osborne addressed them by saying, "What do you want?— Are you hungry? "The answer was, "Yes, white man, yes."

Then, said Mr. Osborne, "Lay down your spears and light a fire and I'll give you some potatoes and butter." At this time a large loaf was in the kitchen, which the deceased begged his wife to cut up and distribute among them; but she was in such a nervous state as prevented her from doing more than breaking it in two pieces and laying it before the sable tribe, with a request that they might fairly divide it. The deceased again said, "Lay down your spears."—"We will," answered Black Tom, "If you, white man, put down your musket." After a short discourse, the gun and spears were placed on the ground, the blacks (each of whom carried a fire-stick) came close to the house, were presented with some potatoes, which they began to roast and seemed quite satisfied. Having eaten them, a party entered the house and asked for more; the deceased went out to get some and on his return, his musket was missing. Apprehensions of treachery were now awakened and the deceased said, "I'm a dead man!"

A moment afterwards Black Tom entered and after saying (as he pointed to many things in the house), I must have this and I must have that, he took Mr. Osborne's hat off his head and wore it himself. Two of the blacks then grasped, as if to shake in friendliness, the hands of the deceased, when a third, who stood at a little distance, forcibly drove a spear into his back, which convulsed him to such a degree, that with a scream he bounded several yards and fell. Mrs. Osborne rushed wildly out, crying, "murder! murder!" was pursued and at length overtaken, after receiving three desperate wounds in the side and, neck.

She was then beaten down with a waddy, robbed of her silk neck-kerchief and nearly deprived of motion. After which, although her loss of blood was considerable, she crawled to the hut of Mr. John Jones, which was at least three miles off; where the most humane attention was shown her and from which several persons, with laudable promptitude, went to the spot where the deceased lay and in pursuit of the assassins; but, were, we regret to add, without success.

HOBART TOWN GAZETTE AND VAN DIEMEN'S LAND ADVERTISER
(TAS: 1821 - 1825), FRIDAY 16 JULY 1824, PAGE 2

Referring to the above, on which, our silence would be criminal, we beg to offer the following remarks; and however invidious they may be thought by the party accused, we have the honour to feel they are strictly just.—It is well known, that on all occasions we are decidedly averse to wound private feelings and that we disdain to add a superfluous link to the chain of slavery; but let it be also known, that we are no less hostile to the violation of those Orders, which are wisely issued in the justice of our Government, to check the depraved and guard the helpless from aggression.

If, therefore, agreeably to our information, an assigned servant has been allowed to roam the woods, at his pleasure, —in avowed pursuit of kangaroos, or for any other purpose, - and in particular at so vast a distance from his master's house, as Jericho from the Tea- tree Brush,—without a pass and subservient to no control,—his master has most culpably infringed a well-known Government Regulation!—and, if he can be proved to have so infringed it, we are bound by both our personal sentiments and Editorial integrity to trust, that condign se-verity will punish an act so fatally operative on the morals, property and lives of the Community.

There is another topic, connected with the above, on which we must express our sentiments, because were we not to do so, the Aborigines in general would by ungenerous report be involved in an odium completely undeserved;—and also, lest the effect of that report should influence unnecessary panic in the minds of our newly arrived Settlers. Perhaps, taken collectively, the sable natives of this Colony are the most peaceable creatures in the universe. Certainly so taken, they have never committed any acts of cruelty, or even resisted the whites, unless when un-sufferably goaded by provocation.

The only tribe who have done any mischief, were corrupted by Musquito, a Sydney black; who, with much and perverted cunning taught them a portion of his own villainy and incited them time after time to join in his delinquencies. And as to Black Tom we may state, that he was brought up in this town by the late Mr. Birch, from whose service Musquito enticed him,—but not before he had become addicted to rum and tobacco, for the procuration of which it cannot be doubted his subsequent offences have been perpetrated.—It however may be hoped, that in a short time both he and Musquito will be apprehended, as a party of soldiers and constables has long been and still is most actively pursuing them.

HOBART TOWN GAZETTE AND VAN DIEMEN'S LAND ADVERTISER
(TAS: 1821 - 1825), FRIDAY 30 JULY 1824, PAGE 2

It must be gratifying to every benevolent mind to hear and it is with much pleasure we are given to understand, that it is the determination of His Honour Lieutenant Governor Arthur to make every effort, through the medium of a very acute black boy, who has been brought up in the family of an inhabitant of this town since he was four years of age, for the civilization of the Aborigines of this Island; and so sanguine are we of the humane measures about to be adopted, that we have every reason to hope and believe they will prove successful.

.....

We learn that the native, named " Black Tom," alluded to in our report of Mr. Osborne's death, was not brought up by the late Mr. Birch, whose servant so called, still remains in the family, not at all inclined to ramble, but very steady.

HOBART TOWN GAZETTE AND VAN DIEMEN'S LAND ADVERTISER
(TAS: 1821 - 1825), FRIDAY 3 DECEMBER 1824, PAGE 3

WEDNESDAY. -- Musquito and Blackjack (the first a native of New South Wales, the latter born on this Island) were placed at the Bar and arraigned as principals in the second degree for aiding and abetting in the wilful murder of William Hollyoak, at Grindstone Bay, on the 15th of November, 1823. Plea -- Not Guilty.

The ATTORNEY-GENERAL described the facts and called John Radford, who de-posed as follows:--" I am and for six years have been a stock-keeper on the run of Mr. Cylus Gatehouse, at Grindstone Bay. I had a fellow servant named Mam-moa, who was a native of Otaheite. I knew the deceased; he was a servant to Mr. George Meredith at Swan Port and came to our hut in November twelve months. He said he was returning home from the Colonial Hospital, where he had been an invalid and begged permission to remain a day or two, as he was not very able to go further. He came on a Wednesday between the 10th and 15th and remained until the following Saturday. The morning after he came, a party of the natives arrived with the prisoners at the Bar.

Their number was about 65. Some of them had spears and sticks about two feet long; but some of the spears, which were wooden ones, might be six and others twelve feet long. I asked Musquito whither he was going? and he said to Oyster Bay. He then begged for some provision and I told him to follow me into the hut, where he should have some bread and meat. After he had eaten some, I inquired how many natives were with him? he answered he could not tell, I then asked if they would kill any of the sheep? He said no. Soon afterwards he retired for that night. On the following morning he again came to the hut and brought two or three women. Some of the blacks were on the opposite side of the creek. He asked for and had some break- fast with me.

He lingered with the party about the plains until 2 or 3 o'clock and then went away to hunt. In the evening he returned and I gave him some supper. This was Friday night. In the hut hung a small fowling piece and a musket, the one by the bed and the other over it. Musquito handled the musket. On Saturday morning early the blacks were in the sheep-yard, sitting round a fire at their breakfast; this was about half-past 5 o'clock. At 6, they came to the hut, with the prisoners at the Bar, over the creek, on the other side of which they had been at their diversions. Some of them still remained there near the stock-yard, which approaches to within 10 yards of the hut. The natives who were playing might be 150 yards from the hut. I walked out to look at them after Mammoa and left the deceased in the hut, but he came out after me. At this time Musquito was on the opposite side of the creek with a number of blacks who were armed; but he had no spear. The weapons he had were a waddy and a stick shaped like the axe of a tomahawk. I had desired the de-ceased to bring the guns should he leave the hut before my return; but he did not. Musquito then called Mammoa to the other side of the creek and he went over. He first, however, asked if the blacks would spear him and Musquito answered no.

They talked to Mammoa for a few minutes, then took up their spears and walked towards the hut. I got to it first. The guns had been taken away.

When I returned, Hollyoak was walking behind me and I asked him if he had put away the guns?

He said no; I made the same inquiry of Mammoa and received the same reply.

At this moment he and Musquito were at the other side of the creek, coming to-wards the hut; when they came opposite they got over. The other natives were by the hut door, so that now the whole body was assembled. I stood with the deceased 2 or 3 yards off. I had three kangaroo dogs and a sheep dog; the deceased had one dog, they were tied to a stump. I saw Musquito untie them and take them into the sheep yard, I heard Mammoa beg him not to take them, but he made no answer.

The natives stood with their spears raised and their points directed to me and the de-ceased. I told him the best thing we could do was to run away and that otherwise we should be killed. We accordingly did run, when one of the blacks threw a spear which pierced my side. I at first ran 2 or 300 yards, but the deceased could not keep up with me;- he called out for me to return and pull a spear out of his back. I did so. The wound was 3 or 4 inches deep. Some of the natives armed with spears were pursuing us: there might be from 30 to 40. I again ran away and the deceased after me. I received another spear in the back of my thigh. At this moment the blacks were within 30 yards of me. The deceased exclaimed "Jack don't leave me." I made no answer, but continued running till I heard him, cry " O my God! the black-fellows have got me!" He was then about 200 yards behind me. I looked back.

The natives were close to him. I saw 5 or 6 spears sticking in him (some in his side and others in different parts of his body.) He was throwing some rotten sticks at the blacks, who appeared to be standing quiet. After looking at them a few minutes, I recommenced my flight and some of them still pursued me: eventually, however, I was lucky enough to escape. When ten days from this time had elapsed, I ventured back to the hut and four days after my return, I found the body of the deceased quite dead, covered with sticks and more than half consumed, as if by vermin. There were some spears bro-ken in it. I am quite positive as to the persons of Musquito and Black Jack. I can swear that no provocation was given to the natives, or any violence shown by me, or to my knowledge by the deceased.

Cross-examined by the Court. -- When the dogs were untied by Musquito, I was deterred from interfering by the whole body, who raised their spears with the points directed to me. I know Black Jack very well by his figure and because his lips are much thinner than those of the natives in general. He had gone into the hut several times and I saw him in it on the Saturday morning, three quarters of an hour before the body of blacks came to it. On being spoken to, he answered me in English quite well. I never heard the prisoner called " Black Jack," but simply " Jack." I call him Black Jack from his colour.

Cross-examined by Doctor Hood (one of the Jury.) -- There were some women with the natives, but neither the deceased or myself had offered any offence, or want-ed to take any liberties. Verdict -- Musquito Guilty, Black Jack Not Guilty.

The same prisoners were then arraigned, as principals in the second degree for aiding and abetting in the wilful murder of Mammoa, the before named Otaheitean.

To prove this charge John Radford was recalled, but as his evidence scarcely varied from that which he had given in the previous trial, we consider that a repetition of it would be superfluous.

Mr. George Wise deposed, that in November last, from information received of the above murder, he, accompanied by Mr. Gatehouse, went off from Pitt Water to Grindstone Bay. Witness reached the bay on, the 17th and on the following morning arrived at Mr. Gatehouse's hut, which was empty, the door of it being open and the former contents strewed about the bush. Witness found Mammoa's body in a pool of water, in the creek, on the 23d; It was buoyant. The head was very much bruised and the body wounded in many places. Seven small holes were in the left side with-in about the compass of witness's hand and there were eight or nine holes in the neck. Altogether the witness counted 37 wounds about the body, which he supposed to have been given by spears. Near the hut; which was 70 or 80 yards from the creek, lay several broken spears, marked with blood. The pool in which Mammoa was found might be nine feet deep. Wit-ness could be positive as to the unfortunate man's identity, having often seen him and also because his features were peculiar.

Cross-examined by the Court. -- The in-formation which witness had received induced him to suppose the wounds had been inflicted by spears; but he might not be able to distinguish them from wounds inflicted by gun shot. The cranium was fractured and the wounds bled which witness had spoken of, he believed must have caused death. All the wounds bled when the body was drawn from the pool. The body was not very offensive. There was no blood on the margin of the creek; but, about 350 yards from the hut, witness found many spears stained with blood and to one of them a piece of cloth was sticking. The deceased had on when found a pair of leather small-clothes, but was otherwise naked. The witness thought Mammoa must have been in the water a long time, because he had understood that a corpse generally became buoyant when putridity was commencing.

His HONOUR the CHIEF JUSTICE then summed up; and the Jury, after retiring for a few minutes, pronounced an Acquittal.

1825

The Tasmanian,
AND PORT DALRYMPLE ADVERTISER.

TASMANIAN AND PORT DALRYMPLE ADVERTISER
(LAUNCESTON, TAS: 1825), WEDNESDAY 12 JANUARY 1825, PAGE 2

In the course of last week about 200 of the aborigines made their appearance in the Town of Launceston and immediate neighbourhood, encouraged no doubt by the accounts of the kindly reception and civil treatment, which their sable brethren recently experienced on the other side of the Island. We certainly should have felt much gratification in recording, had we been able, that these poor wanderers of the woods, on their first approach towards civilization, had discovered in us, on this side of the Island, a disposition savouring more of humanity, if not of hospitality.

What room have we left — we who are an enlightened people and professing Christianity —to express our disgust, detestation and horror, on hearing a recital of the dark and nameless deeds of the untutored savage, who, rude as nature formed him, is left to prowl through the wilderness; while, at the same time, the very threshold of our polished doors are stained with spots of but a lighter hue. Even on their way hither these defenceless creatures (for they came unarmed) were wantonly and maliciously fired at by some of the settlers in the vicinity of Patterson's Plains; and, as if that was not enough for ever to forbid them peeping out from beneath the shelter afforded them by nature, scarcely had they been in and left Town again, before one of their women, in the immediate vicinity of it, was used in a manner, which, for brutality, beggars description.

We are happy, however, in being able to state, that it is the firm determination of His Honour the LIEUTENANT GOVERNOR (who, fortunately for the ends of justice, was in Town at the time), to punish those wretches, whose minds must have been beneath that of the brute creation, with the utmost severity the law can inflict.

The PAKANA *Voice*

BY W.C. SPECIAL CORRESPONDENT—*LUTRUWITA*

The Tyerremotepanner People (Northern Midlands Nation) made friendly overtures to the rytia last week by hoping to visit their village called Launceston. Many Pakana gathered and prepared to enter the place. As a gesture of goodwill they were unarmed and given that others had been received well by the British their hopes were high for a warm reception.

Such optimism was soon dispelled as they began to walk along the makuminya (road) running through the tikaluna (the plain) when a hidden assailant maliciously fired upon the mob.

Later when leaving the village one luna (woman) was taken and brutally raped by more rytia.

It seems unlikely the Pakana will embark on a return visit.

TASMANIAN AND PORT DALRYMPLE ADVERTISER
(LAUNCESTON, TAS¬: 1825), WEDNESDAY 19 JANUARY 1825, PAGE 2

The same body of natives, we have every reason to believe, to which the black woman belonged that was so cruelly treated in the immediate vicinity of Launceston (which circumstance we took occasion to notice in our last), immediately upon quitting Town, bore away in the direction of the Western Tier; with the most resolute and savage determination, no doubt, of avenging upon the first white man, woman or child, that unfortunately came in their way, the injuries sustained by this female attached to their horde.

The following account of the miseries entailed upon two men (sawyers), labouring hard for an honest livelihood and who were no doubt the first that attracted the notice of the savages - together with the providential manner in which they escaped with their lives - occasioned entirely by the bestiality of a villain, not worthy to live, is certainly calculated to inspire us with pity for the sufferings of the poor men; while, at the same time, we cannot traduce, in language sufficiently strong, the conduct of the wretch, who thus makes the innocent to suffer for his crimes. At a place called Lake River, in the direction of the Western Tier, on the morning of the 11th instant, the two men alluded to were at work on the pit, cutting blackwood, about 9 miles from the residence of their master.

The sawpit was not above 20 yards, from their bough hut, but not in sight, the spot abounding with the thickest scrub imaginable. One of them on going to the hut, which he had not left above ten minutes, discovered that their musket had been taken away, as well as several buck-shot that were inside a bag containing provisions and other articles, which was left untouched. Relating this to his companion, on his return to the pit, he treated it as a joke, but soon found it otherwise, on looking in an opposite direction from the hut and perceiving three or four of these sable gentry, in part concealed, behind different trees.

Upon this one of the sawyers immediately retreated towards the hut again, in the expectation of decamping that way and saving his clothes, &c. when he found a large body of them in possession, who assailed him with spears in all directions, one of which entered the lower part of his back; and it was with the greatest difficulty he made his escape by flight, to the nearest stock hut, but about two miles off, severely wounded. The other man made in the direction of the trees, where he knew some others were concealed: and when within about 20 yards of them, three or four of them came from their hiding places and without the smallest menace on his part, as he had no weapon of defence, began a very sharp attack both with their spears and waddies.

He was more fortunate, however, than his companion, receiving only one spear through the fleshy part of the arm; and ultimately made good his retreat to the same stock-hut, although pursued sharply by two of them. The owner's cart was fortunately on the road that morning for a load and getting assistance at the stock-hut, proceeded to the saw-pit, where they found preparations for committing it, with such of the tools as they could not carry away, to the flames; but the noise of the approach of the cart, it is supposed, put then to flight, carrying with them the whole of the men's bedding and clothing, even to their shoes and hats ; an axe, a wedge, saw files, rule and pair of com passes, besides the musket and ammunition.

The similarity of this attack consists in the excessive cunning of the natives to secure, first of all, the musket and ammunition; and in the extreme silence with which the movements of so large a body were conducted, as they are represented to have been 80 or 100 in number.

That their intention was to sacrifice both the men is evident, as those stationed behind the trees, who kept partly showing themselves, could be with no other motive than to drive the sawyers toward the hut, where the main body were then ready to massacre them; and from whom one of the men had so narrow an escape.

We deem it proper to state, in justice to the poor men who have thus suffered only through the misconduct of others that though nearly a month at work on the spot, they had not the slightest previous intercourse, of any description with the natives; not so much as having either seen or heard then hunting; nor had they ever been hunting themselves, having no dogs.

HOBART TOWN GAZETTE AND VAN DIEMEN'S LAND ADVERTISER
(TAS. : 1821 - 1825), FRIDAY 25 FEBRUARY 1825, PAGE 2

EXECUTIONS

This morning Henry Mc'Connell, for bush-ranging and burglary ; James Bryan, Jeremiah Ryan, Charles Ryder, Musquito, a Sydney black and Black Jack, a native of this Colony for murder, John Logan, for shooting with intent to murder Mr. Shoobridge and Peter Thackery, for stealing in a dwelling-house and putting the owner in bodily fear, were executed according to their sentence - a sad example of the fate which sooner or later must overtake the enormities of which they had been convicted. On this occasion, for the first time, the Scaffold was erected within the Gaol walls, but in view of the town; and we should not be doing justice to the newly appointed Sheriff, if we failed to state that the whole of the melancholy arrangements reflected credit to his feelings, as an Officer and a Gentleman. The unhappy men on ascending the Platform, displayed a becoming humility, expressed their deep remorse and, after sing-ing an appropriate hymn, joined in most fervent and pathetic supplications to the throne of mercy. They then requested their clerical assistant, Mr. Bedford, to address, on their behalf, the assembled spectators, which he immediately did in words or to the effect following:-

My dear Friends - It is the anxious wish of these our dying fellow sinners, that I should thus in public, acknowledge for them the justice of their condemnation and that I should call upon you to repent, "for the kingdom of heaven is at hand." They implore you to take warning from their ignominious end; they entreat in this their last hour that you will turn from the error of your ways to the Lord your GOD, for he will have mercy. Yes, my brethren, these poor unhappy fellow-worms whose lives have become forfeited to the laws of violated justice and humanity, implore you all to shun the path that leads to death—to avoid bad company—to be industrious, sober and slow to anger — to be obedient, honest and religious.

> *May their prayers be answered, may their fate be impressed with salutary force on your Recollection and may you now success-fully join me and them in cries to the Redeemer for their, pardon in another world.*
>
> *This address proved very affecting and the hapless offenders after a short interval were launched into eternity. The whole of the officers in attendance were in deep mourning.*

Here I felt compelled to write an obituary for Musquito.[v]

The PAKANA *Voice*

BY W.C. SPECIAL CORRESPONDENT—*LUTRUWITA*

OBITUARY
MUSQUITO 1780 - 1825

The British execution of Musquito on the 25th February 1825 will leave many in the Pakana community angry and disillusioned and perhaps even more determined to fight for their land than ever before. Musquito's life was one of adventure, passion for the rights of his people and betrayal by so many white men.

An Eora (Gia-Mariagal) man born near the northern parts of Port Jackson. He was part of resistance groups fighting against settlers including several raids and reprisals. Eventually captured in 1805 and even though proven not guilty he was exiled to Norfolk Island for eight years and then sent to Van Diemen's Land in 1813 by the Governor. In 1817 Governor Sorell agreed to allow him to return to his Native Place but this did not occur leaving him angry and rancorous.

One man's freedom fighter is another's enemy and no more so than in Musquito's case. Listening to accounts of his life from first abiding with the British and helping to track bushrangers, becoming an outcast, moving to live with peaceful Pakana and eventually joining the wild Oyster Cove tribe. The latter was responsible for killing of several stock keepers in the early 1820s.

After a dubious, kangaroo court he was convicted of murder and executed which needless to say led to further violence from the aborigines.

Musquito was clever, articulate in languages including a sound grasp of English and spent his life fighting for his convictions. He will be sorely missed.

HOBART TOWN GAZETTE AND VAN DIEMEN'S LAND ADVERTISER
(TAS: 1821 - 1825), FRIDAY 25 MARCH 1825, PAGE 2

> *With considerable pain we communicate that the Aborigines, on lately visiting Macquarie Plains, speared a poor man, whose name was Johnson and who had a stock in conjunction with a person named Kinchley. What adds to our regret is, that at the moment the fatal spear was driven, Johnson was providing some refreshment for his murderers.--He died immediately.*

TASMANIAN AND PORT DALRYMPLE ADVERTISER
(LAUNCESTON, TAS: 1825), WEDNESDAY 30 MARCH 1825, PAGE 2

> *A few days ago, two stock-keepers, in the employ of James Cox and Andrew Barclay, Esq. named Arnott and Booth were cruelly massacred by the black natives. When first discovered, their bodies were found to be in such a shocking state that it was impossible to remove them, or even to convene an inquisition, but were interred on the spot.*

A short time afterwards, the same body of natives appeared to an armed party of stock keepers, in the same neighbourhood; and, when pursued, dropped a kangaroo rug and bedtick, the property of the two unhappy men whom they had previously murdered.

HOBART TOWN GAZETTE AND VAN DIEMEN'S LAND ADVERTISER (TAS: 1821 - 1825), FRIDAY 8 APRIL 1825, PAGE 3

Two stockmen, belonging to Messrs. Cox and Barclay have been cruelly murdered by the natives ; and a native woman who has been reared from her infancy among Europeans and who is far advanced in pregnancy, has been speared by the black boy Tegg, of which we promise our Readers full particulars in our next.

HOBART TOWN GAZETTE AND VAN DIEMEN'S LAND ADVERTISER (TAS: 1821 - 1825), FRIDAY 1 APRIL 1825, PAGE 3

To the Editor

Sir,-Induced by the readiness always manifested on your part, to diffuse every local transaction, connected either with the interest or safety of the population of this Colony, I hasten to lay before you and through the medium of your Paper, the Public, a circumstance of a most melancholy nature.

On the afternoon of Sunday the 13th of March, as John Johnson, shepherd to Mr. Jonathan Kinsey, residing at the upper part of Macquarie River, adjoining the Government run and James Taylor, lately stock-keeper to Mr. Cassidy, were at their hut, supposed to be employed in the removal of their bed-ding and other articles from an old hut to one newly erected, they were attacked by a formidable body of natives, about 80 in number, armed with spears and other implements of warfare. The result was, that the two un-fortunate men above-mentioned were most barbarously murdered by this desperate banditti, who afterwards withdrew, as it appeared by traces left, to the distance of about two hundred yards from the mangled bodies, where they feasted and passed the night, taking with them in the morning their wearing apparel, blanket, fire-arms and ammunition.

From this deplorable scene they proceeded to the hut of Mr. D. Lord, situate at the distance of about 2 1/2 miles from the above, which they reached at 10 o'clock, when, it fortunately happened, the stockkeepers were absent, as otherwise they would, in all probability, have shared the fate of the preceding. This place they rifled of every article of provisions, clothing, blankets, fire-arms and ammunition; from thence they directed their course to the hut of Mr. Stocker, half a mile further on-then between 3 and 4 o'clock on the Monday afternoon. One young man only was within, -who, alarmed by the barking of the dogs, hastened out and beheld a band of about 60 in the front of the hut, having, on an average, three spears each ; and another band of 20 or more with two Kings or Chiefs highly painted, at the back of the hut.

The place, in fact, as he reports, was surrounded. As they advanced, he desired them to go away; this they treated contemptuously and still gathering round the hut, with daring and menacing attitudes, would have entered, had he not rushed out with three guns that were loaded. These he placed by the door-post and again ordered them away, upon which, one stepped forward with his spear pointed at him and cried out, " me will," " me will," meaning to throw it; at the same instant a spear, thrown from the back of the house, came through the window and door, which he happily evaded. He then, in defence of his life, used his pieces, containing only shot ; but this would have proved ineffectual, had not another stock-keeper timely arrived, who, discharging his gun at a distance behind, alarmed them, that they fled. It was clearly ascertained that many of these men, were of the party recently participating in the Christian benevolence of the Governor. Their object now, is plunder and fire-arms, with which from their recent robberies, they are tolerably furnished.-I shall forbear any lengthened comment on the various atrocities committed by this body of half- civilized natives, sincerely hoping that as these, a small part only of their deeds, are laid before the Public eye, necessary measures may be speedily adopted for the preservation of the lives and property of individuals in the interior

-I am, Sir, with every respect, your obliged servant, COLONA.

P. S.-I had almost omitted to mention that the bodies of the two unfortunate men were not found till three days subsequent to their decease, when after advising with the Magistrate of the district, it was deemed expedient, from the decay which had taken place, to inter them on the spot. The neighbours being assembled, the interment took place with the strictest solemnity.

As you could imagine I relished reading this letter;

HOBART TOWN GAZETTE (TAS: 1825 - 1827; 1830),
SATURDAY 12 NOVEMBER 1825, PAGE 4

To the Editor,

SIR,--The occasional appearance of the Aborigines in Hobart Town and the kindness they experience from the Inhabitants, cannot but be gratifying to those who feel interested in the improvement of these poor creatures; but it is disgusting to behold, the state of nudity in which they wander about our streets.

Surely something may be done to induce them to conform, in a slight degree, to our ideas of personal decency. Would it not be practicable to give them to understand, that unless they are covered to a certain extent, they will not be admitted into the Town, or receive any food? A positive refusal of the latter, but on the proposed condition, would do much towards effecting this desirable change in their habits.

I remain, Sir,
yours, &c. A. Z.

In one of my more mischievous moods, I simply could not resist rewriting this letter although strangely it was never published;

The PAKANA *Voice*
BY W.C. SPECIAL CORRESPONDENT—*LUTRUWITA*

To the Editor,

SIR,--The occasional appearance of a rytia in our village, and the kindness they experience from the Inhabitants, cannot but be gratifying to those who feel interested in the improvement of these poor creatures; but it is disgusting to behold, the state of dress in which they wander about our camp. Surely something may be done to induce them to conform, in a slight degree, to our ideas of personal decency. Would it not be practicable to give them to understand, that unless they are uncovered to a certain extent, they will not be admitted into our clan, or receive any food? A positive refusal of the latter, but on the proposed condition, would do much towards effecting this desirable change in their habits.

I remain, Sir, yours, &c. W.C.

HOBART TOWN GAZETTE AND VAN DIEMEN'S LAND ADVERTISER (TAS: 1821 - 1825), FRIDAY 5 AUGUST 1825, PAGE 3

A few days since, a large body of the aborigines, led by a one-armed woman named "Nelson," well known here, attacked Cap't. Kelly's farm, at Brune Island and plundered the house of every thing portable, amongst other things a valuable fowling-piece.-They had shortly before speared three of Capt. K's. cows.

CIVILIZATION AND ALL ITS CONNOTATIONS

Upon reflection that evening over a particularly fine nip, I began to contemplate why it is that we as white men believe our civilization is superior to any other race on earth? Why would writers in a small, nondescript penal colony about as far away as it is possible to be from Europe believe so wholeheartedly that their culture, values and beliefs are superior to the people who occupied the land for thousands of years before Western Civilization even existed?

I then began to ponder the true meaning of philosophy. I know that sounds pretentious, but I am writing this at three o'clock in the morning and slightly light-headed to boot, so I beg your indulgence. To understand the writers of the day and their ilk, I needed to appreciate the fundamentals of philosophy. The two go hand in hand. The Pakana people were facing not only guns and disease but the power of ideas.

In the end it comes down to our philosophic perceptions. In the West the term philosophy comes from the Greek, philosoph, love of wisdom. The way in which the British understood the world in which we live had evolved from Greek philosophers and civilization, through to Roman and then to the Age of Enlightenment. Key factors are that it uses written language to convey ideas and logical, analytical thinking as the way to truth, whatever that maybe. The problem with written language is its limitations and vulnerability to reinterpretation. Once written the only way to challenge an idea, an understanding or a philosophy is through more words on paper.

The Pakana people, though, lived their philosophy or wisdom of the universe and conveyed its precepts in oral form. They understood the land, skies, tides, winds and animals which were a part of them and indistinguishable from their being. Such an idea was incomprehensible to the British, who sought their knowledge of the world through second hand accounts in books and literature which often saw the world in terms of absolutes such as good and evil, right and wrong, heaven or hell and so on.

Both have merits in their own right, but the point is that it was a collision in philosophy. I doubt it will ever really be resolved.[vi]

MALE SUPREMACY

My thoughts drifted as I contemplated the notion that thoughts are seeds of ideas drifting through time and space in search of fertile ground in which to land. Some fall on barren ground where they lie dormant, eventually crumbling to dust, while others settle and thrive in different places and eras, adapting to their new home, influencing people, changing lives for better or worse. Some end up far from their origins and are alien and often devastating to their new environment. One such place in which this occurred was Lutruwita.

The lives, culture and land of the Aborigines in Lutruwita were forever changed by one such seed of thought. That is the idea of white male supremacy, germinated in another land, three thousand years before by Aristotle.

As with the master's rule over the slave and humanity's rule over plants and other animals, Aristotle defines these kinds of rule in terms of natural hierarchies: "[T]he male, unless constituted in some respect contrary to nature, is by nature more expert at leading than the female and the elder and complete than the younger and incomplete". This means that it is natural for the male to rule: "[T]he relation of male to female is by nature a relation of superior to inferior and ruler to ruled".[vii]

To be superior infers that others are deemed inferior. Passed down to the Romans, this notion was etched in their laws and psyche until the Protestant Reformation during the 1500s whole heartedly embraced the belief that **white** males were naturally superior to other beings: women, blacks, the disabled and slaves. It functioned well as a way of seeing the world as the rightful preserve of those superior beings, as it provided order, structure and security for all. Everyone had a place and knew where they stood in what they called the 'natural order' and provided no one questioned it, all was as it should be, especially for those self-assigned to the top of the pyramid.

Lutruwita was well suited to enacting the tenets of British culture - with its tiers of white power – government appointed administrators and the army - and those subservient to these - the convicts. This system was superimposed on an island of untouched nature, vulnerability and eminently suitable for their purposes.

These were commanding, uncompromising beliefs which easily assigned Aboriginal people into the nethermost rank in the hierarchy of life. Such a place allowed and was justification enough for those at the top, white males to in effect, treat the Pakana people in any way they considered appropriate to their status. In order to do terrible things to people it is first necessary to assign them a place in the hierarchy and the lower they are the easier it becomes.

In this context the life of an Aboriginal was of less value than that of a sheep or cow, as illustrated by the British murders in retaliation to the killing of their livestock. While a gun may slay the body, it is ideas which motivate and justify pulling the trigger.

HOBART TOWN GAZETTE (TAS: 1825 - 1827; 1830), SATURDAY 11 FEBRUARY 1826, PAGE 4

....

TO THE EDITOR OF THE HOBART TOWN GAZETTE.

Sir — Many of your Readers will re-collect that a meeting was held, about twelve months ago, to take into consideration the best and most effectual means to alleviate the condition of the unfortunate aborigines of this

Island. It must be a matter of regret to all who have any knowledge of the treatment they are subjected to from the assigned servants at the distant stock-runs, that no plan should have been attempted in furtherance of an object so praiseworthy. — From the best information I have been able to collect, these poor creatures have been persecuted from the very moment a settlement was formed on the banks of this River up to the present time. Thus goaded, they have been roused to retaliate; and within the last few years many white men have fallen victims to their provoked rage. They have been driven from their places of resort — and, in a few years, when colonization has extended to the distant parts of the country, they will be deprived (if there be any who have escaped) of the possibility of procuring subsistence. To what then must they have recourse?

Will they not in their desperation seek every opportunity to be revenged, though they cannot discriminate between their friends and their foes? Will they not be driven to have recourse to our flocks and herds for a substitute for that subsistence of which we have been the means of depriving them ?Surely then it is not only our duty as Christians, but our interest also, to strive to put an end to such acts of violence on our part and to afford, in compensation for that of which we have deprived them, our best efforts to induce them to change their mode of life. It is to be hoped that the idea of benefiting these real ob-jects of commiseration is not altogether abandoned and that if there are those who, from principle, cannot assist in the undertaking, they will not oppose those who may try to attain its accomplishment.

I am, Sir, yours, &c.

YORICK

1826

COLONIAL TIMES AND TASMANIAN ADVERTISER
(HOBART, TAS: 1825 - 1827), FRIDAY 6 JANUARY 1826, PAGE 4

THE ABORIGINAL NATIVES.

On Friday last, a party of about 150 natives attacked Mr. Stocker's hut, near the Western Creek and wounded one of his servants, James Cupid, in three places with spears; after which he succeeded in driving them all away by firing at them.

COLONIAL TIMES AND TASMANIAN ADVERTISER
(HOBART, TAS: 1825 - 1827), FRIDAY 17 FEBRUARY 1826, PAGE 4

TO THE EDITOR, OF THE COLONIAL TIMES.

SIR,-It was with much surprise that I observed an article in the Government Gazette, last week, recommending the Aborigines to the notice of the Government of this Island, as I had concluded in common with most of my neighbours, that every possible means had been tried to civilize this degraded race and that it was ultimately found to be of no avail. I received this impression, from the recollection of the Meeting that was called some time since on this very subject and from the knowledge

I had of the great pains and trouble taken by the Rev. R. Mansfield and others, in promoting this most desirable object, the different plans proposed and the one approved, the vote of thanks unanimously given to Messrs.

Bedford and Mansfield, for their assiduity in the business and above all, from the actual appointment of an individual, considered every way qualified to instruct and conciliate these miserable people. Now, judging from the Government Gazette, we would be led to imagine that all these things had been forgotten; and that no further exertions had been made, that the Meeting above alluded to and sanctioned by the Lieutenant Governor, had been called out of pure ostentation and merely to make a shew and parade - an idea which none but the most licentious can for a moment entertain.

My object in calling your attention to this subject, is by no means factious, but merely to ascertain whether the learned writer of the Government Gazette, has forgotten the measure already approved and intends, to make a fresh blaze by calling more Meet-ings, &c.; or whether he is conscious of the ill-treatment of the person appointed at the former Meeting and has adopted a genteel method of refreshing the memory of those whom it may concern and to induce them to make him some compensation for the great loss occasioned by repeated broken promises, by numerous journeys to town and continual detention when there and above all, for the great inconvenience he sustained during the state of suspense he was kept in for several months which prevented him from making these necessary arrangements which he otherwise would have done, if this be the object, it is laudable and reflects more credit on the writer, than the generality of his leading articles; but if it should be to propose a second edition of a former transaction, I would move as an amendment, that the next person nominated as a teacher, should be let into the secret and thereby prevent that great loss and inconvenience which has been sustained in consequence of this oversight.

A SUBSCRIBER.

New Norfolk, Feb. 7,1826

While browsing through pages of newspapers I found it intriguing to see how many would-be poets were lurking in such a small place. Almost every edition published a couple of sonnets and many were locally written with an obsession for love and associated, sentimental nonsense. Occasionally, though, I spotted more serious bards such as the one who penned *The Native's Lament* in 1826.

COLONIAL TIMES AND TASMANIAN ADVERTISER
(HOBART, TAS: 1825 - 1827), FRIDAY 5 MAY 1826, PAGE 4

THE NATIVE'S LAMENT.

Oh! where are the wilds I once sported among,
When as free as my clime through its forests I sprung;
When no track but the few which our fires had made,
Had tarnished the carpet that nature had laid;
When the lone waters dashed down the dark-some ravine,
O'erhung by the shade of the Huon's dark green;
When the broad morning sun o'er our mountains could roam,
And see not a slave in our bright Island home.
When our trees were unscath'd, nor our echoes awoke,
To the hum of the stranger, or woodman's wild stroke
When our rocks proudly rose 'gainst the dash of the main,
And saw not a bark on the wide azure plain;
When the moon through the heaven's roll'd onward and smil'd,
As she lighted the home of the free and the wild.
Oh! my country, the stranger has found thy fair clime,
And he comes with the sons of misfortune and crime;
He brings the rude refuse of countries laid waste,
To tread thy fair wilds and thy waters to taste;
He usurps the best lands of thy native domains,
And thy children must fly, or submit to his chains.
He builds his dark home and he tricks it about,

With trinkets and trifles within and without;
When the bright sun of nature sinks into the main;
He lights little suns to make day-light again;
And he calls a crowd round him, to see him preside,
And our tyrant himself is the slave of his pride!
Oh! dearer to us, is our rude hollow-tree,
Where heart joins to heart with a pulse warm and free;
Or our dew-covered sod, with no canopy o'er it,
But the star-spangl'd sky, - we can lay and adore it!
Or if worn with fatigue, when the bright sun forsakes us,
We lay down and sleep, till he rises and wakes us!
Our wants are but few and our feelings are warm,
We fear not the sun and we fear not the storm
We are fierce to our foes, to our loves we are fond,
Let us live and be free—life has nothing beyond.
Oh I would not exchange the wild nature I bear,
For life with the tame sons of culture and care,
Nor give one free moment as proudly I stand,
For all that their arts and their toils can command.
Away to the mountains and leave them the plains,
To pursue their dull toils and to forge their dark chains.
April 22, 1826.

COLONIAL TIMES AND TASMANIAN ADVERTISER
(HOBART, TAS: 1825 - 1827), FRIDAY 5 MAY 1826, PAGE 2

THE BLACK NATIVES

On Saturday morning last, five Aboriginal natives, who could all speak
English, entered the farm-house of Mr. BROWNING, in the Macquarie
district; and with waddies beat him to death. Mr. B. was at the time
confined to his bed, being seriously indisposed. A poor old man, an assigned
servant, who was also in the house, we are sorry to add, was so shockingly

cut by them on the head, as to leave little hopes of his recovery. They then plundered the premises. Mr. B.'s brother was in town at the time.

The two black Aboriginal natives who are confined in the gaol, on the charge of spearing a man to death, are apparently gifted with a superior understanding to what we have hitherto seen. One appears to have been a Chief. He is very old, has a long beard, long hair in ringlets and is coloured with red ochre; he is ill and feeble, so much so, that he is only able to move about in the prison, by crawling on his hands and knees, with only a piece of loose blanket thrown over his body. The other native prisoner is a youth, tall and erect; he frequently imitates the marching of the sentry in the gaolyard, with much accuracy. He says he is innocent and that his companion is guilty.

COLONIAL TIMES AND TASMANIAN ADVERTISER
(HOBART, TAS: 1825 - 1827), FRIDAY 28 JULY 1826, PAGE 4

MR. EDITOR,

Having, by the intervention of signs, held a sort of conversation with a tame tribe of Aborigines, of whom some appeared more willing to answer my enquiries (so far as I could make them understand my meaning) than any I have hitherto met with, they communicated the terms used by them for the following words :—the head, pericrag-na; eyes, nieburdeirda ; nose, muinna; teeth, capada ; tongue, meina ; chin,cumunda, ear, culubunda ; breast, nomena ; arms, weninda; legs, tieuruna ; toes, perra ; leine, a crow ; eura, a wattle bird.

From the foregoing short specimen it may be seen, that the vowels frequently abound the letter a in particular formed a component part and terminals in a great number of their words; and where it and some others occur, they are pronounced very soft, so much so in fact, that a native of the British Isles can neither spell nor articulate them correctly, or with ease. To the ear their language sounds by no means harsh; on the contrary, it is rather grateful and melodious. I am satisfied that at any event a slight

knowledge of it might be acquired by time and assiduity.
— Yours, &c. A BUSH RECLUSE.

COLONIAL TIMES AND TASMANIAN ADVERTISER
(HOBART, TAS: 1825 - 1827), FRIDAY 15 SEPTEMBER 1826, PAGE 3

EXECUTIONS.
WEDNESDAY MORNING.

We have to record the final exit of seven of the unhappy men, convicted at the late sessions, who were executed on Wednesday morning, for murder and robbery ; and this painful task is left for us to fulfil, deeply sen-sible of the enormity of such crimes in an in-fant colony and that the Law must, in such cases, take its due course: —

Jack and Dick, the two Aborigines, for spearing and killing Thomas Calley, a stock-keeper, at Oyster Bay; William Smith, Thomas Dennings and Edward Everett, for the horrid murder of the unfortunate Mr. Simpson, Settler, at Pittwater ; and John Taylor and George Waters, for robbing a soldier at the penal Settlement at Macquarie Harbour.

. After the elder of the aborigines, named Dick, had received the sacrament, (who has never since his confinement, been able to walk, suffering under a loathsome cutaneous disease, which almost covered his body), screamed out most bitterly, apparently fully sensible of his impending fate and, not withstanding he could climb up the ladder to the platform, he refused, when he was carried up by the Executioner. Being placed on the platform, he would not stand up along with the rest of the unhappy sufferers; he was therefore placed upon a stool, which dropped with him, when the awful moment arrived which plunged them into eternity. —

His partner in crime, an interesting youth, seemed quite unmoved at his awful situation, until Tuesday and Wednesday morning, during which period, the poor lad became quite sensible of his destiny and prayed most fervently to the Almighty, for the forgiveness of his sins. During the period he has been confined in gaol, if any one spoke to him in a friendly manner, he would laugh and appear as cheerful as if he were with his sable brethren in the woods. He declared his innocence both be-fore and after trial. The old black died very hard; and the cord having slipped from the younger up to his elbow, he reached up his hand to his neck and bled profusely from the nose.

The Rev. Messrs. Bedford and Carvosso attended them on the scaffold and performed the last sad and friendly office to these miserable men, when, at 9 o'clock, they were launched into eternity! We can-not but again record, what it has been our fate so often to perform, the unwearied attentions paid by the Reverend Chaplain to the culprits, who, having infringed upon the laws of their country, like these and for other infractions, have been doomed to suffer and to forfeit their lives for an expiration of their offences. Nor can we omit stating a similar strain of sympathy has been felt by the dissenting Ministers; and we trust these unhappy men, by the aid of Divine influence (through their instrumentality) have been induced to fly to that only refuge for frail and perishable mortality.

We witnessed many surrounding the gaol walls as spectators and we sincerely hope the awful end of these miserable men, may be a warning to all, teaching them, if they will for a moment reflect, how beguiling are the paths of temptation and that petty vices, soon lead the unwary youth to greater courses of evil, till perhaps, like these unhappy sufferers, the unbending arm of justice overtakes them and they become examples themselves, to deter others from a life of profligacy and crime, ending, as it generally does, on the scaffold!

And the British called the Pakana uncivilized and barbarous creatures!

HOBART TOWN GAZETTE (TAS: 1825 - 1827; 1830),
SATURDAY 4 NOVEMBER 1826, PAGE 4

MISCELLANY,
ORIGINAL AND SELECT. THE VOYAGE TO SOUTH CAPE.

On the beach of Satellite Island, are also found numbers of the small green-coloured shells, which the black natives string like beads on the sinews of the kangaroo, to wear as ornaments, round the neck and forehead.

HOBART TOWN GAZETTE (TAS: 1825 - 1827; 1830),
SATURDAY 14 OCTOBER 1826, PAGE 2

Dunne, the dastardly thief, has again made his appearance at Mr. Thompson's hut, on the further bank of the Shannon, bringing with him a black native female, whom he had stolen from her tribe. It will of course be among the earliest endeavours of Colonel Balfour to interrupt that silent understanding which so bare-facedly subsists between these abominable wretches, these scabs of humanity and the distant stock keepers. Knowing, as we do, the influence of taunt and reproach upon these men, we call upon the Council, if the law should be found deficient, to enact an exemplary punishment upon every prisoner who shall be proved to have upbraided another man for having taken, or been instrumental in taking, a bushranger, is it possible that a mean coward, as Dunne, or indeed every thief like him, must of necessity be, could be suffered with impunity to enter a room with three men in it and to remain for hours in dalliance with an illtreated woman, whose eagerness to escape from his horrid clutches compelled him to exert every means to restrain? The fact is however too true and such and many such instances, frequently occur.

If the abhorrence, nascent and natural, in the human breast at the bare recital of such enormities could be increased, it would be by the following narrative of a murderous reprisal the evident consequence of such criminal aggression and apparently committed by the aggrieved party. On the next and following day to that on which this audacious conduct of Dunne was perpetrated and within a few miles of the spot, two men, driving a cart with some timber which they had split, in a secluded part of the wood contiguous to the Clyde, were attacked by a party of natives. They were headed by the half- civilized man we alluded to in our last; and coming from ambush, cast their spears at the unfortunate men unawares. The one, F. Burrel, (having a ticket of leave,) escaped unhurt by running to the River, at that time much swollen by the flood; but his companion, William Tidwell (freed by servitude) having a spear thrust through his thigh, was not so fortunate and must have perished from the effect of his wounds in the stream, down , which he was seen, from a distance, to float, with a crowd of natives around to hasten his cruel death.

HOBART TOWN GAZETTE (TAS: 1825 - 1827; 1830),
SATURDAY 11 NOVEMBER 1826, PAGE 2

THE BLACK NATIVES

On Monday the distressing intelligence reached Town, that a tribe of about 250 of these degraded people had attacked the shepherd's hut of Mr. Burns, beyond the River Shannon; and, after being warded off, had watched an opportunity while the unfortunate men were following their flocks, unarmed, to commit the most dreadful atrocities. One young man named James Scott, a free shepherd, who had, not long arrived from Scotland and had the chief direction of the farm, has been cruelly murdered by them. They had first attacked the stock-hut of Mr. G. Thompson, on the same side of the River, where the two inmates were assailed with stones and other missiles. They then attempted to enter by the chimney, when these men, seeing death before-them, fired through the crevices of the hut and wounded one, with whom his companions immediately retreated, but returned next day, evidently with a purpose of revenge and robbed it of every article. On learning the unpleasant news, Lieutenant Dalrymple, from the military station at the Clyde, instantly dispatched a party of soldiers, with a constable to the scene; but their arrival would be too late to prevent the mischief already perpetrated and the natives themselves would have retreated back into the woods. How a repetition of these evils will be prevented is a problem which, in the present state of the Colony, we confess, is most difficult to solve; but that some strong and effective measure must be adopted is evident. Let no inhabitant of the Island flatter himself that he is unconcerned in this matter.

*The hand of these unthinking savages, once imbrued in human blood, becomes hardened and eager for fresh aggression; and though their enormities may now be confined to the outskirts of the settled districts and the more remote and secluded huts, their treacherous habits will, if not timely arrested, soon lead them to attack more populous neighbourhoods. The present tribe is ascribed as being attended by a vast number of dogs, amounting at the least to 60, to which, they are firmly attached and which they teach to surround the huts and attack the inmates. Mr. Thompson's men were completely pre-vented from all possibility of escape by these ferocious dogs. When we con-sider therefore, how they multiply and are nursed by their unthinking owners, we cannot but anticipate the early destruction of numerous flocks of sheep, as well as of the kangaroo and opossums, which have hitherto supported them in the woods; **and that the blacks themselves must, in consequence, perish from want of their usual means of support, or be urged by the calls of hunger and their already strong appetite for wheaten bread, to commit still more and more audacious acts of aggression on the peaceful settler.***

COLONIAL TIMES AND TASMANIAN ADVERTISER
(HOBART, TAS: 1825 - 1827), FRIDAY 1 DECEMBER 1826, PAGE 2

In conducting a Journal, which is understood to express the general sentiments and wishes of the people and in some instances, to regulate and lead them, we are occasion-ally obliged to present those subjects to the attention of our Readers, which the pressing necessity of the case requires, although they may be attended with painful results. It was this feeling which induced us to devote our space in the last two numbers, to the construction and operation of the Council, to the exclusion of our leading article, in continuation upon the political economy of this Government; and it is with the same feeling, that we now beg most earnestly, to draw the attention of all, to the present situation of those poor, wretched, but infatuated savages, the Aborigines of this Island. In devoting a few observations to the cause of humanity — in tracing the dangers to which the Settler must be exposed and in pointing out a remedy, if possible, we are not only doing our duty, as Christians, but as Men ; and if we offer any observations which are entitled to weight, it is also the duty, as we are sure it will be the inclination, of Government, to act upon them.

It would be worse than useless, to shew how different things might have been — it is enough to state things as they are ; and we find by every day's experience, that the natives are no longer afraid of a white man — that they know, how a gun is fired off, it is useless. From attacking stock-keepers, they now attack huts and in many instances, the fight has lasted for hours, until by dint of numbers, they have compelled the whites to retreat. They have tasted the sweets of civilized life, but they have no inclination for the labour of it. They have ceased to fear, and learn to abhor. They look upon the white men, as robbing them of their land, depriving them of their subsistence and in too many instances, violating their persons.

To discuss a question of this nature, it is necessary to look at naked truths. It is too late to discuss the question, whether they might not have been civilized — they have un-fortunately seen nothing but pernicious examples. What intercourse has taken place, has produced only hatred and revenge and nothing, but a removal, can protect us from incursions, similar to the Caffrees in Africa, or the back-woodmen, in North America.

We deeply deplore the situation of the Settlers. With no remunerating price for their produce, they have just immerged from the perils of the bush-rangers, which affected their property and they are now exposed to the attack of these natives, who aim at their lives. We make no pompous display of Philanthropy — we say unequivocally, SELF DEFENCE IS THE FIRST LAW OF NATURE. THE GOVERNMENT MUST REMOVE THE NATIVES — IF NOT, THEY WILL BE HUNTED DOWN LIKE WILD BEASTS and DESTROYED!

Having heard the distinctions in law, laid down by the Chief Justice in the Supreme Court, in the case of Jack and Dick, for murder, we tremble for the consequences to our brother Colonists, on the one hand, whilst we are chilled with horror, with the probable results, on the other. It is impossible to suggest a perfect plan, but having collected the opinions of many intelligent per-sons, we are satisfied, that the first thing, is our own security; the second, the due and proper protection to the natives and last and least, the expense of the measure to Government. In the first place, they must be removed, either to the coast of New Holland, or King's Island. The latter is one of our Dependencies, fertile, well supplied with water and no possibility of escape. There are two parties who have committed outrages — the Oyster Bay and the Shannon parties. We would recommend their being taken, which could easily be effected — placed at King's Island, with a small guard of soldiers to protect them and let them be compelled to grow potatoes, wheat, &c. catch seals and fish and by degrees, they will lose their roving disposition and acquire some slight habits of industry, which is the first step of civilization.

If they are put upon the coast of New Holland, they may be destroyed. If they remain here, they are SURE TO BE DESTROYED. If they are sent to King's Island, they will be under restraint, but they will be free from committing, or receiving violence and we are certainly bound by every principle of humanity, to protect them as far as we can.

We shall hail with joy any measure the Council may devise, to effectually relieve us from this calamity, but they may be assured no half-measures will suffice and as no one Member of the Council can speak upon this subject, experimentally, we hope they will consult those who can, for it is one common interest binds us all.

HOBART TOWN GAZETTE (TAS: 1825 - 1827; 1830),
SATURDAY 2 DECEMBER 1826, PAGE 4

To THE EDITOR.

SIR,--It is perhaps not generally known, that about this time the black natives go to Patrick's Plains and Arthur's Lake to drink the juice of what is called the cider tree. It is a species of eucalyptus resembling the black gum, but with, a smooth, shining bark. The liquor is obtained by cutting a notch in the bark and the stock-keepers, in those neighbourhoods, cut grooves in the trees, to which they fix, cans and into which they frequently find two quarts have issued in the course of one night.

The juice is exceedingly mellow and sweet and if allowed to ferment, it becomes of a strong and intoxicating quality. The wild red currant is also common in those parts. Cherries as white as milk and of a flavour superior to the red native sort, are found growing on the plains.

There is also a tree which bears a sort of apple about the size of a pigeon's egg, which remains green all the summer, but towards autumn it acquires a yellow colour and when of a deep yellow it is ripe and very palatable. Black berries grow in the narrow valleys, where is also found a kind of fruit about the size of a gooseberry, of an oval shape and deep purple colour. But the most interesting of all is the native pepper, which grows on a small prickly bush; and is red until ripe, when it has generally attained a black colour. The pepper corns are then stronger than any from the spice islands.

VIATOR.

COLONIAL TIMES AND TASMANIAN ADVERTISER
(HOBART, TAS: 1825 - 1827), FRIDAY 8 DECEMBER 1826, PAGE 1

Government Notice.

Colonial Secretary's Office, Nov. 19, 1826. THE series of Outrages which have of late been perpetrated by the Aborigines of the Colony and the wanton Barbarity in which they have indulged by the commission of Murder, in return for the kindness, in numerous instances, shewn to them by the Settlers and their Servants, have occasioned the greatest pain to the Lieutenant Governor and called for his most anxious Consideration of the means to be applied for preventing the repetition of these treacherous and sanguinary Acts.

His Excellency has uniformly been anxious to inculcate a spirit of forbearance towards the Aborigines, in the hope that confidence and cordiality might subsist and be conducive to their improvement and the security of the Colonists, but it is with extreme regret he perceives a result so contrary to his hope and expectation.

An impression however still remains that these Savages are stimulated to acts of atrocity by one or more Leaders, who, from their previous intercourse with Europeans, may have acquired sufficient intelligence to draw them into crime and danger. The Capture of these Individuals therefore becomes an object of the first importance and to this point the Lieutenant Governor would particularly direct the attention of those who may be called to aid the Civil Power in the execution of the justifiable measures to which they may have recourse ; and His Excellency deems it necessary to promulgate, for general information, but especially for the guidance of the Magistrates, Constables and Military:

1. *If it should be apparent that there is a determination on the part of one or more of the Native Tribes to attack, rob, or murder the White Inhabitants generally, any Persons may arm and, joining themselves to the Military, drive them by force to a safe distance, treating them as open Enemies.*

2. *If they are found actually attempting to commit a Felony, they may be resisted by any Persons in the like manner.*

3. *Where they appear assembled in un-usual numbers, or with unusual arms, or al-though neither be unusual, if they evidently indicate such*

intention of employing force as is calculated to excite Fear, for the purpose of doing any harm, short of Felony, to the Persons and Property of any one, they may be treated as rioters and resisted it they persist in their attempt.

4. *If they be found merely assembled for such purpose, the Neighbours and Soldiers armed, may, with a Peace-officer or Magistrate, endeavour to apprehend them; and,if resisted, use force.*

5. *If any of the Natives have actually committed Felonies, the Magistrates should make such diligent enquiries as may lead to certainty of the Persons of the Principals, or any of them (whether this consists in knowledge of their names, or any particular marks or characteristics by which their Persons may be distinguished) and issue Warrants for the apprehension of such Principals. The Officer executing a Warrant may take to his assistance such Persons as he may think necessary ; and, if the Offenders can-not otherwise be taken, the Officer and his Assistants will be justified in resorting to force, both against the Principals and any others who may, by any acts of violence, or even of intimidation, endeavour to prevent the arrest of the Principals.*

6. *When a Felony has been committed, any Person who witnessed it may immediately raise his neighbours and pursue the Felons and the pursuers may justify the use of all such means as, a Constable might use. If they overtake the Parties, they should bid, or signify them in surrender; if they resist, or attempt to resist, the Persons pursuing may use such force as is necessary; and if the pursued fly and cannot otherwise be taken, the pursuers may then use similar force.*

By Command of the Lieutenant Governor,

W. H. Hamilton.
Commissariat Office, Dec.1, 1826

Viator was a compulsive letter writer of the day and expressed his views on just about any subject which took his fancy in a witty, thoughtful and clever manner.

Reading this report drew on all the inner strength I could muster because it related to Lowana, the destruction of her clan and her death. I had to step away and detach as best I could in order to complete my work. It is obvious that some bias remains but so be it; I am only human.

COLONIAL TIMES AND TASMANIAN ADVERTISER
(HOBART, TAS: 1825 - 1827), FRIDAY 15 DECEMBER 1826, PAGE 3

THE BLACK NATIVES.
[FROM A CORRESPONDENT.]

On Friday evening last, the 8th instant,

Mr. Laing, the Chief District Constable at Sorell, received information that Black Tom, the native Aborigine, commonly called Birch's Tom, was encamped within about one hundred yards of a hut on Mr. Laing's farm, occupied by a man named Robert Grimes, near the Brown Mountain. Mr. Laing left Sorell at 11 o'clock, p. m. with a party of four soldiers of His Majesty's 40th Regiment and arrived at Grimes's hut, a little before day-break, on Saturday morning ; and at day-light, they proceeded to the spot where Tom and his party lay and got upon them unperceived. They secured Tom and his companions, consisting of four other black men, four women and one male child; who made no resistance; neither had they any weapons or dogs with them.

On being asked where his dogs were, he replied he had lost them. The natives were then conducted to Sorell Gaol, where they now remain, until orders are sent from His Excellency respecting them. It appears, that they came to Grimes's hut on Friday morning and remained nearly all the day. Grimes gave them all the bread he had baked; they eat it and remained quiet about two hours, when Black Tom accosted Grimes and said, "you white b——r, give me some more bread and fry some mutton for us." Grimes being afraid of them, commenced and baked a peck or more of flour into bread for them and cooked three-fourths of a sheep; they devoured the whole and, in the afternoon, went out to catch opossums.-

On their return from the hunt, Tom came to the hut by himself and ordered Grimes to get some more bread and mutton ready for them by next morning (Saturday). Grimes had another damper ready; but Mr. Black Tom was deprived of partaking of it, as Mr. Laing and the Military happened to call upon him before breakfast and his next meal was eaten in the cell of Sorell Gaol.*

** A Colonial term for an unleavened cake, baked under the wood ashes.*

--ED.

I reminded my readers earlier of the need to look for the negative spaces when reading newspapers. Here is a perfect illustration. The article above tells only part of the story and contained very much what readers wanted to hear. Consider what you are expected to see, then look again through the leaves and branches and you will catch a glimpse of sky, clouds and light. Ask yourself, what is the story not telling? What else do you need to know in order to understand the whole story?

In this case, the reporter has overlooked the inconvenient fact that fourteen people had been killed, others held captive and a whole social grouping of humans destroyed for no other reason than they were in the way of what the British wanted: their land.[viii]

My despatch read;

The PAKANA *Voice*

BY W.C. SPECIAL CORRESPONDENT—*LUTRUWITA*

OYSTER BAY NATION
MASSACRE AND CAPTURE
9TH DECEMBER 1826

It is with great sadness that we report another mass killing of people, this time in the Oyster Cove Nation. Reports indicate the attacks were carried out on the Moomairremener Clan in an area known by the rytia (white man) at Bank Head Farm, near the headwaters of Sorell Rivulet, Pittwater. The lunkana took place early at dawn when most families were sleeping and was carried out by the police constable, Alexander Laing and four soldiers.

Upon completion of this action, they had murdered fourteen Pakana, including children, women and anyone within firing range. There was no apparent reason for the attack to occur other than to clear the area of people.

The rytia also took ten people away including the clan leader Kickerterpoller.

It would seem not everyone is equal under British Laws.

The Governor was unavailable for comment.

1827

COLONIAL TIMES AND TASMANIAN ADVERTISER
(HOBART, TAS: 1825 - 1827), FRIDAY 5 JANUARY 1827, PAGE 2

At the beginning of a New Year, it is customary with most people to look back upon the past events of the late one and forward with bright hopes on the one they have just entered. In doing this we shall be very brief; as the past has been such that we can-not look back upon it with any feelings of pleasure and the future presents no apparently cheering prospects. During the last year, it is true bush-ranging, which had arrived to such an alarming and destructive extent, has become annihilated; but to effect this, what have we been compelled to witness? Day after day the dreadful procession of the Sheriff, proceeding to demand some unhappy wretch to expiate his crimes by an ignominious death. Sheep-stealing, however, still continues and we fear is likely to continue, notwithstanding the numerous melancholy examples which have been made of those depredators, with their associates and protectors, who have been detected, until a more vigilant and active civil force is stationed in the interior, for the protection of the property of the Settlers ; and not only so, but their lives - for, no sooner had bush-ranging, which during the last two years and a half, has swept away so many Colonists, including settlers, soldiers and servants, become extinct, than another no less terrible evil has broken out.

The outrages of the Aboriginal Natives have lately kept the Colony in one continual state of alarm. Many lives have been lost on the European side and we doubt not many more on that of the Aborigines. With such mutual hatred do the whites and blacks in this Colony now look upon each other, that little more is necessary to occasion the work of destruction to begin, than for them to meet. The Settler, recollecting the recent murders of his fellow Colonists and servants will, in our opinion, omit no step whereby he may destroy the black tribes even to utter extermination. The stock-keepers act upon the same principle and carnage must inevitably follow on both sides. This is a dismal picture, but it is a true one. We do not wish to sound the tocsin of alarm unnecessarily. But it is a duty which we owe to the Colony generally, the Government and ourselves, to point out the legitimate alarm which these outrages necessarily occasion.

We cannot conceive how the Government Gazette can find grounds for the following paragraph: - " The late enormities committed by the Natives, as we predicted, have ceased and the proper understanding of the steps to be pursued, communicated in the Government Order of the 20th ultimo, whenever they make their hostile appearance, will, we trust, enable the remote settler to guard against any future atrocities from such hands." - In the first place, the enormities have not ceased and in the next, as we have before shown, no person who is not a lawyer, much less an ignorant stock-keeper, can possibly come at the "proper understanding" of the Government Order alluded to. To remedy this evil we have already suggested a most efficient plan, but it seems that the Local Administration do not coincide with our ideas upon the subject, for nothing has yet been done to put a stop to this growing evil.

Week after week accounts reach us of some fresh outrage or another, committed by this useless race, on the Europeans. We have just received the melancholy tidings that Mr. Zachariah Sponsford, a highly respectable settler, connected with Mr. Stocker in the cattle trade, bas been missing these last four weeks. It appears that this unfortunate person proceeded to the Western Tier, for the purpose of collecting cattle for the Hobart Town market at Christmas and has not since been heard of. From the circumstance of between 50 and 60 head of Mr. Stocker's cattle having been found with spears sticking in them, it appears but too probable that Mr. Sponsford has fallen a sacrifice to these barbarous savage people. This and the murder only last week recorded in our Paper, is an additional proof that the outrages have not ceased; as the Gazette unblushingly affirms. We know that the plan suggested by us of the removal of the blacks to King's Island, is approved by most of the settlers and one and all bitterly complain that some more efficient protection has not been afforded them (the Settlers) by the Local Government.

With regard to the morals of the community during the last year, there has certainly been fewer street robberies or burglaries than had been known during the preceding one, occasioned in some measure by the nocturnal confinement of the men in the public works - many of whom, being naturally dissolute and idle and having but a scarcity of provisions, used to resort to dis-honest practices and even personal violence, in order to obtain spirits, which they foolishly think is necessary to support them under their labour.

COLONIAL TIMES AND TASMANIAN ADVERTISER
(HOBART, TAS: 1825 - 1827), FRIDAY 19 JANUARY 1827, PAGE 2

We are extremely happy to find, that Mr. Sponsford who, it was some time ago conjectured, had been murdered by the Natives, has returned to his home. It would appear he fell in with a tribe of blacks and with much difficulty escaped with his life. - Several of his cattle were however severely wounded by the Natives with spears.

A few days ago, about eleven Natives were taken by a party of Soldiers and imprisoned at the Coal River, for having committed some trifling depredation. They have since been liberated; but appear to manifest a strong feeling against the whites, on account of the execution of Tom and Dick, two of their sable brethren, who suffered for the murder of Mr. Hart's stock-keeper.

COLONIAL TIMES AND TASMANIAN ADVERTISER (HOBART, TAS: 1825 - 1827), FRIDAY 26 JANUARY 1827, PAGE 3

ANOTHER MURDER!

The Black Aboriginal Natives have committed another murder. On Wednesday morning letters reached town from New Norfolk, bringing intelligence, that on Sunday last, the 21st, Mr. Thompson's, J. P. shepherd, at the Shannon, was barbarously murdered by the natives, while looking after his sheep. This is not all. On the same day, this furious and savage race of people attacked Mr. Thomson's house there and put three spears into the body of one of his men. One spear, fourteen feet long, entered his side and came out near the spine. Some hopes, however, are still entertained for his recovery, although the poor fellow is labouring under the most excruciating pain. We are happy to add, that a party of soldiers from the Clyde, are in pursuit of the savages, who have repeatedly said they will, sooner or later, murder every white man in the Island!!!— How dreadful it is, that we are again compelled to hand down to posterity the ferocious attacks of these barbarous people.— Surely, the Government cannot reflect one moment on the consequences likely to ensue from laying dormant, otherwise they would adopt some decisive measure to remedy this tremendous evil. Why should a feeling of false philanthropy and humanity towards the blacks be brought into competition with the safety of the lives and property of our fellow Colonists? **While a black Aborigine remains in Van Diemen's Land, there will never be a cessation of their hostilities.**

We have repeatedly pointed out the way to remedy this, by sending the blacks off this Island to some one of the adjacent ones.— And if the Government do not speedily do so, we shall have to record the murders of one half the Colonists, whose blood will lie upon their heads. They might now prevent it by adopting the measures we have suggested.— It must be done, sooner or later and why not at once before more valuable lives are lost.

It evidently appears, by their own words, that they are bent on murder; for they declare, that they will exterminate every white man on the Island.

So began the inkling of exile. My colleagues Andrew Bent and others writing for various newspapers were vehement proponents of this resolution for the Pakana people. It's an age-old solution to the problem of how to deal with difficult and unwanted people. Lepers were sent to remote islands, convicts to distant shores and lunatics locked away in asylums. It works on the principle of 'out of sight out of mind'. This was to be the fate of the Pakana people, for them to be 'removed' from their land to an 'adjacent island'. Shades of white supremacy once again: we will decide what is best for you because we sit on much higher branches of the tree of life than you: my ramblings, take no heed!

And so my reading and thoughts stopped here and at last, with some degree of trepidation, I was to return to Lutruwita as Special Correspondent to London Evening Standard and freelance to other, not so well known, slightly liberal journals in different parts of the world.

*'Hobart' Sketchbook No. 98, 1831-1832 / John Glover. (1831). Images for book
NSW Library Dixon Library, State Library of New South Wales FL436483*

Chapter Five

Return to Nipaluna (Hobart)
1827 – 1830

FROM W.C.'S JOURNAL:

How things had changed in this Colony since I was last here seven years ago! I arrived on the 19th February 1827 on the *City of Edinburgh* under Captain McKellar and immediately became aware of the vibrancy enveloping the Port of Hobart. Ships were loading grain, wool and whale oil. Others were unloading all manner of goods including many luxury items for a growing economy and an increasingly wealthy population. Ships from all over the world were present, trading goods with merchants and farmers, in an ever-expanding market.

By now Sydney was becoming reliant on Lutruwita for food and many other basic necessities. Tasmanian Whale oil lit up the streets of London and wool was in high demand. For the British arriving at this time prospects were good and a comfortable life within reach of all, including many convicts who were able to gain land or positions which allowed them to use their trade or skills. It was an exciting time and the most advantageous to emigrate. Land grants were being given out relatively freely, not only to free settlers but also to ticket-of-leave men keen to prosper or simply live their lives in peace.

Hobart was now far more than a just a penal colony, as ships brought with them more and more free settlers with money to spend, big ambitions to fulfil and egos to match. A far cry from the fledging penal settlement I had experienced on my last visit. Convict ships were arriving on a regular basis and their grudging passengers were all put to work building roads, or as family servants, stockmen and any other occupation to help build this very English community. The thing I noticed mostly from the ship as we sailed excruciatingly slowly up the river was just how much more the hills had been denuded of trees leaving only ghostly stumps further than the eye could see.

This was clearly a town with a bright future. Building and capital works construction were everywhere to be seen; they included a new wharf to join Hunter Island to the town. Bridges were being built and roads carved out of the bush. Importantly for the Aborigines who were my primary interest, the expansion throughout the island had been rapid, insistent and merciless. The *rytia* had encroached into the traditional country of more nations, as you can see in a map drawn only a few years later.

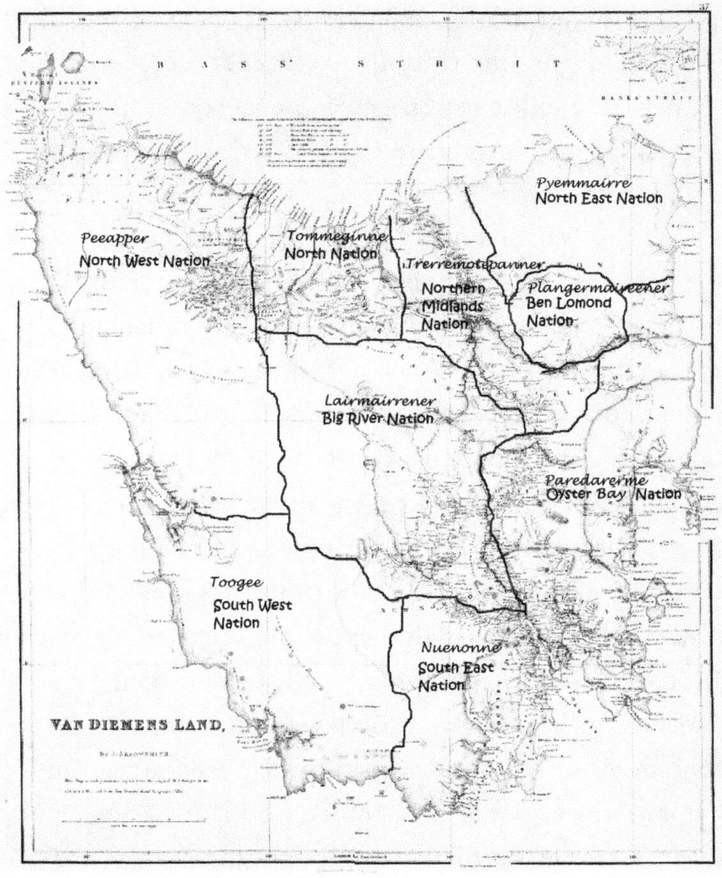

1834 J. Arrowsmith 'Van Diemens Land' modified to roughly overlap with aboriginal nations. Tasmanian Library. Pakana Nations overlay added for this publication only

The impact on the Pakana was dramatic. The white population, as I found out years later, had risen from 49 in 1803 to some 20,000 around 1830 while the Pakana had declined rapidly from an estimated 6,000 when the British first arrived in Lutruwita to around 1,200 people in 1826.[ix] And one million sheep and cattle were now cluttering up the landscape in all directions, eating their way through the feeding grounds of native animals and obliterating traditional Pakana food sources, making it harder and harder for the Aborigines to survive.

Enough of this pontification and tedious facts and figures! I'm beginning to sound like my one-time history teacher Mr Dodderidge, who had the unrivalled ability to make even the most exciting times in history sound as appealing as burnt rice pudding. He was totally deaf and his name perfectly reflected his disposition and physique, which did little to captivate his single-minded charges.

However, my drift is evident. British Tasmania was thriving and filled with enticing prospects for its newly arrived inhabitants. Everyone was looking out for themselves. If you want to know more, I suggest you find a book and read about it yourselves. It's late, I'm tired and Bent is scratching at the door for a pee!

Next evening: clearer head, Malt at the ready. What is interesting is the changing of the guard at the top with the arrival of a new governor, Lieutenant-General Sir George Arthur, 1st Baronet, KCH, PC in May 1824. You will not be at all surprised to know he took an instant dislike to me and the feeling was readily reciprocated.

Governor Arthur was a stalwart of the establishment, dressed in black, a humourless Calvinist and, worst of all, a teetotaller. Can you imagine him? His world was one of order, God-fearing and administrative bliss. Mine was diametrically opposite. I wrote and lived from the heart, grabbed the moment, often to my detriment and thought little of consequences. We were like the opposing ends of magnets, pushing away, never coming close to connecting.

How I longed for the days of Sorell and dear old Knopwood, with their enquiring intellects, relish of life and thorough enjoyment of drink. I disliked Arthur even more when my friend Reverend Knopwood was unceremoniously banished from his beloved Salamanca and sent to Coventry far away across the river to see out his days alone and dispirited. However, as a reporter it is not my job to make judgement on Arthur's rule as I am sure many will in the future and each will vary according to the values and perspectives of their time.

I returned to find Andrew Bent also at odds with Arthur – over the freedom of the press. As you could imagine the Governor was not enamoured with the idea of people having the freedom to criticise his authority and administration. After all, God was on his side and Arthur considered the whole settlement little more than a penal colony for the reform of the convict class. Bent's fight for the right of free speech will I believe be seen by future scribblers as one of the most famous Australian battles for liberty. Spending time in prison and having his life nearly ruined Andrew and his supporters had a win with the Home Government ruling in favour of the right to write. Tasmania became the first colony to gain freedom of the press. Arthur was not happy. He was certainly no friend of reporters and newspaper proprietors – nothing much has changed really.

"plus ça change, plus c'est la même chose"
The more things change, the more they stay the same
(*Les Guêpes, January 1849*).

Despite this I found Andrew Bent in much improved circumstance and surrounds. He was now located in a two-storey brick building on the corner of Elizabeth and Melville Street. He described it himself as being;

"sufficiently large and commodious enough to allow of almost any extent of business being carried on for perhaps a century to come."

He had acquired several fine presses in the previous few years which were a far cry from the original. He had plans to build a new residence for his ever-expanding family. Expanded it had! When I dined with, him and Mary we were inundated with lively noise and excitement from Elizabeth, Catherine, Mary, Andrew, Robert and Hannah was soon to arrive. I should add that this was not to be the end of their progeny with five more to arrive in later years. During our meal I noticed a rather old ginger-grey cat stride boldly across the room to settle comfortably in Andrew's ever favourite chair. It was Daniel still commanding and contemptuously scattering any miscellaneous children in his path.

I found it all to be most amusing and entertaining although at times enveloping me with sadness as I knew such joys were never to be part of my life. Although, if truth be known I had inherited some of my parent's disinclination toward children and would often let out a sigh of relief as I receded from the mayhem of the Bent household. Even so they appeared to adore me and I became known affectionally as 'Uncle C' and frequently commandeered by Elizabeth and Catherine to regale them with stories of adventure and intrigue, which without undue modesty is something I am moderately good at. When the youngest were put to bed we would sit together with a solitary candle and firelight as I spun tales to their wide-eyed delight. I told them of the time I woke to a spear to my heart and a Pakana man standing over me, of sights of sea monsters in the wilds of the

Southern Ocean and of my meeting with the Väddas in Ceylon.
Each child gazed in wonder while I talked of my time with the
Moomairremener people. I told of a girl who could dive into the ocean
and stay under until my heart nearly stopped and return with crayfish
and mussels. Once I let her name slip and at that instant, I caught
Catherine looking inquisitively at me; she instinctively knew Lowana
was special to me. From that time we shared an unspoken secret
which may explain our pen friendship over many years.

Andrew's prosperity had also extended to the status of Landed
Gentry as he now referred to himself seeped in irony after he
purchased one thousand acres at Cross Marsh in 1828 some 40 miles
from Hobarton near a place called Melton and called it Bentfield.
Until recently it had been the domain of the Paredarerme people.
We visited it a few times and found it to be rich in pasture and with
sound prospects which I feared with Andrew's legal debts he would be
unlikely to realise.

A few days later after greetings and chatting about old times,
Bent returned to his black ink and printing machine and I to my
work as War Correspondent reporting on the events which were now
happening all around me. It is only now, as I sit back and look at the
news reports of the day, that I can see the inevitable pattern of human
behaviour which would ultimately almost annihilate an entire race of
people. These are just some of those articles:

COLONIAL TIMES AND TASMANIAN ADVERTISER (HOBART, TAS: 1825 -
1827), FRIDAY 20 APRIL 1827, PAGE 3

THE BLACK NATIVES.

*We have again to regret, that our pages are to be stained by a recital of
the outrages committed by the savage Aborigines. Yesterday week, a tribe,
with Black Tom at their head, visited Mr. Romney's Stock-hut at Jericho, in*

which were three, of his servants - one, James Johnson, a free man and two others. The natives came in a most friendly manner, lit and smoked their pipes and talked with the utmost apparent good-will. Tom then requested Johnson to accompany him, stating, that he had something to shew him. Johnson, deceived by the apparent cordiality of their manner, consented and both went out of the hut together.

They had not got far, when Tom, suddenly turning round, began without the slightest provocation to beat Johnson most unmercifully, about the head and sides, with a waddy. His cries having reached the hut, the other two servants precipitately retreated, leaving the hut and poor Johnson at the mercy of the natives.

On seeing that the tribe was in full possession of the hut, Tom left off beating Johnson and repaired to his sable brethren, who then robbed the place of everything they could carry, taking with them, among other things, two muskets and 16 balls!!! ***This circumstance is an additional proof of the treachery of this uncultivated and truly savage race of people;*** *and clearly points out the necessity of stock-keepers being always on their guard, as the cunning and wiles of the blacks are like those of Satan himself. The poor man, Johnson, lies in the Hospital, in a dangerous state.*

At this time, I also observed how the language was becoming more pointed and extreme as the conflict escalated; something I will gabble more about later in my ramblings.

COLONIAL TIMES AND TASMANIAN ADVERTISER
(HOBART, TAS: 1825 - 1827), FRIDAY 4 MAY 1827, PAGE 3

ATROCITIES OF THE ABORIGINES.
[FROM A CORRESPONDENT.]

It was discovered on Monday, the 12th ultimo, that the Natives had speared two individuals at the Green Hills, near what is called the Eastern Tier, about six miles from Campbell-town, who had been in that quarter tending the flocks of Mr. Walter Davidson; their bodies were found in a very mangled state, with spears still sticking in them. Several persons in the neighbourhood, assisted by a small party of soldiers, made immediate pursuit of the sable murderers and fortunately overtook them at a distance of about ten miles, in a gulley, opposite Mr. David Murray's farm and where for the first time, I believe, trusting to their numbers, they contended a field of battle against European arms and discipline.

They made a most desperate attack on the party which, was disposed in front, with stones and spears, which they, protecting themselves behind trees, received with great sang froid, returning with well directed shots of slugs, their showers of stones and spears. The Natives, thinking they had only the party in front to defeat, which was all they could see, continued their attack with savage fury; when it was considered, from their over-powering numbers, full time for the corp du reserve, which was judiciously placed in ambuscade in the rear, to operate some relief and they commenced firing, with that cool-ness and precision, which reflected the greatest credit on them and which ensured the preservation of their comrades which were in advance, from the inevitable destruction of which, but for this ruse de guerre, they would otherwise, have been the victims.

The consequence of this spirited and well con-ducted, defence was the immediate and complete rout of the Aborigines, who were dispersed in various directions, leaving behind them all their spears, waddies and dogs ; about 20 of the latter, were killed by the party; the waddies and part of the spears they burned. Two or three hundred spears and some knives were brought as trophies from the scene of action; besides the wad-dies, an immense quantity of blankets, rugs and other articles of clothing were destroy-ed. There was also found a carving knife, identified to have been the property of the old man who resided in one of Mr. Gilles's shepherd's huts and who was murdered about six months ago, by the same band. The names of the two individuals thus immediately sacrificed by these would be extirpators of the whites, are Thomas Rollands, free and Edward Green, a prisoner.

About a week subsequent to this event, another detachment of the same squad, showed a disposition to attack two sawyers in the neighbourhood. They with great courage kept their hut, one of them going in the night to the settler for whom they were working for a supply of ammunition; in the morning the Natives attacked them, expecting, no doubt, an easy prey; but they were received in so gallant a manner, that they were forced to make a speedy retreat, leaving behind them a few carcases as a penalty for their temerity.

The consequence resulting from these two affairs is, that dogs are roving masterless in the bush, killing and scattering sheep; and as their destruction is attended with so much difficulty, nay al-most impossibility, as they shun the approach of white men, it is not easy to say when tranquillity will be restored to the surrounding flocks.

A Coroner's Inquest was held on the bodies of the two unfortunate men who were killed - I will not say a mock Inquest, but certainly not a legal one, there being no Coroner in this quarter. The verdict returned was - Wilful Murder by the Aborigines.

COLONIAL TIMES AND TASMANIAN ADVERTISER
(HOBART, TAS: 1825 - 1827), FRIDAY 1 JUNE 1827, PAGE 4

SIR,-As you in one of your late Papers expressed a wish to be made acquainted with any outrages that the Aborigines might commit, I hasten to communicate the following melancholy circumstance, which took place last Thursday.

Two men lately free, named Patrick Lapham and James Ruebottom, in the employ of Mr. W. Brumby, were split-ting shingles about nine miles from the Lake River, when the Natives came on them. Ruebottom made his escape, with three spears in him and now lies without any hopes of recovery; the body of Lapham was found on Wednesday in a state that baffles description -it was one mass of wounds and the head beaten to pieces.-Yours, &c. S. L.

COLONIAL TIMES AND TASMANIAN ADVERTISER (HOBART, TAS: 1825 -
1827), FRIDAY 6 JULY 1827, PAGE 4

THE NATIVES.

*These savages are again at work, carrying slaughter and devastation
wherever they go. On Sunday last, a tribe appeared at Quamby's Bluff,
robbed the hut of Mr. WIDOWSON there and destroyed everything which
they could not take away. Two men, who had gone out in the morning in
quest of their sheep, are supposed to have been murdered by the natives, as
no tidings have since been heard of them and some of their dogs returned
completely speared through, without their masters. This, added to the
circumstance of their cries having been heard amid a great uproar of the
natives, leaves no hope that these unhappy men could escape the fury of
the savages. One was a servant to Mr. Widowson - the other to Mr. Walker.
Another of Mr. Widowson's men, hearing the outcry, went instantly for
his gun and ammunition, with intent to follow the natives. - A mob shewed
themselves at the back of the hut, which he followed and succeeded in
driving them away, but none were killed. While thus engaged in driving one
tribe away, another attacked and plundered the hut, as we have before
described. –*

*A most barbarous murder was also committed by this brutal and atrocious
race last week, on the person of an old man, a stock-keeper to Mr.
SIMPSON, the Magistrate; his body was pierced through and through with
spears and his head beaten flat. The Military instantly pursued the blacks
- brought home numerous trophies, such as spears, waddles, tomahawks,
muskets, blankets, &c., - killed upwards of thirty dogs and, as report says,
nearly as many natives, but this is not a positive fact. - These murders make
six which have been committed near Quamby's Bluff, within the last month,
viz:- Two men of Mr. Brumby's, one of Mr. Field's, one of Mr. Simpson's,
one of Mr. Widowson's and one of Mr. Walker's. - The two men, who we
last week mentioned as having been attacked by the natives, near Michael
Howe's Marsh, while splitting rails, were servants of Mr. J. A. Eddie. One of*

them, named John Flood, has since died of his wounds; and the other poor fellow is not expected to recover, having received nine deep spear-wounds in the back and a dreadful blow with a waddy on the same part. The spear which killed Mr. Simpson's man, went completely thro' his body. Another tribe of natives are said to have attacked and robbed the hut of Captain Thomas, at the Great Western Lagoon. One of the men, named Quin, is missing and it is feared, killed.

We have been favoured with the following extract of a letter from Launceston:- "The people over the second Western Tier, have killed an immense quantity of the blacks this last week, in a consequence of their having murdered Mr. Simpson's stock-keeper. - They were surrounded whilst sitting round their fires, when the soldiers and others fired at them when about 30 yards distant. They report that there must be about sixty of them killed and wounded! They found muskets, cartridges, loose balls and powder, tomahawks, sheep-shears and an immense number of other articles of various descriptions. The man they murdered was formerly an associate of the blacks at Sydney, although himself a white man."

We are thunderstruck when we consider these murders, at the supineness of the Government, in not instantly removing the blacks. We repeat what we have said ten times before, there never will be an end of such transactions till the natives are re-moved - removed, removed, REMOVED.

And the chorus becomes louder and louder until it begins to be heard – REMOVE, REMOVE

The PAKANA *Voice*

BY W.C. SPECIAL CORRESPONDENT—*LUTRUWITA*

Disturbing reports are coming from the Tommeginne (Northern Nation) people of another bloody massacre in the Palittore North area, near Quamby Brook. It is now known that around sixty Pakana people have been killed in reprisal attacks by the British rytia.

Witnesses say the slaughter of young children, older people and all others was brutal and chilling to see. The blood and anguish were indescribable but may soon be forgotten as the nation clans are increasingly diminished and the perpetrators are protected by English Law. They are indeed generally regarded as heroes by the Colonists.

His Excellency Governor Arthur issued a statement saying in part that he deplored violence of any kind and urged restraint from both parties. He said the Government was doing all in its power to see a peaceful resolution to the conflict. God Bless the King.

When asked if those responsible for murdering 30 people would be charged, he made no comment.

TASMANIAN (HOBART TOWN, TAS: 1827 - 1839),
THURSDAY 18 OCTOBER 1827, PAGE 2

We have been informed that a black girl, a native from this Colony, commonly known by the name of Black Kate, is now in an advanced state of pregnancy, by a Lascar [a sailor from India or SE Asia] named Boxhall, a native of Bengal; and that the good inhabitants of Pittwater so far approve of the black match, that many of the generous matrons have already provided white clothes for baby, in anticipation of a safe delivery—a noble precedent to the Ladies of Hobart Town, when necessity solicits their aid.

I was pleased to see that my place of residence, the Hope and Anchor Tavern, was still a thriving establishment;

TASMANIAN (HOBART TOWN, TAS: 1827 - 1839),
THURSDAY 18 OCTOBER 1827, PAGE 3

HOPE AND ANCHOR TAVERN.

THOMAS DIXON (late of the Waterloo Inn) begs leave most respectfully to acquaint his Friends and the Public, that he has removed to the above Tavern, opposite to the Commissariat Office, Macquarie Street, where he humbly trusts the quality of his Brandy, Gin, Rum, Porter, Beer, &c and his assiduous Attention to the Comfort and Accommodation of his Customers, will procure him that share of Public Patronage which it well ever be his utmost Endeavour to merit. –

He particularly solicits Public Attention to his Wholesale Spirit Warehouse, where every kind of Spirit, Wine and Malt Liquor will be sold in any Quantity and on the most moderate Terms. At the Request of his Friends, he has also opened at the end of his Premises, a General Store and Bake-house, where the Public and particularly those coming to Hobart Town by Water can be supplied at all times convenient to the Jetty, with the best articles at the cheapest rate.

A constant supply of excellent Bread and orders from Shippers, Captains and Agents, for Biscuit of both qualities will be thankfully received and executed on the shortest notice. N. B. - Good Stabling provided, Saddle Horses and Horses and Gigs to Let. Hobart Town, Oct. 10, 1827

TASMANIAN (HOBART TOWN, TAS: 1827 - 1839),
THURSDAY 18 OCTOBER 1827, PAGE 3

*We have stopped the Press to insert the following, just received from a
Correspondent, dated Sorell Springs, Oct. 16th 1827 — "On last Sunday
afternoon, the black Natives made their appearance at Curryjong Bottom,
at Mr Presnell's new house, three miles and a half from Sorell Springs.
Mr Bennet the chief District Constable, who lives there, was out about
three hundred yards from the house, with a Capt. Clark, who, I have been
informed, arrived in this Colony by the Research, Captain Dillon. Captain.
C. informed Mr. B., that he had been nearly all over the world, that he
never yet saw any race of savages but he could make friends with; and,
accordingly, went up to them."*

*"While conversing with them, one of them, to draw his attention, called
out,— Kangaroo! Kangaroo! Captain C. turned his head to look, when one
of them instantly threw a spear, which, fortunately, only went through the
side of his arm and broke short off; he immediately knocked the savage
down with a stone and made off, four or five spears were then thrown after
him, but none took effect. Mr. Bennet was returning to the house, when
a spear from one of the cannibals struck him in the back and he now lies
dangerously ill."*

*White writing the above, word has arrived from Lepion Springs that a man
has been speared at Macquarie Springs, near Mr. Weedan's and I have no
doubt that it is the same tribe. "Something has to be done to put a stop
to these barbarities, for it now gets quite alarming and, without some
measures are promptly taken, we shall next hear of their spearing the
travellers on the road; especially, after this alarming attempt, at a place
close to no less than four houses and shepherds with their flocks all
around them.*

This tribe is headed by that notorious fellow, Black Tom."

TASMANIAN (HOBART TOWN, TAS: 1827 - 1839),
FRIDAY 21 DECEMBER 1827, PAGE 3

TO THE EDITOR OF THE TASMANIAN

Sir - The late news from various parts of the Colony, relatively to the outrages committed by the black natives on some of the white people has excited considerable alarm and as you, in one of your late numbers invited information on the subject, I beg to introduce my views of the case I frankly confess, that, during the time I have resided in this country,-I have remarked, from the several arguments and doctrines held forth on the subject, that the public are not properly acquainted with the true cause of the disagreement between the parties ; sweeping charge of treachery and an eager desire of blood, are made against them — the press teems with horrible tales,—and when the accounts of the stock-keepers reach town, painting, in vivid colours, the hostility and depredations of the natives, not a voice is heard—not a single pen is exerted — in behalf of a race of men, whose crime is that of repelling the invaders of their country and preserving that liberty of hunting and acting which it daily more circumscribed.

To hear men say, that, because we have chosen to take possession of this country the natives must be put to death, does little honour to the character of Britons and cannot raise it in the estimation of other nations. Were we to inquire into the temper and disposition of the black natives when we first settled in this country and trace the history of our transactions with them we should, perhaps, have reason to blush and be at a loss to fix the blame of all the mischief that has happened on the right shoulders. We have and can defend ourselves;— we have the use and superiority of arms; and the advantage of a regular intercourse.; by means of the press and otherwise and where is the person (except a coward) who will use the former; but in cases of extreme necessity, against tribes who can scarcely offer a resistance.

The philanthropist and the man of justice and humanity, would find some better means than those proposed, for the accomplishment of the object and one which if properly conducted, would prove as beneficial [?] might be conducive to the well-being of the natives. I am truly sensible of the dangerous situation in which many of the stock-keepers are placed; I am sensible, too, of the urgent necessity which exists to afford them every possible protection; and I know, that some innocent men have suffered for the crimes of others; but the prejudice which has taken hold of a great number of people in this Colony leads to no favourable conclusion towards a perfect reconciliation.

I have heard some say, that they would never give a black fellow the chance to approach them but level him to the ground without hesitation; others exclaim, that the Government order protects the natives at their expense, merely because it conveyed an intimation that the whites should be careful not wantonly to kill a black. It behoves us,—before we proceed to measures which may, either by legal process or arms, deprive our black fellow-creatures of life,— ? to weigh the nature and condition of those laws, by which we pretend to regulate our conduct towards them; and then, from a due consideration of these subjects and from what knowledge we have acquired of the country, endeavour to point out the method by which the natives are most likely to come into our views and obtain for themselves the benefits of civilization, founded on principles that will secure them from relapsing into their former habits.

Among the schemes proposed respecting the aborigines, one, I am told, is that of banishing them to some island in the neighbourhood and leave them there (for any thing I know to the contrary) to starve ;—this is cruelty with a vengeance: - I am, by no means, satisfied in my own mind, respecting this plan; but if ever it be tried, I would suggest that kindness, attention and support be afforded them and every possible attempt made at education and rural instruction, under the management of men of principle, with qualifications suitable to such a responsible employment. I will take upon me to say, that, with proper care and judicious arrangement, much good could be done, provided they can be got hold of without bloodshed.

I have heard it argued that such a measure would be attended with too much expense to Government; but this objection will only be made by a certain description of economists and to which I shall answer, that, as we have taken possession of their country, it is our bounden duty to use every means in our power, not only to keep then in as comfortable and content a condition us they were in before we deprived them of their inheritance, but also, if possible, much better. I have thus given you my opinion on this important subject and which, if you think worth so much notice, you will please give publicity to, in your rapidly improving Journal; and I trust, if it does no other good, it will provoke discussion and bring forth the remarks of abler hands.—I am, Sit;, your's &c.

A Border Settler. [We reserve our opinion on this subject, until we hear from more of our Correspondents, which we again invite.—E».]

1828

TASMANIAN (HOBART TOWN, TAS: 1827 - 1839),
FRIDAY 25 JANUARY 1828, PAGE 2

Important Change.—The civil officers of the Colonies and all who are employed by Government on the civil establishment, we believe, are to receive rations no longer, but are to have a stated salary in money, adequate to the support of those employed and the nature of the employment.—This is as it should be—every person can now buy his meat and bread where he pleases, which will cause a regular and constant circulation of money and bring the wealthy as well as the poor settler into the public market-place, which, we trust, will be got ready for that purpose with the least possible delay.

Black Natives—We have just learned that six men and one woman of the aborigines, came up with a poor man in the interior, last week, whom they speared and abused until they thought he was dead and after searching his pockets and taking all his money, (six shillings,) they left him. As they were going away the woman said—"the money they got from white man would buy sheep."

We have this day recorded another murder committed at that dreadful place—Macquarie Harbour, under circumstances of the most horrid and cruel description. The unfortunate man was stabbed in the body, in three different places and finally, his throat cut from ear to ear. We think, the very idea of being sent to such a place, ought to prevent every description of crime amongst us.

COLONIAL ADVOCATE AND TASMANIAN MONTHLY REVIEW AND REGISTER (HOBART TOWN, TAS: 1828), SATURDAY 1 MARCH 1828, PAGE 43

THE NATIVES.

These black savages commenced the new year and their depredations together, by setting fire to the forest, which did much damage about Bagdad. On the Macquarie River they were chasing the stock-keepers and shepherds in the most malignant manner—near the latter end of January, a poor man was dreadfully ill-used and robbed by a native man and woman. They have on several other occasions acted with great violence and outrage, killing and pursuing the stockmen and shepherds in all directions.

On Monday night, they made their appearance at Bagdad, surprised and attacked three of the road party, one of whom was speared to death, the other two narrowly escaped. Another man, named Brisco, a smith, was killed by them on the preceding Saturday, they also wounding two other men, at the same place. A party went in pursuit, but the sable murderers had fled, after stripping their victim, Brisco, of all his clothes. Another tribe, which infests the neighbourhood of Launceston, attacked a number of women who were washing clothes and some men who were bathing at the basin, on the Cataract River, about half a mile from Launceston.

They robbed them of all the wearing apparel that they could lay hands on, making them run for their lives with what they could first catch hold of. A few hours previously, a tribe of blacks robbed a hut on the North Esk. about two miles from Launceston the tenant fortunately (thanks to his heels) narrowly escaped with his life.

HOBART TOWN COURIER (TAS: 1827 - 1839),
SATURDAY 8 MARCH 1828, PAGE 4

SWAN PORT FEB. 07 1828.

You have often asked me for something for your Paper. I now state as fact, for you to put forth, in your own very impressive way, that the Natives, after an absence of nearly twelve months, are in this district, & creating the greatest alarm. Twice have they plundered one of my Stock-huts, the Stock-keeper escaping the first time, through great presence of mind.

Once they have been at Mr. Lynes s, knocked down & stunned one of his children which was happily rescued in time to save his life. Mr. John Amos's children were driven home by them this week. Also, my head shepherd chased within 100 yards of the barn. The same night, about midnight, they approached close to the Stock-yard and hut and were chased away, the people rising from their beds: and I have now received intelligence that they have burned young Mr. Allen's hut and wheat stack, first stealing his guns and pistols.

The local Government has no time to lose in the adoption of some decisive steps in regard to these creatures and for the sake both of the Governor and the governed, you cannot express yourself too strongly upon the subject to rouse the Government to energetic measures. Every Paper you print should reiterate your call for something to be done more effective than mere proclamation. Every week's delay will only add to the loss of lives and destruction of property and render the final determination more difficult of execution.

TASMANIAN (HOBART TOWN, TAS: 1827 - 1839),
FRIDAY 11 APRIL 1828, PAGE 3

TO THE EDITOR.

SIR,—On Thursday last, a Messenger from Wallace, came to this place and reported that the Natives were holding a Corrobory, about a mile to the Northward of Mr. Makersey's Farm. A party of the 40th were immediately despatched in quest of them. They scoured the adjacent Gullies and found —not the much dreaded Natives, but a group of Neighbours who were enjoying the pleasures of the Chase: between whose hunting halloo and the wild yell of the Blacks, some cowardly keeper, had not been able to distinguish. I believe that one half of the dreadful accounts that are promulgated about the Aborigines, are built on as fragile foundations. I have known some of our Farmers tremble at the sight of a fire in the bush.

A shepherd loses his sheep, flour is missing from the stock hut; the Servant dreads his Master's anger; and the poor Natives, who never saw it, must bear the blame. I am not insensible to the depredations that the Aborigines have committed; they have stolen our goods, plundered us of our flocks, burned our habitations, yes and they have even dyed their spears in our blood. How shall we put an end to these incursions? Shall we kill the Blacks wherever we meet them and blot their names from the face of the Earth?

Humanity revolts at this, we shudder to imbrue our hands in human blood, shall we hunt them with our blood-hounds? Shall we remove them to some place of security? The idea is absurd and impractical: we may as well attempt to catch all the Kangaroos in the Island, as the cunning light-footed

Aborigines. I am of opinion that the Blacks may yet be civilized. About the Western Coast the Blacks are settled and friendly; they reside in the same huts for months together; subsisting on the fish that are caught by their women.

During their stay at these parts, much good might be done amongst them. At these times the attempt to gain their confidence, would be highly practicable and, if matters were properly managed, we might succeed. It only requires the Government and our philanthropic Colonists, to put their hands to the Plough. I am, Sir, Yours, &c.,

A Constant Observer

HOBART TOWN COURIER (TAS: 1827 - 1839),
SATURDAY 22 MARCH 1828, PAGE 3

UPPER CLYDE MARCH 10 1828.

On Friday last Mr. Russell's hut, at the Regent Plains, was robbed of every article, including two muskets, by the blacks. The men unfortunately were absent at the time and on their return discovered what had happened. The stock-keepers finding it would be un-safe to remain without fire arms, immediately made off for Dennis town. On Sunday one of them was sent back on horseback and on his arrival at the farm discovered the hut in the possession of the natives, who immediately gave him pursuit and he in consequence came down again to the Clyde to give the information. A military party was despatched on Mon day along with Mr. Russell's men, but it is very doubtful whether they will get up in time to prevent the blacks destroying the buildings, which are numerous and substantial; the barn is shingled and well filled with oats.

The blacks who are supposed to have murdered Mr. Franks' man, are gone to Abyssinia and from the want of military Mr. Curtin has not been able to send in pursuit of them, having been obliged to take off his sentry to send all the men he could spare to other quarters. Our magistrate too has had about an acre of his potatoes taken out of the ground by the blacks, a few days ago, although the field is very near his house, which is a great loss where there are many pigs kept.

GREEN PONDS, March 10.

The natives have lately became so dreadfully bold and daring, that un-less some decisive step be immediately adopted for the protection of the interior, the sound of murder will ever and anon be ringing in our ear. Many and desperate have been their attacks during the summer, which have never been recorded in your columns. A short time ago a man belonging to Messrs. J. and C. Franks, encountered a party, when a black more courageous than the rest, rushed in and seized his musket. It appeared quite doubtful for some time who would gain the mastery. Had nothing more fatal than this occurred I should not trouble you with the account, as. the man, after boldly defending himself with his back against a tree, for upwards of an hour, escaped unhurt; not so with the unfortunate man Whose death I am now about to relate.

On Tuesday last Mr. John Franks and his stock keeper, left the lakes, both mounted, with a number of fat steers and sheep for the Cross Marsh Market. Mr. Franks was on first with the cattle, when about five miles from Capt. Wood's he observed a large party of blacks, eight or ten behind him, forming a line across the road to prevent his retreat; each of them had his spear uplifted and a small bundle of spears in his left hand. Mr. F. turned his horse and faced them, when they all as if actuated by the same spring, dropped on one knee, still holding the spear in a threatening attitude over their heads.

It appeared to him that they intended to let him pass unmolested but it is quite clear that they were only gaining a little time and endeavouring to divert his attention until they had completely surrounded him and thus make their work more sure; however, he again began driving the cattle and the moment he cracked his whip, the blacks instantaneously rose with the same precision with which they had dropped and commenced running towards him in the most exact order. Mr. F. at this instant could not help admiring their discipline, not even yet aware of the imminent danger that threatened him. On looking round they again stopped, to use his own words, " in the most beautiful style." It now appeared evident to him that they must have some hidden design for this conduct and on examining each side of the road he perceived they were gathering round from all quarters.

This was the critical moment-one more and he would have added to the number of those already sent into eternity by this blood-thirsty race, for on his right hand within thirty yards stood a fellow in the very act of delivering a spear, which was, already quivering in the air; the spurs were instantly applied and, most providentially, the rider saved. In consequence of the thickness of the scrub, the exact movements of the natives could not be observed, but it is supposed there were many more close by the one seen by Mr. F. who imagines several spears were then thrown, as the cattle made a rush at the time he galloped off; in all probability some of them were speared, (some have been since seen speared,) at was the case with some of the sheep that were afterwards found.

His horse received a spear in the thigh ten feet in length, which brought his hind quarters to the ground. Mr. F. now gave up all hopes of escape, but fortunately the horse recovered and after two or three more falls of the same nature the spear fell from him, he arrived safe at Capt. Wood's, who with Mr. Russel most humanely rendered every assistance, providing both for man and horses and kindly taking charge of the wounded animal, at whose stable he has since remained. He is much injured, but it is likely he will recover. Mr F. accompanied by Mr. Russel, directly set off to protect the man who was bringing down the sheep and who had been left a long distance from the blacks, but, melancholy to relate, the work of death had been completed before they arrived at the fatal spot.

The horse was found scarcely able to move, having been speared in numerous places: the poor beast died a few hours after. The force with which these weapons are thrown appears almost in-credible. One spear penetrated the flap of the saddle and entered above four inches into the body of the horse. The man not being immediately found, they entertained a slight hope that he had escaped on foot, until a dog barking about three hundred yards distant, led them to a creek, where they found the body of the poor-creature most dreadfully lacerated. Eight spears had- entered the breast, the head was literally beaten to pieces, the flesh of the upper lip entirely knocked off and in every respect presenting most appalling spectacle. I fear you will think me exceedingly prolix, but the subject being of so momentous a nature, must plead my excuse. I really cannot fully express my feelings upon this occasion.

When we reflect that a fellow creature has lost his life, whilst engaged in his master's service, that in the morning he was in perfect health and a few hours after we behold him; a cold and lifeless corpse, thrown across a horse's back, covered with blood ; it certainly calls loudly on those witnessing such sights to state every particular connected with so dreadful an occurrence in the hope that the proper authorities will give this subject their most mature consideration.

The PAKANA *Voice*

BY W.C. SPECIAL CORRESPONDENT—LUTRUWITA

Lungkana Lakarana (To Kill Big)

MASS MURDER COMMITTED BY BRITISH

Reports are emerging from the Lairmairrener people (Big River Nation) of killing on a massive scale which occurred on the 4th March 1828 in the

Clyde police district. It appears likely the Braylwunyer clan may have been hardest hit with up to seventeen being randomly executed. The stockmen attacked the clan in an area known by the rytia (white man) as the Lagoon Lower Marshes near the Jordan River.

Witnesses say muskets, with bayonets and pistols, were used to kill as many people as they could and this was carried out in two raids first murdering seven and then later following the clan to a lagoon, killed ten more. Many of the victims were women, children, old people and those unable to escape.

A government spokesman said they were looking into the matter but at this stage believed the men were acting in self-defence.

HOBART TOWN COURIER (TAS: 1827 - 1839), SATURDAY 3 MAY 1828, PAGE 3

There is no duty more incumbent on a public writer than to combat vulgar errors. One of the most unpardonable which it behoves us to subvert, is the prevailing belief that the natives of this island are of peculiarly mean intellect and of debased capacity. The great Buffon and many other of our most celebrated naturalists, have lent their aid to propagate this error. We maintain however, that it is totally devoid of truth. - Providence is more equal in its blessings than is commonly supposed. It is the proper and profitable use of them that forms the difference among mankind, depending chiefly on ourselves in this world of trial. But to suppose that a whole race of people was originally created with a deficiency of intellect, is to suppose what never has been nor ever will be, while the world lasts.

The boy whom we mentioned as lately caught by Mr. Batman, at Ben Lomond, evinced the most lively disposition, the most acute intelligence and the finest and most tender affections. The two natives whom Mr. Roberts brought up last week from the channel, displayed great quickness of understanding and force of mind. That their happiness is circumscribed must be evident from the limited resources which their habits of life afford, nevertheless, they have enjoyments in their savage state, which many of the most civilized whites would envy.

The five who came up the other day belonging to the same tribe, betray an equal share of intelligence and it is gratifying to see their late prevailing dread of the whites giving way and voluntary journeys undertaken to satisfy curiosity. We rejoice to learn, that a sort of depot, or place of refuge, is forming for them on Bruné island,- under the sanction of Government, where those who, are inclined will be supplied with food and most probably be inured to useful labour. Everything depends on the persons with whom they at first associate! who must treat them with kindness, attention and even respect, if they would conciliate; and by such means, if properly followed up, we doubt not their present hostile feelings may be gradually obliterated.

It seemed the Government was not short of helpful and self-assured advice coming from all quarters, including Z, who wrote;

TASMANIAN (HOBART TOWN, TAS: 1827 - 1839), FRIDAY 16 MAY 1828, PAGE 2

TO THE EDITOR

SIR—I perceive in the Hobart Town Courier of the 10th instant, an article respecting the Black Natives, written I suppose, by some one resident on the Elizabeth River, as the observations point entirely to those in that district. The object of that letter, I confess, I am unable to discover. He says—"The natives have been kindly treated, but have committed murder in every shape. We rejoice that the matter has been taken up so earnestly by the Government and submit that it is useless to enquire who struck the first blow; our object is to stop the effusion of blood.

To this and this alone, our attention should be directed;" and concludes with an ill-timed sentence, which he mistakes for wit, in calling to his aid the services of Mr. Lightfoot. Throughout the whole of the article there is an attempt at the pathetic, but mixed up with the satirical, unbecoming a manly and Christian feeling and useless as to the object wished for—putting an end out to the distressing situation of the Settlers who are exposed to the atrocities of savages. I consider what has been done by Government of no avail. When the people are exposed to murder in the most horrid shapes, the Government issues a proclamation—and against whom? —Against savages, who know as much about its nature as the cattle who range the mountains.

The plan, Mr. Editor, I would recommend is this. Let Government call on the Settlers who have stock-keepers and get them to accompany parties of soldiers and constables, each party 15 in number, to apprehend the Black Natives, giving the reward of freedom for every certain number of the blacks that will be apprehended alive. From experience (and I have for several years been among cattle and stock-keepers in the interior and seen and known more of the savages than I think necessary to state at this time) I resolve to assert that, to the stock-keepers, the Colony will at length owe its relief from the depredations of the Black Natives.—

None know so well as stock-keepers, how to track them by their fires and come upon them when asleep. This knowledge, melancholy as has been the effect, is not the less true. It is to them, therefore, that the Government and the Settlers must look for that riddance which is now so necessary and so much desired by all parties. If the matter be protracted, the difficulty will just the more increase. I therefore, as an interested member of society, call upon Government now to set about the matter with all its energy.

I am, Sir, yours, &c. Z. ●—oo—

Z.

The human condition is indeed a complex one. If you think it is possible to understand history from one viewpoint only then I fear your naiveté will lead to bleakness of mind and spirit. After reading Z, now take heed of 'A CURRENCY LAD'; a term used for children of convicts born in VDL whose name was derived from their demands to be paid in hard currency for their work.

TASMANIAN (HOBART TOWN, TAS: 1827 - 1839), FRIDAY 23 MAY 1828, PAGE 4

TO THE EDITOR

*SIR—By the Proclamation of the 25th ultimo, I perceive it is the humane intention of the Lieutenant Governor to ameliorate the condition of the Aborigines of this Colony; and may heaven prosper the undertaking, for these poor creatures lead a most miserable life to my certain knowledge. **I have travelled through the greater part of this Colony during the last nine years and am personally acquainted with many of them and know enough of their language to understand the many sorrowful tales they have related of their treatment by the white men.***

I have no hesitation in asserting, that, by proper and conciliating measures, the black natives may be yet guided; and if Government would offer, through a proper medium, to provide for them in peace and safety, they would willingly come and accept of it. I know an old man who is even better acquainted with the black natives than myself and who, I dare say, would volunteer in this humane service, if required; and if I can be of any use in forwarding their amelioration, I am quite ready; for which purpose, Mr. Editor, my address I now make known to you and which you have my leave, if you think proper, to communicate to His Excellency.

I am, Sir, yours, &c. Richmond, May 15, 1828

A CURRENCY LAD.

ABORIGINES.

The wife of a man named Dingle, belonging to the 40th, was speared in the head this week, by the Black Natives, near the Western Mountains.

A few days ago a party of the Blacks attacked Mr. Reynold's stock hut, at the Break O'day Plains but were defeated and two of them taken prisoners, who were brought in custody to Campbelltown, from which, we understand, one of them has since made his escape.

[By His Excellency Colonel George Arthur, Lieutenant Governor of the Island of Van Diemen's Land and its Dependencies.]

A PROCLAMATION.

WHEREAS the Black or Aboriginal Natives of this Island have for a considerable time past, carried on a series of indiscriminate attacks upon the persons and property of divers of His Majesty's subjects and have especially of late perpetrated most cruel and sanguinary acts of violence and outrage; evincing an evident disposition systematically to kill and destroy the white inhabitants indiscriminately whenever an opportunity of doing so is presented; --

AND whereas, notwithstanding the Proclamation made and issued by me on the Fifteenth day of April, last past, -- and that every practicable measure has from time to time been resorted to, under that Proclamation and otherwise, for the purpose of removing the Aboriginals from the settled districts of the Colony and for putting a stop to the repetition (sic) of such atrocities, --repeated inroads are daily made by the Natives into the said settled Districts and acts of hostility and barbarity there committed by them, as well as at the more distant stock runs and in some instances upon unoffending and defenceless women and children. -- AND whereas also, it seems, at present, impossible to conciliate the several tribes of that people ; and the ordinary Civil Powers of the Magistrates and the means afforded by the Common Law, are found by experience to be wholly insufficient for the general safety ; and it hath therefore become at length unavoidably necessary, for the effectual suppression of similar enormities, to proclaim and keep in force Martial Law, in the manner hereinafter proclaimed and directed:

NOW THEREFORE, by virtue of the Powers and Authorities in me, in this behalf vested, I, the said Lieutenant Governor, do by these presents, Declare and proclaim, that from and after the date of this, my Proclamation and until the cessation of hostilities shall be by me hereafter Proclaimed and directed MARTIAL LAW is and shall continue to be in force against the several Black or Aboriginal Natives, within the several Districts of this Island; excepting always the places and portions of this Island, next mentioned, (that is to say) --

1st. -- All the country extending southward of Mount Wellington to the Ocean, including Brune Island;

2nd. -- Tasman's Peninsula;

3rd. -- The whole of the North-Eastern part of this Island which is bounded on the North and East by the Ocean and on the South-West by a line, drawn from Pipers River to Saint Patrick's Head;

4th. -- And the whole of the Western and South-Western part of this Island, which is bounded on the East by the River Huon and by a line drawn from that River over Teneriffe Peak to the extreme West-ern Bluff; on the North by an East and West line from the said extreme Western Bluff to the Ocean and the West and South by the Ocean.

AND, for the purposes aforesaid, all Soldiers are hereby required and commanded to obey and assist their lawful superiors and all other His Majesty's subjects are required and commanded to obey and assist the Magistrates in the execution of such measures as shall by any one or more of such Magistrates be directed to be taken for those purposes, by such ways and means as shall by him or them be considered expedient, so long as Martial Law shall continue to exist. -- BUT, I DO, nevertheless, hereby strictly order, enjoin and command, that the actual use of arms be in no case resorted to, if the Natives can by other means be induced or compelled to retire into the places and portions of this Island herein-before excepted from the operation of Martial Law; that bloodshed be checked, as much as possible; that any Tribes which may surrender themselves up, shall be treated with every degree of humanity; and that defenceless women and children be invariably spared. -- AND, all Officers, Civil and Military and others person whatsoever, are hereby required to take notice of this, my Proclamation and Order and to render obedience and assistance herein accordingly.

PROVIDED nevertheless and it is hereby notified and proclaimed, that nothing herein contained, shall, or doth extend to interrupt or interfere with the ordinary exercise of the Civil Power, or the regular course of the Common Law, any further or other-wise than as such interruption shall, for the purpose of carrying on military operations against the Natives, be rendered necessary.

GIVEN under my Hand and Seal at Arms, at the Government-house, Hobart-town, this first day of November, One thousand eight hundred and twenty-eight.

"GEORGE ARTHUR."

By Command of His Excellency, J. BURNETT.

GOD SAVE THE KING!

The PAKANA *Voice*

BY W.C. SPECIAL CORRESPONDENT—*LUTRUWITA*

DECLARATION OF WAR

The British Government has effectively declared war on all the Nations of Lutruwita. Their representative on this island, His Excellency Governor Arthur issued a proclamation on the 1st November 1828, pronouncing Martial Law across many of the areas now occupied by rytia (white) people.

This comes after several years of escalating conflict as British incursions into the Pakana nations continue to rise.

Martial Law places full command of the Army and all its associated resources directly under the Governor's control whose orders are to forcibly move Pakana people from their home nations to other foreign parts of Lutruwita. Resistance will be met with an armed response.

Such action may seem somewhat extreme considering there are now over 20,000 British and perhaps 1,000 or so Pakana people remaining.

HOBART TOWN COURIER (TAS: 1827 - 1839),
SATURDAY 17 JANUARY 1829, PAGE 1

THE COUNTRY POST.

OATLANDS,-John Danvers and Constable Holmes who were sent as guides with a party of military in pursuit of the Natives returned to Oatlands on Saturday, after being absent 29 days. This party traversed the greater part of the island from the Eastern marshes and Blue hills to Oyster bay, calling at Maria Island, then proceeding to St. Patrick's head and Schoutens seek, without perceiving any Native fires, or the traces of the Natives anywhere is the direction followed. The party might have proceeded farther, but as no signs of natives could be discovered and as martial law does not extend beyond the limits where the party then was, they returned, carefully examining the country in their route back. It is now pretty evident, that the Natives who recently infested the Eastern parts of the island, must have crossed the country and sought a retreat in the Western parts beyond the Big River.

Danvers observed during this journey the manner in which the Aborigines point out the road they have taken, when travelling, to those who may be straggling behind, or left, hunting opossums. They fix a small stick in the ground, about two or three feet in length, giving it an angular direction, the top leaning towards the road they are pursuing. About a hundred yards from the first stick another is placed in a similar manner and position and so on, so the Natives by following these sticks cannot help falling in with those who went before them.

Ensign Lockyer with his party, James Hopkins, guide, returned to Oatlands on Sunday last without having fallen in with the Natives, In a solitary and sequestered spot beyond the Eastern tiers, Ensign Lockyer came upon a hut constructed by some white person, wherein was found the skull of some white man, probably murdered some time or other.

BOTHWELL -The natives made their appearance at the river Ouse on the 6th instant and robbed Capt. Ramus's hut of two muskets and Mr. Jamieson's hut of one musket and speared one of the men. Being hotly pursued they divided into two mobs, one of which crossed the Ouse towards the Clyde, the other went into the interior towards the river Dee.

There are 14 parties out in all directions from this station. We have got an increase of two sergeants and twenty five rank and file, to the military party here, making three sergeants and about 80 rank and file belonging to this station, under the command of Lieut. Williams, Police Magistrate, who is most active and zealous in pursuit of the natives.

On Sunday evening a native man and woman arrived here as guides from Brune Island. They seem very cunning and express themselves very determined to find their countrymen out. I believe they are to he sent in the direction of the Big Lake. His Excellency is to be here on his way from the Big Lake, on the 23d inst. He will find this place very much altered since his last visit nearly three years ago. Our township is increasing very fast; Mr. Vincent has got the brick work of his new inn in the township up. It is 40 feet by 40 and two storeys high. We still want a church, which I hope his Excellency will forward when he arrives here.

COLONIAL TIMES (HOBART, TAS: 1828 - 1857),
FRIDAY 30 JANUARY 1829, PAGE 3

It has reached us by a settler, that Boomer, the black native, having struck the Serjeant of the detachment which he was acting as guide, in pursuit of the Aborigine, endeavoured to escape and received the merited reward of his treachery and presumption, by being shot dead. So much for reliance upon the fidelity of a native!

THE BLACK NATIVES_A Correspondent at Great Swan Port, says-"The grand topic of local interest here is the blacks and the general combined movements against them.-These savages in the district are particularly annoying.-They rob every [?] but they can succeed in drawing the inmates away from but there have been no murders since Mr. HAWKINS'S man. Parties are continually out in quest. We saw but one black during the whole of our journey and he escaped among the scrub. There were doubtless others, but they would not show themselves. Two of Mr. MEREDITH'S huts and Mr. ALLEN'S have been robbed within this fortnight.

Mr. DAVID RAYNER shot a black man near Mr. LYNES'S on Monday last. Nine were killed and three taken, near St. Paul's River, two days back and about the same time ten were shot and two taken near the Eastern Marshes. A few weeks ago, a tribe attacked Mr. MEREDITH'S horses, which had been tethered and barbarously put two of them to death. We are daily expecting them round on the Schoutens, when all hands will be out in pursuit. You cannot think how cunning the black devils are. When the first of Mr. MEREDITH'S huts was robbed, they set fire to the fence, to entice the men out of the hut!"

In other parts of the Island, the natives have robbed the stock-huts of Messrs. Humphrey, Ramus, Triffit and Shorns and speared one of Mr. Jamieson's men. A Mrs. Walton and family, which were in Mr. Triffit's house, providentially escaped these savages. Ensign Lockyer, of the 40th and his party, as well as John Danvers and Constable Holmes, who went as guides with a military party in pursuit of the natives, have returned to Oatlands, after an absence of 21 days, without perceiving a single native in any direction to the Eastward.

COLONIAL TIMES (HOBART, TAS: 1828 - 1857),
FRIDAY 30 JANUARY 1829, PAGE 3

The town is quite en qui vive [on the lookout for] in anticipation of a splendid and good dinner, in commemoration of the restoration of the Freedom of the Press. We know of no room more suitably adapted than at the Dallas Arms, New-town road, kept by Mr. MORRIS

Life is full of ironies. Here amongst the chaos, murder and mayhem, a young Pakana youth is seen to find pleasure in William Collins *Ode to the Passions*. Mind you, if I had it read to me, my expressions too may well have been pantomimic – the poem is well beyond my sense of understanding.

The Aborigions of Van Demonds land endeavouring to kill Mr John Allen on Milton Farm in the District of Great Swanport on the 14th December 1828; Dixon Library, State Library of New South Wales CALL NUMBER DL Pe 279

CORNWALL PRESS AND COMMERCIAL ADVERTISER
(LAUNCESTON, TAS: 1829), TUESDAY 17 FEBRUARY 1829, PAGE 3

ON Saturday, the Police Magistrate, (P. A. MULGRAVE, Esq.,) accompanied by DUDLEY FEREDAY, Esq. (Sheriff) and the Rev. WM. BEDFORD, attended St. John's Church to witness the manner in which an Aboriginal youth would be affected by the organ and we are reliably informed that his gestures and demeanour throughout the performances (which were extremely pleasing and respectable) was in fine keeping with the music. His ear seemed most delicately sensitive; and although so pantomimic were his grins and shrugs as to repeatedly excite a smile, there is no reason Collins' " Ode to the Passions" was never before acted in dumb show so well or unaffectedly.

ODES. 67 THE PASSIONS.
AN ODE FOR MUSIC. WHEN

Music, heavenly maid, was young,

While yet in early Greece she sung,

The Passions oft, to hear her shell,

Thronged around her magic cell,

Exulting, trembling, raging, fainting,

Possessed beyond the Muse's painting:

By turns they felt the glowing mind

Disturbed, delighted, raised, refined;

Till once, 'tis said, when all were fired,

Filled with fury, rapt, inspired,

From the supporting myrtles round

They snatched her instruments of sound;

And, as they oft had heard apart

Sweet lessons of her forceful art,

Each (for Madness ruled the hour)

Would prove his own expressive power.

And that is just the first verse of many...I feel for the boy!

CORNWALL PRESS AND COMMERCIAL ADVERTISER
(LAUNCESTON, TAS: 1829), TUESDAY 23 JUNE 1829, PAGE 3

BLACK NATIVES

We have been favoured with a long and interesting letter from Mr. Davis, at New Plains, respecting these degraded creatures. But however willing and; desirous we may be to insert it, our limits compel us to merely state some of the particulars.— It appears that about a fortnight since, at mid-day, Natives to the number of about 200 surrounded a dwelling in which were Mr. D.'s overseer, shepherd and others, but were providentially discovered by a little girl, the overseer's daughter, who instantly gave the alarm and with the rest made off for Mr. Davis's dwelling House.

Messrs. Davis and Russel then armed themselves and the men, but so overpowered were the servants by fright that not one of them could fire his piece. The Blacks were still hemming them in, but upon Mr. R. discharging his musket upon them they fled in confusion to the place where they were when first discovered. They were finally driven off and happily. There were no lives lost on the occasion.

I read this article riddled with despair. Murders, reprisals, hatred and stupidity of war and violence between humans.

CORNWALL PRESS AND COMMERCIAL ADVERTISER
(LAUNCESTON, TAS: 1829), TUESDAY 10 MARCH 1829, PAGE 4

A person who came into town a few minutes ago from Bonney Flats, reports that the natives made their appearance there yesterday and perpetrated a most barbarous murder.

Launceston, March 20.—I know you wish to hear the news from this quarter: I have some of an awful description to tell you about those cruel and merciless savages the Blacks. After they had speared Mr. Bell's man a few weeks ago, they gave chase to Mr. Charles Dry, who escaped them by the speed of his horse; they, however, a day or two afterwards surrounded his hut, near the Western river and although there were four men in it with arms and ammunition, they blockaded the huts from 11 o'clock in the forenoon until sun-down, when they disappeared. During this interval the white people fired several times through holes they made in the roof, but with-out doing any execution. One of Mr. Dry's men was induced to go out of the hut with a loaf of bread, intending to throw it towards the Blacks, when he received a spear in his right knee from an artful boy who was crawling by the side of a tree near the hut. As the poor fellow was wounded, the Blacks gave a great shout. Many of them spoke good English, but their words were extremely indecent.

On Tuesday last they made their appearance near Launceston and robbed one or two huts near the Cataract and on Friday they were seen on the North Esk river, a short distance from Launceston, when they robbed three or four farm houses and killed a woman and two men at the farm of a man named Mellor. They also speared a man in his master's barn and another who was on the road to Patterson's plains with a bag of flour upon his back; both those persons are badly wounded and are now in the Hospital. Two stock-keepers are also missing and are supposed to have been killed by the Blacks in the same neighbourhood.

Several parties have been sent in pursuit, but the soldiers and constabulary were unsuccessful. Yesterday morning a party of volunteers came up with the murderers about 12 miles from hence, at a place called Bullock's hunting ground, **where four men, a woman and a child of the Black people were killed**. One of the men that were shot had on a red coat which was stolen from the Commandant's stock-keeper, in a hut near the Cataract hills. I am told there is a woman amongst them who formerly lived at Launceston for several months.

Ibid:[The same source] The black natives on Friday about mid-day went to the farm of a settler named Miller and killed Mrs. Miller and two men named James Hales and Thomas Johnson. Miller came up to the house whilst the blacks were there and made his escape by running. The blacks then went to the farm of a settler named Russel and severely wounded two men.

There are also two stockkeepers missing, one of them servant to Mr Towers, the other to Mr. David Williams. Several small parties went after them. One party overtook them and killed five. The blacks then took post on a hill, (it is said to the number of about 150) and set the party at defiance. Finding them make so formidable an appearance and having broken one of their muskets, they were compelled to retire. Some fresh parties have since gone in quest of them. Miller's house is only about 2 miles from Launceston, but on the further side of the South Esk.

I think this is what is referred to colloquially as Black Humour although in this case it may offer credibility ill deserved

HOBART TOWN COURIER (TAS: 1827 - 1839),
SATURDAY 21 MARCH 1829, PAGE 2

TRADE AND SHIPPING.

It is now the prevailing taste in Paris, closely imitated in London, to have a black woman for a cook, a black boy or girl for a femme de chamber and another for a lacquey. If this fancy continues there might be some chance of disposing of a few of our Aboriginal blacks, if we could manage to produce them for sale about Park lane or Bond street.

THE COUNTRY POST.

Richmond, April 27, 1829, A coroner's inquest sat yesterday on the body of one of the native Aborigines, who died in the gaol at this place on Thursday morning last. The jury returned a verdict of - Died by the visitation of God.

One of the jury strenuously endeavoured to establish a charge of the man's death having been occasioned by the want of sufficient nourishment and Dr. Garrett, hearing after the jury had given their verdict that a feeling of censure had in consequence gone abroad upon the conduct of the keeper of the gaol not having afforded the man sufficient attention and food, judged; it necessary to suspend the interment until this morning, when on again opening the body and proceeding further than he had before done in his examination, he opened the chest and discovered the lungs to be in a very diseased state, arising from an old spear wound which had penetrated the chest and which was the actual cause of his death.

The PAKANA *Voice*

BY W.C. SPECIAL CORRESPONDENT—*LUTRUWITA*

It would appear the Christian God is now responsible for taking lives of the Pakana people 'by the visitation of God.'

Apparently being imprisoned in an alien, damp, cold and friendless structure such as a prison and being fed foreign food had little to do with his death. It is also worth noting that he was nameless, and referred to only as 'one of the native Aborigines' and yet this was a coroner's inquest!

CORNWALL PRESS AND COMMERCIAL ADVERTISER
(LAUNCESTON, TAS: 1829), TUESDAY 19 MAY 1829, PAGE 4

ABORIGINES.

On Saturday afternoon last, the Blacks again made their appearance at the back of Miller's farm, in the immediate neighbourhood of the Town. They fell in with and speared in the arm, a boy of about 12 years of age, belonging to Mr. Brugh, near to the farm of Dr. Aldridge and within a hundred yards of that of W. E. Laurence Esq.

HOBART TOWN COURIER (TAS: 1827 - 1839), SATURDAY 12 SEPTEMBER 1829, PAGE 2

MORVEN, Sept. 7. — On Wednesday last Mr. Batman, with the party under his orders, fell in with the black natives on the east side of Ben Lomond. They saw the smoke of their fires about 3 o'clock p.m. and lay in thick scrub until after sun set, when they crept down upon them within twenty yards. The dogs at this time (upwards of 40 in number) came barking at the party and the natives arose. Mr. Batman then gave orders for the men to fire which was done and then rushed forward; only one woman and a male child about two years old were taken that night. James Clark, a very active and determined young man, rushed into the scrub and seized the woman and child.

The woman bit his hand in several places severely, but he still held her until another man came to his assistance. The next morning James Gumm found a man and brought him up to the party. He proved to be a most notorious character and well known as a chief. He had a number of ornaments about his body. Shortly afterwards Pigeon, a Sydney black, found another young man about 20 years of age, very stout and strong, severely wounded in the body.

Mr. Batman learned from these, that 10 men and two women were wounded in the body and were dead or would die. The party found several traces of blood in different directions and places where they had lain down and had bled much. They shot upwards of 20 large dogs and took a great number of spears, waddies, blankets, rugs, knives, &c. The party fell in with upwards of 80 huts in different places. Above 300 buck shot were fired at them, at the short distance above stated. The woman and child were brought away with them. Mr. Batman and his party are proceeding to Oyster bay, in order to fall in with that tribe.

BOTHWELL, Sept.5.-Last week the natives surprised one of Captain Wood's servants, at a stock hut on the Jordan, beat him and speared him and left him for dead, but he is likely to recover. The day before yesterday they attacked Mr. Allardice's shepherd within 300 yards of his house and speared him twice in the loins, but he escaped with life by plunging into the Clyde. Parties of military and constables have been dispatched in various directions by Lieut. Williams, but up to this hour no tidings have been received of these black wretches being overtaken. They seem to have Jack the Giant's in-visible coat and also his seven league boots.

A few years later I was able to interview John Batman when I returned to Lutruwita in the 30s. I would frequently see John at the Cornwall Hotel in Launceston. The centre of attention, he was constantly wheeling and dealing with some gentlemen about his next ambitious scheme or some way to improve his standing in society. I noticed he was regularly bought a drink by one or other patron, handshakes accompanied by much back slapping for his successes. It takes little imagination to realise that we were unlikely to ever become acquainted on peaceable terms. Privately I thought he was a man of disagreeable disposition and disreputable character with calculating eyes and a cold sneer in his smile.

COLONIAL TIMES (HOBART, TAS: 1828 - 1857),
FRIDAY 18 SEPTEMBER 1829, PAGE 3

THE NATIVES.

We omitted last week to notice that Mr. Batman and the party under his orders fell in with a tribe, comprising 70 in number, of the Native Blacks, at Ben Lomond. The sable tribe had no less than 40 dogs, whose barking alarmed the party.— The natives, so formidable in point of numbers, made the first attack with their spears. By their cunning, they succeeded in creeping down within 20 yards of the party, when they were obliged in their own defence to fire and rush forward, when a complete rout of the blacks ensued; about 15 were killed and wounded and several taken, among whom were one or two most notorious Chiefs, with many ornaments about their bodies.

The party succeeded in killing upwards of twenty of their large dogs and taking a great number of their spears, waddies, blankets, rugs, knives, &c.; and also fell in with upwards of 80 huts in different directions.

We now almost despair of seeing any number of these miserable, uncultivated, human beings taken alive, in order to their civilization, from the formidable position they take of attacking an armed party of Europeans. Without making any serious reflections on the enormities they have committed on the Stock-keepers and other Settlers' servants from time to time, we trust that no effort will be left untried by the numerous parties in pursuit of them to capture the whole ; and we hope that the persons at the head of the parties will always keep humanity in their minds, while on this very unpleasant duty. Accounts have just been received, stating that the Natives have been very troublesome at Great Swan Port, where they have speared several persons.

Being a diligent reporter, I made myself known to him and to my surprise he was very congenial and accommodating. However I did notice a perceptible change when I told him I was the Special Correspondent for *London Evening Standard* and would very much like to interview him. He was torn between utter contempt for the press and his ego calling out to be revealed to the world. Needless to say, the latter won. He insisted emphatically that I call him John. We were about the same age, which perhaps made such familiarity bearable.

We set our next meeting for a few days' time at a mutually convenient place, the cosy, smoke-filled corner of the bar at his hotel. There our discussion ranged widely. From his humble birth and convict parents, to his large estate at Kingston nestled below the mountain of Ben Lomond in the Fingal Valley. He became enraptured regaling his capture of the infamous, gentleman bushranger, Mathew Brady and other worthy adventures he had undertaken in his life.

He was even more animated on the subject of his plans with Gellibrand, Simpson, Wedge and Swanston, who called themselves The *Port Phillip Association*, to colonise the lands around the Yarra River just across Bass Strait. I broached the subject of the people already living there, the Wurundjeri, but he assured me this time there would be a treaty. John went to script in his reply;

'We have told the British Government that our aim is to establish a nucleus "for a free and useful colony, founded on the principle of conciliation, of philanthropy, morality and temperance calculated to ensure the comfort and wellbeing of the natives'."[x]

I wondered how compatible this was with their stated goal, which 'was to depasture [graze] stock as profitably as possible'.[xi]

He talked and talked about himself, his ambitions and accomplishments with rowdy encouragement from his gaggle of followers. That was until I cinched my eyes to his, smiled and asked what was to be my final question;

'John, in many years to come, do you think you will be remembered with bridges and monuments built and numerous places named in your honour as a leading founder of Melbourne, or will you be remembered as a mass murderer of Ben Lomond Nation women, children and men and killer of the wounded?'

The whole tavern froze; you could have heard a pin drop. Batman grew red in the face, his eyes fiery and body stock still. He leant so close, finger pointed within inches of my face that I thought he was going to thump me but instead he said in barely controlled anger:

'What I did was within the Law and make sure you print that in your sh**ty rag!'

I thought it an opportune moment to thank him for his time and make a quick exit. Feeling a chill in the air as I strode along Cameron street I wondered if John and I were still on first names but then I really didn't care too much.

We never spoke again. Soon after he and his fellow peacemakers left for new pastures and did indeed set the foundations for a village in the Yarra. It is believed he died of syphilis a few years later aged thirty-eight. Humans are indeed perplexing beings!

Then I came across this distressing news item.

HOBART TOWN COURIER (TAS: 1827 - 1839), SATURDAY 23 MAY 1829, PAGE 2

Mr. Gilbert Robertson has returned from his second expedition in quest of the blacks. He pursued his course, we learn, to the west, passed near the great lake, explored the western borders of Lake Echo, reached within about 15 miles of the hill called the Frenchman's cap and returned by the Shannon.

He was frequently close upon the natives and in one part came upon a small village of their huts which had been built about 4 weeks before, but did not capture any of them. As a strong proof of the rapid decrease of this benighted race, their temporary villages which a few years ago consisted sometimes of from 30 to 40 wigwams or huts, (each containing on an average 4 or 5 inmates), are now seldom found to consist of more than 4 or 5 huts. Numerous herds of wild cattle, without any brand mark, were found around Lake Echo and on the beautiful and extensive plain of rich pasturage to the West and south.

I read this over several times and still find it hard to respond. I thought about posting a piece to my editor but I was filled with such mixture of emotions that I thought I will leave it for later contemplation. Now I shall leave it for you to draw your own conclusions; if indeed you can.

The reports that the Pakana villages are now so much smaller is sobering indeed although it ends on the positive note that there are herds of wild cattle on 'beautiful and extensive plain of rich pasturage to the West and South'. So things are not all bad after all!

Newspaper editors sometimes fail to read beyond their own stories or think about the improbable and contradictory nature of what they are actually saying. While one paper is reporting there is clearly a rapid decline in the numbers of the Pakana people another is sensationally reporting three hundred black natives appearing at the girl's school, Ellenthorpe near the village of Ross which of course is a great story. The message is that there are still large numbers of blacks threatening us all and we are likely to be killed in our beds. Although the report was retracted a week later it had done its work. Who reads or believes retractions anyway? And so, untruth engenders fear which leads to reactive responses and later justifications of those actions.

COLONIAL TIMES (HOBART, TAS: 1828 - 1857),
FRIDAY 23 OCTOBER 1829, PAGE 2

A tribe of Black Natives, of no less than three hundred in number, made their appearance at Ellenthorpe Hall last week. We have not heard that they committed any offence there.

COLONIAL TIMES (HOBART, TAS: 1828 - 1857),
FRIDAY 30 OCTOBER 1829, PAGE 2

We were misinformed in stating, that a tribe of 300 natives made their appearance at Ellenthorpe Hall. -

We are further requested to state, that an instance was never known of any natives being seen there since Mrs. Clark's Academy has been established.

You will be pleased to know I am not completely sedentary in my old age. Bent makes sure of that and takes me with him for his daily walk in search of new scents and his insatiable quest for rabbits or foxes to chase. After reading the last article once again, I needed time to think, agonise and then forget. I am good at searching my soul over things I have absolutely no control over. You could liken it to hitting your head against a stone wall; it feels better when you stop, or, in my case, imbibe a little, although only for medicinal purposes, or so I tell myself.

It is now mid-winter in Martock and the air refreshing, in other words, bitterly cold. On my walk the wind was so strong I had to work hard to push against its force as we fought our way along the dark, wet track. As Bent began training me again in the never-ending art of stick tossing, my thoughts began to deliberate once again over the idea of civilization.

THE QUANDARY OF CIVILIZATION

It may be an odd train of thought, but so many of the articles I have been reading talked about civilization. The implicit assumption was that the British were civilized and the Pakana people were not. What does it mean to be civilized? My reading says it is when a human society is at an advanced stage of social development and organisation. The British Empire was without doubt extraordinary in its power, structure, government processes and industrial ingenuity. Culturally it was alive with literature, music and worldliness.

This is of course the paradox: to see yourself as civilized you naturally require the counter to exist, that is, the uncivilized. Who better to fit that description than tribal people who live with their natural surroundings, without any apparent desire to radically modify them, speak incomprehensible languages, have no written communication, walk around naked and, most of all, are unpardonably black! And yet how do we define 'advanced'? Perhaps this might come down to how we see ourselves and our place in nature. Do we live with and within nature, or do we live apart and alter nature to serve our own purpose? The difference may be summed up in the way white people talk about living on or in the island of Tasmania while Pakana may see themselves living **with** the island of Lutruwita. This is an observation and a feeling I gained from those I met.

And yet the Pakana had lived with their island for thousands and thousands of years while most civilizations are fortunate if they to stay in place for a couple of centuries. Which one then is more 'advanced'? I really don't know the answer but, as any steadfast reporter would, I posed the questions and left others to seek the answers. I came to no conclusions, except that it was too bloody cold to stay throwing this wet and slimy stick any longer. We needed to retreat to the warmth of my beloved attic!

***

Returning once again to the ongoing saga of Lutruwita. Difficult times generate inventive, often harebrained ideas and this one would top the list, but apparently it was considered with all due diligence at a public meeting in 1829. The proposal was for the civilized British to bring in blood thirsty, fearless, man-eating Maoris from New Zealanders to capture and sell Pakana people as slaves for the price of one musket each. They would in turn greatly benefit by learning how to become civilized.

Well considered and thoughtful idea!

Interestingly, Major Gray who seconded the motion also thought up the 'Black Line', another crazy idea but one which was taken seriously and carried out in all its glorious absurdity, resulting in dismal failure.[xii]

 The difficulty which our troops have experienced while Bush fighting with the Maoris calls to mind a project brought forward in June, 1829, by Mr Horace W Croft and seconded by Major Gray, to introduce a number of New Zealanders into Van Diemen's Land.

It was contended that, as they would sell slaves for a musket each, they would be quite willing to catch Black-fellows at the same rate. Their great intelligence, their crafty policy and their warlike bearing, with the use of weapons better adapted than "Brown Bess" [flint lock musket] to forest contests, made the plan acceptable to many. Mr Croft added a plea of benevolence.

The Maoris were then regarded as about the most bloodthirsty savages and cannibals that the world could furnish; so without reflecting upon the consequences of contact to the poor Tasmanians, they declared that "much good would result to the New Zealanders by their intercourse with us and would probably sow the germ of civilization among an energetic and enterprising people". But the humane Colonel Arthur feared the massacre of the Black subjects and rejected the proposal.

THE BLACK NATIVES. (1829, NOVEMBER 6).
COLONIAL TIMES (HOBART, TAS: 1828 - 1857), P. 3.

THE BLACK NATIVES.

On Monday last, a tribe of these barbarous and uncivilized savages, consisting of not less than one hundred and fifty in number, made their appearance at Blinkworth's Hunting Grounds, about three miles from the Cross Marsh. It appears, that they had been for some time previously pursued by different parties of the Field Police and the Military. The depredations which they have committed in this neighbourhood in so short a time and with such increased symptoms of daring outrage are unparalleled in any former instance of attacks perpetrated by the natives. In the first place, this very formidable tribe, whose very appearance was enough to frighten any respectable settler's family, attacked the farm house of Captain Clark.

This Gentleman finding that his premises were so suddenly beset ere he could find means for defence, instantly fastened all the doors and windows of the house. The blacks, not being able or even inclined to venture to break open the house, artfully burnt all the brush fence contiguous thereto, doubtless with a view to entice the family to come out and expose themselves to their attack. Not succeeding in this scheme however, the natives decamped, without fortunately doing any further injury.

They nevertheless proceeded to the stock run of Mr Philip Pitt. Their approach not being perceived, they deliberately went up to and opened the door; and, without a moment's hesitation, instantly speared two of his men; one poor fellow, who was just recovering from the effects of a broken leg, received a spear in the body, from the cause of which he died the following day : the other was not however speared so dangerously and escaped with his life. Not satisfied with this revenge, they hastened to the farm-house of Mr. Field, where their approach was fortunately discovered in time. Mr. Field and his wife, dressed in men's wearing apparel, with their servant man, continued parading in the front of the house, with only one loaded musket, during their stay. Although every artful plan was resorted to by the natives to induce Mr. Field in discharge the contents of his musket, he was resolved not to fire till they commenced an attack; and, having been thus deterred, they made off, leaving Mr. Field, his wife and servant, in peaceable possession of their 'homestead.

Upon arriving at the Broad Marsh, they dispersed themselves in three separate parties of about 50 strong, each mob taking different directions. At this settlement, each tribe, by some private signal of their own, succeeded in plundering, at the same moment, no less than three farm houses; namely, Mr. Chapling's, Mr. Davis's and the German's hut, which are all in sight of each other. We are happy to have to state, that none of their inmates were however speared, the whole of the respective families having escaped previously to their coming up. The blacks nevertheless plundered each of these poor Settler's farms of everything they could carry off, even to their bedding and they are consequently left almost destitute of clothing. Nothing further was seen of them until the following day; when they were discovered in the Paddock of Mr. Murdoch, there waiting for a favourable opportunity of rushing upon and robbing the residence of that Gentleman. It is singular that the moment they saw Mr Murdoch ride up, the whole of them ran off, as if a regiment of soldiers were at their heels.

Since writing the above, we have received accounts stating, that the natives have killed a servant woman, belonging to Mr. Triffitt, of the River Ouse; that they speared and burnt to death a poor old man named Clark; that the remains of the woman, named Newport, were also found in the ashes of the same fire; - that they have speared one of Mr. Thom-son's men at the Hollow-tree - killed several sheep and cattle belonging to Dr. Sharland and robbed many huts in the neighborhood, where many of the settlers and particularly the stock keepers are dreadfully frightened. They also made a very artful attempt to attack Mr Sherwin's house, but we are glad to find, without effect.

COLONIAL TIMES (HOBART, TAS: 1828 - 1857),
FRIDAY 13 NOVEMBER 1829, PAGE 3

THE BLACK NATIVES.

Mr. Editor,-I request you will allow me to correct an error in your statement of the outrages committed by the Natives in your last paper. Neither my dwelling at the Clyde nor that at the Hunting Ground was attacked. An attempt indeed was made by the Aborigines to rob a neighbouring house at the Clyde. The Natives wished to carry their object by stratagem; they watched the man and his servant in to dinner and then set fire to a bush-fence, in order to draw the inmates from the house, while some of their party should slip in and plunder the dwelling.

This in part had the desired effect and while the people stood wondering who could have made the fire, the wife suggested that it might be the Natives and that they would rob the house during their absence. They instantly returned and saw the Natives close to the house. An alarm was given, assistance immediately rendered and the Natives fled; and, although they were pursued for two or three hours, they could not be overtaken.

I owe the preservation of my hut at the Hunting Ground chiefly to its position, which could not easily be surprised ; and I think if Settlers in general paid more attention to the site of their stock-keepers' huts, it would tend materially to lessen the number of outrages committed by the Natives.

They should never be placed at the foot of a scrubby hill ; and all the trees and underwood (particularly the tea-tree, which affords the best shelter for the Natives), should be cut down, to the distance of two or three hundred yards and together with all the dead wood, so as not to leave any cover, under which the Natives could make their approach ; and if the remote stock-huts, in which there are seldom more than two men, were surrounded by a slight stockade, it would guard the inmates from surprise. This might be erected by the stock-keepers themselves with little trouble and no expense.

Let a sufficient number of spars, of about ten feet in length and pointed at the top, be set up as close as possible, all round the building and the earth rammed well about them; then a piece of black wattle, something thicker than a man's thumb, bound all along near the top of the spars, with a piece of bullock-hide, would keep all tight and afford the inmates of the but an effectual guard against surprise from the Natives.

COLONIAL TIMES (HOBART, TAS: 1828 - 1857),
FRIDAY 13 NOVEMBER 1829, PAGE 3

Two or three men, well armed, need never fear an open attack from them, however, numerous; and if the fence were made to form small circles, about four feet in diameter, having an opening to the inside, at any two of the opposite angles, they would form flanks, which would completely rake four sides of the stockade and prevent any approach. The fence should be far enough from the building to prevent the Natives from throwing a fire-brand upon the thatch and a final wicket, fastened with a bullock chain and padlock, would afford the hut some protection when the stock-keepers are necessarily absent. I have known this kind of fence, useful in other countries; for we are not the only people, that meet with annoyance from Aborigines-those in this Island are not formidable; the chief thing to be guarded against is surprise.

-I am, Sir, your most obedient humble servant,

W. Clark. Clyde, November 3, 1829.

One must never let the facts get in the way of a good story and no more so than in times of conflict and war. I am not doubting for a moment the essential truth of much of the article published in the *Colonial Times* on Friday 6 November 1829 and the account of the killing and wounding of the British is terrible to read. However, William Clark had the fortitude to not only correct the reporting but to make some obvious suggestions in relation to the Aboriginals. He made it clear his properties were not attacked and then reaches out to others by sensibly inferring that leaving stockmen isolated in their huts unprotected was indeed a recipe for disaster.

Clark was confident in his status and would not flinch from stating his controversial views openly. His pedigree and standing in British society were impeccable and he was well liked by the Governor. In fact, his daughter Jane became governess to Governor Arthur's children. For readers who desire a little family background, Clark and his wife Ann came to Tasmania in 1824 and eventually lived near Bothwell at a property called Cluny and before acquiring another, The Hunting Ground, later called Mauriceton, on the River

Jordon. Clark had been a prisoner of the French in 1812 and served in South Africa before selling his captaincy and bringing his family to the colony. Their life was not however without tragedy, they lost their son, William and his wife to yellow fever in Jamaica and later their grandson, William George, who died in India aged 26. Charles another son, drowned in the shipwreck of the *Lady Munro* in October 1833 on his way to join his parents in Tasmania.

I tell you this because it is important to acknowledge that the British, whom I often portrayed in a less than positive light, were also people with families and their own personal triumphs and misfortunes to contend with.

I sometimes wonder though just how many Britons, as individuals, had much control, if any, over the events happening around them, particularly the savage treatment meted out to Aboriginal Tasmanians. Henry Windowson's observation as a visitor, for example, noted that very few people living in the colony during the 1820s had ever actually seen an Aboriginal, let alone one who lived in their own domain.

Those who acted directly against Aboriginal people may well have had some choice, but were their actions predetermined by the culture, values, beliefs and context in which they lived? To kill or not, to exterminate or not? Again, I have no answer and, if I had, as a reporter I certainly wouldn't share it.

CHAPTER XXI.

THE ABORIGINES OF VAN DIEMEN'S LAND.

So little is known of these children of nature, and still less has been done to gain any knowledge of them, that not much can be offered as to their present numbers or condition. From what I have seen and read, the natives of Van Diemen's Land are unlike any other Indians, either in features, their mode of living, hunting, &c. There are many hundreds of people who have lived for years in the colony, and yet have never seen a native. The stock-keepers, and those who frequent the mountains and unlocated parts of the country, now and then fall in with them; and sometimes a tame mob,* as they are called, visit the distant settler, to beg bread and potatoes. An aborigine has occasionally been seen in Hobart Town, but not of late years.

The features of these people are any thing but pleasing: a large flat nose, with immense nostrils; lips particularly thick; a wide mouth, with a tolerable good set of teeth; the hair long and woolly, which, as if to confer additional beauty, is besmeared with red clay (similar to our red ochre) and grease. The limbs of these people are badly proportioned; the women appear to be generally better formed than the men. Their only covering is a few kangaroo skins, rudely stitched, and thrown over the shoulders...

* These unfortunate beings have a native or two with them, who have either lived or been brought up with a settler; but, tired of work, which they dislike amazingly, have left their employers to rove about, as nature intended them to

Windowson Henry Present State of Van Diemen's Land London 1829

The PAKANA *Voice*

1830

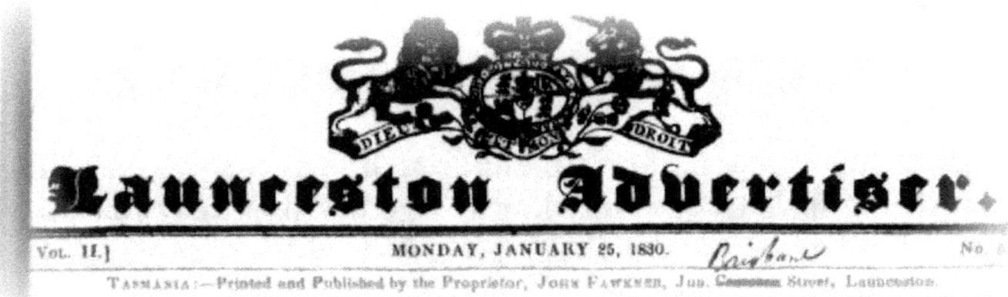

Vol. II.] MONDAY, JANUARY 25, 1830. *Brisbane* No.

TASMANIA:—Printed and Published by the Proprietor, JOHN FAWKNER, Jun. Cameron Street, Launceston.

HOBART TOWN COURIER (TAS. : 1827 - 1839),
SATURDAY 2 JANUARY 1830, PAGE 2

The Legislative Council, we hear, is summoned to meet on Monday. Mr. Robinson, the superintendent of the establishment for the civilization of the Aborigines at Brune Island, is we are happy to learn, about to proceed, on an expedition towards Port Davey and other parts of the interior with the hope of forming some pacific arrangement with the several tribes, he having already acquired as much of the language as will enable him to make himself understood amongst them . Eumarrah or Tamiua, as he is called and 15 other Blacks accompany him in the expedition.

COLONIAL TIMES (HOBART, TAS. : 1828 - 1857),
FRIDAY 19 FEBRUARY 1830, PAGE 2

HOBART TOWN

We confess that we wish we knew what measure to recommend, with respect to the Aborigines of this Colony, for the present state of the relative connexion between themselves and the whites, is anything but what it ought to be. Scarcely a week passes that does not bring us acquainted with some new violence offered by them, either to the persons or property of the Settlers; and still no remedy appears to be presented. Twelve months ago we heard much, although at the time we expected little, of what the sort of Guerilla parties, under the command of Mr. GILBERT ROBERTSON and others, were to accomplish.

Next, we were led to believe, that the Military and Field Police, every where stationed in the interior, would be all that was required-and last of all, we were taught to hope, that the Establishment on Bruné Island, aided by the advice of the- Standing Committee, for the amelioration of the condition of the blacks, would be of efficacy, towards putting an end to the atrocities now weekly recorded. But unhappily, neither of these separately, nor the whole of them collectively, appears to have been of the slightest avail and it really becomes matter of consideration with all classes, to offer such suggestions to the Committee, as they have expressed, through the official organ, their desire of receiving - thus hoping, that in the multitude of Counsellors, there may be wisdom.

For our own parts, we should say that, if we only catch them, no plan would be half so good as that which we have so long and so repeatedly re-commended, viz. to transport the whole race to some or other of the Islands in the Straits, where they might have quiet and undisturbed possession and live in their own way and according to their own customs, but the difficulty seems, how to come in contact with them, for they are ubiquitous and active in the extreme have acquired a great degree of cunning in all their movements, by their partial intercourse with their invaders and are so well acquainted with fastnesses or inaccessible places, that it is like a warfare with the Chamois Goats of the Alps, to undertake to pursue them.

The Head of the Government has already found unspeakable advantage in stirring up a spirit of exertion among the prisoner population, under the hope of pardon or other indulgences and the promise of these held out to this class, or of grants of land, free of all restrictions to others, of sizes proportionate to the numbers of Aborigines they may have taken alive for the purpose of removal, might possibly tend to the effect we are recommending. Whatever measure may be adopted, should in our opinion be one of peace rather than war, but something should be acted upon and that quickly, otherwise, the evil will increase and each year will bring fresh cause of regret that the present state of things should have so long continued.

Since writing the preceding article, we have received the communications published in another part of our Paper. If any thing further were wanting to show the necessity of some immediate and strong measures being adopted, it will surely be found, in the alarming conviction afforded by these, communications, that the blacks have, at length commenced the system of firing and have dared to move by night, under the light of torches.

We trust and cannot doubt, that the Settlers and Inhabitants, of all classes, will evince a proper spirit and promptitude in coming forward to aid the efforts of Government and the Standing Committee, both in devising and carrying into effect all necessary steps to prevent further mischief from their increasing hostility and consequent outrages. Pacific measures and the exercise of that humanity, which doubtless all the European and Native-born classes would prefer we fear cannot be long entertained; but that the sentiments of our Correspondent, "A Settler" will become but to general; and that self-preservation will be found to present itself with an urgency of claim too imperious to give way to other considerations.

Let it ever be kept in mind, however, that to spare the effusion of the blood even of those Natives, is our bounden duty, in every attempt to take them, or conflict with them, as far as is possible, consistently with due regard to that self-preservation.

At least the next letter started well! I wonder if the editor added the cryptic quote *vox et praeterea nihil* which loosely means all talk without substance.

LAUNCESTON ADVERTISER (TAS. : 1829 - 1846),
MONDAY 15 FEBRUARY 1830, PAGE 3

vox et praeterea nihil .

Mr Editor— So much has been said about the Savages, whom by the mere right of power we have bereaved of their dominion and against whose defenceless wretchedness we have waged a war directly tending to extermination— so many fine things have been said and so very little done to ameliorate the hardships to which those deeply injured owners of the soil we cultivate, have been subjected by our national ambition; or by our individual cupidity, that one is induced to all but laugh at even the most respectable paragraphs in which either officially or otherwise their situation and sympathy are connected.

But it would of course Sir, be highly reprehensible in me, an obscure Individual, to treat with levity a subject which has won so many Tickets of Leave for Bush Constables-— so many tramps for the Soldiers-–~so much land, deservedly I own, for Mr. Batman and so much celebrity as I think undeservedly, for the quasi scientific Experimentalist in agriculture, whose practical essays on one of the Government Farms rendered him very Dear to his employer. I do therefore propose, with suitable gravity, that as none of Mr. Gilbert Robertsons ingenious plans to capture the Aborigines, have been crowned with that success for which I admit the Public at large are solicitous and as the Committee for ameliorating their condition invite communications, that a party of fifteen mounted on Horses, having pack-saddles and carrying, each, from ten to twelve red night-caps, shall be sent out with all convenient expedition and that when they come up with the Natives, they shall dismount and after drawing the said red night caps over the eyes of every man, woman and child, lead the whole mob into either Hobart Town or Launceston. I am. Sir, Yours, &r. PHILANTHROPOS.

I think I should just leave you alone for a while to read the next few letters in quiet solitude, without my constant and irritating interjections. They make confronting reading so be warned. I find I can only read a few at a time. So, I will sit here and try once again to fill and light my stubborn pipe while adhering to Bent's demands for me to use my big toe to rub the exact spot on his scruffy tummy.

One final point before I leave you to your reading. You will find mention of George Augustus Robinson many times in these articles. He became known decorously as the Chief Protector of Aborigines, a title which well suited his ego and sense of self-importance. There is no need here to repeat his story which is well documented and you most certainly should follow up with further reading. Suffice to say his influence and actions in relation to the Pakana people remain riddled with controversy and will no doubt do so for many years to come.

HOBART TOWN COURIER (TAS: 1827 - 1839),
SATURDAY 20 FEBRUARY 1830, PAGE 2

(We have been favoured with the following).

Committee Room, Feb. 15, 1830.-Sir, The members of the committee on the Aborigines, have the honour to acknowledge your letter of the 3d inst. and beg leave to return you their sincere thanks for the suggestions therein contained and the humane interest you so laudably take in the fate of these our wretched fellow creatures. They furthermore are induced to express their sentiments thus publicly in the hope of prevailing on other resident settlers of similar humane feelings to follow your example and communicate to the committee all incidents and information which may come within their knowledge.

The committee avail themselves of this opportunity of calling on all as Christians and us men to prevent by every possible means the hostile attacks of their servants and to compel them to adhere to a system of self-defence and not of wanton aggression and in all cases of confidence or surrender to treat them with every kindness and preserve towards them the most inviolable good faith.

Many instances have occurred, which clearly demonstrate that they can and do discriminate between their friends and their foes; thus leading to the gratifying hope of future conciliation and mutual good will.

William Bedford. James Norman. Jocelyn Thomas, Col.Treas. P. A. Mulgrave, Chf.-Pol.-Mag. Janies Scott, Prin.-Col.-Sur. Samuel Hill, Port-Officer. To Arthur Davies, Esq. J. P. The Lawn.

We have to add with regret, that the blacks have burned down Mr. Howell's house at the Shannon, with property estimated to the amount of from 3 to 400 pounds and also within a short distance of it the destruction of Mr. Sherwin's hut, on the out farm at Weasel's plains.

COLONIAL TIMES (HOBART, TAS: 1828 - 1857),
FRIDAY 26 FEBRUARY 1830, PAGE 3

BLACK NATIVES.

MR. EDITOR,—Your desire for information respecting the Aborigines has induced me to state what I conceive to be a proper view of the matter. In our neighbourhood every day affords some proof of their determination to destroy and their declaration to war with the whites. Whenever an opportunity presents itself they have invaded our district in almost every direction, during the last eight months, with considerable success as respects their hostile attacks, particularly in taking the lives of several individuals and in having accomplished the ruin of whole families.

It appears that the only use the native hunting parties can be of in this service, (if their number were sufficiently augmented), is to keep a vigilant watch and chase after the Natives, when once the party have fallen in with the track of their retreat and the pursuing party should harass and follow them well up and give such daily information of the retreat and the direction it is in to any of the Military advance posts they may approach in the pursuit, which are eight in number and consist of three rank and file at each station, viz.—Mr Thomson's, Shannon; Mr Patterson's, ditto ; Mr. Young's, Ouse; Mr Torlesse's; Mr. Nicholas's, M'Guire's Marsh; Mr. Smith, Mead's Bottom Mr. Mood's, Abyssinia ; and Mrs. Burn's, Ellen Gowen.

These stations constitute, as it were, the frontiers of the inhabited portions of the district and I think, that by the moving parties keeping a constant pursuit of the Natives and driving them from their fires and their half-dressed kangaroo, a speedy notice of their anticipated approach in any direction might be given and the Settlers thus prepared, could afford them a warm reception. To travel after the blacks without the scent of them is of no use, they are so very subtle. The gangs in this quarter can speak Colonial English with tolerable fluency. They told Mr. Sherwin, when burning his dwelling-house and dancing before it, to go away and that he was not game to fire on them ; on the other hand it should be observed, that a party might be of great service in checking their approaches from one division of the country to the other, by being stationed in am-bush at the common passes where they make their appearance on their route to and from their resorts.

The inhabitants of stock runs and those parts where they are most likely to go, might be supplied with three or four men from the Public Works, in charge of one soldier well armed and let them be strictly careful to keep within doors and avoid all appearances of a hostile nature and let no one but one man go out of the hut in the same dress and I will be answerable that many gangs of the Natives may be taken in this way and let the rewards or indulgences for the Crown prisoner on this service be in proportion to the number of blacks captured and you will very soon see an alteration.

The Natives sneak upon the lone hut in small advance parties, reserving their force and the formidable appearance of their numbers until the damage is done, or the murder accomplished. To present the blacks with British luxuries and to entice them to partake of our comforts, is the very way to induce them to plunder the Settlers for these very comforts, we have sought them to regard as essentials to life. Blankets and sugar and all such presents are mere stuff; no overtures of mercy or conciliatory promises will ever tame or soften the incorrigible heart of the Van Diemen's Land savage; he never felt the struggles of a conscientious remonstrance after the commission of a horrid deed, but his contemptuous ignorance laughs a hideous grin at the dying victim, as he lingers in the jaws of a cruel death. These observations, I trust, will excite the notice of the Authorities, by distributing parties of Crown prisoners under the orders of the Military, in the quarters most liable to be invaded by the savages. - I beg to remain, Mr Editor,

your most obedient servant,
A SETTLER.
River Clyde, Feb 22, 1830.

COLONIAL TIMES (HOBART, TAS. : 1828 - 1857),
FRIDAY 26 FEBRUARY 1830, PAGE 3

RIVER CLYDE, Feb 22, 1830.

Since the last, the particulars of the outrages at Mr. SHERWIN's have been fully made known. It appears that on the Sunday afternoon about three o'clock, the woman servant was alarmed by a crackling noise and upon running out discovered the roof of the house, which was thatched, to be on fire. The family followed her and perceived at some distance a mob of ten or a dozen Natives, with their hands upraised, hallooing with shouts of delight. One of them had succeeded in throwing a lighted stick into the thatch, which caused their merriment and the house to be burnt down in a few minutes, allowing time only to remove a few articles of wearing apparel and bedding.

In order to protect the stacks of wheat, the family could not pursue the Blacks, which gave the latter time to set fire, in several places, to about 1000 feet of American fence and then to make off. This has been a sad visitation to Mr. Sherwin, much useful property, amongst which were his cheese vats and dairy utensils having been destroyed; and Mr. Sherwin now believes that the burning of his barn about twelve months ago, was by the Natives.

His Excellency the Lieutenant Governor, with much humane feeling, has generously afforded private assistance to Mr. Sherwin and, we understand has promised on the public account, that if one of Mr. Sherwin's sons and young Doran, whose father was lately speared, will each head parties and bring in a mob of Natives alive, they shall have liberal grants of land. We have no doubt that this principle will be acted upon to some extent; it has already been recommended by us, as one of the most promising plans and there are doubtless many spirited youths in the Colony who would give their aid, under a certainty of such encouragement.

On Wednesday evening information was received by express, that the barn of Captain CLARKE, at the Upper Clyde, containing 1000 bushels of wheat, was burnt on Monday last, supposed to have been by the same mob of Natives that fired Mr. Sherwin's premises.

On the same day, a boy named Plaistow, ten years of age, was speared to death, near the Swan Inn, Constitution Hill, upon which a number of the neighbours armed themselves and joined in pursuit of the aggressors. On the preceding Saturday, a party of the Natives were within a mile of Bothwell and broke into Mr McRae's house, carried away his boxes and opened several of his trunks and not knowing glass to be tangible, pushed their hands through the windows. We understand, also, that a stack of wheat at the Green Ponds has been set fire to.

We forbear any further comments the present week, upon this important subject ; it is one that interests every Settler in the Island and is capable of almost endless remarks, but we trust that the attention so generally excited towards it now, may spare us, at least for a season, after our unwearied labours in reference thereto for so long a period.

COLONIAL TIMES (HOBART, TAS: 1828 - 1857), FRIDAY 9 APRIL 1830, PAGE 2

We had hoped to be spared the painful necessity of recording further atrocities by the Aborigines, but on Friday a poor man was brought to town by boat be longing to the Commandant of Maria Island, from a part of the coast nearly opposite to that Settlement who had been so beaten with waddies, in an attack from a party of these mis guided wretches, that he was found in the bush almost sense less, having remained there without food for several days. Upon enquiry we learn the man has died of injuries he had received, notwithstanding every possible care was taken of him after being received into the Hospital.

It appears, from the Launceston Advertiser that the landholders, merchants and inhabitants of Launceston, have been, petitioning the Lieutenant Governor concerning some improvements required at their, Wharf and also relative to the state of their roads and streets. His-Excellency's answer was to the effect that, if he could in any degree remove the difficulties pointed out, it would be done with pleasure.

A letter from the interior states, that the Native tribes have been very quiet near the settlements and that their hostile movements are confined to their own hunting grounds and that the stock-keepers and settlers in general, at remote stations; were now so well prepared, that the Aborigines find it extremely difficult to commit any depredations of the nature hitherto practised.

HOBART TOWN COURIER (TAS: 1827 - 1839), SATURDAY 17 APRIL 1830, PAGE 2

We regret to learn, that Black Tom, the native, who has for some time acted as a guide to Mr. Robertson's party, has absconded from his companions and joined the incursive tribes. Several of the out-stock huts about Swan port and Prosser's plains have been robbed, we fear, in consequence of

being led on by him. One man who was pursued by them, saved himself by crossing the river and succeeded in shooting a black in the very act of throwing his spear at him.

COLONIAL TIMES (HOBART, TAS: 1828 - 1857),
FRIDAY 16 APRIL 1830, PAGE 3

ABORIGINES.

It is with great concern we have to record fresh instances of outrage by some of the Aboriginal tribes. - On Wednesday last, a party made their appearance in hostile array at Mr. Sharland's hut, at the Lower Clyde, which they robbed; from thence they proceeded to Mr. Triffet's hut, which was subjected to a similar depredation. After com- mitting these robberies, the party made their appearance near Mr. Dixon's, who was in his barn with three men, thrashing grain. They made their approach unperceived by those in the barn, but fortunately a servant girl in the house discovered them and gave the alarm.

Mr. Dixon immediately ran towards the house, to protect his family from the expected attack, he succeeded in reaching the house, but received a spear wound before he arrived thither. The blacks, finding their scheme of surprisal frustrated, went away without attempting any further molestation. We are glad to find that the wound of Mr. Dixon is not likely to be attended with any very serious consequence.-It is reported that a soldier has been speared by the natives, in the neighbourhood of Mrs. Burns' farm, in the same district.

Last Friday, a mob of upwards a hundred strong appeared before Mr. HOOPER'S hut, at the Hollow-tree bottom, but retired without making any attack, this is the most formidable body seen for some time.

Forgive me for this intrusion but I have to say I found the next letter to be the most incomprehensible, convoluted drivel I can remember reading. I have studied it and still cannot work out what they are saying, but I think in the end it is simply a justification for what was happening. It's worth reading but far too long to print here: I wish you luck![xiii]

COLONIAL TIMES (HOBART, TAS: 1828 - 1857), FRIDAY 23 APRIL 1830, PAGE 4

THE RELATIVE SITUATION IN WHICH THE WHITE INHABITANTS OF THIS ISLAND STAND TOWARDS THE ABORIGINES

The law of nature or the law of GOD (terms synonymous) is that primitive law coeval with eternity itself, which has regulated and will continue to regulate, all the motions and operations of the universe. This great law must of necessity be immutable and perfect, but although it appears Manifestly to us, that this law, as far as applies to the universal system, acts upon one unerring principle , yet, as far as individual worlds are connected, we can merely form some rational conjectures, in no shape amounting to certainty.

Reflection would reasonably suggest to us that the inhabitants of the great planet Jupiter (twelve hundred thousand times larger than our little globe) cannot partake of the same nature with us. The length of the winter and summer, day and night, in Jupiter, would seem to indicate, that the creatures in that planet must differ widely from those on our earth, in species, in bulk, in appearances and in every other degree , but, as we have before observed, this is mere conjecture -But whatever regards individual worlds and whatever may be the various and distinct subordinate laws which govern each separately and individually, yet these subordinate laws are and can be, nothing more nor less than modifications of the primitive law, how much soever they may vary in appearances.

The subordinate laws are, in fact, parts, parcels and branches of the great law of nature and of these there are numbers which apply to this world and its inhabitants, but it will fully answer our purpose merely to notice two, viz. the law of necessity and the law of nations......

The law of GOD is inflexible and admits of no evil. It therefore behaves us to shew by what right we have taken possession of this country and having established that right, to discuss the question how far we stand justified, not only in repelling the aggressions of the Aborigines, but even pursuing them to death, in case they should not desist from invading the settled habitations of the white Colonists.

During this time, I began hearing more and more about massacres of the Pakana people. Whole clans, small groups and individuals were murdered by stockman, settlers, soldiers and police, not only in retribution for the actions of the Aborigines but also simply as a way of ridding the land of a perceived menace.

However, the press rarely reported these events and if they did there would be scant details, merely reporting '30 natives killed' or similar matter-of-fact accounts. I later found out that these shootings occurred far more frequently than most people were aware of; ignorance is bliss.[xiv] Were the papers complicit or did people simply not know what was actually happening? There may have been an element of both. The details provided about the attacks on white people were usually explicit and extensive and made compelling reading. They certainly sold newspapers. But to be fair, newspaper proprietors were hardly in a position to elicit much information from the Pakana themselves and the perpetrators of ill-treatment were unlikely to show much empathy for their victims.

The PAKANA *Voice*

BY W.C. SPECIAL CORRESPONDENT—*LUTRUWITA*

Our correspondent from the Tommeginne Nation has informed us of the massacre of another six people from Pallittorre clan located not far from Deloraine.

It appears that stockman took it upon themselves to kill using shotguns, muskets and bayonets.

Witnesses say two of the Pakana men were shot and another stabbed to death. There was no definitive motive for the bloodshed other than the fact that the stockmen knew they could get away with it with impunity, especially as they were in the employ of the local magistrate, M.L. Smith.

Government House refused to comment on the matter while it was under investigation.

COLONIAL TIMES (HOBART, TAS: 1828 - 1857), FRIDAY 23 APRIL 1830, PAGE 2

Early yesterday morning, a party of natives entered the hut belonging to Mr. P. Dalrymple, at Connie Flats, during the temporary absence of the men and robbed it of everything moveable, including some muskets and ammunition. The military were dispatched in pursuit of them, but without success.

ABORIGINES.

We have again to record fresh attacks made by these misguided creatures. Mr. ALLEN, of Oyster Bay, has had his hut robbed by them and property taken away and destroyed to the value of £60, among other articles carried away by them was an excellent key bugle, which having no other use for will serve as a splendid ornament to decorate the person of some one of the tribe -Mr. SIMPSON.at the 2-mile Creek, has also suffered by their depredations.

It appears the Aborigines watched the inmates out and then made their attack, but, they were fortunately disturbed and only enabled to carry off a few articles, the greater part of their booty consisting of blankets. It appears that a dog particularly attracted their attention and being determined to carry off their prizes, finding it impossible for them to undo the collar or chain, they by constantly shaking the part to which the chain was fastened, loosened it so as to enable them to draw it up and thus with dog, chain and post, decamped into the woods.

On Fri- day, the 23d, a party of constables who had stopped all night at a hut built by Mr. ADEY, situated on the Little Swan Port River, left the place without having fallen in with any of the natives.

It appears that the latter were not far from them, but much too cunning to allow themselves to be seen by those who were in search of them and that they must have watched the departure of the constables, for they enter-ed the hut almost immediately after and robbed it of some flour and sugar and in searching for a farther quantity, in a flour cask one of them, unluckily for himself, put his hand into a large vermin trap, which the overseer on leaving the hut had set on the top of the cask , unfortunately he had neglected to fasten the trap to any place, or the depredator would have been held secure. On his return the trap was found about 100 yards from the hut and the hand in it, the companions of the native having, it appears, actually resorted to the desperate expedient of severing by main force his hand just above the wrist and thus enable him to escape.

The unfortunate creature must have undergone dreadful agony, as we hear that, the sinews and tendons of the arm were drawn out by main force and to use the expression of our informant, resembled those of the tail of a kangaroo.

TASMANIAN (HOBART TOWN, TAS: 1827 - 1839), FRIDAY 14 MAY 1830, PAGE 7

THE ABORIGINES.

We lament to have, to announce another outrage committed by these savages. A few days ago a number of them visited Mr. Hobbs' farm at the Blue Hills and shocking to relate barbarously killed two men and a woman in the employ of that Gentleman.

COLONIAL TIMES (HOBART, TAS: 1828 - 1857), FRIDAY 28 MAY 1830, PAGE 3

THE ABORIGINES.

We have been favoured by a gentleman with a letter written by a friend of his resident in the country, giving some in-formation upon an alarm that had been felt in the neighbour-hood of New Norfolk, in consequence of the appearance of one of these unfortunate beings a few days ago, at Charlie's Hope the residence of Mr Thomson and from which he has obligingly allowed us to make the following extract : -

"About the middle of the day on Sunday, just as we were preparing for dinner, ... arrived from New Norfolk breathless and looking as white and trembling as though he had seen a ghost and hastily entered the house and casting his eyes everywhere around, as though apprehensive of pursuers, said in a hurried perturbed manner, ' I have some bad news to tell you ' You

know, that for my part, having seen so much of the world as I have, I am not now very easily thrown off my equilibrium and perhaps not appearing at the moment to partake of poor...............'s fright quite so eagerly as he had expected, he stared at me with a sort of surprise and repeated in a more energetic tone, ' I have some bad news for you, the blacks are all coming, they are on the hills all around, I have been to Mr. Thomson's and I don't know what they haven't done.' ' Well,' replied I, ' I am glad your news is no worse, for it was plain enough that something or another had frightened you, long before you reached the house , but set down , you are safe now, at all events and let us know all about it.' 'Safe! do you say,' be exclaimed, '

Why there are at least a hundred of them some say two. One of their leaders has been taken and the parties are everywhere in pursuit of them. I have brought you a supply of ammunition and now I'll be off, if you please, directly to Hobart Town, as I would not stay here tor the world.' It was in vain that I endeavoured to soothe or quiet his alarm and, after a short while he took leave, accompanied by one of the men as a guard, until he gained the high road, when he made the best of his way to town, every now and then, I understand, stopping and looking be-hind him, doubtless in full expectation to seeing the cruel savages, with whom his imagination was possessed. The long and short of what he had to tell me, stripped of all embellishment was, that one day last week an Aboriginal youth went to Mr Thomson's asking for bread, when he was immediately taken and proved to be one who had already been in our hands, but had made his escape and it was reported that the lad, who could speak a little English, had given information of there being a considerable party in the neighbour-hood.

This occurrence, inconsiderable as it was in itself, was however enough to set rumour's tongue at work and what with the alarms of old women, the fiery impetuosity of young men and the readiness of all to believe whatever is said, our little district became, within a few hours, one scene of stir and bustle. In the course of a few hours, one more hardy than the rest, having dared to go so far as his next neighbour's dwelling, established a code of signals between each other-the firing a gun-the blowing of a horn the lighting of a bonfire-or even the more simple and all expressive coo-eh being settled to he used, according to the situation and circumstances of the several inhabitants. All this happened on Sunday and these measures being adopted, Monday passed over quietly and although many a look out was given throughout the day and many a ' Run, Jem, you little varlet you and see if the blacks be a coming,' was dinned into the ears of some of the unbreeched urchins around us, by their watchful mothers or grandams, Monday night came and still no appearance of the Natives.

But Tuesday brought with it, a sad termination of this state of repose from previous alarm, for scarce had the sun half reached its meridian, when a messenger ran through the district at full speed, spreading the direful intelligence that the Aborigines were in great force, two miles the Hobart Town side of New Norfolk - that they had rescued the man previously taken -had murdered the guard who had attended him, with I scarcely know what besides, the catalogue being so dreadful. I listened to all this, with a nonchalance that was evidently very provoking to him who told it and when he had finished his story, expressed my determination to proceed to the spot, where the affair was said to have taken place.

Those around me, thought I was mad and said all they could think to dissuade me, but I was sceptical upon all I heard and could not conceive such a feeling as fear, with any rambles in the neighbourhood stated to have been the scene of action. So accordingly I went, unarmed and unattended. As I proceeded along my way and passed some of the cottages near the path side, one good dame stood, at the door-way, blocking up ingress or egress to all others and called to me, 'Oh! Mr. -------, where in God's name are you venturing to! Do be advised, Sir and go back again, for my little Betty saw their fires over yonder hills, not more than an hour ago.' I thanked her, but still travelled on, till again interrupted by some other neighbour, who, alarmed for my safety and seeing a spear or a waddy, in every bush that grew, would fain have dissuaded me from my errand. At length, however, I reached the spot and found things just as I expected. The lad who had been taken at Mr. Thomson's, had contrived to make his escape, between New Norfolk an Hobart Town, from the constable who had him in charge and the latter apprehensive doubtless, of the consequences to himself, had stated at a house near the road side, that he had been set upon by two other Natives who darted suddenly out of the scrub and knocking him down, had rescued his prisoners.

This story, however, plausible as it might at first seem, failed in certain essentials towards obtaining for it, credence; and none more strongly than that, the marks of one man's footsteps were clearly discernible along the road, up to a certain point, when they entirely ceased to be apparent, but no additional footsteps either at the spot described by the constable, or elsewhere, could be traced, as must have been the case, had two other Natives been there. In many other points, the constable's story exhibited similar discrepancies; so that, should you and my other friends at Hobart Town, hear the atrocities of the Blacks in the neighbourhood of New Norfolk and be alarmed for my safety, rest assured I am safe and well and that it is all 'Much ado about nothing." - Your's truly.

COLONIAL TIMES (HOBART, TAS: 1828 - 1857), FRIDAY 16 JULY 1830, PAGE 3

ABORIGINES

The attacks and the depredations of the Aborigines on the white people of this Colony and on stock-huts, remote only a few miles from the townships and Military stations, assume a regular and alarming consistency and evince on the part of the blacks a cunning and superiority of tactic which would not disgrace even some of the greatest military characters.

The week before last a tribe of the Aborigines fell suddenly on Mr. Evans's hut on the Big River, when Mr. Evans was engaged in the field and only for the courage he display-ed in fighting his way into the hut, himself and his servants must have been killed. From eleven o'clock until four in the afternoon, Mr Evans was surrounded by the Natives and although he fired at them five shot, he made no impression on them till near sun set. A servant was immediately dispatched to Captain Young, of Hunter's Hill, River Ouse and that gentleman, with his usual zealous activity and alacrity, did not lose one moment in proceeding with a party of the military in search of the Aborigines, although the weather was wet and the rivers swollen.

In the course of last week a man was dangerously speared by some of the Aborigines at Mr. Nicholl's stock-run, on the River Ouse. On Thursday last, the 8th instant, a tribe of the Natives came down upon the men in the employ of Lieutenant Betts at the Big Lagoon, who were in the act of chopping wood for their fire, at a few yards distant from their habitation; the Aborigines, no doubt, seeing the men unarmed and taking advantage of this circumstance, placed themselves between them and the building ; fortunately for the men, a cart screened them, or most probably they would have been instantly speared, after some few moments dodging, they however were enabled to take to their heels and made the best of their way towards the adjoining stock-hut of Mr. STOKELL, which is only a few hundred yards distant ; at the latter place, all the arms and men were procured and they hastened back in order to fall in with the depredators, but on their coming to the place, not a sign of them was perceptible, they had decamped, taking away everything moveable along with them; the men then again returned to Mr. Stokell's and to their astonishment, found that in their absence, which had only been for a few minutes, the same depredations had been committed upon them, with the addition that the Natives had attempted to set fire to the hut; all this happened in so short a space of time that it is evident the mob must have been well organized and of considerable number and that watchmen must have been regularly placed to give notice of what was going forward.

On Saturday afternoon last a tribe came down upon Captain Wood's hut, in Poole's Marsh and three of them proceeded fearlessly to the door of the hut, but could not get in as it was fastened. Jemmy and another of Captain

Wood's assigned servants, were then in the sheep-yard and fortunately had with them their pieces and ammunition. Six or seven shots were fired, but all missed.

There was among these blacks one of tall stature and long hair, whom Jemmy recognised as having twice before been at the hut. They were finally repulsed, but must have remained close by in some gully during the night, for early in the forenoon of yesterday morning they robbed the splitters' hut in the tier, not more than two miles off and carried away some flour, blankets and other things.

(Extract from a letter from Green Ponds, dated July 12.) > One should imagine that the increased activity of the roving parties and the judicious manner in which Capt. Vicary, the Police Magistrate of Bothwell, has stationed the military' detachments for the protection of various stock-huts within the district of the Clyde, would overawe the natives and render it almost impossible for them to conduct their operations with any chance of success, but it is really impracticable for the Police Magistrates and the Military Commander to effect any sensible good, by reason of the apathy which exists so visibly amongst some of the settlers, their overseers and their man, in not affording speedy communication when the Aborigines make their appearance.

Although Mr Betts's hut had been robbed as well as Mr. Stokell's, no one took the trouble to proceed to the military commandant at Oatlands, Major Douglas, to acquaint him with the occurrences and the distance is only five miles. Old West, in Poole's Marsh, could not see the necessity when the danger was over, to send his companion to Mrs.Jones, residing half a mile from Captain Wood's hut, to put her, on her guard and to acquaint her that the Aborigines were in the vicinity ; much less to dispatch him off to the military detachment stationed at the Sideling Hill at a distance of only three miles. Another settler on the Jordan, not more than two miles from the military detachment at Sideling Hill could not spare one man out of three to communicate the above trans actions to the soldiers; and although the natives had attacked Captain Wood's hut on the Saturday afternoon, yet on the Sunday afternoon, Mr. Broadribb, the Division Constable, five miles off only and all the other stock-keepers through the whole line to Bothwell were unacquainted with the movements and appearance of the Aborigines in Poole's Marsh. The roving and military parties cannot be everywhere at the same time and if settler and others will not transmit by their assigned servants speedy information, they must thank themselves for many of the mishaps which occur.

In the case of the robbery on Mr. Betts's hut, only four blacks made their appearance and in that on Captain Wood's hut, merely three or four. ; All the rest of the tribe are distributed on the adjacent hills, so that by signalizing from one to another, they can give timely notice of the approach of danger. These facts show that the Natives go on with increasing courage, derived from long success and increasing craft.

However, the utmost exertions are made for repelling the aggressions of the Aborigines; Peter Scott with a full party are increasingly roving in the Eastern Marshes, Rushy Lagoon, the Blue Hills, sometimes debouching towards little Swan Port, but within the District of Oatlands. John Danvers with another full party are roving near the Quoin beyond the Cross March, stretching sometimes across to the hunting ground and ranging along the Jordan within the District of Oatlands.

Benjamin Allinson with a small party, all but one or two concealed within a recently constructed hut, a few miles from the Big Lagoon, are erecting a small sheep-yard with a brush fence, so to try if this scheme will not decoy some of the Aborigines into the hut and thus make capture certain.

The Police Magistrate of Oatlands, by calling out five of the Police Constables (very inconveniently spared, especially at this, season of the year) has been enabled to dispatch a party, with a black guide, into the Oyster Bay District in search of the Aborigines, some of whom visit this part of the Island at this particular season for the purpose of gathering Cygo.

This party is under the charge of James Hopkins, accompanied by Field Police Constable George James. In the District of Clyde, independent of the numerous military parties so judiciously distributed by Captain Vicary.

Mr. Sherwin, Junior, an active and indefatigable young man, is roving with a party between the Rivers Ouse and Clyde, under the more immediate instructions of Captain Vicary. Doran with another party, is ranging in another direction, within the same district

I did warn you! Only the soulless could not be troubled by such tales and it gets worse. If you want happy endings perhaps now might be the time to purchase a ha'penny novelette and surrender to the world of make-believe.

If you are still with me, I will continue with my melancholic account.

I needed to move beyond the claustrophobic confines of Nipaluna with its stifling society and narrowness of thought. You may think me arrogant and an intellectual snob; well you're right on both counts. I was at an age when humility rarely mellowed my confidence and self-assurance; that would come later, much later.

Now though I could afford to be cocky and brash and my job required me to be thus. I was there to challenge the establishment, set the world right and confront the lies and deceptions blanketing the world around me. I was idealistic, dedicated and painfully naïve. If only I had taken another path, blinded myself to the merciless quest I set, maybe I would have saved myself so much pain and agony.

In hindsight, the cracks were beginning to show even then. I had started drinking alone which I had never done before, as well as spending more time in any watering hole that still welcomed me. Sleeping too was dispersed and restless, although the nightmares were to come later. To meet me you would never have known of my inner turmoil. I retained my beguiling persona, witty and charming and I was pitiless in my work. Why am I telling you this? Because I was there; I smelt the blood and tramped for miles to follow the stories to which there was a human cost so why should you get it all for free?

My colleagues and friends Andrew Bent, Robert Murray, Henry Melville et el were what I call pub reporters.[xv]
That's where they found most of their stories; they hardly ever ventured beyond the town walls. To be fair, they had a paper to publish so they weren't able to take weeks to travel in pursuit of a story but I could! Hence, the seriously deleterious effects on my well-being that I were to eventually sustain.

By Spring of 1830 I needed to move. My restlessness and inner disquiet required physical release. I also wanted to be closer to the action, to talk directly to people from both sides for my stories and to establish a sense of professional credibility.

My journey took me into the South East, Big River and Northern Midlands Nations as we travelled north through the centre of Lutruwita to Kanamaluka, called Launceston by the British. There I stayed for some time meeting with many of the locals and arranging contacts with Pakana clans.

Chapter Six

Tour of Duty
Northern Lutruwita 1830-1833

I arrived in the Tyerremotepanner Nation (Northern Midlands) a few weeks after leaving Nipaluna at the town of Launceston on the banks of Kanamaluka, known to the British as the River Tamar. I wanted to report on what was happening in this nation and others close by, including Ben Lomond. Until now I had spent most of my time in and around Hobart and observed the conflict from the administrative centre and the capital, but what of the regional perspectives? Was this going to be any different; would I find my reports varied, reflecting an even smaller community with an essentially rural outlook? I needed to find out and as I came into the town I discovered a close-knit society based on the success of large farming properties with traders and merchants whose livelihood depended on wool, wheat and cattle. In other words, everyone here needed the farms to succeed and any encumbrance such as tigers, native animals and savage natives needed to be controlled.

In the north, I stepped straight into a full-scale war. There can be no other description for it, as the newspapers show below. The killings on both sides were now unstoppable with one inevitable end in sight.

The white population of the colony had continued to grow while the Pakana people were rapidly declining. Only a few hundred people were now scattered across the land.

The newspaper articles I read give the European version of events, but again I began to for look for the negative spaces. I wondered what was not being reported here and whether I was missing another viewpoint, which may be gleaned from the words sprawled across the pages and how as a reporter I could remain objective in my thinking. But then I was an unashamed idealist, which may partly explain my distinct lack of material wealth in the latter part of my life!

There are simply too many articles, letters and commentaries to publish here so I have randomly picked a few at random for you to read and see what you can make of it all. I have also taken the liberty of adding a few of my own cryptic comments which, of course, you are welcome to interpret from your own perspective or simply dismiss as nonsensical gibberish.

However, it warmed my journalist's heart to read this prominent line at the head of the *Launceston Advertiser* the day I arrived and in many other editions:

"It is the public duty of a Journalist to dispel delusion: but in the discharge of this duty he must not expect to find his road perfectly free from the arrows of those who are interested in preventing the Ægis[xvi] of truth from confronting and dissipating their power."

And this from the *Colonial Times*:

Let it be impressed upon your minds, let it be instilled into your children, that the Liberty of the Press is the Palladium of all your Civil, Political and Religious Rights.

Junius.[xvii]

Freedom of the press was certainly alive and well in this microcosm of Britain.

COLONIAL TIMES (HOBART, TAS: 1828 - 1857), FRIDAY 27 AUGUST 1830, PAGE 2

The country about Bothwell is in a sad state. The repeated attacks of the Aborigines on the Settlers of that District are every day getting more and more frequent. Indeed, the commencement of the spring seems to have given these misguided wretches a fresh impetus to commence their warfare upon their enemies. At present, one of their chief holds is about the Den Hills, between the Black Marsh and the Den.

It is said that Captain WOOD's men have had several skirmishes with the different mobs and we are sorry to say that several of the Natives have been killed. We do not wonder at these men taking revenge upon the Aborigines, when we consider in how many instances they have been sufferers by their attacks; but we fear the plan at present adopted will leave no other chance of obtaining peace than the annihilation of the whole race; for we imagine that the Settlers have had convincing proofs that the Aborigines are a most brave and resolute people, who cannot be intimidated, but will continue their warfare to the last moment. Something must be done! we have long exclaimed; but the question is, what is best to be done? The military are not the most proper persons to be employed, being unaccustomed as they are to the fatigues of the bush.

Parties of the old inhabitants, with persons who are acquainted with the country as well as the Natives themselves, would be the right kind of men to employ in capturing them and in the end these must be the persons fixed upon; not one party but scores should be regularly appointed, who would be able to watch all the different passes at once and not as has latterly been the case, every here and there one insufficient and struggling party, prowling about seeking after the Natives, who are generally better acquainted with their manner of acting than they are aware of.

It is with great pain we have to record another instance of the dreadful attacks of the Aborigines; it more particularly happens just at the time the Government are attempting to bring about some peaceable reconciliation and we are fearful that by some the lately published Government Notices will be considered as too lenient towards these poor misguided wretches. "Mr. HOOPER, who is well known to many of your Readers, with the female with whom he lived and his assigned servant, were, in the road, opposite the farm, (to which he had latterly removed,) when, the blacks made their appearance. The man and woman ran away and got to the Lovely Banks, leaving Mr. Hooper to his fate, who went up to the house and procured a double-barrelled gun and fired upon them, after which, they instantly rushed upon him and murdered him with their waddles, leaving an axe stuck in the back of his skull. Mr. BATMAN and Mr. THOMAS PITCAIRN rode by Hooper's just after he was murdered, but too late to save him."- A small tribe of about twelve made their appearance yesterday night at the Cross Marsh, upon Mr. CURR'S farm, where they for some time chased two of Mr. BENT'S' farming men, who fortunately made their escape, after firing upon them and taking some of their spears.--This is supposed to be part of the same tribe that murdered Mr. Hooper.

TASMANIAN (HOBART TOWN, TAS. : 1827 - 1839),
FRIDAY 27 AUGUST 1830, PAGE 6

THE ABORIGINES.

On Sunday last, Mr. Hooper, an old Settler, was unfortunately killed by the Aborigines, at his farm Spring Hill, near Jericho. During the last week, the huts of Mr. Hudspeth, (brother to Dr. Hudspeth) and Mr Bisdee, were robbed of everything they contained and a fine Entire Horse of Mr. Stocker's, which cost him 100 guineas, was wantonly speared by these unhappy and benighted people.

THE INFAMOUS BLACK LINE

COLONIAL TIMES (HOBART, TAS: 1828 - 1857),
FRIDAY 24 SEPTEMBER 1830, PAGE 2

HOBART TOWN:
SEPTEMBER 24, 1830.

The course adopted by the Government with respect to the Aborigines in many recent Orders that have been officially promulgated has hitherto been suffered to pass without any particular notice from us, under the idea that, going on to amend what well required amendment, we should have had another edict or two upon the subject and we were willing to make one occasion serve for all; nor have we been altogether disappointed.

What is it that is really intended, by Order after Order, so quickly following each other in succession, as is frequently the case, from that by which each is immediately preceded? We very much doubt whether or not this is known to the framers of the Notices of which we are speaking - how then, we wonder, is it to be expected that those for whose guidance or instruction they are professedly put forth are to be edified or directed by them? We will briefly review the whole proceedings of the Government upon this question.

First - about two years ago we have a Proclamation creating an imaginary division of the Colony into two parts and stating, that one side of the supposed line is to belong to the English inhabitants and the other to the Aborigines - that if the latter attempt to pass this line and are seen in the territories reserved for the others, they are to be considered as under Martial Law and to be treated accordingly - that there is to be a chain of Military and Police posts along this boundary, in aid of the Settlers, towards driving back the Aborigines, should they attempt to cross it - and lastly, calling upon the Inhabitants to keep themselves and their servants well armed and to use force if necessary, in order clear the country of their sable visitors - "the dogs of war being thus let slip," all was ardour and emulation among many of the Whites, trying who should hunt, kill and destroy the most.

To be an Aborigine and to once be in the neighbourhood of a settled district, was a sufficient cause for being chased down if possible, with savage ferocity; no matter whether the disposition of the individual had been friendly or not - whether his errand had been merely to indulge tastes and- habits that had been acquired by mixing with Europeans, or had been for the purpose of rapine or mischief. So dangerous, no indiscreet a latitude as was thus allowed to a class of persons so totally unable to discriminate as most to whom this Proclamation was particularly addressed, or at least, by whom its purport would have to be carried into effect, could only have had one result.-It was a result that was foreseen at the moment by cool and reflecting persons, it ought not to have escaped the sagacity which presides over the collective wisdom of our Executive Council - but it did escape and the consequences has since been, an ineffectual endeavour on the part of Government to re-trace its steps; and by subsequent Orders and Notices- serving to bewilder the faculties of the Public, one contradicting the other, as has been frequently the case - to partially do away with the object of the original measure.

But we will go a little further back in our review of the inconsistent and ill-advised conduct of the Government towards this benighted race and refer to an occurrence which is and ever will continue, an indelible stain upon the history of this Colony. We allude to the execution for murder of two of them, about three years since, than which a greater cruelty was never practised - no, not even by the Spaniards upon their first settlement of America - in all our reading we have met with only one parallel case and that is related by a traveller who wrote of Italy, in the last century. He is speaking of Turin and says, "the circumstances attending a criminal prosecution, that took place du-ring my stay in that city, are of so singular a nature as to excite at once the pity, contempt and. risibility of the reader.

"On the 21st June, 1774, were publicly executed, after being duly tried and convicted of having wilfully, maliciously and at the institution of the devil, devoured a child a short time before. They were tried according to all the forms of law, by the superior tribunal and sentenced to die by the hand of the public executioner and then to be quartered. The Judges, unwilling to burden their consciences by the effusion of innocent blood, thought fit to submit the case to one of the most eminent Lawyers of the City. His opinion was as follows :-That the sentence pronounced by the Judges was consistent with justice and sound reason - fully agreeing with the ancient laws of Solon and Moses - and confirmed and strengthened by the opinion of the oldest and most enlightened philosophers, no less than by the sentences pronounced at different times by many European tribunals."

Thus much for our parallel. The laws of Solomon and Moses might very possibly have authorised the trial and execution of the two Aborigines equally as of the dogs that devoured the child; but we are under a higher code of laws; and where, we will ask, will a sanction for making beings little removed from savages and of a different nation and language to ourselves, amenable to laws, of which they neither understand the purport; effect, or meaning, be found in that religion of which we profess to be followers? where either in that reason, of which we vaunt ourselves, constituting our superiority over the wretched creatures whose fate we thus reprobate?

In good truth, the subsequent proceedings, adopted under the same auspices and by which instruction and persuasion have been referred to, as means of civilization, instead of the cruel experiment that had been thus tried, seems to argue that the futility (to say the least) of sanguinary measures had been felt and fully acknowledged.

We come now, however, to events of a later date. In February last, a Government Notice was issued, offering certain rewards for the capture of the Aborigines, which - differing as it did from much that had preceded it, both in spirit and in substance - has naturally enough been misunderstood by many into whose hands it had come and it therefore became necessary to correct certain of its provisions and to ex-plain what was meant. Accordingly, on the 20th Ultimo, out comes another, (No. 161.) calculated to effect this purpose - at least, insomuch as it drew a very marked distinction, that "It is His Excellency's particular desire and most peremptory order, that no violence or restraint shall be offered to the inoffensive Natives of the remote and unsettled districts," &c. and that any "wanton attack or aggression would be severely punished.

As might have been reasonably expected, this Order was the almost immediate precursor of another, to prevent the " misinterpretation" to which it gave rise and we were therefore not surprised to read the following in the succeeding Gazette:- " The Lieutenant Governor has learned that the intention of the Government, in issuing the Notices 160 and 161, has been misinterpreted, &c." - And then going on to draw certain distinctions, by way of explanation, which we conceive were only opening the door for whatever treatment individuals chose to practice towards the Aborigines with impunity. To wind up all, we have the long Notice that lately appeared and although we fully go along with the general measures as promulgated - are quite disposed to award praise to the Government, for having thus aroused its energies and given the Public something like a defined plan of operations for general guidance - yet it neither changes nor con-firms the many different Orders by which it has been preceded and a man may unwittingly do too much, or too little, merely from ignorance, as to which Orders are or not still in force.

COLONIAL TIMES (HOBART, TAS. : 1828 - 1857),
FRIDAY 17 SEPTEMBER 1830, PAGE 2

On Friday last an old man was brought into town from Swan Bay, on the Tamar, almost beat to pieces, by the native Blacks. They had thrashed him with their waddies, in a most dreadful manner, about the head and shoulders, - he is not expected to live.

There were two other men with him splitting, one of whom received a spear, but made his escape; the other by the name of Freeman, a noted boxer, was knocked down by a waddy, but recovered his feet and got away, thus has alarm once more visited the banks of the Tamar and this danger will add very considerably to the price or all kind of timber, which requires the workmen to live in the wood to split, at the very imminent risk of their lives, for the caution and vigilance of these bloodthirsty marauders is so very great, that no man, however courageous, can reckon his life safe from them one minute, for they seldom disappear until they have succeeded in dipping their hands in the blood of some person or other.

The old man has died since writing the above. - Launceston Advertiser.

COLONIAL TIMES (HOBART, TAS: 1828 - 1857),
FRIDAY 24 SEPTEMBER 1830, PAGE 2

There are one or two provisions of this last edict, which we shall make subject of separate notice; but what we at present wish to convey is, that the Public should not be perplexed by some half dozen different Government Orders and thus left in an uncertainty which to follow, but that, adopting the example of consolidation set by Mr. Peel with the Criminal Law of England, we should have one and only one, clear, comprehensive, well defined and easily-to-be-understood Order; cancelling or repealing all former ones and of a nature to give the Public a reasonable chance of effectually seconding the Government in its endeavours towards restoring and preserving the tranquillity of the Colony and at the same time of exercising proper humanity towards the miserable beings, by whom it is unfortunately at present but too much disturbed.

As things now are, we ourselves really do not understand, nor have we been able to meet with any who could explain to us, whether the sword or the Bible is meant to be the means of instructing the Aborigines in their relative duty to ourselves. In other words, whether destruction or civilization is to be the order of the day - are the numerous parties which are soon to scour the interior, to destroy or save these misguided creatures? Whatever may be the intentions of the Government, we are fully convinced, that most of those who are now preparing for the interior are not aware of the manner in which the Government expect them to act.

We trust, that as we know we speak the sentiments of many thinking persons in what we have now said, all possible misconception upon so important, a question may be removed ere the order to march be given, as otherwise it may be too late to remedy unintentional errors. As to whether any force that could be mustered on the Island, would be sufficient to intercept and way-lay even a trifling few of the various tribes, it is not now for us to question; but we sincerely wish that the hoped-for success may crown the operations; but were we to give our candid opinion, as to what we consider likely to be the result, we might be accused of foreboding bad success; we will therefore sum up by saying, that whatever may be the result that attends the unanimous endeavours of the Government and Settlers, to bring to a close the distressing scenes so frequent in the interior, one thing is most certain, which is, that every individual in the Island must, directly or indirectly, be benefitted by the present operations, causing as it will so large a proportion of the enormous sums to be put in circulation, which are now lying idle and useless in the iron chests of the Treasury.

We have elsewhere given an ample detail of the proceedings which took place at the Public Meeting of Wednesday. It was with pleasure we noticed that the general feeling was to act decidedly in conjunction with the proposed measures of the Government and we trust the result will be, that the body of military that can be decorously spared and whose services can be performed by the Inhabitants, may forthwith be allowed to proceed into the Interior, in furtherance of the present plan. The whole of the resolutions were unanimously agreed to and no signs of discussion or difference would have been shown, had the Gentlemen who called this Meeting of the Public, allowed the Public themselves to have chosen their own Committee, instead of palming upon them a list of - we will allow, very respectable - Gentlemen, many of whom have not yet even tendered and perhaps never will tender their services. Such a step was impolitic and the spirited manner in which it was opposed, by a body of respectable Inhabitants who had previously suspected what was likely to take place, we think, will - at all events for the present - put an end to the imprudent and unpopular system of a party first calling a Public Meeting and then, without the sanction of, or rather, perhaps we should say, without properly proposing to that Meeting, proceed as a matter of course to nominate a Committee to control over a body of fellow citizens, but few of whom having as yet come forward to enrol their names as volunteers. Want of room will not allow us at present to make the remarks which such proceedings call forth from the pen of a Journalist and which we would otherwise make. That the line of distinction, however, latterly so decidedly visible between the aristocracy and the democracy of this Town may be speedily lost sight of in the sincere wish of every good and loyal Citizen; but when a Committee is appointed in such a manner as was that of Wednesday, can it be at all wondered that the feelings of the people, when they can claim to be heard, should be demonstrated in the manner it then was?

The Gentlemen who tendered their services for the Battery station did not even stipulate any time, but offered to supply, the place of the Military on that Outpost so long as they may be required in pursuit of the Aborigines; we say they most willingly came forward so to do, not knowing at the time that any other guard would be relieved by their Fellow-Citizens; - and we further say, that if their services are accepted, they will undertake and perform that duty in a most efficient manner; they want no such Committee as that appointed by the Public Meeting to control their movements; we say, what they offer to to carry into effect will be done in a creditable manner and. if they find it expedient, as they naturally will, to elect officers, let them do so from among their own body, which they no doubt can accomplish without any distinction and without endangering the good understanding which prevails among them.

We understand that some time since a Settler at the Black Marsh offered to bring into Hobart Town twelve of the Aborigines prisoners, provided the Government would allow him five ticket of leave men. The reward that he required was that the whole of the men, if successful, should receive their emancipation and he himself a grant of 1000 acres of land - the offer was refused. We think this would have been a cheaper plan to the Government than the present mode of operations.

When I began to reflect on this massive military exercise, I thought once again how isolated the Pakana had been for thousands of years and how unprepared they were for such an event to occur. The threat of invasion, war and the associated political manoeuvrings had long been part of the British psyche. Every place in Europe had been invaded and invaded others with dramatic effects on either side, so the occurrences here were pretty much a normal part of life. While the nations in Lutruwita most certainly had conflicts with each other, these would never have been on the scale experienced in Europe. Just think of the Napoleonic War, the numbers killed, in single battles were at times far greater than the entire Pakana population. Remember too that many of the settlers had experienced some of the extraordinary conflicts of this war and bought that knowledge to play in the Pakana War.

The Aborigines were clearly adept at fighting and learned the art of European warfare quickly with effective results, but they were alone and secluded. They were fighting the most powerful nation on earth, with its wealth and military apparatus, guns and fire power. Whereas the British had a seemingly endless supply of soldiers and military power at their disposal, with regiments deployed and placed at the disposal of the governor. Of course, they also had their God on their side and an unwavering faith in their own 'civilization', both of which were useful in such a situation of conflict.

And so the Black Line was mobilised; a hair-brained scheme of Arthur's which involved militia, settlers, convicts and just about any white person who could stand up, walking in a line across the wilds of Lutruwita with the sole object of rounding up the remainder of the Pakana people. Needless to say, it was a poorly executed endeavour, it cost a fortune and was a rip-roaring fiasco.[xviii]
I wondered if there was a desire to reconstruct a 'real war'. The British considered that a war should be conducted according to rules of battle and sensible agreements on the best way of dealing with armed conflict. For centuries battle lines were established with troops lined up on either side, with assorted regiments and weaponry, waiting until daylight. Then they indulge in a killing spree until one side surrenders. It had been so since the days of Rome and that's the way they believed it should be until they were faced with uncivilized savages who fought in ways completely at odds with their convention. The Black Line restored this imbalance: There was a battle line, the British on one side and the enemy on the other. The Army was in control. Those involved acted under orders and they were clear about what they wanted to achieve. Life and war were as they should be: there is beauty in order.

This is my modest contribution to the topic:

The PAKANA *Voice*

BY W.C. SPECIAL CORRESPONDENT—*LUTRUWITA*

WHITE LINE

October 1830

Reports are emerging from several Lutruwita nations of a long white line of over 2000 British soldiers, free settlers, their servants, convicts and partly freed convicts attempting to march across country in order to 'capture' Pakana people.

If it wasn't so important, or such a grave matter, it would indeed be laughable. In fact, a comedy sketch would probably receive giggles and gasps of audience incredulity. This is exactly what the few Pakana people left would have done as they observed such a display of the British in their ridiculous red coats and carrying heavy packs and weapons and struggling through dense bush and wilderness.

According to informed sources the whole affair cost an extraordinary amount of money and resources and resulted in the claiming of an elderly man and a child. It is sometimes hard to believe that a race of people who claim to be superior in their civilization, religion and culture can be so stupid!

W.C.

25. *The inhabitants of the country, generally, are requested not to make any movements against the Natives, within the circuit occupied by the troops, until the general line reaches them and the residents of the Jordan and Bagdad line of road will render the most effectual assistance, by joining Capt. Wentworths force, while yet on the Clyde.*

26. *The assigned servants of settlers will be expected to muster, provided each with a good pair of spare shoes and a blanket and 7 days' provisions, consisting of flour or biscuit, salt meat, tea and sugar; so, also, prisoners holding Tickets of Leave; but these latter, where they cannot afford it, will be furnished with a supply of provisions from the Government Magazines.*

27. *It will not be necessary, that more than two men of every five should carry fire arms, as the remaining three can very advantageously assist their comrades in carrying provisions, &c. and the Lieutenant Governor takes this opportunity of 'again enjoining the whole community to bear in mind, that the object in view is not to injure or destroy the unhappy Savages, against whom these movements will be directed, but to capture and raise them in the scale of civilization by placing them under the immediate control of a competent establishment, from whence they will not have it in their power to escape and molest the White Inhabitants of the Colony and where they themselves will no longer be subject to the miseries of perpetual warfare, or to the privations which the extension of the Settlements would progressively entail upon them, were they to remain in their present unhappy state.*

THE COURIER. (1830, SEPTEMBER 25). THE HOBART TOWN COURIER (TAS: 1827 - 1839), P. 2.

On Wednesday, one of the most numerous meetings which has yet been held in the colony was assembled in the Court of Requests' room, for the purpose of carrying into effect the proposal of the inhabitants to undertake the duty of the Town Guard and so to place a proportionate additional number of the military at the disposal of the Government in the approaching movement against the Blacks. Mr. Hone being voted into the Chair explained the object of the Meeting and briefly, but strongly enforced the imperiousness of the present call on every inhabitant of the colony.

Mr. Kemp then rose and in moving the first resolution, pointed out in strong co- lours, the jeopardy in which the welfare of the settlers is now placed from the atrocities of the Blacks; and while he called upon all to come forward in the cause and expressed his own readiness to lend every assistance in his power, he lamented that much of the hostility of the Blacks was in the first in-stance to be attributed to aggressions on the part of the Whites and mentioned a circum-stance of a brother officer of his belonging to the 1021. regt. in the early periods of the colony who committed an outrage upon them by firing on a tribe which had assembled at Cove point, where he was stationed.

Mr. Gellibrand seconded the motion and said he intended to go in the interior and join the expedition himself in person, but he wished that the plan of operations had been clearly laid down before him, that he might have known exactly what he was to do for he deprecated all idea of shooting at such of the blacks as might endeavour to make their escape by running away from their white pursuers Mr. Stephen explained that the object of the meeting was merely to contribute aid to the government and to leave it to the proper authorities to decide how that aid could be best applied.

Mr. Hone said the blacks now unfortunately made no distinction in their attacks upon the white population. Women and children were alike their victims and he mentioned as an instance that the grass could not have yet grown on the graves of the poor woman and her twin babes who were lately butchered by them at Regent plains. Dr. Turnbull condemned all such vacillating and half measures as had hitherto been adopted.

A determined hostility against the whites evidently existed in the breasts of the blacks which had now grown up into an open and cruel warfare of the worst kind, because it was a warfare of individual against individual, but a strong decisive general movement like the one now projected, was the best and most merciful means of eventually putting a stop to the ef-fusion of blood. A considerable discussion then took place upon the point first started by Mr. Gellibrand as to the legality of shooting at the blacks, in which Mr. Horne, Mr. Stephen, Dr. Turnbull, Mr. Thomson and others took a part.

Mr. Hackett regretted that so few efforts had been made by the whites to learn the language of the blacks and to go among them and explain the really benevolent intentions which we have to them. He did not think there were 5 persons in the island who could converse with or make themselves understood by them. Had Van Diemen's land been colonised by Frenchmen, the case would have been very different. Dr. Ross denied that the French or any other European nation would have done more or so much as the English had done and mentioned a promontory in Grenada, called Sauteurs or the leapers, because the last remnant of the Caribs, the Aborigines of that island about 40 in number, had been driven over its precipice and dashed to pieces on the rocks in the sea. He lamented that so much time of the meeting had been occupied in discussing legal points, for the very purpose of their assembling was one of the purest humanity.

The lives of both blacks and whites were in jeopardy and the present measure was to preserve both and he urged in strong terms the danger in which the very existence of the colony would be placed, if we did not one and all come forward upon the present occasion with every possible aid. Shew all mercy said he, but let not a black escape. Mr. Murray scouted the idea of fear or danger from the natives and declared that 2 or 3 defenceless women

*would be sufficient at any time to put a whole tribe of them to flight. Dr.
Ross explained, that though he was deeply sensible of the hazard in which
the colony was placed from the atrocities of the blacks, Mr. Murray had
misunderstood him in saying that he was afraid, for fear was a sentiment
foreign to his nature.*

The following is a copy of the Resolutions which were passed at the Meeting

1st.-Moved by Mr. Kemp, seconded by Mr. Gellibrand,

*That inasmuch as no measures for repressing future aggressions on the part
of the Aboriginal Natives, can reasonably be expected to attain complete
success, without the most zealous and extensive cooperation of all classes
of the community, it is, at this juncture, peculiarly the duty of every man
cheerfully to contribute to the common cause, every assistance within
his power.*

2nd.-Moved by Mr. Hone, seconded by Mr Collicott,

*That, so far as it respects the inhabitants of Hobart town, such assistance
may, in the opinion of this Meeting, be advantageously afforded, either by
personal service in the country, or by performing a portion of the ordinary
duties of the military in town, by which last-mentioned means, a most
valuable accession to the number of troops might, as it appears to the
Meeting, be for several weeks, placed at the disposal of the Government
for duty in the interior.*

3d.-Moved by Dr. Turnbull, seconded by Mr. Hewitt,

*That, with this view, the present Meeting, on behalf of themselves and their
fellow townsmen, agree to undertake for the period of five weeks from the
2nd. of October next, the performance of such portions of the ordinary
military duties in Hobart town, as the number of volunteers subscribing to
this re-solution shall be ascertained to be equal to.*

4th.-Moved by Mr. Stephen, seconded by Mr. Thomson,

That, in the opinion of this Meeting, the contemplated force will more readily and advantageously be raised and kept together in an efficient state, by such a plan as, (one officer or person in charge being selected for each guard), shall enable every individual, so far as may be practicable, to select his own particular guard and the particular officer, or person in charge, under whom he would prefer to enrol himself.

That, for the purpose of carrying the objects of the preceding resolutions into effect, a standing committee of fifteen gentlemen be appointed, with full powers to make such further general arrangements and adopt such particular measures of detail; upon the subject, as may appear to them to be most expedient ; —that Messrs. Hone, Kemp, Stephen, Wilson, Adey, Hewitt, Turnbull, Bell, Cartwright, Gellibrand, Horne, Westbrook, O'Connor, James Ross, Capt. Boyd, Capt Nielly, W. Sorell, P. A. Mulgrave, J.T. Collicott, J. Scott, Lieut. Hill. be such Committee; that they have power to add to their number; and that five of them be a quorum.

6th --Moved by Mr. Mulgrave, seconded by Mr. Jennings.

That, the Committee; or such of them as can conveniently attend, be requested to wait upon His Excellency the Lieutenant Governor and communicate to him the proceedings of this Meeting.

A deputation of the gentlemen of the Committee waited on the Lieutenant Governor

on Thursday, when Mr. Hone addressed His Excellency and having introduced the subject by a short account of the meeting and the purposes for which it had been assembled, read the above resolutions. To which His Excellency was pleased to reply as follows:-

"GENTLEMEN

*"GENTLEMEN**

*It has given me great gratification to learn the resolutions which were
yesterday unanimously carried at the meeting of the gentlemen of this town
and in consequence of which you have now, in so patriotic a manner come
forward and tendered your services in assisting to perform the military
duties of the garrison, in order to enable me to augment the force which
will shortly commence active operations in the interior. I gladly accept the
offer which has been made in so laudable a spirit and, in entrusting such
important duties to the gentlemen of town, I shall repose the most entire
confidence in the vigilance with which I am sure they will watch over the
security of the community."*

*His Excellency was then pleased to explain the nature of the proposed
arrangements which we have been since enabled to lay before our readers
in the Government Order and the reasons which had induced him to adopt
them in preference to any other plan. Our limits prevent our enlarging up-on
it this week, farther than to say it meets with our cordial approval and under
all the circumstances is in fact perhaps the only feasible method that could
have been taken.*

*Whatever may be the result of the present measures against the blacks,
we have the satisfaction to know that they have not been undertaken until
necessity rendered it no longer safe to forego them and the mode in which
they are to be conducted has been devised with the concurrent knowledge
and judgment of the most worthy and intelligent persons in the colony. The
extent of research, the unwearied pains and unceasing anxiety which his
Excellency has bestowed, before the plan was brought to its present state of
perfection, must have been very great.*

*We are sorry to learn, that the three black youths whom Mr. Wedge, the
surveyor was endeavouring to instruct and civilize, ran away from his
house last week, taking some things with them, after having learned some
of our customs.*

FURTHER SUGGESTIONS

On the approaching movement against

THE BLACKS.

There was one material point which we omitted to touch upon in the course of our remarks on this subject last week. We mean that of dogs. It is well known that   the Blacks, since the Whites have introduced dogs into the island, having found out the great assistance they afford them in hunting the different animals in the bush; on which they subsist, have reared them in numbers, so that now, not only every tribe, but almost every individual of that tribe is attended by a crowd of them and these animals are now more numerous among them than themselves. Having in the first in-stance been obtained mostly from the stock keepers' huts, the original breed for the most part was derived either from the shepherds' or the kangaroo dogs. But they have been allowed to increase in so careless and indiscriminate a manner, that together with associating with their black owners, they have dwindled into a sluggish, ugly, mongrel race, with character and habits peculiar to itself. So that the Native dog, so called from being bred up and living with the Natives, has grown up into a new variety of the canine species, easily distinguishable from the different kinds reared by Europeans.

As every tribe is thus attended with its pack of these creatures, which will set up a loud barking at the first appearance of a stranger, giving their masters the alarm and timely notice to escape; it would appear at first sight that, the difficulty of catching the Blacks would be much increased by this means. But on consideration, we are inclined to think that, if the business be properly managed, instead of being a protection they will be the means of betraying their owners. We will suppose that a party which has been on the outlook has discover-ed from the summit of some clear hill in the night-time, the fires and encampment of a small tribe of Blacks; and that as they are commencing their movement before break of day to surprise and apprehend them, their dogs begin barking and the whole tribe take to their heels in an opposite direction. But then, if the party is also accompanied with a pack of well-trained strong, lively dogs, will be seen the truth of our maxim of our fighting the enemy with his own wea-pons. For though their dogs may commence a barking in return and betray the immediate situation of the Whites, they may be urged on to pursue them and will not only speedily overtake the Native dogs, but will lead the party in the best direction to follow their masters up, until probably they encounter one or two neighbouring parties, who coming up thus timely, would assist in surrounding and securing the whole tribe. For in this we take it will consist, on the present occasion, the grand hope of success in the chance supplied by the numbers who will be out on the, expedition of one party meeting unawares a tribe of Blacks that has been put to flight and is making its escape from another party. Whereas, from the fewness of those hitherto in quest of them, they have on former occasions been mostly enabled freely to make their ultimate escape without hindrance or opposition. But the moment they found themselves thus unexpectedly met by an opposing party, then they would be taken aback and not knowing which way to turn, would remain panic struck and motionless.

On these considerations, therefore, we would recommend that every party should be attended with dogs, of the best and fleetest kind that can be procured, as well as some of a smaller and slower description. Because for instance while the hounds or kangaroo dogs and others follow up the blacks and get out of sight, the smaller dogs would hasten after them at a slower pace, with which the party might be better able to keep up; until they overtook them. Then would appear the necessity of being well provided with the means of securing the captives until they could be placed on the peninsula or some other place of security in the meantime.

And the only sure mode of keeping them that occurs to us is, by fastening each by the wrist to the wrist of a white person, either by a strap, handkerchief, or manacle. We do not indeed see that a temporary act of bondage of this kind can with any safety be dispensed with. For it is not to be expected that these poor creatures, if we were to allow them to march at freedom before us, could be instructed all at once in the abstract information contained in the cry, "If you run off I will shoot you," and that too expressed in a language of which they are ignorant. Their native cunning is more-over so great that more care and watchful- ness would be necessary to guard against their attempts to escape at night than could be expected from persons worn out perhaps with the fatigues of a previous day's journey.

If indeed sufficient numbers could be obtained to form a cordon across the island, so as to sweep the whole of the blacks without exception, like a net, into the receptacle pre-pared for them at Tasman's peninsula, these unpleasant compulsory measures would not be necessary. Acting as the net ourselves, we should gradually, as we advanced, drive them before us until they arrived at their destined home. But then the greatest pos-sible caution would be requisite lest the meshes of our net should be large enough to allow them to escape back, for the farther we proceeded and the more we took them from their original ground these poor people would be filled with a stronger and stronger desire to return and like eels, the most subtle and slippery kind of fish, they would evade our grasp. It is however worthwhile to calculate the extent that would be necessary for such a cordon and the numbers that could be mustered to form the links of it.

In making such a general sweep of the island, we should commence in the first in-stance at Cape Grim and Circular head, gradually extending our wings to the north-west and south east until we reached Launceston on the one hand and the head of Macquarie harbour on the other, making a distance in a direct line of about 100 miles. At the same time we should start another arrangement from Cape Portland, carefully extending our wings as we advanced first along the coast, progressively until we arrived with one end at Launceston and the other at St. Patrick's head. The greatest extent of this line would be from Low head, at the entrance of Port Dalrymple, to the head land opposite the Black reef; on the north east of the island, a distance in a direct line of about 80 miles. But perhaps it would he preferable to commence at Low head itself, gradually bringing the south wing of the cordon up to Launceston in the first in-stance and then stretching out the other wing all round the coast to St. Patrick's head, while the first remained fixed, like the leg of a pair of compasses. The greatest extent of this line would be from Launces-ton also to the head land opposite the Black reef, little more than 60 miles, a saving up- on the other plan of nearly 20 miles. Here then we have on the most direct computation a distance of 160 miles as the largest measure of our cordon. For having completely crossed the island from Macquarie harbour on the west, through Launceston to St. Patrick's head on the east, we have an angle at Launceston and by bringing up the parties to the straight line about Campbell town, we reduce its extent to about 120 miles and from that point every advance from coast to coast would reduce it within still smaller compass.

Because the end of the wing at Macquarie harbour should not move from its position until the other had arrived at Waterloo point, or Spring bay, which would then so contract its limits as to allow it to extend down the south side of Macquarie harbour to Cape Sorell and thence along the coast to Port Davey and so on to the top of the Huon. Or probably as the blacks about Port Davey and Brune island are known to have the power of crossing at short distances in small boats or coracles, as from the main to De Wit's or other islands and across D'Entrecasteaux's channel to Brune island, it would be safer and more advisable when the party reached the mouth of the South port river, to ex-tend the cordon to Brune island and embrace the whole at once, rather than first going up the south bank of the Huon and then down the north and subsequently sweeping Brune island, because it is not impossible, that while we had cleared the region about South Cape and were ascend-ing the Huon, a tribe of blacks might cross the river or channel behind us and render our labour nugatory.

If then, we may calculate on the ardour expressed by the settlers generally and the interest of every inhabitant of the island which is so in intimately concerned in the pre-sent undertaking, we should imagine that without exaggeration about 3000 persons would turn out upon the service. We have we presume about 600 military, or perhaps more, if the inhabitants of Hobart town and Launceston do the duty of town guards - about as many constables and field police and it is hard if the settlers do not make up the remainder. In a distance then of 160 miles and supposing that we have 3200 per-sons, we have a cordon of 20 individuals to each mile. But as in many parts of this ex- tent, there are plains over which the eye can easily discern if a black should attempt to pass and there are numerous clear hills where a commanding view might be had, as well as lofty snowy and stony mountains over which even the blacks never attempt to go, the necessity of even this number in some places might be dispensed with so as to enable us to render the links of the chain closer where the danger of the blacks escaping between would be more imminent.

We are scarcely sanguine enough, how-ever, to hope that this attempt will be made, although upon reflection it is not only the most effectual and complete in itself, but on the whole the most easy. If it were but well and judiciously arranged the result would be certain and decisive. From the short distance between the links, it would be perfectly practicable even by hailing from one to another to pass intelligence through the whole cordon from end to end in a few hours. And as the cordon advanced and the blacks were crowded before it, the links according to our plan, would become closer and closer, to the number of 30 or 40 in a mile, rendering their escape still more impossible. For although some persons have told us that the blacks have latterly begun to travel by night, we have never yet had any authentic proof of the assertion and are un-willing to believe it. However we think that even should an escape by night be attempt-ed, the dogs on both sides, of the natives as well as whites, would give the alarm and deter them from attempting it.

As the cordon advances, however and captures are made, if they are secured ac-cording to our plan by attaching every black to some one or other individual of the party, its strength will in that way be in some degree increased. For it is a singular fact, that almost all these blacks, especially the most hostile of them, can speak English, more or less and although thus restrained against their will, they would readily point out any others that might come in view of their more discerning eyes. And this they would be still more likely to do when they were brought beyond the limits of their own district or territory, in the midst of a tribe with which they were probably at variance. Most of our readers are of course aware that the aborigines of this island consist of 4 or 5 distinct nations, the boundaries of whose territories are not only clearly defined and understood among themselves, but even their languages are completely distinct.

Much will no doubt be effected by availing ourselves of every favourable circum- stance as it arises in the process of the expedition. In the event of the capture of a chief or other person of authority among his tribe, the greatest care should be taken to gain him over, for the influence of the rulers of these people is of the most complete and despotic kind. Their nod is law and the simple waving of their hand will bring the whole tribe from one side of a mountain to another, with the greatest speed. And here we have a most encouraging suggestion in our forthcoming attempts at civilizing these poor creatures, for we have the experience that the same authority can speedily be ac-quired over them by a stranger as by one of their own native born chieftains. So that a person of some skill and discrimination, some acuteness and knowledge of human nature, may shortly with due management ac-quire such an ascendancy over them as to lead them from their present barbarous habits, to civilized and useful occupations. Mosquito, the Sydney black, who lately perished here, acquired such a command over the Oyster bay tribe, that he led them where ever he pleased and in two or three instances made them actually perform some simple agricultural labour. He certainly had the qualifications of sable nobility in his veins, for he both considered himself to be so and acted as a great man. He has been known frequently to enter the cottages of the settlers, ordering his followers to the amount perhaps of 150 or 200 to await his motions on a neighbouring bank and having seated himself with all the familiarity, or rather with all the claims to the rights of unbounded hospitality at the board of the land lord, would help himself bountifully to the best fare of the house and cast with an air of condescension the bones and offal's to his people, who submissively and thankfully gathered them up from his hand.

And this leads us to mention, what we have long strongly suspected, our belief that many of the late incursions of the hostile tribes have been instigated and directed more or less by unprincipled, traitorous men, who have escaped from their employment with the settlers and have gradually insinuated themselves among the blacks, until they have accustomed themselves to their habits and acquired an influence over them. How else can we account for the knowledge of the English language which many of these people possess, that have seldom or never been seen or lived among the settled districts and apparently have never had the slightest opportunity of learning it? About two years ago, it will be recollected, that a man was observed among a tribe which appeared about Jericho, whom various persons declared was white and we ourselves have more than once seen among the bark huts in remote parts of the interior, marks and delineations which no native black that we have yet seen could have made. If the present measure prove successful, which we confidently expect it will, the result will prove the truth of this suspicion.

A great deal will depend on the due arrangement of the supplies of provisions and very active steps have, we learn, been already taken by the Commissariat to place ample depots in the most convenient parts. We intreat the Government to make these supplies very liberal, for in this stage of the undertaking it is impossible to tell the extent of the drafts that may be made upon them. The captives themselves as they increase will of course require also to be fed out of them. If sumpter horses, laden with provisions, could also be provided to attend such of the parties as undertake the most remote and unsettled parts, it would very much assist the expedition. Because the horse being loaded could be led by turns by the different persons of the party to which it be-longed and when the provisions which each had carried with him were exhausted, re-course might be had to the supply from the horse, by which means they would be enabled to keep the field much longer than they otherwise would.

We had proposed to enter upon the best mode of treating the blacks when they were securely placed at the Aboriginal establishment on Tasman's peninsula, but we have already extended these observations to too great a length to admit of our touching on so important and extensive a subject in the present number.

Formerly, the unsettled state of the slaves, no doubt caused the necessity of many severe examples; I should be very sorry were it to be supposed for one moment, that I was advocating the cruel practice which were so commonly believed to exist towards the slave. All such as may have been educated in Europe, can look back to the time when they shuddered at the mere bare recitals of some of the horrible tales published about the severity with which slaves were treated; but now, let such, I say, only picture to themselves what touching tales, under able hands might be now written on the pleasant measures we are adopting towards the Aborigines of this Colony.

Picture, I say, any of these poor creatures singly, with all his harassing opponents searching to destroy him and guiltless as he may be, endeavouring to exterminate him, because one or two of his fellow creatures have been revenging the atrocities that the robbers of their country, the destroyers of their peace and happiness have committed - and who are now endeavouring to sweep away the whole race of sable inhabitants.

*Christians as the settlers pretend to be, let them think of what they are now on the point of undertaking - let them call to mind all the atrocities ever committed by the Spaniards in America - deprive those horrid histories which have been handed down to us in their proceedings of the co-louring given to them by the authors - and, in real truth, **the inhabitants of Van Diemen's Land must acknowledge that they at all events equal those*** *whom they abhor - whom they loath for their cruelty, yet the time will come when the manner the settlers of Van Diemen's Land behaved towards the legal possessors of the soil, will be coloured and recorded to their disgrace.*

What views may now be construed into advisable measures - whatever feelings the English Parliament may have towards the operations now adopted towards the Aborigines - there is one thing very certain, that to them the meanest slave now existing under an English master, is to be envied by the whole race of the wretched original possessors of this Island.

POLICE INTELLIGENCE. (1830, DECEMBER 13).
LAUNCESTON ADVERTISER (TAS: 1829 - 1846), P. 3

A report has reached town that the Government cutter Opossum has been wrecked on the East coast, near Swan Island, to which place she was conveying provisions for the use of the Aborigines lately captured and placed there by Mr. James Parish and his party. We are happy to state, that the crew were saved. TO THE PUBLIC OF CORNWALL. A meeting has been called by our brother Colonists at Hobarton, in order that the sense of the people may be taken as to the propriety of a 'vote of thanks', to His Excellency, Colonel Arthur, for his strenuous endeavours to arrest the murderous course lately pursued by the Aborigines of this country against the white population ; and also, the very painful personal exertions of His Excellency having excited the earnest attention of all parties who had an opportunity of witnessing it, we trust that our thus calling the public attention to this, point will not fell to have that food effect which every well wisher of the Colony can desire, viz,—

The PAKANA Voice

PUBLIC MEETING.

On Wednesday the Public Meeting of which we spoke in our last, to address His Excellency the Lieut. Governor, expressing to him the thanks of the Colony for his arduous exertions in the late expedition Against the Aborigines and urging him to proceed until the great object of capturing them is accomplished, was hold in the Court Room. It was by much the most numerous and respectable meeting which ever yet assembled in Van Diemen's Land; much interesting discussion took place principally upon matter of form, for in respect to the object of the meeting, all were cordially invited, the Resolutions having all passed without a dissentient voice. A proposition for adjournment was made by Mr. Gregson and seconded by Mr. Kermode, when, the 1st resolution but one was put and was negatived by the whole meeting, the mover and seconder excepted. We are unable to give our readers the details of what took place upon this interesting occasion until our next, when the whole proceedings will be fully reported.

....

THE ABORIGINES,—Two of Mr Allardyec's shepherds were last Sunday attacked and speared by these savages, at the Lagoon of Islands. Mr. Howell of the Shannon, who went in pursuit of the Aborigines, with six of his men, fell in with a party of them on Sunday last, a little below the junction of the Shannon and the Ouse and captured a man and a woman, with a great number of spears, waddies, &c.

1831

The Tasmanian

AND SOUTHERN LITERARY & POLITICAL JOURNAL.

Vol. V.]   FRIDAY EVENING, JANUARY 14, 1831.   [No. 202.

COLONIAL TIMES (HOBART, TAS: 1828 - 1857),
TUESDAY 15 FEBRUARY 1831, PAGE 2

The Aborigine question seems entirely at rest and the expense, trouble, great exertions - meritorious exertions and all that, which three months ago absorbed the entire attention of all classes, have not only subsided, but are as if they had never been. What will all the address gentry think? What are the Colonists to think of the assurance with which the last Government Order that was issued upon the subject terminated? what will be thought of the affair in England, when, after, receiving the ac-counts that will have reached it of the ardour and emulation which converted even grave senators into sentries, in place of common soldiers - placed the pike and halberd in hands that had heretofore been chiefly employed in measuring tape by the yard, or making out bills of parcels for figs of tobacco - enabling persons of staid experience all at once to make the discovery, that for six years they had looked at local politics through a glass and darkly and that, now the film was removed, that which had always been condemned, was suddenly warmly applauded ;- what, we say, will be thought of us, when, after all this hubbub and noise, it shall come to the knowledge of our home

Readers, that, having caught two natives, everything is as still and quiet here, with respect to our side of the question, as it is in England? And further, we might say, what will be thought of the whole affair - of the marches and counter-marches - of the three weeks in Paradise Scrub - of the order of the day, with all the pretty romance of Savage and the white men to boot - when it shall appear, as it has upon the authority of one of our contemporaries, who may be justly considered a sort of demi-official upon such subjects, that three hundred and fifty-four is the extent of the male population of our sable neighbours and that a portion even of these (for it cannot be pretended that the whole were ever included within the lines) contrived not only to check the pursuit, but eventually to baffle ten times as many of our white inhabitants, " armed at all points and burning for action?"

Truly, the whole affair has been very extra- ordinary and it is made doubly so by the apathy and indifference that have succeeded the bustle and activity that at one time held sovereign rule here. The summer has been frittered away and winter is already on the approach ; the Natives have re-commenced their depredations and yet nothing has been done ! nor are there any visible signs of anything doing, either in fulfilment of the pledges that have been given, or of the hopes and expectations that have been reasonably formed by the Colonists at large.

TASMANIAN (HOBART TOWN, TAS: 1827 - 1839),
SATURDAY 17 MARCH 1832, PAGE 4

That a sum not exceeding £10,818 3s. be appropriated to defray the Expense of the Episcopalian Clergy and Catechists for the Year 1832. Resolved— That a sum not exceeding £5,953 be appropriated to defray the Expense of Schools for the Year 1832. Resolved—That a sum not exceeding £286 be appropriated to defray the Expense of the Establishment for the civilization of the Aborigines for the Year 1832. Resolved—That a sum not exceeding £831 15s. be appropriated to defray the Expense of the management of the trust of the Clergy and School Lands for the Year 1832.

LAUNCESTON ADVERTISER (TAS: 1829 - 1846),
MONDAY 28 MARCH 1831, PAGE 99

TO THE EDITOR OF THE LAUNCESTON ADVERTISER.

*As it appears to me that there is no subject which more demands the attention of the Public, at the present time, than the hostility which now exists between the Aborigines and the Colonists, (nor ought there to be any on which greater unanimity should prevail among the People) I take the liberty of writing to you by way of submitting a few ideas which have occurred, to me. with regard to the practicability of putting a stop, to the slaughter on both sides which prevails. The enmity of this benighted race to our People, although in the instance, no doubt excited by wanton cruelty on our part, has now attained such a pitch, that **nothing short of the extermination of the white inhabitants, seems to be the aim of the Savages**. The warfare with them has therefore every prospect of being interminable. Where two nations are at war, they always have some bone of contention, which is known to both.*

*The one seeks to obtain something from the other which being withheld is sought to be taken by force when treaty has failed and ensures a termination of bloodshed by giving up the thing contended for. In regard to the Blacks however, it is impossible to form any plans of concession to them which shall satisfy them, because **we have no means of negotiation. It is really shameful that during the whole time this Island has been Colonised, great part of which time the Natives have in many in stances been associated in life with the Europeans, for the most diabolical purposes, not an iota has been learned of their vernacular tongue**. Not so much as even a vocabulary of words in common use has been reduced to writing, although there must have been abundant opportunities for framing such, when we consider the number of half caste children, the progeny of Black females, which there are in this Colony.*

This mixture of blood I have heard severely reprobated, but for my own part, however much I might feel disgusted myself in such an intercourse, I cannot on the score of Policy condemn it; and it occurs to me that this very circumstance is capable of being converted into a great benefit to the Colony, for the following reasons. The fathers of these children are without doubt many of them in existence and might be found. They must, in the course of their cohabitation with the Aboriginal females, have acquired a knowledge of many of their words. These if collected from a variety of sources might be, in the hands of a studious man, it does not require any great ability, form the materials for reducing the language of the Aborigines into a written dialect. Besides the above sources of information which should be carefully sought for, there are Natives under Mr. Robinson and those with whom that gentleman is said to have conferred. His journal, if his conduct has merited the encomiums passed on it by the Government must be rich in specimens of the various vernacular tongues, of the different tribes and with such materials what difficulty would there be in reducing the language of the Blacks to a written tongue, teaching those which have been captured the use and power of a written language; and finally sending, them with a proper escort among the friendly tribes with whom Mr. Robinson has already conferred.

These would in their turn be instructed in the use of characters; and the common roman Alphabet seems quite sufficient for the purpose, by which means knowledge, be it in ever so limited a degree, would be disseminated among the Blacks. This object once attained a negotiation, might be entered into and ultimately the natives be raised in opposition to their prejudices, to some rank in civilized life. The idea of instructing them in the English tongue, in order to spread knowledge among them, is too ridiculous to be long entertained. No sir, we must take first the labour of learning their language; and in that language instruct them, if we wish to do so.

The work is I will confess most arduous but it is highly and intensely interesting; and there are many who would undertake it with pleasure if remunerated properly for their time and trouble. It may perhaps be said that while this is going on, for it will necessarily take time, the Colonists may be all murdered. Not a bit of it, if a sufficient protective force is stationed on the defensive at the remote huts and farms, acting only in cases of attack first, made by the Blacks agreeably to your suggestions a week or two back.

I am Sir, Your's respectfully, A. Settler. Quamby's March 22nd, 1831.

LAUNCESTON ADVERTISER (TAS: 1829 - 1846),
MONDAY 28 MARCH 1831, PAGE 101

In our — page appears a letter signed a Settler, which appears to us very well worthy of attention The subject is at once novel and important; and the enquiry which it involves highly interesting. We perfectly fall in with the opinion given by "A Settler" that civilization can be spread among the Blacks by our learning their language only. If we want to instruct them we must do it in their "vernacular tongue," for they are so averse to everything European that there is not the slightest hope of their ever becoming sufficiently acquainted with the English language, as to become thoroughly master of it. Whereas on the other hand, if we were to succeed in writing their own dialects; and teaching them how they might, to use their innocent phrase "make paper talk to Black fellow," it would induce such a degree of curiosity on their part as would go far to ensure success. Any improvement in their tongue, they would readily learn, but the task of persuading them to pursue the difficult study of the English language is we consider hopeless.

Deeply impressed with the necessity of the native language being acquired, we call upon every man let him be high or low, bond or free.to come forward with whatever words he may be acquainted with. We ourself will always feel proud to receive any words. Should there be any persons who knows the least of the Native language resident near us, we request they will favour us with a call at our office, as we pledge ourself to collect all the minutia possible; and having arranged it, to transmit it to the authorities to be placed in the hands of any gentleman, who may undertake to form a vocabulary. Were all the journalists to adopt this method they might render an essential service of the Colony. While upon this subject we cannot pass by the continued outrages of the Natives, as recorded authorities to send Military to be stationed at the remote stock huts and farms, with orders not to molest the Natives unless they first make a hostile movement.

Let every protection be afforded to the Settlers, but on no account let the Natives be harassed in the first instance by the Whites; if the success of the friendly missions and the lives of those employed in them are deemed of any, importance. We are constrained to urge this, because we are fearful lest the exterminating zeal, of some, may endanger the success and safety of others.

LAUNCESTON ADVERTISER (TAS: 1829 - 1846),
MONDAY 16 MAY 1831, PAGE 157

THE ABORIGINES.

The Natives appeared at Dixon's, near Jacob's Sugar loaf, within a few rods of the high road, on Thursday, speared and beat his daughter, about thirteen years of age, in a dreadful manner; but were eventually driven off. We trust the girl is doing well towards recovery. The Natives were afterwards seen prosecuting their route, by a man of Mr. York's, who concealed himself in a tree until they had passed, about eighteen in number. Some Soldiers from Auburn went in pursuit immediately - no success.

COLONIAL TIMES (HOBART, TAS: 1828 - 1857),
WEDNESDAY 25 MAY 1831, PAGE 4

CORONER'S INQUEST.

Before the witnesses were examined, the Coroner and Jury, in the presence of a large concourse of people, took a view of the bodies of the two murdered men, Moses Boss and William Carter. When seen in a mutilated and emaciated state, a glance of indescribable emotion passed over the features of every person present. A feeling of indignation, mingled with horror, was visible in every countenance. Carter had three spear wounds in the back, three in the breast and one from a bayonet in the belly. His head was beat to a mush by waddies and weighty stones, his nose and whole face disfigured; and when the bandage about his head was removed. the gore, in pure colour, flowed from the gashes inflicted. Boss's head was emaciated in a similar manner; a spear had been thrust in his neck and another into his breast and the whole of his back shewed the blows he had received. The most hard-hearted could not behold the mournful spectacle without inwardly cursing the perpetrators of murders so foul and barbarous.

On Monday, the 9th inst., two soldiers who had the previous evening, arrived at Mr. Kemp's hut on the Sorell Lake, took their departure early in the morning. About 10 o'clock in the forenoon, Joseph Barlow, (Mr. Kemp's overseer,) Jenks and Evesy left on horseback, in search of cattle. The witness, Daniel Flinn, had by this time got in all the water required for the hut, as there is great danger for one man, when by himself, to leave huts to go for water. The two deceased men, William Carter and James Boss, were employed in a field about 300 yards distant from the hut. These two men had often been cautioned to take their fire-arms with them, when in the field, but they always neglected it. - About half-past 10, Daniel Flinn went into the barn to bring a piece of salt beef out of a cask for dinner and placed his gun against the door-post outside, as he could reach the meat from the door. The barn and stable are under one roof and a loft above the stable containing oats and straw - there were two dogs kept in the barn, that had been kangaroo hunting the day before - they attempted to get out, bristling their hair at the same time and seemed very uneasy, Flinn therefore shut the door. - He then heard a sort of galloping noise outside, which he at first imagined proceeded from a foal in the paddock. - He, however, put down the beef again and opened the door, when to his great surprise, he saw his gun in the hand of a black man, who had two others under his arm. He observed seven blacks between the barn and the hut. One of them, a tall man, who had some shells round the crown of his head, walked up and down leisurely, seeming to be a chief, having a spear in his hand and was directing the movements of the others

Flinn now got up in the loft, where he could have secreted himself, but being certain that the Aborigines had seen him, he seized hold of an adze, putting himself in a posture of de-fence. All this, time, none of the dogs made the slightest noise, the black took away five of them and two puppies with the greatest ease. A black man entered the stable and asked Flinn to come down and tie the dogs; he spoke good English. Flinn flourished his adze and the black said "No good, no good, come down." Shortly after there came in more blacks, with a woman, endeavouring to persuade Flinn to come down, one of them had four waddies in his hand, watching to have a fair throw at Flinn, who piled up some oats and straw to ward off the waddies.

- The men now appeared to leave the hut and the woman called to Flinn saying " pretty white man, pretty white man, come down to tie the dogs - we no hurt you - me give you a kiss." – She then to induce him further, exhibited the most lascivious gestures. He looked down from the loft and saw two or three blacks concealed underneath. One attempted to get up into the loft through the manger, but was beaten down by Flinn.

They then went out and presently the woman returned by herself. To intimidate Flinn, she told him, "damn soldiers go away this morning," and she made some signs, indicating that the blacks were aware that Barlow and the other two men were away on horseback. -

When she found she could make no impression on Flinn, she began to chatter, grin and threaten. Flinn seeing the barn clear, descended and placed some bags of oats and some logs, against the door, to prevent the Aborigines entering again. He then got on the loft and made all the noise he could, to give notice to Carter and Boss to be on their guard, but unfortunately he was not heard. - Looking through the shingles, he saw the blacks coming out of the hut with wearing apparel, flour and sugar. A red night-cap, belonging to Mr. George Kemp and which the witness stated that the young gentleman set great store by, was converted into a sugar bag.

Shortly after Flinn saw Carter near the garden fence; he had been wounded by the blacks and nearly murdered. The chief, walking with a spear in his hand, made a motion to the others and instantly as Carter endeavoured to rise, his head was crushed with large weighty stones and in a few minutes he was motionless. Boss was killed about four yards from Carter, but Flinn did not see him at the time, as he was covered by a tree.

Flinn's situation now became truly alarming. The Aborigines attempted to make their way into the barn through a window about four feet above the ground. Two of them raised a black up to enter, but Flinn cut him across the head with the adze, when the blacks all set up a howl and desisted. Eleven were now seen, but some more were evidently concealed in an adjoining scrub. Being foiled they returned to the hut, from whence they brought out some fire-sticks, which with brush-wood they pushed through the window, but Flinn succeeded in defeating their object at that time. They again returned to the hut and having provided themselves with four or five fire-sticks and brush-wood, they again went to the barn, pushing the sticks and brush-wood through the logs, when in a moment the barn was in a blaze of fire. Flinn's jacket and waistcoat and trousers caught fire. He quickly pulled off his jacket and waistcoat and extinguished the fire in his trousers; the burning shingles were falling down upon him. In this distress he forced a log away at the back part and happily got about 100 yards away before he was seen by the blacks, who were all in front of the place, rejoicing at their own handy work. A race now began and speedily Flinn was overtaken. A spear was darted at him, which he caught and broke in two.

A second spear was thrown, which took be-tween his shirt and body and this he kept, making with his adze, a defence for him. The stones now came flying about him, but one of the blacks coming within some yards of him, received a stone from Flinn in his stomach with such force as to make him bend double. Flinn then made for a scrubby hill and when on the highest elevation, the Aborigines ceased the pursuit.

The blacks carried away from Mr. Kemp's hut, four muskets, two pistols, one bayonet, seven pounds of tobacco, about two hundred and sixty weight of flour and seventy pounds of sugar. Barlow and Flinn positively refused to return to the hut, as nothing can remove from their mind the sense of horror they naturally felt on the occasion. Mr. Anstey, as Coroner, has held twenty-four Inquests, but the mutilated and emaciated state of Carter and Boss exceeded any thing he had seen before.

Verdict - Wilful Murder against some of the Aboriginal tribes whose names are unknown, by certain spears and wad-dies made of wood and a bayonet made of iron.

We have been very minute in our statement of the above affair, so as to render the public fully acquainted with the practices of our sable enemies.

A few days previously, Mr. Alwright's hut in Patrick's Plains was burned to the ground, with a large quantity of provisions belonging to Government.

Forty of the Aborigines made their appearance on the Saturday before, at Mr. Howell's on the Shannon. Mr. Willowson's shepherd was run by them a few days ago. Mr. Franks's man, at the Crescent Lake, narrowly escaped their hands a few days back and the following day two other of his men came up with the tribe, which was immediately after pursued by Mr. Anstey's splitters and fencers.

The appointment of Mr. O'Loughlin as King's Sergeant, in Ireland, has, we understand, given great satisfaction to the Catholics.

INDEPENDENT (LAUNCESTON, TAS: 1831 - 1835),
WEDNESDAY 1 JUNE 1831, PAGE 3

Mr. Meredith remonstrated on the hardship of the dog tax. I am obliged, said that gentleman, to pay a sum of nearly 10/- annually for I cannot, living as I do in a remote part of the Island, do without my dogs. No settler would be safe unless provided with these necessary animals and yet a heavy tax is laid upon them. He then read a list of dog licenses he had been compelled to takeout and observed that if the tax had been 10/- each dog he should still bare been obliged to pay it. No tax is imposed on a watch dog in England and why should we have such imposed upon us? He then alluded to the absolute necessity of having dogs to protect the Settler from the attacks of the black Natives.

I became increasingly puzzled by the fact that there were so few *luna* (women) present in the clans I visited, especially along the northern coast. I thought at first they might be hiding from me through shyness or for protection. Eventually I realised that many *luwana* (girl) and luna had been taken to the islands by sealers and were kidnapped for sexual intent and enslaved for their lifetime. This practice had apparently started many years ago even before any formal settlement on Lutruwita by the British. The clans had now been so depleted of *luna*, especially those of child-bearing age, that it was having a devastating effect on the population of the Pakana people.[xix]

TASMANIAN (HOBART TOWN, TAS: 1827 - 1839),
SATURDAY 23 JULY 1831, PAGE 7----

THE ARORIGINES.

We are happy to be enabled to state, that by the judicious stationing of the military at the most exposed parts of the Interior, the incursions of the Aborigines have been so completely repelled, as that the settlers now consider themselves to possess entire protection. The conduct of the 63d Regt. thus detached, as it is into numberless parties, is spoken of with the greatest commendation and is highly creditable to the discipline of that fine Regiment and to the whole of the officers by whom it has been effected and is maintained.

The principle now adopted by the Local Government, is, in our view of the subject, the true one. It is strictly defensive. We have a right to this and to the whole of this, but to no more; and we are in sanguine hopes, that by a steady perseverance therein, the great object of a friendly intercourse may be finally fully established. It is highly gratifying, however, to know that the whole of the most exposed of the settled frontier, is now most satisfactory protected.

HOBART TOWN: SEPTEMBER 7, 1831.

Let it be impressed upon your minds, let it be instilled into your children, that the Liberty of the Press is the Palladium of all your Civil, Political and Religious Rights

THE ABORIGINES.

Mr. G. A. Robinson, (we have our information from one of his party, who came into Launceston yesterday morning) with Lemena Bingna, (an aborigine) who has been for some time in pursuit of the natives on the eastern coast and has been following in their track backwards and forwards from the Bite of Ben Lomond for about 400 miles. at last, on the 27th ult. had the good fortune to come up and capture, between Forrester's River and the Little Piper, the fugitive Yumarrha, the Chief of the Stony Creek mob, with five other men, one woman and 16 dogs. As soon as they were sufficiently near, Yumarrha recognised Mr. Robinson and immediately ran forward to and shook hands with him, when the rest gave themselves up without the least resistance. It appears there are now but three natives belonging to the Stony Creek tribe in the bush, to whom Yumarrha promises to lead Mr. R's party.

The captives (now 24 in number) seem quite satisfied with their situation and pass the greater part of their time in hunting, returning with the spoil at night ; they are said by our informant to be a fine set of men and have luxuriant long black hair; **Yumarrha is very communicative and stated to Mr. Robinson that they would not have committed so many murders as they have but on account of the women being kidnapped from them by the Sealers; and that had they continued free they would have taken into the bush every white woman they could have caught!** *They report that it was a woman who some time since murdered Mr. Fitzgerald - that she died about a fortnight (now three weeks) since. Yumarrha, it appears renders himself useful in keeping those that were with him, for not long after the capture (if such it may be called) an armed party of Sealers made their appearance, when, but for Yumarrha's assurance that they were safe with Mr. Robinson, they would have decamped.*

The party learnt from Yumarrha that the capture of the whole of the Big River tribe may be easily accomplished and he offers to conduct Mr. Robinson to them. If all this is true, (and we have every reason to believe it is) we rejoice; inasmuch as there are so many fewer at large ; but the idea that the whole of the Aborigines in the Island may be caught in like manner, we consider Utopian. Nevertheless, as it is the object of Mr. Robinson's mission, we consider him entitled to the highest praise for so undauntedly following it up. We have during the week received one or two communications from correspondents to the westward, giving information of the appearance of the natives in that quarter and of a commencement of hostilities on their part.

The PAKANA *Voice*

BY W.C. SPECIAL CORRESPONDENT—*LUTRUWITA*

The Tyerremotepanner people (Northern Midlands Nation) report an increase in the number of kidnappings of luwana and luna from their clans. Women are taken against their will from their home and family to be exploited by the sealers in every way possible.

Many waypa (men) are threatening to capture rytia luna (woman white) for revenge but in more rational moments understand that such action would achieve only more deaths and hostility from the rytia and will not bring their luna back to them.

No one from the government was available for comment.

COLONIAL TIMES (HOBART, TAS: 1828 - 1857),
WEDNESDAY 7 SEPTEMBER 1831, PAGE 2

HOBART TOWN: SEPTEMBER 7, 1831.

Let it be impressed upon your minds, let it be instilled into your children, that the Liberty of the Press is the Palladium of all your Civil, Political and Religious Rights

They are however very scant of particulars, not even stating whereabouts they were seen ; one letter, however, dated from Westbury, says that "on Monday the Aborigines visited Mr. Stocker's stock hut, when they speared a child, who was standing at the door, through the thigh ; the mother, known by the name of Dalrymple, fired six shots at them before the man in charge arrived to her assistance ; they attempted to burn the hut, in which fortunately they could not succeed ; and in the flight slightly speared two horses that were near them. The following day they visited Mr. Gibson's, hut and speared the stock-keeper, Cupit, (who has been once before speared whilst in the service of Mr. Stocker,) in the thigh." This correspondent is the only one affording the least intelligence, but all uniting in praise of the exertions made by Captain Moriarty, Police Magistrate of that district to capture the savages.

These accounts but ill accord with the Government notices elsewhere inserted, calling upon the Colonists to treat them with kindness - nor does it hold out to them anything remarkable for the encouragement it may give to attempts at conciliatory measures. - The Independent of that district to capture the savages. These accounts but ill accord with the Government notices elsewhere inserted, calling upon the Colonists to treat them with kindness - nor does it hold out to them anything remarkable for the encouragement it may give to attempts at conciliatory measures. - The Independent.

TASMANIAN (HOBART TOWN, TAS: 1827 - 1839),
SATURDAY 10 SEPTEMBER 1831, PAGE 6

DREADFUL EVENT

It is with the most unfeigned regret we have to announce, that Captain B. B. THOMAS, brother of our respected Colonial Treasurer, has been murdered by the natives. While there was the slightest hope that it was possible the intelligence received in town of this dreadful event might be unfounded, we hesitated to give it utterance. We fear it is impossible to indulge even the shadow of such. It is too fatally confirmed by the arrival, this morning, of a gentleman from Launceston that Captain Thomas, Mr. Parker, his overseer and three of his men have been killed by the natives, at his estate on the northern coast of the Island, a few miles west of Port Sorell. We believe that Mr. Moriarty was the nearest neighbour to this ill-fated gentleman, at a distance of at least thirty miles.

The beauty of the place, its numerous natural advantages and Captain Thomas's anxiety to retrieve, even in the dismal solitude of the inmost recesses of the Island, the very great losses, pecuniary and as respected the expectation he had a right to entertain, as the original managing partner of Colonel Gibbs, Messrs. Latour, Elphinstone and Keate's association, commonly known here as the Horse Company, induced him to fix his abode in so exposed a situation. We are not acquainted with the circumstances of this deeply afflicting event; but we shall not fail to furnish our readers with them in our next.

Captain Thomas was a brave and accomplished cavalry officer. He served for several years, with high reputation, in the 9th Dragoons, with which Regt. he per -formed the South American Campaign. His next eldest brother is Colonel Thomas, of the 20th Foot, commanding a large and important district in India. He was highly connected in Ireland, being nearly related to several noble families, to the O'Connor family and to Sir Henry Parnell, the new Secretary at war, by all of whom this deplorable event will occasion the deepest regret.

INDEPENDENT (LAUNCESTON, TAS: 1831 - 1835),
SATURDAY 17 SEPTEMBER 1831, PAGE 2

THOMAS AND MR. PARKER.

The bodies of these unfortunate gentlemen were brought up to Launceston from George Town on Wednesday last, having been found—by means of a partly civilized Aboriginal woman, who persuaded a woman of the tribe, who was taken prisoner by Captain Thomas's servants, to conduct them to the spot where they had killed them—two days previously. The next morning, the bodies were removed from the boat to the Commercial Tavern and a Coroner's Inquest was instantly convened by Mr. Lyttleton, at the Police Office. The Jury (which was highly respectable, being composed of— Captain Ritchie, foreman, Captain Kyle, Dr. Westbrook, Mr. Gunn,

Mr. Dowling, Mr. Cameron, Mr. Robson, Mr. Sherwin, Mr. Beveridge, Mr. A. Wales, Mr. Robertson and Mr. Wilson) having been sworn, proceeded to view the bodies and upon their return took the following evidence:

— George Warren, sworn. Started, from George Town on Sunday last, by order of Mr. Clark, in search of Captain Thomas and Mr. Parker; got to Port Sorell on Monday morning the 12th Instant, when I saw Dr. Smith and Ensign Dunbar; two women offered to take us (that is, Alexander M'Kay and me) to the bodies; they took us into the bush about 2 miles, when they stopped and cried and would , not go any farther, but pointed to the place where the bodies were to be found; we went and found the body of Mr. Parker, on his back, the head towards the root of a tree; he had on no hat, handkerchief, coat, or waistcoat; saw blood under the head; saw 10 spear wounds in his body; I found a spear at about 10 yards distant from the body then; asked the women to show us where the other body was on my way, I found the, tail of a coat ; found Captain Thomas's body about 100 yards off, among some long grass ; saw some wounds about the body. and a black stake under the head; there were 12 wounds by spears—3 in-the right thigh, 2 or three in the right side, 1 in the back, &c.; the head was not bruised so much as Mr Parker's, but a quantity of blood, was under him; from the appearance of the bodies, thought they had been dead a fortnight ; part of the neck of Captain Thomas was destroyed by vermin; some notes were lying about him (one. produced); we left the bodies and returned with the women to Dr. Smith, at Port Sorell; on the way the women appeared sulky.

Dr. Smith then accompanied us to the bodies, together with several others; this time, the women thought the soldiers had come to kill them; one of the women said, (through the other who interpreted,) that Captain. Thomas and Mr. Parker came to one of their tribes—that one of the black men took a gun which the stout man, meaning Mr. Parker, had under his arm and ran away it—-that one of her own tribe speared Mr. Parker in the back —that Captain Thomas then ran away, but was overtaken and knocked down; the bodies were removed to George Town ; the women told us Turm assisted in

*spearing them; Turm is now in Gaol at George Town; This woman exactly
described the position the bodies lay in before reaching the place [here
the skirt of a coat was found and certified as being to part of that worn
by Captain Thomas.] Thomas Carter, sworn. Assigned servant to Captain
Thomas; I was at Port Sorell on the 31st ult.; I was at Port Sorell with
Captain Thomas and Mr. Parker; I was in charge of the boat with three
others of the crew; before*

*Captain Thomas came down two natives came into our tent we were eating
some damper ; they called out for Breadlie" ; we told them to come in ; they
did come in ; we gave them some damper and some cheese; at this period,
or within a quarter of an hour, Captain Thomas and Mr. Parker arrived
on horseback and, then Captain Thomas said, have you seen the natives? I
replied, I have two in the tent; he then got off his horse; he asked the blacks
if there were any more; when they held up all their fingers and said " good
many more' Captain Thomas asked them to take him to them, which, they
readily agreed to do; Mr Parker then advised him not to go by himself;
Captain Thomas said " I will go myself" Mr. Parker, however, fearful of
trusting Captain Thomas amongst the natives by himself, walked behind at
some little distance, with a double-barrelled gun under his arm; this is all.*

*I saw of Captain; after being absent two days and one nighty returned, but
without success. Thomas or Mr. Parker;—about two hours after, the two
native men who went with the Captain, returned with three others besides—
two women and a man; M'Kay shook hands with them;, in a few minutes we
saw another woman, who we enticed to us and gave her some bread; before
we left, (which was about two hours) we cooed, but were not answered ;
after having started, taking with us the horses belonging to Captain Thomas
and Mr. Parker, about 300 yards homewards, another native came up,
whom we enticed, but he ran away before we reached Northtown Beach,
where Captain Thomas resided; we then asked, what had become of the
white men? they said they had " tabbity," meaning ran away; we did not ask*

them before we started; the next morning Mrs. Parker sent four men out in search of Captain Thomas and Mr. Parker; after being absent two days and one nighty returned, but without success.

Dr. Smith, sworn. On the. return to George Town of Chief Constable Freestone and Mr. Haims, (who had been in search of the bodies of Captain Thomas ;and Mr. Parker) on Thursday last, I was requested to see Mrs. Parker, who was very ill: I left George Town on Friday last, with Ensign Dunbar and arrived at Port Sorell about 2 o'clock, where we found Mr. J . Thomas, jun. and Captain on the beach, who had not found the bodies, but were waiting for a man (M'Kay) and a partly civilized native woman; next morning they arrived, when we proceeded to Port Sorell in search of the bodies, but did not succeed in finding them: we then returned to Northtown Beach, with the exception of M'Kay and the native woman who were sent on to George town for one of the native women, who had been taken there. He returned with the two women and upon his firing a gun, we sent a boat over for them: McKay said one of the women had told them where the bodies were to be found and then went with Warren and the two native women by my order ; they returned in about an hour and said they had seen the bodies; I then proceeded with them and a man of the name of Jones, to look at the bodies, about a mile up from the Creek, in the direction of the Northtown Beach) but to the left of the road : this was about 4 miles from Northtown Beach: the women conducted me straight to a body which I recognized as that of Mr. Parker: I called one of the constables to remove the dress, so as to enable me to examine the body :

I found on his breast, five or six spear wounds, on the left side, near the heart: every wound would have caused death.— I found six open wounds on the back and an extensive contusion on the side of the head : we then proceeded with the women eastward about 50 or 60 yards and found another body, lying dead, which I recognized to be that of Captain Thomas upon removing his dress, I found one wound very near the heart and three others on the right side, one of which had bled profusely : one wound by-the clavicle : I then had the body turned and found five spear wounds on the back: the upper part of the throat was eaten by crows or native Cats: on the following morning the bodies were conveyed by my orders to George Town.

The evidence of the native women was then called for and in consequence of their not having yet arrived from George Town, the inquiry was adjourned to 11 o'clock on Saturday, ("this day,) when it was again adjourned to Monday, in consequence of the Meeting of the Quarter Sessions for the purpose of granting Licenses to the Publicans. The murdered bodies of the much lamented Captain THOMAS and M. PARKER were buried yesterday morning followed to the grave by a numerous concourse, comprising nearly the whole of the public officers, civil and military and a great number of the respectable inhabitants of Launceston. Such an unequivocal mark of the public sympathy on this truly melancholy occasion, cannot but be highly gratifying to the friends and relatives of the unfortunate deceased gentlemen.

COLONIAL TIMES (HOBART, TAS: 1828 - 1857),
WEDNESDAY 14 SEPTEMBER 1831, PAGE 3

TO THE EDITOR OF THE COLONIAL TIMES.

MY DEAR FRIEND, - The Blacks have again commenced their murderous operations. My family have become so alarmed and so constantly upbraid me with allowing them to remain in such a perilous situation, that should any calamity occur and that I myself should escape slaughter, I should never forgive myself, or again hold up my head. My poor wife is in such a state from constant apprehension for the safety of our little innocents, that I certainly shall decamp as soon as possible.

Pray look out for a cheap lodging for us. As my land is so near, indeed, close to -------'s run, I have no doubt of being able to drive a bargain with him ; and, as you know, I was once extensively concerned in the spirit trade at home, perhaps an opening may be found to begin the business again. At all events, here I have come to the determination of not remaining.

After eight years of hard struggling in the wild bush, all my anticipations of independence in old age and leaving a comfortable subsistence for my family, are at an end - all my golden dreams have vanished.

You will perhaps reply - "Do not be dis-heartened. The Government is most anxious in its solicitude to conciliate these Aborigines.

Do you not know that a Black Committee have been sitting for the last two years and that they have Black Robinson dressed in a full suit of black and a flaxen bob wig employed as an emissary? All will yet be well." " Yes," I reply, "but in the meantime fancy our situation. The moment I get up, instead of going about the farm looking after the men, the sheep, the cattle, &c and other various occupations, my daily business is to see that the muskets are primed and loaded and then I repair to my post of perpetual sentry, with the exception of meal times, when the cook chap mounts guard in my place. My poor wife is so frightened that she will not al-low me to stir for an instant. I pray to be al-lowed to take up a book. No; the Blacks may be in before I could take to the muskets."

So here I am, with a family to provide for, bills to pay, numerous engagements to make good, converted into a common sentinel. In the meantime everything is in disorder. The men have become masters and all around wears the aspect of discomfort and dismay. Thus circumstanced, without any hope of relief, (all the soldiers who afforded us such ample protection during the winter, when there was no occasion for them, having been marched off to Launceston, there to embark for India.)

We have, after many heart-rending struggles, determined on flying from an inglorious enemy and, "as we cannot bear the ills we have, must fly to others that we know not of."

I remain, my dear friend, your's,
JACK DISMAL

From Under the Tiers, Sept. 8, 1831.

COLONIAL TIMES (HOBART, TAS: 1828 - 1857),
WEDNESDAY 14 SEPTEMBER 1831, PAGE 3

THE ABORIGINES.

We lament to have, to announce another outrage committed by these savages. A few days ago a number of them visited Mr. Hobbs' farm at the Blue Hills and shocking to relate barbarously killed two men and a woman in the employ of that Gentleman.

I know this report on a public meeting held in Hobart Town is atrociously long and I did my best to cut it down and even considered leaving it out altogether but I in the end I believed it is worth reading because much of the discussion is well considered and thoughtful. Clearly many of the 'gentlemen' present are trying to deal with the moral and practical conflicts which they were faced with during this period. It also offers a refreshing change from the, at times, hysterical demands by some writers, or the over-dramatization of situations white settlers were dealing with.

TASMANIAN (HOBART TOWN, TAS: 1827 - 1839),
FRIDAY 24 SEPTEMBER 1830, PAGE 5

PUBLIC MEETING. 1

Our readers are aware that an advertisement appeared in our last, which was repeated by printed hand-bills affixed all over the town, calling a Meeting of the Inhabitants for the purpose of taking into consideration the necessity of forming a Civil Town Guard, sufficiently strong to take all the duty usually performed by the military, whereby to place at the disposal of the Government, the soldiers which otherwise must be left in Hobart town for that purpose. This meeting took place on Wednesday in the Court of Requests' Room. At about 2 o'clock, the inhabitants began to assemble and soon after, that large room was completely filled [Some processes and opening of meeting deleted here]

Mr. Kemp then stood forward and opened the immediate business of the day, by moving the first Resolution. He introduced it by remarking upon the necessity which existed, in consequence of the atrocities which had been committed by the Blacks in the interior, for the inhabitants to stand forward in support of the Government; and in order to enable the Military force sent into the interior upon the great object now to be undertaken, to be as numerous and as efficient as possible, it was desirable that the Town duty should be taken by the Inhabitants.

Mr. Kemp commented at some length upon the aggressions committed by the blacks, which he attributed, in a great degree, to some officers of his own Reg., (the late 102d) who had, as he considered, most improperly fired a 4-pounder upon a body of them, which having done much mischief, they had since borne that attack in mind and had retaliated upon the white people whenever opportunity offered. Mr Kemp referred to the zeal of the inhabitants, which he was satisfied would actuate them upon the present occasion and he had no doubt that a body of volunteers would be formed, quite equal lo the object in view. Mr. Kemp was received with much applause, evincing as he did, by taking the leading part on this occasion, that the present measure of the Government had his entire support. Mr. Gellibrand—I have been requested to second this motion, which I will do accordingly ; but I confess I feel some difficulty on the subject, which I feel it due to myself and to the occasion, to express plainly and without reserve.

It has been stated by Mr Kemp, that we have been aggressors in the present unhappy state of hostility which prevails between the white people and the black Aborigines. This reflection cannot but give rise to the most painful feelings. How dreadful is it to contemplate, that we are about to enter upon a war of extermination, for such I apprehend is the declared object of the present operations and that in its progress, we shall be compelled to destroy the innocent with the guilty. All are to suffer equally, the poor black who may never have been present at any single hostile aggression may and probably will, be equally a victim with the most guilty.

When a party of the military, or of the civil force, aiding in the operations against this unhappy race, falls in with them, they will, of course, run away and no doubt the black will run much faster than the white can follow him. Is it intended that the pursuer shall, when he finds he cannot overtake the fugitive, level his piece at him and take his life! If this is to be, it behoves us seriously to consider what it is which we are about to undertake and how far we may not be placing ourselves in a situation of considerable peril, by acting as I have stated. In what situation are we at present, as respects the Government Orders and Proclamations? (Mr. Gellibrand here referred to the three last published orders, which he commented upon at considerable length and described as being utterly incompatible with each other.) Mr. Gellibrand continued.

It is my intention, if the Supreme Court adjourns, so that I am enabled to get away to join the parties proceeding to the interior, I shall certainly do my utmost to forward the great object in view; but I think it right to state, that by no inducement whatever shall I ever take away the life of a fellow creature, unless that it is either in repelling aggression or in a struggle. I shall do my utmost to capture these people, to the utmost of my ability. But I repeat, I never will shed their blood, if I cannot succeed in taking them, unless under the circumstances I have stated. Indeed I consider that a great legal question arises upon this subject. I do not wish to give my opinion upon this point, there being so many others who are perhaps more competent so to do. But I should be strongly disposed to think, that before the proposed operations are commenced, some change in the existing law should be effected.

I do not understand how it is possible, under the law as it now stands, for any man who has not committed a felony, to be killed, if he cannot be captured. I admit, that if any of the blacks who have committed the dreadful atrocities, which no man laments more than myself, could be identified and were pursued and could not be captured, that it might then be justifiable to shoot them. But I doubt very much, whether, if, unless such identity was ascertained, that any individual who should shed the blood of one of these unhappy people, would not, in the present state of the law, be guilty of murder. It is therefore, I think, of considerable importance, that the law upon this point, should be distinctly understood; because it would be very disagreeable for any of us, in the course of the proposed operations, to be led into the commission of acts, to answer for which, we maybe brought before the Criminal Court and if so, I have little doubt that the Judge would find it his duty to tell the Jury that such acts were murder.

With this view of the subject, I cannot but consider, that until the state of the law, well understood, we are acting at least with precipitation. I speak now, solely and entirely in reference to that part of the resolution which refers to our proceeding to join the parties in the interior. In respect to the formation of the Town Guard, I have no hesitation whatever in seconding the present Resolution and in strongly recommending it to the adoption of the meeting. (This is a mere outline of Mr. Gellibrand's speech, which our limits compel us to abridge into the shortest possible compass, as also indeed, all the other speeches which were delivered in the course of the day.)

Mr. Stephen—I rise to address you. Sir, a very few words in reply to what has fallen from Mr. Gellibrand, on the subject of shooting the miserable people whose atrocities have now reached a point, which renders some strong measures absolutely necessary to the very safety of the Colony. I cannot perceive what possible connection there is between whatever measures the Government may have in contemplation to adopt, for the purpose of repelling the aggression of the blacks, with the object of the present meeting, which is solely to take into consideration the formation of a Town Guard, in order to enable the Government to send away disposable soldiers into the interior.

No doubt it is highly desirable, that every person who can, by any possibility, proceed to join the force in the interior, should do so, if his affairs or concerns can by any means permit him, but I apprehend the present object is to call into operation the services of all those who are unable to leave the town. I cannot therefore perceive, what the measures proposed by the Government, have to do with the object which has brought us together to-day. I beg that it may be clearly understood, that in whatever falls from me on the occasion, I speak without any reference whatever to my capacity as a public officer. Indeed my duties as such, are of a description so wholly different to the present purpose, that it is impossible that I should do so.

I address myself to the meeting entirely in my capacity of a private individual, having however a considerable stake in this town, with a large family and a number of servants. But even as a public officer, I should consider that I am fully entitled to express my sentiments truly and altogether uninfluenced as they are by any persons or by any consideration whatever, than those strictly connected with the object of the meeting. I find then, by the Government order of the 9th inst., that an important simultaneous operation is intended, upon as large a scale as the resources of the Colony will permit. What the nature of that operation is, I declare I am in as perfect ignorance as any other gentleman present. But I consider the formation of a Town Guard highly necessary and to afford every possible facility to the carrying that operation into effect, be it what it may. I am aware that it cannot be effective unless it receives the cordial co-operation of the great body of the in-habitants. I hope and believe, there are many of them who can go and will go, to join the force in the interior. But there are many others who cannot do so; who cannot leave their homes and their families and all such I trust, will come forward and join the Town Guard. I cannot see how any person can object to the resolution, even if he is in the same ignorance with myself, of the nature of the plans of the Government. The Chairman, Mr. Hone, then read the first resolution, which was carried unanimously.

It was as follows:— Moved by Mr. Kemp ; Seconded by Mr. Gelliibrand. I.—That, inasmuch as no measures for repressing future aggressions on the part of the Aboriginal Natives, can reasonably be expected to attain complete success without the most zealous and extensive co-operation of all classes of the community, it is, at this juncture, peculiarly the duty of every man cheerfully to contribute to the common cause, every assistance within his power. Mr. Hone.— I have been taken somewhat by surprize in being requested to move the second resolution. It appears to me, that even in addition to the military, if all the civil force was to be sent into the interior, there are enough around me able and willing to preserve the peace of this town. Mr. Gellibrand spoke of the criminality of shedding the blood of the Aborigines, with that eloquence by which he is on all occasions distinguished. But surely he forgets, when he speaks of the indiscriminate slaughter of the blacks, how indiscriminate has been their slaughter of the whites. Surely he cannot have forgotten that the grass has hardly yet grown over the graves of the two children who were recently so barbarously murdered.

But there is another object which I consider of very great importance. It is generally admitted, that our wool is the staple commodity of the Island. I have heard, that so alarmed are the shepherds in the interior, in consequence of the dreadful atrocities which have been committed, that they peremptorily refuse to go out with the flocks of sheep, which are thereby left to wander and stray away. I agree fully with Mr. Stephen, that the plans of the Government have nothing whatever to do with the object of the present meeting and that Mr. Gellibrand's observations, however eloquently urged, are quite irrelevant thereto. I am always opposed to appeals to the passions in the way of argument. On the present occasion, that appeal has been most powerfully made, but entirely on one side, in favour of the blacks against the whites. If therefore, extermination is necessary, horrible as is the alternative, I do not see that other means of protection exist. I have therefore great confidence in moving this resolution and I trust that Mr Gellibrand's eloquent address may fail of its intended effect.

Mr. Collicott seconded the resolution, which was carried unanimously. It was as follows:— Moved by Mr. Hone; Seconded by Collicott.

II. —That, so far as respects the Inhabitants of Hobart-town, such assistance may, in the opinion of this meeting, be advantageously afforded, either by personal service in the country, or by performing a portion of the ordinary duties of the military in the town; by which last mentioned means a most valuable accession to the number of troops might, as it appears to the meeting, be for several weeks placed at the disposal of the Government, for duty in the interior Dr. Turnbull—I beg leave to move the 3rd resolution. In respect to what fell from Mr. Gellibrand, I consider that his views are at variance with all established rules. What is the invariable custom in Parliament? If any particular expedition is brought under consideration, the object of it is alone discussed and the plans of operation invariably left to the Executive. So also here. It is obvious, that a full explanation of the plan of the Government would tend essentially to cripple their operation. It has been said by Mr. Kemp, that to us is owing this unhappy state of warfare. But that does not alter the existing state of things. The war must be a war of extermination. It is so already; and a movement upon a large scale as at present pro poses, is infinitely preferable to a lingering warfare, in the course of which, the blacks are cut off little by little, but still it is a war of extermination.

The present plan will strike them with dismay. They will be either taken, or destroyed, or driven into some of the recesses in the interior. The present warfare of the stock-keepers is infinitely more one of extermination, than the present one will be. It is the war to the knife, which is always a war of extermination; the simultaneous movement will excite terror, not rage. Two interests are concerned, the black and the white and the simultaneous attack, will be the means of saving, not shedding blood. The blacks will be less injured, the whites more secured. Another argument has been adduced, in reference to legal points.

With these I consider we have nothing whatever to do, nor can I conceive that Mr. Gellibrand's observations are at all relevant to the question before us. I now beg leave to move the 3rd resolution. Mr. Hewitt.—I beg leave to second the motion of Dr. Turnbull. For myself as an inhabitant, I will do all that I can upon the present occasion and as to the plans of Government, I think we have no business to interfere with them. I propose however, to amend the resolution, by changing the time for the inhabitants taking the Town Guard from the 7th to the 2nd October, in order to allow time for the military to proceed to the interior, previous to the day fixed for commencing the operations. [Some discussion commence in relation to the practical matters related to the establishment of the Civil Town Guard]

I am compelled to say this, lest it should be supposed that I speak those of others, or that there is any wish or opinion elsewhere, which I give utterance to. I beg that this may be distinctly understood, I speak my own private individual sentiments, without any reference whatever to those held in any other quarter. I take this opportunity of noticing Mr. Gellibrand's observations as to taking the lives of the blacks. I agree with Mr. Hone, that their slaughter of the whites has been as indiscriminate as any which can be the result of the proposed operations and I say, that as they have urged such a war upon the settlers, you are bound to put them down. But there is another consideration, which weighs strongly with me. I say that you are bound to so do, in reference to the class of individuals, who having been involuntarily sent here, are compelled to be in the most advanced position, where they are exposed to the hourly loss of their lives. I say, Sir, (Mr. Stephen here spoke with much animation,) that you are bound upon every principle of justice and humanity, to protect this particular class of individuals; and if you cannot do so without extermination, then I say boldly and broadly, exterminate!

I trust I have within me as much humanity as any man who hears me, but I declare openly, that if I was engaged in the pursuit of the blacks and that I could not capture them, which I would endeavour to do by every means in my power, I would fire upon them, I again and again say, I know not whether this is the opinion of others. I expose myself I am aware thereby, to much attack upon the ground of humanity, but I am satisfied that we are bound to afford all possible protection to those who are exposed to the atrocities of the blacks and therefore I am of opinion, capture them if you can, but if you cannot, destroy them.

Mr. Thompson.—I am to second this resolution. If there is an imperative necessity to destroy the Blacks, then, I say, we are bound to use the means which providence has placed in our hands for that purpose. Mr. Gellibrand.—Before this question is put, I beg leave to say a few words in reply to the attacks which have been made upon me in my front and upon my right and upon my left. The remarks of Dr. Turnbull are all very well where they are applicable. But they are anything but so here. His reference to Parliament and to the operations of civilized regularly military warfare, are so opposed to the state of things to which I refer and which I look forward to as about to be carried into operation, are so totally different to the case which Dr. Turnbull has imagined, that it is really utterly unnecessary to notice his objection. If the question had been limited solely to the formation of a town guard, then I should not have troubled you with one word upon the subject. But it is mixed up with a proposition as to our proceeding to the Interior.

I have already stated that it is my intention to proceed thither if any public duties will enable me so to do; and I have not heard one syllable from any of those who have spoken in answer to the important questions I asked, I consider that the extermination which is spoken of involves a most important question. Either it is legal or it is not so. I am of opinion that, as the law now stands, any man who may kill one of these Blacks would place himself in a very dangerous situation. I well remember the time when the Gentleman who now presides filled that high office against the power of the functions of which no man can stand. At that period a very strong feeling existed in respect to the atrocities which had been committed upon the blacks; and I take upon myself to assert, without fear of contradiction, that if any man who had killed a black native had been brought here under such a charge, that the Attorney-General would have brought him before the Chief Justice for murder and that the Judge would have directed the Jury to find him guilty. I assert, then, that the law being now exactly as it was then, the greatest consideration is necessary, that we may not place ourselves in a situation of very great peril in the furtherance of the object before us. Mr. Hone has complained of my appeal to the passions and yet he himself fell into the same error, if such it is.

Can there be a greater one than his reference to the green graves of the murdered children! But I wish to set him right upon that point. (Mr. Gellibrand here went into a full detail of that unfortunate event, at the place where it occurred he had been present but a day previously and with the whole circumstances of which he was fully acquainted and which he described to have arisen entirely in retaliation for atrocities of the most horrible some committed upon the blacks by the stock keepers.) Under these circumstances (continued Mr. Gellibrand) this dreadful event took place. But how does it apply to my question as to the state of the law, to which I have referred in the anxious desire that it may undergo that consideration which I consider necessary, to place those who may proceed into the interior to the assistance of the Government, from being placed at the bar of the Criminal Court upon their return.

To this I have not received one word of answer. I know there are those present whose legal opinion may be much better than mine; but I have only asked for information and in doing so I do not consider that the slightest reply has been made to me. Mr. Hone explained. Mr. Stephen.—In respect to the legal question which Mr. Gellibrand has introduced, I can only say that I have not replied to it, because I do not consider It expedient so to do. It is a mere question as to the law and if I was to enter upon it, the meeting would not understand me. But because I do not reply, I beg to be understood not to assent to Mr. Gellibrand's statements,— neither to dissent from them. I forbear to reply to them altogether, because I consider them totally inapplicable the subject before us. At the same time I have no hesitation in stating that I have been called upon for my legal opinion upon the subject and having given it, I do not consider it either fitting or expedient to discuss the matter here.

I admit that the atrocities of the whites against the blacks, particularly in the instance which Mr. Gellibrand described to me this morning, to be dreadful beyond belief: and if I could discover the monsters by whom they had been perpetrated, I should only wish that they had each ten lives, to expiate with them the horrible crimes they had committed. But the question now is as to the formation of a Town Guard and I forbear to reply to Mr Gellibrand's legal questions not only for the reasons I have stated, but also because I do not consider that they have anything whatever to do with the subject under discussion. Dr. Turnbull.—-I differ entirely with the view. Mr. Gellibrand has taken upon the subject of extermination. That measure has been adorned in the Sister Colony with the greatest success The Natives having committed great atrocities, the Government sent out a military force against them, by whom they were so destroyed that all inhabitants of Sydney have since boasted of the tranquillity which has resulted therein. Hav-ing therefore the example of New South Wales before us, I consider that the legal questions of Mr. Gellibrand are totally irrelevant.:— IV.— That, in the opinion of this meeting, the contemplated force will more readily and advantageously be raised and kept together in an efficient stale, by such a plan as, (one officer or person in charge, being selected for each guard,) shall enable every individual, so far as may be practicable, to select his own particular guard and the particular officer or person in charge, under whom he would prefer to enrol himself. Mr. Sorell.—In moving the 5th resolution I have only to observe, that its object does not require any remarks. It is merely for the appointment of a Committee to carry into effect the proposed arrangements. Mr. Hackett.—The duty of seconding this resolution having been thrown upon me, I beg leave to offer a few remarks, being of opinion that in a meeting of this description every man is at liberty to declare his sentiments. The proceedings of this day will have a material influence on the public opinion. Previous to the adoption of the measures of extermination which have been spoken of, I am desirous of being informed whether everything possible has been done in way of conciliation, I ask, what attempts have been made to effect so desirable a purpose?

Not one! It is a national disgrace to us that this has been omitted. I believe I may venture to assert that there are not 6 persons in the whole Colony who are able to communicate with the blacks in their own language. Had we been a Colony of Frenchmen how different a policy would have been adopted. This, I think, is a matter deserving the most serious consideration. Dr. Ross.—I differ with Mr. Hackett on this subject. I think, looking at the evidence of history, that the French, Spanish and Portuguese Colonists have treated the Aborigines in all the countries where they have settled very differently to what Mr. Hackett seems to be aware of. I was a member of a Corps of Volunteers in one of the West India Islands some years ago, raised, for purposes similar to the present and the result was most satisfactory. We are blind to the situation of the settlers in the interior, which demand the strongest measures of protection. So necessary do I consider it that every individual of this town should proceed to the interior to aid in the great operation now about to take place, that I would have every man, free, ticket-of-leave, or assigned servant dispatched immediately for that purpose. No man should be permitted to say that his business prevents him, or that his affairs render his presence here necessary.

Every ticket of leave man who should hesitate should be put into the gaol gang. I say again, that the whole of the inhabitants of this town and all their servants should proceed at once to the interior and that no excuses should be accepted of— Mr. Murray —Printers excepted of course. (A general laugh) Dr. Ross.—Oh! certainly,

Printers excepted. But if would even go myself if the arduous duties of printing the Gazette did not require my presence and if my subscribers would consent to let their subscriptions go on in the meantime. Mr Murray—I would waive the subscriptions if the business could be carried on. Dr Ross.—I cannot agree to that. The exigency is most serious and requires the co-operation of every individual. Why, to such an extent have the aggressions of the Blacks been carried that if they are not prevented they will come and drive us from this very Court-room and compel u to take refuge in the ships. The present situation of things is extremely alarming and I trust the strongest measures will he adopted, without any reference to the legal question which Mr Gellibrand has raised, with which I consider we have nothing whatever to do.

Mr. Murray —I differ entirely with Dr. Ross on the subject of alarm he feels as to the Natives driving us from this room to the shipping. No doubt that they are enabled to commit many atrocities most frequency by the exercise of that cunning by which all savages are distinguished; but to talk of 6 dozen of miserable creatures and never was a larger body seen assembled than 72, driving us from this room is of course a joke. Mr. Murray then requested to be informed, whether there was any resolution in the series which were to be proposed as to the distribution of the different posts or guards. Mr. Stephen replied that he did not perceive any resolution to that effect, indeed that the one now under consideration was the last which appeared to be prepared. Mr. Murray —I hold in my hand,

Sir, a paper signed by 24 individuals, one of whom I am myself, in which we beg to tender our services to the Government to undertake the duty of the Battery. It is the advanced post and one of considerable responsibility, all which we are ready and willing to undertake and for an unlimited period, so long as our services shall be considered necessary. The Gentlemen of whom I am the humble organ, desirous to shew how zealously they are disposed to support the Government on the present occasion, will cheerfully undertake this duty; and they will perform it, they trust, with accuracy and assiduity. They have prepared their offer of service and signed it. I hold it in my hand and I beg leave now to move that it be received and attached to the proceedings of the day. [The meeting continues with discussion on procedural matters]

One of my great pleasures in life is meeting people whose uniqueness and quirks of nature compel me to pen their stories and delight my readers. At this time Lutruwita appeared to have amongst is meagre population a plenitude of such characters. Perhaps for those who chose to partake in such an adventure were by their very nature individualistic, determined and often just a little eccentric. Others whose choice to come to the island was determined by forces beyond their control also needed considerable fortitude and ingenuity to survive and succeed as many managed to do.

James Erskine Calder was one such person whom I met on several occasions. Appointed as assistant surveyor to the Colony James' dedication and application to his work became legendary even in his own time. Just shy of two score when he stepped ashore in VDL both his physical prowess and sharp intellect were forces to be reckoned with. Clearly at odds with establishment views on the treatment of Aborigines he was strong enough in himself and social standing to express his views openly and with thoughtful vigour. Which is why I have included this letter written soon after his arrival and would, I imagine, have been received with some degree of scepticism. His sketches of Pakana people are also displayed within these pages.

LAUNCESTON ADVERTISER (TAS. : 1829 - 1846),
MONDAY 26 SEPTEMBER 1831, PAGE 299

*[From a Correspondent. James Erskine Calder]

THE ABORIGINES.

The verdict, of the Coroner's Jury has attributed the deaths of the late Captain Thomas and Mr. Parker to the male natives, Wowwee, Maccamee, and Callimarowie who are now in custody, and to the rest of their tribe. The evidence adduced before the coroner is so conclusive, on this head, that there can be no doubt of those two gentlemen, whose loss we deplore, having been killed by these benighted and treacherous people. My feelings prompt me to wish the extermination of the blacks ; but on a mature reflection on the subject some solemn questions present themselves.

Are these unhappy creatures the subjects of our king, in a state of rebellion? or are they an injured people, whom we have invaded and with whom we are at war? Are they within the reach of our laws ; or are they to be judged by the law of nations ? Are they to be viewed in the light of murderers, or as prisoners of war ? Have they been guilty of any crime under the laws of nations which is punishable by death, or have they only been carrying on a war in their way? Are they British subjects at all, or a foreign enemy who has never yet been subdued, and which resists our usurped authority and dominion? Have we a right to try them for murder in our own way ? Would not such a trial be a solemn mockery ; seeing that the criminals, if such they can be called, do not understand our language nor our customs, and cannot make any defence ? Ought we to avenge the death of our friends, by the death of these natives, or ought we to secure them, to prevent their doing further mischief, and to conciliate and civilise them, having them in our power ? By this time His Majesty's Attorney General is in possession of the evidence taken before the Coroner ; to him therefore I would seriously propound the above questions. Much as I am prejudiced against the savages, I cannot on principles of justified and humanity, refrain from coming forward on this occasion as their advocate, to plead in their behalf, that they are not amenable to our laws, as they are ignorant of them—that they are not murderers under the laws of nations, having killed the white men while following upon a war in their own way—that they are therefore only prisoners of war—that indeed they cannot be justly tried as they can make no defence, and ought not to be tried as murderers.

I also plead that the English Government have no right to look upon these men as criminals ; and that the utmost which can justly and conscientiously be done to them is to confine them as prisoners by the fortune de la guerre. The Aborigines were originally the rightful owners and possessors of the island—they were inoffensive, innocent, and happy. The British Colonists have taken their country from them by force ; they have persecuted them, wantonly sacrificed them, and taught them to hate the whites. The savages are ignorant of our laws ; they have never lived under the protection of them ; it is questionable if they even know what laws are, according to our acceptation of the term. They consider themselves, and justly so, ill-used. They seek to avenge the deaths of their relatives. We are at war with them ; they look upon us as enemies— as invaders—as their oppressors and persecutors— they resist our invasion. They have never been subdued, therefore are they not rebellious subjects, but an injured nation, defending in their own way, their rightful possessions, which have been torn from them by force. Let us not then act unworthily of the country whence we sprung. Who ever heard of a prisoner of war being put to death by the English for acts committed in the field of battle ? Shall we, an enlightened nation, descend so low as to imitate the barbarity of the Algerines and Turks, whom we consider so far behind us in civilization ? Surely not. Away with prejudice, away with all feelings but those of justice and humanity.

The three men are in our power, let us keep them so, but not have recourse to the only security of tyrants—the death of our enemies. These men merit our compassion, they have done nothing worthy of death by the civil law. What we call their crime is what in a white man we should call patriotism. Where is the man amongst ourselves who would not resist an invading enemy ; who would not avenge the murder of his parents, the ill-usage of his wife and daughters, and the spoliation of all his earthly goods, by a foreign enemy, if he had an opportunity ? He who would not do so, would be scouted, execrated, nay executed as a coward and a traitor ; while he who did would be immortalized as a patriot. Why then shall we deny the same feelings to the Blacks? How can we condemn as a crime in these savages what we should esteem as a virtue in ourselves ? Why punish a black man with death for doing that which a white man would be executed for not doing? Is there such an effect produced on the soul by wearing a black skin, that it converts into vices those acts and feelings which are virtuous when done or entertained under a white one? I think not.

The same God made both, the same God protects both, and the same God will judge both. I beseech the Authorities, and especially Lieutenant

Governor Arthur, by all that is humane, just, and honorable, not to stain the nation with the blood of these unhappy people by making them amenable to laws which they neither understand, nor are subject to ; for acts which in reality, according to our own laws, are those of the highest excellence and virtue, and which they, poor creatures, consider not to be crimes. Secure them, but spare their lives. They are in our power ; they cannot do any more mischief ; their death could answer no good end ; it would not operate as an example to the rest, nor would it check the atrocities of the savages. Rather would it create a more lively hatred towards us, and it would be an unnecessary and a barbarous MURDER !

Had they fallen before the fire-arms of our parties, in the bush, they would have fallen as enemies in the field of battle. But they are taken : the great object of the Government is attained ; and surely that Government which holds out humanity and conciliation as the rule by which those employed to capture the Aborigines should be governed, will never imbue the hands of the nation in the blood of three prisoners of war. I may probably stand alone in this advocacy and intercession for the lives of these men. Public feeling is much against them ; but in appealing to the Lieutenant Governor I appeal to a humane man, and trust my pleading will not be made in vain. In short I feel convinced that His Excellency will never sign the death-warrant of three prisoners of war, (for a murder committed in the field of battle, although by a treacherous stratagem,) after a trial in a language which they do not understand ; under laws of which they are ignorant, and to which they are neither subject, nor bound to pay obedience. If the Attorney General prosecutes, the law must take its course ; but even then the Chief Authority can, thank Heaven, SPARE THEIR LIVES. J.E. Sept. 22.

[We give insertion to the foregoing, although far exceeding the limits generally allowed to correspondents, believing that the writer really felt what he has so charitably penned in defence of the native prisoners — However, the Proclamation, of the year 1829 we think, negatives the charge of murder. It is most probable that they will be placed on Furneaux's Island.]

HOBART TOWN COURIER (TAS: 1827 - 1839),
SATURDAY 15 OCTOBER 1831, PAGE 2

The Blacks attacked Mr. Bilton's hut in the Blue hill marshes, on Sunday week, having it appeared previously watched the overseer and one of the men away. One man named Perry was left in the hut, who went out for a pail of water, taking his musket with him, which he laid down a few yards from him, whilst he dipped out the water. On turning round he saw several blacks, (one of them with the musket in his hand) apparently much pleased. The poor man ran towards the hut, which he fortunately reached in safety and seizing another musket, which luckily happened to be loaded he fired at them, when they made off being no doubt prevented from repeating their attack by the timely return of the overseer.

......

Mr. Robinson started this morning in prosecution of his mission of conciliation with the aborigines. His expectations of success with the Oyster bay and Big river tribes, which are said to have united, are most sanguine.-'Laun. Independ.

Mr. Batman has resigned his charge, the Sydney natives he had under his command, which is given to Mr. Anthony Cottrel, a gentleman admirably adapted to the undertaking. Campbell town is to be the central point of these operations. The natives, when caught, are to be placed upon an island in the immediate vicinity of the one at present occupied as a depot for the Aborigines, known by the name of Great Island, being about 50 miles in length,-Gun carriage island being too circumscribed to afford a livelihood for those placed thereon. Meanwhile, we understand, the greatest possible disposable force, civil as well as military, is to be distributed about the country for the protection of the settlers,

We are surprised to find that nothing has yet been done towards the protection of the numerous half-caste children in this island — sons and daughters of sealers and others. Numbers of these poor little beings are under the care of the most abandoned of our population and are allowed to remain in the haunts of vice and profligacy, which it is to be lamented abound, without the least exertion being made in their behalf as we hear by our Christian government, or Christian population.

We trust something will speedily be done towards removing such a stigma from us as a people; and rescuing this portion of our race, which of all others should excite our commiseration from the scenes of debauchery and vice which they witness; and in which, it is to be feared too many have become hardened and depraved If Government do not feel justified in appropriating a portion (and it would be a small portion) of the public funds to their relief, still surely there remains a sufficiency of means for the exercise of charity— and we trust we may soon have a proof that there is charitable motive sufficient in Tasmania to raise a PRIVATE fund for the government and education of the black native and half-caste children of Van Diemen's Land.

My blood ran cold when I read this. A matter which I had not faced, through cowardice and denial, was the question of whether I had left Lowana with child. I had no way of knowing since communication between us was impossible after we parted. I had left for Ceylon soon after and did not return to Lutruwita for several years during which time Lowana and many of her clan died in a massacre. But had she born a child? Had it survived the killing and become one of the numerous half caste children on this island? I tried to find out, but to no avail and the question and torment will remain with me forever.

I wondered occasionally what would have happened if we had stayed together. But how? I remember vividly the picture of Lowana free from encumbrances, sliding gracefully into the ocean and returning with the spoils of the sea; the sense of self and wisdom she held within her natural world. Could you imagine snaring such a spirit with heavy cloths, stripping away her name, denying her family and friends and living in a closed, oppressive civilized society with all its prejudices and conceits? On the other hand, consider how I would fare in her realm. I have never killed anything in my life. I can't use a weapon of any sort, nor do I have the dexterity to survive in nature. It's one thing to live with a community for a few months but quite another for life. Logically and rationally our lives were mutually exclusive even if our hearts were not.

COLONIAL TIMES (HOBART, TAS: 1828 - 1857),
WEDNESDAY 26 OCTOBER 1831, PAGE 3

TO THE EDITOR OF THE COLONIAL TIMES.

SIR, - As the Colonists at large look to your paper for the fair and candid publication of all accounts of the atrocities committed by the natives, fearless of official displeasure, I transmit you the following report made some of their re-appearance in this district, take verbatim from the mouth of the reporter.

About 2 o'clock on Thursday the 5th inst., the natives made their first appearance, at the premises of constable A. Reid and having dis-covered and taken away the arms which he had in the field with him, (being ploughing at the time) they then proceeded to and plundered the hut. Reid immediately went to inform district constable Amos, who made up a party of his sons and Mr. Watson Jun., who chanced to be at his house and lost no time in going in pursuit, at the same time taking the very necessary step of sending a man over to Capt. Watson, (at the head of Swan Port) to warn him of their appearance. The latter gentleman himself set off the same evening, to give the alarm to Mr. Lynes, (above Moulting Bay,) and who he expected would send up to the grant of Mr. Amos Jun., a few miles higher up, that night or early in the morning, to warn the people there. Had he done so, those men would have remained at home and could have defended themselves against any numbers, as that hut is purposely built for security and defence; but he sent no notice and they proceeded out as usual next morning.

On Friday forenoon, the pursuing party having traced the blacks all the way from Reid's hut to that of Amos Jun., found it also plundered of everything, including a considerable quantity of flour; and having been out all night, they then went down to Mr. Lynes, to report this robbery there.

About 2 p.m. young Lynes with two soldiers (stationed there) set off, as he said, to visit Amos's hut and see after the men; but after proceeding part of the way, returned without doing so. In the evening, however, the soldiers proposed going up themselves with a guide, when Mr. Lynes observed, they had better wait till morning, as probably the men had been killed and thrown into the river. However, the soldiers did go and happily found the men safe. On Saturday one of these men proceeded to report this robbery to the Police Magistrate at Waterloo Point and called on Mr. Lynes to ask why he had not warned them of the natives, as Capt. Watson had warned him. He replied he intended to do so, but somehow forgot it. On Sunday morning the same man attended upon Lieut. Aubin, the Magistrate, to give him particulars and carrying with him a message from Mr. Meredith, to state that there was no doubt the natives would proceed round to his fishery at the Schootens and applying for a party to be sent there before hand, as that situation afforded the most probable chance of capturing them and Mr. Meredith tendered one of his boats for their conveyance ; but Lieut. Aubin stated he could not send more force out, until some of those he had sent returned; these were understood to be two constables and four soldiers, besides the two at Lynes's; and none of these, the man stated to the Magistrate, would go round to the Schootens he knew.

> *Should anything further transpire before a conveyance for this offers,*
> *it shall be added by Your obedient servant,*
>
> *A SUBSCRIBER. Great Swan Port, Oct. 17, 1831.*
>
> *P.S. - Wednesday 19th Oct. - This morning a signal appointed by Mr.*
> *Meredith with his people at the fishery on the Schootens, was made, to*
> *notify the appearance of the natives there, as expected and information*
> *was sent of such fact to Lieut. Aubin, the Magistrate, at Waterloo Point,*
> *when strange to say, he had departed for Richmond. The Government boat*
> *was represented to be out of repair and three of the crew absent; and this*
> *at the time when the natives were actually known to be committing their*
> *atrocities in this district. However, our Military Magistrate's representative,*
> *the Sergeant in command, ordered a small party to be in readiness and they*
> *were sent off without loss of time, in the best way, the boat and remaining*
> *crew admitted. The natives are now at the place where they might all have*
> *been captured in Capt. Hibbert's time, had the Government proclamations*
> *been such as to have justified that officer in acting as he was inclined to do;*
> *and the whole district would now rise as one man and act cheerfully under*
> *proper authority and guidance.*

I am still to this day incredulous when I realise how fiercely independent the press had become in the colony and how strong was their determination to express views contrary to the government of the day and to their rival publications. It was a badge of honour to be contrary and stand up for your editorial rights and a tribute to Andrew Bent and others of similar persuasion had won the right to press freedom and to print without government censorship. People relished every opportunity to write freely and to challenge those with opposing views.

Below is an example of press freedom at its best; a fierce and fiery letter to the editor, savaging the editor of the *Tasmanian* over his views on the treatment of Aborigines.

What a letter! You can almost feel the sweat and his grip on the quill as he dips for ink and scribbles another line.

COLONIAL TIMES (HOBART, TAS: 1828 - 1857),
WEDNESDAY 2 NOVEMBER 1831, PAGE 3

TO THE EDITOR OF THE COLONIAL TIMES.

SIR, - The learned Editor of the Tasmanian, in a late number, has not only not out-Heroded Herod, but he has taken upon himself all the attributes of a sucking dove. Even the doctrines of our Blessed Saviour do not come up to his ideas of patience and kind forbearance. Good soul! Our Saviour says, "if a man slaps you on the right cheek, turn your left to him also." But, the humane Editor of the Tasmanian goes farther. He exclaims, "We have invaded the possessions of these peaceful happy Aborigines - no law, human or divine, allows it, therefore on no account retaliate ; submit to be butchered with a good grace - suffer their spears to run you through - much better is it to die, than have the sin of murder on your head, by shooting these unoffending creatures - these rightful possessors of the soil:" I reply, this looks very pretty upon paper. It is like Political Economy, "Immigration and other nice theories; but, will it stand the test of practice. When I call to mind, the flowery speeches made by the powerful orators at the Court-house about twelve months ago, on their "black" subject - when reflect

LINE OBSCURED.

part then taken by the learned Editors of the Tasmanian and the Courier and the beautiful classical illustration of "being shortly driven to our ships," if we did not annihilate these now poor simple creatures, I confess, I am in "amazement lost." It would now appear, ac- cording to the humane Editor of the Tasmanian, that we have invaded the right of others - that we never had rightful possession of the soil - that we are in an enemy's country and may and indeed ought to be butchered with impunity - that all is fair in war and that, in point of fact, we deserve nothing short of death, for thus invading the territories of others.

*Now, Mr. Editor, as I am no hero, but a peaceable tiller of the soil, I beg to state in my own justification, that I applied to the Colonial Office in London for permission to come out here, shewed the certificate from the two Members of Parliament of my county, (no rotten borough,) received a letter from the then Secretary of State for the Colonies, authorizing me to receive from His Excellency the Lieutenant Governor the number of acres of land in Van Diemen's Land that my capital entitled me to. Having thus obtained an order from the English Government to take possession of as much land as I could bring into cultivation, am I now to be told I am an invader? that I am not to be afforded any protection against the incursions of the Aborigines; and that I may either live or die as I best can? This, then, is the boasted end of Colonization and " Pauper Immigration." If this is a conquered Country and that we came out as Colonists on the faith of the British Government, surely every protection ought to be afforded to us. **If it is still the property of the Aborigines, how come it that the Government has taken upon itself the right of disposing of it, without having first made a treaty with the rightful owners?***

However, here we are and the next question to be put, is, are we to abandon our possessions or not? The only satisfaction we poor settlers have, is, that the usurers (as we learn by the Tasmanian) have nearly all the land of the Colony mortgaged, so much so, that scarcely any " maiden" can be had as security; and therefore we shall leave them to fight it out with the Blacks as they think proper.

I am, Sir, your obedient servant,

BLANCO.

Whatever else we have been left with, this is a rich and extraordinary legacy of the most fundamental tenant of democracy: freedom of speech, gained in a fledgling British penal colony thousands of miles from home.

LAUNCESTON ADVERTISER (TAS: 1829 - 1846),
WEDNESDAY 30 NOVEMBER 1831, PAGE 37

It is with great pleasure we report the capture of ten more of the hostile natives, 8 men and 2 women, by Surridge and party consisting of 2 friendly native women and 5 whites. After following this tribe for some days, says our informant, they lost all trace of them and gave up the chase. A day or two after, however, when strolling down the bank of Forester's River, they again observed the fires of the natives on a hill a very short distance to their right. The women were sent up by Surridge and they succeeded at once enticing down 4 of the ten natives of which the party consisted.

The remaining six soon after followed them. Surridge succeeded in getting the party into the boat, in, two divisions and landing them all safe on Waterhouse Island. M'Kay has again left the town with his 2 native women as guides, in pursuit of, the blacks. We are glad to hear that the Lieutenant-Governor has signified his intention to reward this man handsomely.

His free pardon having passed His Excellency's approbation, previous to the capture of the four natives near Circular Head, His Excellency will decide in Council as to the extent of reward which shall be given him, on account of that service. We hope it maybe liberal: men in M'Kay's situation will be found to have the greatest share of perseverance of any men that can be employed; and it is to such we must look if we would have the scheme of taking the natives alive succeed.

HOBART TOWN COURIER (TAS: 1827 - 1839),
SATURDAY 10 DECEMBER 1831, PAGE 2

As predicted in the valuable information we were enabled to lay before our readers in our last, the blacks have continued, in their accustomed route, their course to the westward ,and it is a matter of infinite satisfaction us that in consequence of the inhabitants being thus put upon their guard no lives have been lost. They have gone indeed by the exact line of road pointed out, viz. through Bothertom's Marsh -Bettsholme where they murdered a man last year and near which they sometimes before murdered two women and a girl - Springhill bottom, where they murdered Hooper - Brady's Sugarloaf, where they murdered the servant of Jones, the lime burner and near the place where they formerly murdered Matthew Osborne.

In Bothertom's Marsh, where they were on Sunday, they made two attacks simultaneously four of them attacked Mr. Story's hut, while 6 others attacked Bothertom's old hut, about a quarter of a mile distant. At the former place they surprised the cook, named Buckley, while he was feeding his master's pigs and struck him with a spear in the back of the head, which fortunately took a slanting direction just behind the ear and went though the flesh but did not injure the bone. He is since pronounced out of danger. They were near the Jordan Big Lagoon on Thursday.

A small party of seven blacks have been prowling about the Greenponds for some time, chiefly between the Quoin and Jerusalem They were seen on Monday at Urquhart's farm, belonging to Mr. Joseph Johnson between, Stockman's farm and Logan's Marshes(so called from Malcolm Logan, who was murdered by the bushrangers) where they burned an uninhabited hut.

BOTHWELL, Dec. 6. - Perceiving by last week's Courier, that some apprehension has been felt on account of Mr. Robinson and his party, it will no doubt be gratifying to learn that a few days ago he was near the Lakes, (15 miles west of Lake Echo) endeavouring to procure an interview with the Big river natives. The black female who was present at the murders of poor Captain Thomas and Mr. Parker and who is now with Mr. Robinson, succeeded in leading him three several times upon this tribe but the blacks invariably fled on his approach. On the last occasion (ten day's ago, fifteen miles from Lake Echo,) such was their hurry to escape that they left behind them a considerable quantity of arms, &c, consisting of eight stand of fire arms! viz. the identical double barrelled gun which was snatched from Mr. Parker at the time of his death, (and which is identified by the woman above mentioned,) another gun said to have be-longed to Captain Thomas, two other fowling pieces and four muskets, together with a bag of bullets and shot and a large looking glass, &c. The party fell in with traces of several considerable villages or encampments of the natives; from the number of the huts it is supposed they take up their winter quarters in that neighbourhood. The guns were all in good order and appeared to have been recently cleaned, except Mr. Parker's, the tumbler of one of the locks of which was overshot, the other barrel was fit for immediate use.

The PAKANA *Voice*
BY W.C. SPECIAL CORRESPONDENT—*LUTRUWITA*

It is with great sadness that we report the capture by the British of ten more Pakana people from the Pyemmairre tribes (North East Nation), eight men and two women, by Surridge and party consisting of two native women and five whites. After following the tribe for some days, says our informant, they lost all trace of them and gave up the chase. A day or two after, however, when strolling down the bank of Forester's River, they again observed the fires of the Pakana on a hill a very short distance to their right. The women were sent up by Surridge, and they succeeded at once enticing down four of the ten Pakana of which the party consisted.

The remaining six soon after followed them. Surridge succeeded in getting the party into the boat, in, two divisions, and isolating them on Waterhouse Island. M'Kay has again left the town with his two native women as guides, in pursuit of more Pakana people. We hear that the Lieutenant-Governor has signified his intention to reward this man handsomely for removing people from their family, home and land.

W.C.

1832

THE INDEPENDENT.

Ⅴ. II.]   SATURDAY, JANUARY 28, 1832.   [NO. 45.

COLONIAL TIMES (HOBART, TAS: 1828 - 1857),
WEDNESDAY 11 JANUARY 1832, PAGE 2

On Saturday last the twenty-six Aborigines captured by Mr. Robinson, march-ed into town. A more grotesque appearance we have seldom witnessed, than the arrival of these natives. At an early hour the inhabitants were expecting them; but it was 10 o'clock, when we observed a crowd of persons descending the hill and soon after we discovered our worthy Chairman of the Quarter Sessions in his gig, followed by " the strange band." The number of blacks, including the tame mob, amounted to forty, all of whom, with the exception of trousers that had been presented to them a short distance from town, were arrayed in battle order, each male carrying three spears of twelve to fifteen feet long in the left hand and only one in the right. As they continued advancing they shrieked their war song and if report says true, the view with which they were induced to accompany Mr. Robinson, was, that they should seek redress from the Governor, whom, next to Mr. Robinson, they had been to con-sider the greatest man in the Island.

These men, it is said, were bent upon spearing His Excellency, provided he did not grant them the redress they were seeking. The whole mob immediately proceeded to Government House, when His Excellency came out to meet them and after consulting some time with those of the tame mob that could speak English, he gave to each of these savage looking warriors a loaf of bread, after which they retired to the green sward, at another part of the premises, when the band was sent for; on the first sound of the musical instruments the astonishment with which they listened was truly wonderful ; there was a degree of fear portrayed on their countenances, but as the music continued they became more calm and at the conclusion of the air, applauded the musicians with a most hideous yell, after the first few minutes it became very evident that the music was not lost upon them; we noticed one savage chiefs countenance, which appeared the very picture of de-light, while at the same time a sterner looking object began to beat time with his head.

The slow music was evidently preferred by them. After the band had ceased playing a shutter was placed against a tree and the warriors were re-quested to aim with their spears at a mark chalked upon it; the immense force with which these instruments of destruction were darted through the shutter was truly astonishing, but the men did not perform well, the crowd pressing too closely upon them and the wind being very strong at the time. After having thus amused the company, unfortunately a spear broke in the hand of one of the blacks as he was throwing it, the consequence was that part of the instrument took an oblique direction and a foolish lad who was standing within a few feet of the target received the spear (after its having, touched the ground), in his leg; the wound was not very serious, but the natives finding that they had hurt the lad, could not be persuaded to throw any more. Soon after this the natives were persuaded to go on board a vessel in the harbour they consented, understanding that they were to be sent to a place where there is plenty of kangaroo and no work. It is now some years since the inhabitants of Hobart Town have witnessed a tribe of Aborigines in their native state.

COLONIAL TIMES (HOBART, TAS: 1828 - 1857),
WEDNESDAY 11 JANUARY 1832, PAGE 2

The hair of the women was shaved closely and their covering a blanket; the hair of the men, on the contrary, was clotted with a sort of red ochre and grease, resembling very much little strings of bugles ; the up-per part of their bodies was also well greased and reddened with, a portion of the same earth. On the whole the arrival of these natives in Hobart Town cannot but be highly satisfactory to the Colonists and although some imagine that Mr. Robinson has been too well paid, still on such meritorious under-takings we are not of that party who would calculate about pounds, shillings and pence. But before we quit this subject, let us strongly recommend to His Excellency's attention one of the individuals who accompanied Mr. Robinson - we mean M'Geary.

This person is willing, if His Excellency will provide him with rations and undertake to ship the natives as he may deliver them up, we say this M'Geary will enter into a con-tract with the Government to deliver to them one hundred of the Aborigines, if in return the Government on receiving the natives will give him a grant of five hundred acres of land. So much for the offer on the part of M'Geary, but we think that will not be the only reward this man will receive, if a subscription be not raised for him, if he be successful by the Settlers, we unhesitatingly say that the Colonists will be ungrateful to the extreme. As to the reward of £5, generally under-stood to be given on the capture of the Aborigines, it is all nonsense - we believe the instances are very few where the re-ward has been given. Recommending such men as M'Geary to the consideration of the Government, we leave the subject, only regretting that such measures were not undertaken before the £30,000 expedition, for which the black boy was the only return.

INDEPENDENT (LAUNCESTON, TAS: 1831 - 1835),
SATURDAY 14 JANUARY 1832, PAGE 2

The Colonial Times of Wednesday contains an interesting account of the march into Hobart Town of the lately captured tribe of Aborigines, Mr Robinson at their head. They were cozened into Hobart Town under the idea of laying a statement of grievances before the Governor, whom, next to Mr Robinson, it appears they have been accustomed to consider the greatest man in the island and if redress was not afforded they had determined upon spearing him.

They were persuaded to go on board a vessel in the harbour with an understanding that they were to be sent to a place where was plenty of kangaroo and no work. Thus far Mr. Robinson's expectations have been realized contrary to those of most other people - ours included. We wish him as much success in his future operations, considering the small deceit that has been played off upon the Aborigines as the merest possible bagatelle, in comparison with their removal from the scene of long continued barbarous and unrelenting outrages.

LAUNCESTON ADVERTISER (TAS: 1829 - 1846),
WEDNESDAY 25 JANUARY 1832, PAGE 29

The last Gazette contains the following highly complimentary para: " Mr. G. A. Robinson, having rendered a very important service to the whole community, in conciliating and bringing into Hobart Town, the Oyster Bay and Big River tribes of Aboriginal natives, the Lieutenant Governor has directed the great satisfaction he feels at Mr. Robinson's success to be thus publicly expressed. 'His Excellency relies upon Mr. Robinson's confident belief that there are now no hostile natives remaining in the settled Districts either to the Eastward or to the South side of the Island and His Excellency feels assured that many lives will be preserved by the zeal, perseverance and intrepidity which Mr. Robinson has displayed in the performance of the important duty with which he has been intrusted.' There is little doubt that Mr. Robinson is fully entitled to the public praises here bestowed upon him, or that he has not hardly and wearily earned the more substantial rewards which have been lavished upon him. His task has been arduous and hazardous in the extreme and therefore he justly merits all the encomiums which the Government in its gratitude for his services, can pass upon his conduct; but, at the same time and by the same rule, the exertions of Surridge and M'Kay ought not, to have, been passed over in silence.

These men have actually more praise due to them than Mr. Robinson : what they have done could not have been expected from them, situated as they were; whereas, Mr. Robinson was, from the commencement entrusted with full power— he was looked upon as the man whose prowess was to deliver, the Island from the hostile natives and to save the Colonists from their aggressions, by his pacific diplomacy.

He has succeeded —he says so and we have no right to question the truth of his assertions: he has been rewarded, substantially rewarded he is now publicly held up as an object of admiration, while poor Surridge and M'Kay, who have actually done as much as he has, if not more, are not even noticed. Is this the way to induce men to volunteer their services in hazardous undertakings for the general good? Is this the way that superior conduct shall be rewarded? Is this justice-to heap all the praise upon Robinson, while his more humble compeers receive no acknowledgement or reward? Surely the Lieutenant Governor, must have, overlooked these and other men and we trust, that he will now, when reminded that such beings are in existence hasten, to heal the breach which neglect has hitherto occasioned

HOBART TOWN COURIER (TAS: 1827 - 1839),
SATURDAY 17 MARCH 1832, PAGE 2

We wait with some anxiety to learn some news of the condition of our truly interesting colony of the Aborigines at Great Island, at soon as the vessels return which have carried Mr. Robinson, the Superintendent and Lieut. Darling, the Commandant of the settlement. We trust that this establishment so truly creditable to the Government and the colony, will be conducted on the soundest and purest principles of reason and humanity.

We could fill whole numbers of our journal with our lucubrations on the best mode of treating these interesting people, but we may content ourselves here with saying in brief, that a leading feature of their education should be, especially with the adults, manual employment even under the character of amusement, in the open air, ac-companied with gradual and judiciously timed attempts to instruct them in the art of reading and writing as leading to a knowledge of Christianity.

By the help of this double aim they would ultimately be brought to be both intelligent, manageable and productive, so as to contribute mainly to their own support and to save that expense which in the first instance in particular as far as the engaging of properly qualified persons to dis-charge the important duty, must on no account be niggardly.

The common reproach to most colonies in modern times, established in savage countries, of annihilating the Aboriginal tribes, will not now, we hope, by means of this establishment (of which we have some satisfaction in having been the first and most strenuous, advocate many years ago) be attached to Van Diemen's land.

TASMANIAN (HOBART TOWN, TAS: 1827 - 1839),
SATURDAY 17 MARCH 1832, PAGE 4

MONDAY, 6TH FEBRUARY, 1832.—Council met pursuant to adjournment and His Excellency the Governor took the Chair.

Resolved—That a sum not exceeding £286 be appropriated to defray the Expense of the Establishment for the civilization of the Aborigines for the Year 11332.

LAUNCESTON ADVERTISER (TAS: 1829 - 1846),
WEDNESDAY 28 MARCH 1832, PAGE 101

ABORIGINES.

We lately paid the natives now in Launceston with Mr. Robinson, a morning visit and was much delighted with the happy and healthy appearance they presented ; through the medium of interpreters (several of the blacks speak English), they conversed freely with us and expressed a degree of satisfaction at the idea of going to the Islands. They have no hesitation in speaking of the mischief they have done, which, they say they were instigated to by the dreadful treatment they have experienced from the white people.

It gives us much satisfaction to find that these people are laid under no restraint, but proceed of their own free will. Mr. Robinson starts shortly to the Westward for the purpose of bringing in the inoffensive tribes in that direction.

INDEPENDENT (LAUNCESTON, TAS: 1831 - 1835),
SATURDAY 25 FEBRUARY 1832, PAGE 2

SHIP NEWS. LAUNGESTON- FEB. 20

the cutter Charlotte, for Great Island, with Mr Robinson 16 Native Blacks and Stores for the Establishment.

And so the process of removal begins.

LAUNCESTON ADVERTISER (TAS: 1829 - 1846),
WEDNESDAY 21 MARCH 1832, PAGE 91

THE ABORIGINAL SETTLEMENT AT GREAT ISLAND.

The accounts brought up by the brig Tamar from the Aboriginal Depot at Great Island are of a nature to dispel all fears respecting the quietude of that settlement. The disturbance to which we had occasion to allude, some time back, was, it seems, by no means so serious us was imagined, having originated in a dispute between the natives and the boat's crew, in consequence of the improper conduct of the latter towards the "gins." The appearance of Mr. Robinson and Lieutenant Darling effectually put a stop to all hostility and when the Tamar left, this very interesting but expensive settlement was perfectly quiet. We think, however, that too great caution cannot be used to prevent a recurrence of any thing like hostile feeling; nor can any steps be censured which may have for their object preparation for any sudden burst of feeling on the part of the Blacks. It is no disparagement to them, to say that they are a treacherous race and cannot be too much guarded against. Under this view of the settlement, we deem the present force which is stationed there, to be insufficient, in case the natives should rise against their keepers. After becoming partially civilized, they would be the more formidable as antagonists because knowing our plans, they could with their peculiar tact in the bush, more-easily evade and overthrow them.

Without the utmost precaution being used, instructing the Blacks is putting arms into their hands against ourselves and therefore in proportion as they are instructed our caution should be increased; always being provided for the worst. While on this subject, we should like to enquire what course the Government means to adopt with the Blacks at Great Island? Are they to be kept there mere prisoners of war and allowed to range about the Island as they may think proper, without restraint, or are they to be schooled into the habits of industry and the profession of Christianity?

At first, it would be indeed Quixotic to suppose the Blacks could be set to work- their former habits and known principles being so decidedly averse to any thing of the kind; but by a gradual and judicious train of instruction they might be led to prize the comforts of civilized life; so much, as to be induced to work for them; and by this means rendered a useful set of people who would provide for their own support in a short time.

This is what we wish to see ; and therefore we say it might be done: but, really there are so many difficulties to combat and over come before the deep-seated prejudices— vindictive feelings — and indolent habits of the Blacks could be rooted out, that the idea seems almost Utopian But, perseverance will do much and rather, therefore, than cast any damp upon the ardour of those who are engaged in the work of civilization, we would urge them to push forward - to smile at difficulties— and not to be cast down or turned from their purpose by any disappointments.

*It is a good - a Christian work. If (and Heaven grant it) the effort made and making to raise these people to the standard of civilized society and to bring them as rational, created beings, to the knowledge of the existence of a God and of a Saviour be successful, the era will be a brilliant one on the pages, of our history and the event a glorious feature in the escutcheon of Colonel ARTHUR. It is our best wishes - it shall have our most cordial support and we trust that every member of the community will feel and unite with us, in urging all parties concerned, to persevere, until the work be accomplished, which has been undertaken— **and until the savages of Van Diemen's Land shall be lost in a race of useful and well conducted beings, differing only from ourselves in the colour of their skin.***

The PAKANA *Voice*

BY W.C. SPECIAL CORRESPONDENT—*LUTRUWITA*

FEAR OF LOSING PAKANA SPIRITUALITY

Thousands of years of spiritual thinking and understanding of the world may be lost forever if the British continue to impose their Christian religion onto the Pakana people according to clan leaders.

Since arriving on Lutruwita the white people have steadfastly ignored and disparaged the spirituality of the Aborigines and none have taken the time to learn about the rich and deep beliefs of those who appreciate the importance of nature and the world which they inhabit.

For those readers who are unfamiliar with the teachings of Christianity some of the following may help. Essentially they hold with the notion that there is only one god. Why this is the case no one can really explain but wait it gets even more confusing. Apparently this God, who by the way is all loving and omnipotent, sired a son with a virgin called Mary apparently without her consent or the knowledge of her husband to such an enterprise. His father evidently had plans for his son Jesus who spent the latter few years of his life prophesizing and suggesting better ways to live your life. Apparently as depicted in most Western Art Jesus appears to be the only Caucasian in Galilee at the time which may be an indicator that his father was white.

Then there is even a more bazar twist when god allows his son to be killed by the Romans to save everyone from their sins. Obviously this makes perfect sense to the rytia and naturally their beliefs should be respected although at times it is little it is little hard to follow.

However, it must be said, the actions of Christians at times seem contradictory to the tenents of their religion. For example, a basic command is, 'Thou shalt not kill' and yet they are killing the Pakana people to the point of extinction. 'Thou shalt not steal' but they take all the land. They also believe in the saying, 'Love thy neighbour, as thyself', while they kidnap Pakana women for their own desires. Jesus is reported to say 'Bring the little children unto me' but the British steal children from their families.

These are just a few of the mixed messages the Christians are giving as they relentlessly smother the ancient beliefs of the people of Lutruwita. They are indeed a contrary race!

W.C.

Needless to say, my editor was none too pleased with such blasphemous sentiments and immediately dispatched a less than flattering letter written in the perfunctory dictate of a displeased editor. The gist being that I was to write something our readers wanted to hear or find another job.

Indignation and journalistic self-righteousness came to the fore that evening as I sat alone in the Hope and Anchor Tavern bar. It lasted until Mrs Fox the landlady fixed me in the eye as she passed over another malt saying in her Irish lilt,

'Ah, so you'll be paying your rent tomorrow WC?'

Built with the all the grace and power of an oxen, Ida had a reputation for throwing seaman through windows followed by their possessions for far less.

I have neither the fortitude nor courage of Andrew Bent and others who are willing to go to gaol or risk disgrace for their principals. It is the unending quandary for journalists: principles versus practicalities of living. If I lost my job over this I would never work as a journalist again and the truth is it's all I know.

I succumbed and to make amends to appease my editor I sent a series of mindless pieces on society weddings, funerals of prominent people and other quizzical trivia which fills the pages of our newspapers. I kept my position.

EUMARRAH[xx]

HOBART TOWN COURIER (TAS: 1827 - 1839),
SATURDAY 31 MARCH 1832, PAGE 2

We regret to learn by the Launceston Advertiser, the death in the hospital there of Eumarrah, the well known Aboriginal chief.

The PAKANA *Voice*

BY W.C. SPECIAL CORRESPONDENT—*LUTRUWITA*

OBITUARY
EUMARRAH (1798-1832)

It is rare in these troubled times to find a person who is universally respected by both sides of the divide in this terrible war. Eumarrah, or Kanneherlargenner or Maleteheerlaggenner, was the chief of the Tyerer-note-panner (Stoney Creek) people from the Northern Midlands Nation.

He campaigned hard against the British and developed a formidable reputation for not only his fighting skills but command of English and ability to communicate and negotiate effectively with his enemies. On many occasions he cleverly created a world of subterfuge playing ruses and outwitting both Arthur and Robinson. Even so both men seemed to have developed a fond, although cautious, liking for Eumarrah.

It is said when travelling with Robinson he would sing hour long stories of amorous adventures and exploits in war. Eumarrah died of dysentery in Launceston Hospital on the 24th March 1832 leaving his second wife Woolaytoopinneya. His first wife had died in an inter-Aboriginal fight in 1831.

Quite a character and one who will be sorely missed.

LAUNCESTON ADVERTISER (TAS: 1829 - 1846),
WEDNESDAY 4 APRIL 1832, PAGE 109

In our sixth page, we have extracted from the Tasmanian a notice of Mr Sharland's expedition to the westward to discover the quality of the land reported by Mr. G. A. Robinson. The successful researches of that gentleman, are of the first importance of Colony, as they have opened to new settlers, a most valuable tract of unequalled country here to before unknown; and it cannot be a little gratifying to Mr. Robinson and to the Government, that Mr. Sharland's report so fully bears out the statement of Mr. Robinson, as to the advantages or the New Country, which, are described in more glowing terms by the Assistant Surveyor General, than by the original discoverer.

The way in which this land was discovered, is rather singular : While Mr. Robinson was searching for the Oyster Bay and Big River tribes, he was led by the natives to a fine open country, about 30 miles from the Peak of Teneriffe, to the N. W., which it seems had been chosen by the Blacks for their strong hold, after they had been so much disturbed in the settled districts ; and from the summit of a hill in the vicinity, Mr. Robinson described fine pasture land, in the direction of Macquarie Harbor, which the natives told him extended farther than he could see — "plenty far." This seems to be the identical sheep land of Mr. Sharland.

From the northern end of Lake Echo, this land is not difficult of access, although on the southern it is inaccessible. The land in the immediate vicinity of the Lake is said to be good cattle pasture, but must be very wet in the winter; while on the other hills, a short distance eastward, the pasture is fine, open and dry. Many herds of cattle were seen about.

There can be no doubt of this newly discovered country proving a most valuable acquisition, as from its position between Macquarie Harbor and the settled districts, it forms the key of communication across the Island, from east to west. But we have some forebodings, that the present land regulations, under which no more land can be granted, will, by putting a stop to emigration, prevent the benefits of this discovery being felt as they otherwise would.

COLONIAL TIMES (HOBART, TAS: 1828 - 1857), TUESDAY 25 DECEMBER 1832, PAGE 3

TO THE EDITOR OF THE COLONIAL TIMES.

SIR.-It is a perfect matter of astonishment that, an editorial article should appear in the Colonist newspaper of Friday last, sneering at its having been made a boast that all the natives had been taken - allow me Mr. Editor, to contradict so erroneous a statement. To a resident in town and who has taken no interest in the success of so desirable an undertaking as that of freeing the settlers from the incursions of the aborigines, because he felt safe from their murderous attacks, it may not be matter for congratulation, but he must know little of this Colony who can for one moment attempt to turn the acts of the Government as far as the blacks are concerned, into ridicule.

The fact is, those who are at all conversant in the matter are aware and have been all along, that there were tribes of natives, along the Western Coast, from Macquarie Harbour to Circular Head and all around that quarter. After Mr. Robinson had been so successful in ridding the settled districts of the aborigines, he and Mr. Cottrell entered into an agreement with the Government to bring in these Western tribes. How therefore could the Government boast of having freed the Island from its native inhabitants, when they entered into a bargain to capture those who still remained out?

That Mr. Cottrell has succeeded in taking part of them is now apparent and it is earnestly to be hoped that he may complete a work which has been so happily commenced. Those who were in the Court-house in September, 1830 and heard the eloquent speech which Mr. Hone delivered on that occasion, can never forget that part of it, where he so beautifully expressed himself, as to the blood of the murdered " blushing on the earth," (and which speech if I mistake not the learned Editor of the Tasmanian allowed to be equal to anything ever delivered by Cicero or Demosthenes).

Who would not have lent all his assistance to an undertaking to rid the Colony of such foes, when he drew the picture of the woman and her little innocents who had been so cruelly butchered at the " den," by the sable monsters and whose grave was but newly covered ? No one can forget the impression this speech made, the public came for-ward, were unanimous in their declaration, rendered every assistance and although at first the attempt to capture them failed, effort after effort was renewed until the whole of the aborigines who had infested the settled district were taken without bloodshed. The truth is, snarling abuse is one thing, calm dispassionate argument is another and which of the two the Editor of the Colonist has resorted to, a liberal and discerning public will best judge.

-I am, Sir, your obedient servant,

A BUSHMAN.

1833

THE
TRUMPETER GENERAL.

Published every Tuesday and Friday Mornings.   All Advertisements intended for publication, must be sent to the Office before 1 o'Clock the day previous.

No. 1.)   FRIDAY, NOVEMBER, 29, 1833.   (Gratis.

INDEPENDENT (LAUNCESTON, TAS: 1831 - 1835),
SATURDAY 2 FEBRUARY 1833, PAGE 2

On Sunday night last the three aborigines, whom many of our readers have seen perambulating the streets of Launceston, made their escape. Mr. Robinson it appears, had formed so good an opinion of these men, that he was induced to take them from the jail and place them under little or no constraint. The blacks had shewed every sign of being perfectly satisfied till Sunday morning, when one of them observed some fires on the North Eastern hills, which were immediately pronounced by all of them to be black men's fires. They appeared particularly elated, jumping about and dancing for joy, telling everybody that black men were not far off.

Towards the evening a dispute arose between one man and his " gin'," which ended in the usual manner, viz., the man first banging his lady rather unceremoniously with his fist and then making her leave the fireside. This little domestic broil did not, however, last long for tranquillity and a good understanding prevailed within a few hours. Towards midnight it was observed their fire, which they always kept burning, had gone out, but this did not excite suspicion and it was not until the following morning that it not discovered a retreat had been, effected without beat of drum—both the men and woman having absconded, the former taking with them a favourite hound belonging to Mr. Whitcomb and the latter her little interesting picca ninny.

It has been stated by several persons, that the aborigines were dissatisfied with the provisions supplied them by the government; had they been kept to their rations they would not only have been dissatisfied, but in all probability they would have been almost starved. Happily, however for the poor creatures, they were left partially under the protection of an, individual, through whose kindness a sufficiency of food was always at their command ; and whatever blame their might attach to the pen find ink system, in the present instance we say private charity prevented these poor creatures from suffering that absolute want which the system would have enforced.

Only conceive muscular human beings, accustomed to most violent exercises—accustomed to slay the kangaroo and devour it till they became scarcely able to move from the spot from repletion and then lying down sleeping till again sufficiently hungry either to finish the remaining portion of the animal, or to seek for others in the bush — only conceive we say such men placed upon the liberal government rations—men who have in all probability, committed no crime—who ought to be free as nature made them—only conceive such men with their pound of meat and their pound of flour, food which they are not accustomed to, with an equally liberal allowance of wood and water per diem.

Does such treatment towards a poor unoffending race of human creatures emanate from a government? Yes and from a government which is considered as desirous of inculcating religion and morality. We are sorry that these men have betaken themselves again to the bush, not so much on account of fearing their future attacks, for from the treatment they have experienced, we fancy a good feeling prevails on their part towards the white population—but the reason we are sorry, is. on, account of the poor creatures themselves, who have now again become targets for the aim of any man who carries a musket and chooses to fire at them

LAUNCESTON ADVERTISER (TAS. : 1829 - 1846),
WEDNESDAY 4 APRIL 1832, PAGE 109

DOMESTIC

Mr Robinson leaves this town, today, on his intended route to the westward, for the purpose of bringing in the Aborigines of that part of the island. He proceeds first to the Hampshire and Surrey Hills and from thence to Circular Head and Cape Grim, but his ultimate destination; appears to be on the western coast, in the direction of Macquarie Harbour and Port Davey.

INDEPENDENT (LAUNCESTON, TAS: 1831 - 1835),
SATURDAY 2 FEBRUARY 1833, PAGE 2

As soon as Mr. Robinson arrives it is believed he will set out in search of the party and with his well known experience he will doubtlessly soon be enabled to find traces which will ultimately lead to their recovery.

Blacks on Flinders' island— 8 on board the government cutler Charlotte, which recently sailed from Macquarie harbour to the establishment, It is computed that there are about 60 yet at large on the western coast, between 30 and 40 (females) in a state of slavery and tyrannical subjugation among the sealers on Kangaroo island and the other small islands in the straits and a very few (less than a dozen) still in the central part of the island. Mr. G A. Robinson has 10 of the domesticated ones with him at Macquarie harbour assisting him to conciliate and bring in those who are still roaming on that part of the coast. These, as accurately as can well be arrived at, comprehend the whole number now remaining of these interesting people, once so formidable to the settlers.

Every friend to humanity must rejoice that the dreadful hostilities which so long subsisted between them and us have been so happily terminated and that the Aboriginal colony, now settled, is proving so hap-py and prosperous. We cannot however allow ourselves to conclude this brief account of them without again renewing our appeal to the good feeling of our country-men to induce them to come forward and present Mr. Robinson, whose persevering services have been the main means of bringing the glorious achievement about, with some public testimony of the benefit the colony has, received at his hands, if the thing is permitted to pass over in Silence we say candidly and distinctly it will be discreditable to our nature. Mr. Robinson is now out assiduously engaged in the arduous duty, striving his best by bringing in the remainder to put the grand finish to the great work and we most sincerely trust that before his return, be when it may, something effective will be done to inform him and his children after him that the colony is not forgetful of the services he has rendered it.

If I had a heart left by now these few lines would surely have broken it forever.

AUSTRAL-ASIATIC REVIEW (HOBART TOWN, TAS: 1833),
TUESDAY 5 MARCH 1833, PAGE 3

THE NATIVE CHIEF.

We regret to state, that the Tasmanian Native Chief, who was for sometime in this town and whose manly appearance excited great admiration, died on the 20th of February, at Great, on Flinders Island. His death is supposed to have been consequent upon the excitement occasioned by his change of habits. His [?] failed him and he sank to the grave, having by his whole demeanour obtained the good will of all at the Aboriginal establishment.

The time had come to leave. My sentiments were in turmoil with excruciating highs and lows I could not explain. I would have days of blackness existing in a deep, deep hole, only to emerge when friends literally dragged me into light and life again. Then I would fly high in a writing frenzy till all hours with shattered sleep and a feeling of purposelessness. I would wake in a sweat seeing the faces, the tears always but I was only watching, never rescuing – neither hero nor villain.

I recently visited a quack to see if he had any way to overcome my demons and emotional troubles. His remedy was clear and direct.

'Drink water. Give up the grog.'

Thoughtful and compelling advice which I contemplated later that night as I refilled my pipe and observed in front of me a glass of water and in another a three-finger drop of my finest malt.

After some time, well as long as it took to light up and with a dose of healthy smoke filling the room, I decided the best thing to do was compromise; so I poured the water into the Whiskey which meant sticking partly to the good doctor's advice to drink more water! Personally, I can't abide the stuff but it can be tolerable when added cagily to my drink of choice.

It turns out the doctor in question is a Biblical teetotaller and prescribes exactly the same advice to every patient regardless of ailment. The moral of this story is if you want the right answer choose your doctor well, although providentially speaking it's probably better not to go to a doctor at all.

It was time for me to have Home Leave and return to family and forgotten childhood memories. My father had died some years ago and mother was now alone and pining for her son. I hoped to return someday but not for a while. There was now little to keep me here to see the final, inevitable devastation of the people of Lutruwita.

Perhaps I would become a reporter of gardening and write effusively about rose gardens or Mrs. B's prize for dahlias at the local fate or the merits of sheep manure on tomatoes. Maybe I should write about cooking and enter agonizing debates over the best way to make a Spotted Dick! At least that way I would be able to ignore the horrors which swirled uncontrollably about in my head.

We would see, but first I needed to get home and so I embarked on the Norvel under Captain Ross on the 6th March 1833, for my long and arduous journey home.

Arriving back in Gravesend I was greeted by a smiling, overjoyed Sophia who was a far cry from my childhood soulmate. She stood with an infant snuggling into her breast while a little girl took refuge in the protection of her long flowing dress. Beside them was her husband Nicholas Bright sporting a clergyman's dog's collar. The irony was not lost on her. After being raised next door to a church by agnostic parents and a sceptic of a brother, she had married the local vicar! However, it should be said in his favour, Nicholas was a sensible sort of chap who held a very C of E approach to his vocation. The only criteria for being a Christian is to be a gentleman or indeed a lady.

All else it would appear is of little consequence and a far cry from the bleakness of Governor Arthur's brittle Calvinism. We were aware too of the absence in our lives. Father was no longer with us and our mother spent much of her days in their beloved library lost to the world.

Chapter Seven

Finally a Short Visit 1839

Many years have now passed since my last visit to Lutruwita. I feel restored in my heart and strong enough to return and see what has occurred with the Pakana people during my absence.

Needless to say, reporting on flower shows or cooking did not eventuate. Instead I retreated to the seclusion of my study for some time before venturing to write more about my experiences in Ceylon and even trying my hand at fiction again. With some success I might add!

I arrived in Nipaluna (Hobart) aboard the brig *Louisa* commanded by Captain Roach on the 29th December 1838 after leaving London on the 14th August. As was my habit I made straight for the offices of the Colonial Times only to find my friend Andrew Bent had been forced to sell it some years ago to pay his debts.

I did meet him though and found a very different man from the one I had left behind. His fight with Arthur over the freedom of the press, his prison term and paying huge fines for libel had almost ruined him financially. Bent had had to sell his newspaper to Henry Melville and also his property Bentfield, at Cross Marsh to pay his debts and his town house disposed of by the sheriff. He was still resolute and the old spark would re-emerge with the vigour and vitality of yesteryear. He was soon to leave for Sydney and a new life. I wished him well as his ship was about to set sail, although inwardly I feared for him and his family.

In time I managed to read much of what had been written in the press about the Pakana people and their plight over the last few years. The most noteworthy impression I gained was just how greatly the number of articles written about them had declined during that time. It really was a case of out of sight, out of mind. In the intervening years the few remaining people from the Lutruwita nations had been taken to Wyballena on Flinders Island.

The experiences of the people on the island are well documented so I will concentrate on the newspapers of the day and how they reported these events.

COLONIAL TIMES (HOBART, TAS: 1828 - 1857),
TUESDAY 16 APRIL 1833, PAGE 3

TO THE EDITOR OF THE COLONIAL TIMES.

SIR.-AS I was "trotting along the road" the other day towards Richmond and Jerusalem, to look at some places recommended to me, having my heart filled with outrages, perpetrated by the aborigines of the Island and about which I had been reading the night before, I chanced to pass a " black person" carrying a blue bundle with him, knocking the dust about strangely as he walked along and, as seemed to me, he had rather a fierce look ; but as the road chanced to be pretty tolerable just there, I did not stop to examine him much. I rode on, thinking about black natives, scalping and all manner of horrible things-how-ever, I had not gone far when I overtook a jockey- kind of a looking gentleman, rather well mounted-and finding him disposed to be chatty, I mentioned about the strange person I had lately passed and enquired if any of the " real" natives had been so far civilized as to make such an appearance. The gentleman having mused a little and asking me if I was a "stranger" in the Colony, said- "Well, Sir, I will tell you a thing which will surprise you That very man you speak of is a Magistrate." " A Magistrate!" I exclaimed, " surely you are joking with me."

" No Sir," he replied, "it is no joke I assure you. The fact is, that our Antipodean Government, here, oftentimes soar altogether above the comprehension of ordinary minds-and it must be admitted, sometimes descends altogether as much below again. Now, Sir, you must know, that they took into their wise heads awhile ago, that the aborigines of this Island were possessed of most extraordinary endowments; that they were capable of understanding languages, by intuition, as it were and could read English at first sight, if it was printed-and so they actually sent off Proclamations amongst them, by which their chiefs must govern the tribes.-Nay more, it was also supposed that they were Artists, by nature and paintings were hung up among the trees of the woods 'for them to study and improve; and now, lastly, in order to give a proper colour to justice, one of them has been appointed a Magistrate and must be returning from Court, perhaps, after receiving the Governor's thanks for some especial service probably on account of quelling, or at least trying to put down, the last of the Oyster Bay tribe of natives, a very troublesome set and which it has been long attempted to bring into subjection, without success.

It is supposed the appointment that makes you stare so, has been a kind of experiment-all military efforts having failed." Having listened with much attention to my communicative companion, I was about to ask a few questions for further information, when coming to a turn of the road, he suddenly turned off and galloped away, calling out, as we parted, " a strange-country, Sir, this--strange people - strange government-strange everything. However, if you doubt what I have been telling you, why-apply to any of the Editors of the public Journals and they will tell you all about it"-and understanding that yours is the oldest in the Colony, I make my first application to you accordingly.

-I am, Sir,
your obedient servant,

A STRANGER.

[We remember Mr. Bill, Mr. Pigeon and Thomas Beck, or persons named somewhat in that fashion, receiving grants of land for certain services and we were fully aware at the time, that they were the Aborigines of New South Wales ; but it was unknown to us (till "a stranger" informed us) that any one of our black Aborigines was elevated to the Bench of Magistrates ; perhaps however, he will do his duty quite as well, or even better than some of our white skinned Magistrates-ED.]

HOBART TOWN CHRONICLE (TAS: 1833), TUESDAY 28 MAY 1833, PAGE 2

We have had the pleasure since our last to receive some further information regarding the truly interesting little colony of aborigines at Flinder's island.

At first the settlement was placed as a temporary measure, until a better situation could be fixed upon, on a little spot on the coast which at this season would have been unavoidably cut off from all communication with the main part of the island by a large lagoon; besides that in itself it did not afford any good land fit for cultivation. In consequence, the commandant (Ensign Darling) after carefully exploring all the other parts of the island that were likely to prove at all suitable, as a permanent settlement, recommended the government to remove the establishment to a spot about 15 miles northward, as being the most eligible for the purpose that could be found.

It is a projecting point formerly known among the sealers by the rude name of " pea-jacket point," but has since very properly been named from the native more harmonious and appropriate appellation of "Wyballenna," (which being translated into English means "black men's houses.") The total removal of the establishment was completed in February last and the result which has already taken place proves how judiciously the change has been made. An excellent garden has already been enclosed and in a great part laid down mostly by the labour of the blacks themselves, under the immediate guidance and superintendence of Mr. Darling. There is an abundant supply of excellent water at all times of the year. The village is already beginning to show itself, four excellent huts being completed—28 feet long by 14 feet wide, with a double fire-place in the centre and a partition. Each apartment is calculated to accommodate six of the natives, though until more buildings are erected a greater number must of course take shelter in them. They are very neatly built with wattles, plastered and white-washed. The wattles and the grass for thatching were procured and brought in entirely by the natives themselves, who took a very lively interest in the progress of their new habitations. The furnishing of them with rustic bed places, tables, stools, &c, was affording additional opportunity to amuse and arrest the attention of these poor creatures.

A neat little garden was laying out also in the front of each cottage and by the ensuing spring it will, we may fairly anticipate, afford one of the prettiest and most interesting spots for the "ullima Thule" of an aquatic excursion from our little metropolis that can well be imagined. The women are already so far inured to the arts of civilized life as to be able to wash not only their own clothes but those, of their husbands and "get them up," as the laundress would say, quite as well as a white woman.

A person visiting the little colony does not now find its inhabitants in a half state of nudity as formerly, everyone being well and decently clothed. The general character of the whole island of Flinders', which is extensive, is rugged and mountainous. The rocks of which it is mostly composed consist of granite, which geologists or rather farmers know to indicate a barren country. But few parts of this large island are accordingly susceptible of cultivation. Besides, however, the tract of good land where the village of "Wybalenna" is situated, there are several others of small extent near enough to be available, as well as many good spots on some of the neighbouring little islands that are scattered near and are readily accessible by boats, far more than sufficient indeed to supply with agricultural produce the small remnant of the Aboriginal tribes that have been saved or may be saved from Van Diemen's land. There are now about 120.

HOBART TOWN CHRONICLE (TAS: 1833), TUESDAY 18 JUNE 1833, PAGE 2

We regret much to learn by the last accounts from the Aboriginal establishment at Flinder's island, that several deaths have recently occurred during the last few months.

Since the first commencement of this interesting colony from 10 to 12 deaths have occurred and only four births. On the whole, however, they are a very healthy and happy little society.

AUSTRAL-ASIATIC REVIEW (HOBART TOWN, TAS: 1833),
TUESDAY 30 JULY 1833, PAGE 4

THE ABORIGINES.

We have much pleasure in being enabled to publish the following extract of a Letter from Mr. Robinson, (of whose exertions no terms of praise can he too strong.) by a gentleman here, by which it appears that he has completely effected the important object of capturing the whole of the Aborigines in the Island, with the exception of 40 individuals, of whom also he expects shortly to be in possession. TO THE EDITOR. Macquarie Harbour. 26th on June 1833. Sir— I have much pleasure in acquainting you with the circumstance of my having removed from the main Territory, (without force or violence) the whole of the Port-Davy tribe of Aborigines. consisting of seven men, nine women, two infants and two children making a total of twenty individuals. Whom I have forwarded to the Aborigines Settlement at Flinders Island, per Government Vessel "Shamrock" and Tamar.

These people were removed at two separate periods. six on the 25th ult. when twelve Aborigines were brought in. On this occasion the expedition has to travel through considerable part of the interior and four last days of their return, the expedition suffered considerably from want of food. On the 20th Instant the remaining eight were brought in, on this occasion also the expedition had a long fatiguing journey to within a days march of Port

Davy and it is a source of much satisfaction to me that during the course of those?, not the slightest casualty has happened to any of my people. The only Aborigines now at large, are two tribes in the vicinity of Macquarie Harbour Heads, consisting of about [?] individuals, whom I propose proceeding inquest of with the least possible delay In the course of this service, I was accompanied by my two sons and my Aboriginal attendants and one white man as messenger.

G. A, Robinson

1834

THE INDEPENDENT.

VOL. IV.]   SATURDAY, JANUARY 4, 1834.   [NO. 145

LAUNCESTON ADVERTISER (TAS: 1829 - 1846),
THURSDAY 3 APRIL 1834, PAGE 3

THE ABORIGINES AGAIN.

The following information has been forwarded to the authorities by Mr. J. B. Thomas, of Everton, near Perth; and we are indebted to that gentleman for the copy, with which he has been so obliging as to favour us: — On Tuesday the 18th inst, at 4 p.m., my hut at Native Plains, on the Mersey, was surrounded and plundered of every article by the natives, who took away one carbine, powder and buck shot, flour and several other articles.

One of the men in charge of my cattle, (Samuel Brown) was with the cattle; the other man (Thomas Thomson) had gone to the well, a distance of a hundred yards; when on his return, he saw twelve men round the hut: presently two came out; one of them coolly levelled the carbine and fired at him ; he then ran away, pursued by two of the blacks for upwards of a mile *and he concludes that he owed his safety to his two dogs, who attacked the pursuing blacks and impeded their progress. This is the third time this hut has been robbed. The blacks were accompanied by dogs which were taken away at the last robbery. _*

LAUNCESTON ADVERTISER (TAS: 1829 - 1846), THURSDAY 8 MAY 1834, PAGE 3

CAPTURE OF TWENTY-ONE ABORIGINES

Mr. Robinson has succeeded in capturing twenty-one hostile natives — the whole of which party were brought up in the Edward, V. D. Land Company's schooner, from Circular Head, on Saturday last; and were transhipped on board the government cutter Charlotte and forwarded immediately to the black establishment at Flinder's Island. It will be gratifying to every lover of humanity to learn that this service has been effected by Mr. Robinson without violence or force; on the contrary, the natives were allowed to hunt and follow their own amusements, without the least restraint, during the journey from where they were taken to Cape Grim, which occupied six days. The party taken consists of seven men, five women... (two of whom are enceinte,) one male youth and seven children; and form the greater portion of a tribe which has all along manifested the most determined hostility to the whites and have committed so many outrages on the V. D. L. Company's lands. They were the most conspicuous in the diabolical attack upon Mr. Robinson, on a former expedition, at the Arthur river; and upon another occasion in an attempt to spear the Sydney natives, who were in pursuit of them.

They also attacked the missionary party on its way to Macquarie Harbour. They had, it is said, declared their determination never to be brought in; and, it is added, had resolved, having plenty of dogs, (eleven of these animals were taken with the blacks,) to retire for a time to the mountains and live on badger [wombat]; or, quoib, in the native tongue. Finding Mr. Robinson's party in pursuit of them, they concerted a plan to entrap him and his Aboriginal attendants by making false roads, in which tracks they stuck sharp pointed slicks in order to wound the feet of his party and laid in ambush alongside. Mr. R's blacks soon discovered these sticks and manifested great aversion to pursuing the journey, arguing the difficulty of falling in with the hostile tribe and the certainty of losing their lives. Even in this discouraging situation Mr. Robinson's mind was not diverted from the great object of his mission and with his usual finesse, necessary to be resorted to with the domesticated blacks, succeeded in quelling their fears and pushing onward, eventually succeeded in the work. The expedition is described to have been most harassing— the hostile natives having lately divided themselves into small parties.

Besides his inland excursions, Mr. R. made three journeys down the western coast to Sandy Cape; and on one occasion he nearly reached Macquarie Harbour; returning from that station by an inland route to the coast, ten miles northward of Pieman's river: during the whole of this long journey following on the track of the hostile blacks. The party taken were fallen in with at three different periods: on the 28th of February, eight were secured; on the 14th March, three others; and on the 12th April, nine more. After reaching that part of the coast opposite the Hunter islands, several days intervened before an opportunity occurred of removing them from the main land ; those islands having been chosen by Mr. Robinson for their encampment, until he could bring them down here; but none of the party attempted to leave and appeared in the highest good humour with Mr. R. and his party. After seeing them safely on board the Edward, Mr. R. started in search of two or three other natives, reported still to be out; and we are confident every colonist will desire that success may attend him in this journey.

1835

THE

True Colonist.

Van Diemen's Land Political Despatch, and Agricultural and Commercial Advertiser.

The first Daily Paper published in the Island.

Price, 6d.   Hobart Town, Saturday, January 10, 1835.   No. 55.

In the end it comes down to money!

TRUE COLONIST VAN DIEMEN'S LAND POLITICAL DESPATCH AND AGRICULTURAL AND COMMERCIAL... (HOBART TOWN, TAS: 1834 - 1844), TUESDAY 20 JANUARY 1835, PAGE 3

THE ABORIGINES.

In our publication of Saturday, we quoted a paragraph from the Launceston Advertiser, on which it was our intention to have offered some very necessary observations. Believing, as we then did, that there did not exist the slightest ground for Mr. Robinson's firm conviction that there are no more Aborigines at large, ' it certainly would be very desirable for Mr. Robinson to impress the same conviction on the minds of the Government, for on their entertaining the same ' firm conviction' depends his receiving the sum of £700, being the balance of £1000, which the Government contracted to pay him on condition of his capturing all the natives in the Colony within three years from January 1831, of which £1000 he received £300 in hand, besides his salary of £250 a-year, bonus of £100 and 2560 acres of land, which he sold for £1280 and ample salaries for his two sons. The period of three years has now expired and we assert, notwithstanding the firm conviction, that there are now at least sixty natives, known to be at large in the Colony- -namely, the ' Pieman's River, Sandy Cape and Hampshire Hills tribes.' And in confirmation of our own ' conviction' we can adduce the testimony of Alexander M'Geary, who ac-companied Mr. G. A. Robinson in all his excursions, until they separated in consequence of a difference about the capture of the Hampshire hill tribe, which M'Geary said might have been effected, but the Commander in Chief, for certain reasons, did not think it expedient at that moment'.

M'Geary is now willing to engage, within a given time, to bring 'in fifty of the wild natives, stipulating only for a moderate salary and provisions for himself and party, with the present premium for the capture of each individual and 500 acres of land on his bringing in the fifty. We hope the Government will consider of this (as the period has expired within which Mr. G. A. Robin-son was to have fulfilled his contract) before they pay the £700, for we question whether they can get it back after they have heard of a few murders by the spears of the Hampshire hills tribe, which is by no means improbable before winter is over. We shall have a great deal to say on this subject at an early opportunity; in the meantime, we ex-press our sorrow to hear that the Colony on 'Great Island' is far from being in a desirable condition. We will make farther enquiries and then trace the whole of the proceedings relative to the Aborigines, from the hanging of Musquito, down to the present time, when we think a good deal of deceit, humbug and mismanagement will be brought to light.

HOBART TOWN COURIER (TAS: 1827 - 1839), FRIDAY 20 FEBRUARY 1835, PAGE 2

THE COURIER.

FRIDAY MORNING, FEBRUARY 20, 1835. Ten little children of the Aborigines, now domesticated at Flinders' island, were last week brought up and placed with the four others already in the Orphan school, to be educated. It is of course a most desirable thing that these poor children should be properly instructed, for they have the intellectual faculty as strong as a European and at first sight we were ready to applaud the committee for adopting apparently so benevolent a measure

It is delightful to a man of feeling to see these 14 little black children intermixed and taught in classes with the other little or-phans in that noble institution ; and were they all orphans and without another friend or relation to care for them, our satisfaction would be unmixed, But this is not the case, most of them have parents or near relations dearly attached to them at the Establishment, by whom their separation is looked upon as the direst affliction that could befall them - a removal almost as painful as that of death it-self would be. We are too ready to suppose, that because those poor people are of n different colour, they have not the same warmth of sentiment the same tenderness of heart as ourselves-when the very opposite is the fact.

The passions of the breast are even keener than ours and we know that the parents and relations of these children daily and hourly lament their removal so much, that susceptible as they are, it is not unlikely to accelerate their death. It is for this reason, that looking calmly at the matter we disapprove of the measure and should rejoice to see the committee restore them to their homes. There is already a properly qualified schoolmaster on the island, or catechist to undertake that duty and if it was desirable to teach them in conjunction with white children, it would have been easy to send some of the orphans from this place to stand in the classes with them.

These people are or ought to be as free as ourselves and we maintain that we have no right whatever to take away their children without first consulting them-without the leave and consent of their natural parents and guardians first asked and obtained. This was the great and laudable principle on which the government all along went, in the mediations of Mr. Robinson with all the tribes which brought about the present happy arrangement unprecedented in the annals of man and it is not one of its least gratifying features, thus to seize remnants of various little states, formerly in open hostility with each other now living in social community (in all but the loss of their children) happy and contented.

And this leads us to look at the present state of the numerous black nations that in-habit the immense continent of New Holland, around which in all directions the English are daily planting themselves and forming encroachments. We have seen at Sydney and we see at Swan river and other settlements, with the best possible precautions under the old system, what heart rending rencounters and barbarities are committed-and see what might have been done-what enormities might such a mediator and protector as Mr. Robin-son has proved himself to be with the tribes of this colony, had been employed from the first ! Unless a man, with a zeal like his, make up his mind to go among the blacks, to be familiar and associate with them, living and doing as they do and learning 'their language, little good can be expected. To the want of this, we presume, is to be attributed the failure of success with the missionaries of New South Wales.

But it is not less the duty of these colonies than of England, to take some measures at the present crisis, when the increased emigration from the mother country is likely to renew, unless opportunely prevented, all the outrages and barbarities of the past times. It is with deference we suggest it to the authorities, but we do think, considering the number of deaths that have occurred at Flinders' island, that the finger of Providence seems to point out to appeal to the better feelings-the just-ness of our nature, to employ the present handful of domesticated blacks, scarce, we believe, amounting to 150, with Mr. Robinson as an instrument-a nucleus in New Holland, for mediating with and ultimately civilising the yet harmless natives of that vast continent.

We would remove by degrees, that is with their own consent, both the people now here with Mr. Robinson and those at Flinders' island to an easily accessible convenient station in New Holland, A peaceful halo would play around such an establishment and gradually, under the guidance of a prudent, active, superintending hand, its civilising and missionary influence would be felt in the remotest corners. All promiscuous mixture, unfortified and premature, as now occasionally takes place with the whites at Sydney or Fremantle, ought carefully to be avoided. We look upon these meetings as no better than vain show-injurious, guilty parade. If you cannot teach them our virtues, our religion, do not, we entreat you, teach them our vices. We speak in the broad and liberal view of the matter-as regards our duty to our neighbour. But contingently, see what advantages such a measure as we now advise might ultimately confer in eliciting the resources both geographically and physically of these comparatively yet unexplored, singular countries!

Can we expect to prosper when we leave such a bounden duty as this neglected, unconsidered, unregarded? Are we, like the Goths and Vandals of old, so engrossed in our own pursuits, to run down and exterminate these unoffending, de-fenceless people, without one thought of poignancy or remorse-without one single effort to save them?

HOBART TOWN COURIER (TAS: 1827 - 1839), FRIDAY 28 AUGUST 1835, PAGE 2

THE COURIER.
FRIDAY MORNING, AUGUST 28, 1835.

"We refer the reader to our last page for the particulars of the singular fact of a white man residing for a period of thirty-two years among the aborigines of Port Phillip. This will perhaps hold out an additional inducement to some to try their fortune in that new country, as they may have the means of availing themselves of the local knowledge which a European, under the peculiar circumstances must have acquired. We have no wish to discourage enterprise - to lay the smallest restraint on the motions or most unbounded speculations which every man has a right to indulge in as he pleases. We certainly rejoice to see our favourite, our adopted colony, prosper, but to learn that our fellow creatures are happy, whether in Hobart town, Port Phillip, or elsewhere, must always be a source of plea-sure to us.

Nevertheless, we consider it a duty incumbent on us, not as censors, but as observers of passing events and guardians of the public, to caution them, without due consideration, against being induced by any prevailing mania, though sanctioned by the example of older heads, from taking any important steps in life, which after experience may force them, when too late, without severe losses, to retrace. Let them weigh well the pro-probable advantages (solely we conceive pastoral) they are likely to derive from emigrating to that new country and embarking their means in it, with - we do not say the inconveniences, for these of course they calculate upon - but the risks, the dangers as to the safety of both life and property, which they must unavoidably encounter.

It would be madness to expect that savages such as the aborigines of these countries, when once they have acquired a relish for our civilized comforts, will be restrained in their endeavours to obtain them, by any principle of restraint which operates on the educated, to say nothing of the religious mind of the civilized European. The comparatively slight impression which the long sojourn and association of Buckley has had upon them is a lamentable proof of this.

HOBART TOWN COURIER (TAS: 1827 - 1839), FRIDAY 28 AUGUST 1835, PAGE 2

Indeed though this man is evidently superior in his class, he has verged far more back into the savage state, than they have been elevated by his means into the civilized. Does any man in his senses sup-pose, when these people have tasted the sweets of the annual tribute agreed upon as the price of the fancifully bounded tract of land, that they will wait the return of the thirteen moons to demand a second? Who has ascertained that they can count to the number of thirteen? Should it be demanded in as many days, as it is probable it will be, how do you expect will the refusal be received? Do you suppose, when they have acquired a relish for mutton and can help themselves with ease to carcases from your flocks, that they will be induced by any persuasion of yours or Buckley's to leave them alone and continue instead the trouble of hunting kangaroos, opossums and emus? Theft with them, so far from being a crime, is a virtue.

Do you expect that the distinctions of meum and tuum, which all the labours of your schoolmaster and your lawyer abroad and at home are able to impress but on a portion of your own white community, are, as if by a miracle, to be instilled into their brains? What idea can savages like these have of your compact for land - of a deed of conveyance, which special pleaders among yourselves only can comprehend?

And even among yourselves, as your numbers increase, do you anticipate that human nature will be different at Port Phillip from any other part of the world? - that jealousies, animosities, contentions, inroads, strifes, assaults and aggressions, will not sooner or later arise among you? Are you all perfect men? Is there no chance of a press an emanation from some of our beautiful Van Diemen's Land ones, starting a fourth estate amongst you? It is all very well for people in the abstract - for writers who seek for excitement, or for the restless, disappointed men at home who call themselves patriots and advocate destructiveness, as the phrenologists call it, to inveigh against the pension list, public expenses, Government printing and what not but a moment's reflection tells us that no society, no safety of life or property can exist without laws and regulations - without a provident Government. To this it must come at last and though a few in the first instance, as has already taken place at Two fold and Portland bays, may for a time and so long as two or three separate interests do not clash together, do very well, it is utterly impossible that a colony of disjointed individuals with-out the bond of mutual laws, or a common refuge for protection, can exist for any length of time without the most annoying differences and even outrages arising amongst them for which there will be no redress. Let old heads do as they like, but we feel it our duty to say to all, but especially our younger readers, not to be led away by the yet untried example of others, but to consider for themselves before they take an irremediable step-to look before they leap.

There are many great stories from this part of the world and that of William Buckley (1780 – 1856) is hard to surpass. There is a saying 'you've got Buckley's' or 'Buckley's Chance' meaning that your chances are pretty slim. This idiom is aptly derived from William's experience when he escaped from Collin's brief settlement in 1803 at Sorrento in Port Philip Bay with seemingly little thought about his future. When the ships left for Hobart a few months later he remained there for the next 32 years living amongst the Aborigines who believed him to be a spirit from the dead, although one with earthly needs and thoughtfully provided him with a wife and allowed him to live in peace.

The *rytia* (white people) began to arrive again in the mid 1830s from Tasmania and after trying in vain to mediate between the two groups William returned to live within his own culture in Tasmania. Hence 'you've got Buckley's chance' of surviving.

THE AGRARIAN REVOLUTION

The Pakana way of life was also deeply affected by what is loosely termed the Agrarian Revolution which had rapidly changed European farming practices in the previous half century. The British began to use science and rational processes to improve their crops and animal food production. It was highly successful and many of the principle ideas were brought to Lutruwita.

Common land for all to use had once been a feature of the English countryside but as farming changed the need for fencing and private ownership took priority and much common land was lost to private land owners. Communal land also appears to have been an important feature of the Pakana culture. Although there were clear boundaries and a system of agriculture informed by the boundaries of nations and clans, the notion of individuals owing private land was unfamiliar and the idea of fencing, imposing straight lines across the landscape, was an alien practice to the people.

Fencing was an essential aspect for agrarian developments to occur on a large scale and began crisscrossing the untethered landscape. Livestock reproduction could be controlled with the rotation of crops which needed to be fenced off from sheep and cattle as well as wildlife. The latter were killed as quickly as possible in order to allow wheat, barley and other crops to flourish.

For the Pakana this meant they were not only prevented from traversing the land but their food sources, which had for ever been available, now being systematically decimated. Neither would they take the British animals to eat. Rytia held the belief that as individuals they could 'own' animals a notion alien to the Pakana and meant that killing them would result in calamitous consequences.

With this came technology: the plough, irrigation and the unequivocal right to change the environment to suit the needs of the agricultural. This had been a feature of much of human kind for thousands of years and although the Pakana knew how to manage and cultivate the land effectively, their practices were not appreciated by the Europeans. The plough dug the land and replaced natural grasses with foreign seeds while irrigation redirected water streams to different parts of the land. Such features were a normal part of British life and seen as necessary for an increasing world population. For the Pakana it was a desecration of their land and spirits.

Directly related to this was the displacement of peasants from their traditional homes throughout Great Britain and their being forced into urban poverty. The outcome was desperation and crime, leading to executions on a massive scale, overcrowded prison hulks on the Thames and the creation of a transportation system to the other side of the world. For half a century the British sent over seventy-five thousand convicts to Lutruwita, perhaps ten times the entire pre-British Pakana population. At least the convicts were deemed to be civilized!

1836

TRUE COLONIST VAN DIEMEN'S LAND POLITICAL DESPATCH AND AGRICULTURAL AND COMMERCIAL... (HOBART TOWN, TAS: 1834 - 1844), FRIDAY 26 FEBRUARY 1836, PAGE 63

ABORIGINES.

We recommend to the attention of our Tasmanian Lawyers, the following very ingenious and unanswerable plea, put in by Mr. Sydney Stephen, on behalf of one of the Aborigines, who was arraigned for the murder of one of his countrymen before the Supreme Court of the British intruders upon the soil of the Aborigines. **Chief Justice Pedder will find in this plea some matter that will afford him no very comfortable reflection when he looks back to the awful proceeding of trying, sentencing and executing some of the miserable race here, without counsel and without any interpreter.** *Verily, the earth of their native Island, which received their bodies from the hand of their slayers, will not cease to call for vengeance to Heaven, until insulted justice is appeased for this awful sacrifice : — 'The King v. Jack Congo Murrell. 'And now the said Jack Congo Murrell in his own proper person comes and having heard the in-formation aforesaid read and protesting that he is not guilty of the premises charged in the said information, or any part thereof, for plea, nevertheless saith that. he ought not to be compelled to answer to the said information, because, he saith that the said Territory of New South Wales before and until the occupation thereof by his late Majesty King George the Third, was inhabited by tribes of native blacks who were regulated and governed by usages and customs of their own from time immemorial, practised and recognised amongst them and not by the laws or statutes of Great Britain and that ever since the* *occupation of that said Territory as aforesaid, the said tribes have continued to be and still are regulated and governed by such usages and customs as aforesaid and not by the laws and statutes of Great Britain. And the said Jack Congo Murrell further saith that he is a native Black be-longing to one of such tribes aforesaid and that he is not now, nor at any time heretofore was a subject of the King of Great Britain and Ireland, nor was, nor is subject to any of the laws or statutes of the Kingdom of Great Britain and Ireland.*

And the said Jack Congo Murrell further saith that the said Jabbingee in the information named and with the wilful, murder or whom the said Jack Congo Murrell is and by the said information charged, was at the time of such supposed murder, a native Black be-longing to one of such Tribes as aforesaid and was not then, nor at any time theretofore a subject of the King of Great Britain and Ireland ; nor at any time was subject to any of the laws or statutes of the Kingdom of Great Britain and, Ireland, or under the protection of the same. ' And the said Jack Congo Murrell avers that agreeably to and under and by such usages and customs, he, the said Jack Congo Murrell is suspected of the murder of the said Jabbingee, can and may be made to stand punishment for the same and can and may be exposed to such and so many spears as the friends and relatives of the said Jabbingee, with the supposed murder of whom the said Jack Congo Murrell is and stands charged in and by the said information may think proper to hurl and throw against the body of him the said Jack Congo Murrell, may be endangered and brought into jeopardy for the said supposed murder of the said Jabbingee.

And the said Jack Congo Murrell also avers that no proceedings may be had or taken against him the said Jack Congo Murrell, in the said Supreme Court of New South Wales, for the said supposed murder, nor any verdict of acquittal which may be had or follow thereupon will or can operate as a bar, or be pleaded as such to the proceedings which will or can be had against him the said Jack Congo Murreli, by the said relatives and friends of the said Jabbingee, with the supposed murder of whom the, said Jack Congo Murrell stands charged in the said information, agreeably to the before-mentioned usages and customs and this he is ready to verify. Wherefore he prays judgment and that by the Court here he may be dismissed and dis-charged from the said premises in the said information specified. ' His Honour the Chief Justice said the plea was a very ingenious one and asked the Attorney General how he should proceed, when that gentleman re-plied that he must take time to consider the plea.'

LAUNCESTON ADVERTISER (TAS: 1829 - 1846),
THURSDAY 17 MARCH 1836, PAGE 3

Flinder's Island — We have been highly gratified this week by the reports of the general prosperity of the Aboriginal Establishment at this Island; and of the great progress made in the education and civilization of the blacks since their indefatigable friend, Mr. G. A. Robinson, has had charge of the Establishment. Both male and female natives are becoming cleanly and industrious in their habits. The male blacks have, within the last two months cleared a road from the establishment to the beach half-a-mile through a dense forest, beside some cross roads of minor importance: a portion of them have been engaged lately in reaping several acres of barley, which they are stated to have cut and housed admirably : and it is a singular fact that those natives engaged who were brought from that part of the main the most remote from the settled districts, were the most clever in this agricultural pursuit. The female blacks have become' attentive to domestic matters — are cleanly in their persons and in their dwellings, which they sweep out twice every day; they wash the clothes for their families; and are already so proficient at the needle as to make all their own garments and keep them in repair.

Within the last month they have been taught knitting by the Catechist's wife and already they have made such progress in this useful art, as, although labouring under the disadvantage of an absence of proper materials, to produce specimens well worth seeing. In addition to the day-school for women and children, an evening-school and Sabbath-school have been commenced; each of which, the attendance being with great judgment made perfectly voluntary, is well attended. The former was first opened so lately as the 7th of February and the anxiety of the natives to learn is said to be indescribable.

Be sides the officers of the establishment and their wives, who act as teachers, there are two native youths (one 9, the other 12 years old) who are so advanced as to have classes entrusted to them ; and they are to be seen, perched upon stools, engaged in the interesting occupation of teaching the English alphabet to 7 or 8 native adults ; who have so far been led to forget former ferocious habits as to pay the greatest attention to their juvenile teachers and to evince an intense anxiety to secure their approbation by progressing in their learning. We are highly gratified in being able to make this statement of the condition of the ancient inhabitants of the country. Mr. Robinson has made the Colony doubly his debtor.

TASMANIAN (HOBART TOWN, TAS: 1827 - 1839), FRIDAY 3 JUNE 1836, PAGE 6

THE ABORIGINES.

We have already drawn the attention of the people to the injustice of subjecting the Aborigines of these Colonies to laws, of the very nature of which they are not only in the most perfect ignorance—but the subjecting them to be tried by Jury not their " Peers," is of itself a flagrant violation of those very laws themselves, under which every foreigner is entitled by express statute to be tried by a Jury, one half of which are to be foreigners. Thus therefore, monstrously absurd as it is to subject the Aborigine to laws utterly incomprehensible to him, to try him legally under those laws he is entitled to a Jury of one half of his own countrymen.

The Jury very sensibly got rid of the difficulty by acquitting the prisoner. The following is the report from the Sydney Gazette:— "Jack Congo Murrell, (an Aboriginal) stood indicted for the wilful murder of (another

Aboriginal named) Jabingi, upon the Windsor road, by striking, him on the head with a tomahawk, on the 21st December, 1835. Mr. Therry, in stating the case to the jury said, he believed they were the first, jury impanelled to try an Aboriginal for the murder of another. But however unpleasant it might he to sit upon a charge made against a person who was not conversant with our language and who did not possess the same degree of intelligence as ourselves, yet, still the Judges of the Supreme Court had decided, after solemn argument, that such persons were amenable to the English law for such offence as the prisoner stood charged with. He then proceeded to state the particulars of the case which will be seen from the following evidence.

John Solly.—I am a settler residing at Richmond; on the 1st December last, I was near Mr. Baylis's, between Richmond and Windsor; there were five or six black men and two black women; prisoner got up off the ground and struck another on the head with a tomahawk; his name I did not know; the man did not fall with the first blow, but to the best of my knowledge, prisoner struck him again on the head; I then went towards Baylis's door and remained there until all was quiet; 1 then went to the spot where they were; the man was dead; he had a brass plate on his breast with the names of Jabingi; there was a wound on the back part of the head; it appeared to have been inflicted with a tomahawk. Cross-examined.—There was two blacks dead when I went up; all the blacks were there except one, who ran across the adjoining paddock; that was not the prisoner; the affray did not continue more than ten minutes; did not know the origin of the quarrel; the other black had no plate on his breast; I am positive it was the prisoner who struck Jabingi.

TASMANIAN (HOBART TOWN, TAS. : 1827 - 1839), FRIDAY 3 JUNE 1836, PAGE 6

Edward Jeffery.—I live with Mr. Baylis {on the 21st December last, some blacks came there between 10 and 11 o'clock ; there might be nine or ten of them; Baylis keeps a public house; they sat down on the side of the road opposite the house for two or three hours after that they began to cut capers with tomahawks; the first blow I saw struck way by a gin, when Bummery struck the man on the head and he fell; prisoner then struck another man on the back of the bead with his tomahawk, but as he did not fall prisoner struck knee, when he fell; he never moved hand or foot afterwards; deceased did not strike the prisoner during the affray; I was in the front room of Baylis's house and saw the whole of it through the window; I cannot say whether they were drunk or sober; they had three or four pots of sour beer from the house; I believe a small matter makes them drunk. After some further evidence, Mr. Windeyer submitted that so far from a case of murder a case of manslaughter had not even been made out.

The Acting Chief Justice said lie must let / the case go to the Jury and called upon the ' prisoner for his defence; having nothing to say, be was asked if he had any witnesses. Mr. Windeyer said, that they had no witnesses, because the only parties they could would be the blacks who were present and he understood such evidence would not be received, they not believing in a future state His Honor said that the British laws were to be enforced here so far as they were applicable to the circumstances of the Colony ; .and certainly if a black man was to be tried, black witnesses might be called, Mr. Wyndeyer said if they had been aware of the fact, they would have been better prepared, but he understood they could not be examined for the reason already stated. His Honor replied that such a point had never been decided by that Court, this being the first case of the kind which had ever come before it; but as they had no witnesses now, he would not then state his opinion, it would be quite time enough to argue the question when it comes regularly before the Court.

He then commenced addressing the jury, by explaining the authority which the Supreme Court possessed over all parties within its jurisdiction and the power they had to try the blacks for offences committed within it; after having gone through the whole of the evidence, he left it to the jury to try whether the prisoner was guilty, or not guilty. If guilty, whether of murder or manslaughter. The jury after an absence of a few minutes, returned a general verdict of Not Guilty.—Prisoner was discharged.

His Honor observed that probably this trial would be of great service; as it might tend to teach the blacks, that if they came into the civil parts of the Colony, they would be made amenable to the laws for any outrages they might commit *The Crown prosecutor declined proceeding with the case of Buramerv, the evidence in that case being the same as above. He consequently was discharged from custody."*

TRUE COLONIST VAN DIEMEN'S LAND POLITICAL DESPATCH AND AGRICULTURAL AND COMMERCIAL... (HOBART TOWN, TAS: 1834 - 1844), FRIDAY 9 SEPTEMBER 1836, PAGE 286

TO MR. JAMES HOBBS.

"Thou shalt not bear false witness against thy neighbour."

SIR, - By the receipt of some volumes of Parliamentary Papers, my attention has been again directed to your evidence given before the Aborigines Committee on the 9th of March, 1830, wherein it appears that you made the following gratuitous statement, which had done me great injury in this Colony and may, have done me some in England. You, say, "Mr. Gilbert Robertson has never exerted himself in pursuit of the Natives; he has done much' mischief in not following them up; he has been more employed in looking after grants of land than the natives." Now, Mr. James Hobbs, I call upon you, in the face of the whole Colony before Colonel Arthur leaves it, to state publicly the grounds on which you took upon yourself to give this testimony against me, behind my back, in a secret Committee.

Such secret, got up testimony, has been the ruin of hundreds of honest men in this Colony; and now that the hatred system is, I trust, at an end, it becomes, the duty of every honest man to trace out the authors of these secret slanders and put them to the proof; let them shew that they had reasonable grounds for what they state, or let them sink at once to that infamy and degradation, which is the merited station of a lying slanderer, a false witness. I call upon you to shew that you, from your own know-ledge, had any opportunity of being acquainted with the truth or falsehood of what you stated when under solemn examination as a witness; or that you were deceived by others and who the parties were that so deceived you. Now, Sir, I have, through every vicissitude of fortune and against much wicked persecution, preserved something which I value more than anything of which you could deprive me - I mean, a character; and regard to this compels me to demand from you an answer - a public answer, to this letter; establish what you have said, or shew that you were deceived and publicly retract this slander. When, on a former occasion, I made some remarks on your evidence in this case, I am told that you smoke very big and threatened to thrash me in the street.

Now, Mr. James Hobbs, I must have some more satisfactory answer than this, for you claim to be a gentleman; and although I should not, when prepared to expect it, be much afraid of an attack from a street bully, even of your prowess, yet I have never learned that even the, more gentlemanly means of powder and ball, much less sticks or fisticuffs, was a satisfactory or rational method of clearing character. I have set before you a very simple method of settling this matter - if you believed at the time that you spoke the truth; shew upon what grounds - if you were deceived, acknowledge it and express your regret. Do me justice, it is all I ask; but be assured, that until you have done so, you shall have little rest while you and I live in the same country. I will neither kill you nor maim you and I will always be ready, as I trust I am able to defend myself, should you attempt to put in execution the threat which you made on a former occasion.

Do me justice and I will forget and forgive the injury; deny me this and be assured you will be sorry for it, if the people of Van Diemen's Land should ever recover from the effects of the present system, so far as to place any value on truth, candour and honesty, yours, as you take this,

GILBERT ROBERTSON. I address you thus publicly, because the slander, which I wish you to remove, was first brought under my notice in a public official document, printed and published by the House of Commons.

1837

TRUE COLONIST VAN DIEMEN'S LAND POLITICAL DESPATCH AND AGRICULTURAL AND COMMERCIAL... (HOBART TOWN, TAS: 1834 - 1844), FRIDAY 31 MARCH 1837, PAGE 514

ORIGINAL CORRESPONDENCE
TO THE EDITOR OF THE TRUE COLONIST

Sir, - The reappearance of the aborigines, at Bushy last week astonished the whole colony. The Government, who had so patronised and paid Mr. Robinson with money, land and honours, as well as several districts in the interior, had praised and subscribed, to him, did expect and had a right to expect that he had finished his work according to his assertion. I am informed there are three tribes at large in the colony, viz: — The Pieman's River: tribe, the Sandy Cape tribe and the Hampshire Hills tribe; beside several stragglers - about 120 individuals! A ? the public sentinel, the colony calls on you Mr. Editor to make equity into this mysterious affair— I am, sir, etc. QUID NUNC.

[It has been several times reported to us, that there are three tribes of natives still at large as represented by our correspond-ant. We do not wish to offer any opinion as to the merits of Mr G. A. Robinson, compared with the rewards, has received. But all must admit, that the party under his

charge were eminently successful. We do not grudge. Mr. Robinson the rewards he has received, but we know that there are other persons who have done and suffered much in the same cause and whose success at least furnished the means of doing all that was accomplished in bringing in the natives— but who have, been most unjustly refused the compensation which they had been promised for their labours. But we are certain of one thing, that not one half of the natives who were known to be in the island in1828; have even been accounted (for - it is too probable that numbers have been slain, whose fate has never been publicly known. Ed]

TASMANIAN (HOBART TOWN, TAS: 1827 - 1839), FRIDAY 28 JULY 1837, PAGE 7

THE ABORIGINES.

We find the following excellent article in the Cornwall Chronicle of Tuesday. We rejoice to perceive that one public journal has the manly bearing to venture to lift up even a corner of the shroud, covering that miserable "humbug the Aborigines Establishment: — "BRITISH HUMANITY—THE FLINDERS' ISLAND BASTILE.—In passing our eye over the minute on the subject of Finance, as laid before the Honourable the Legislative Council, we observe, in allusion to the Establishment at Flinders' Island, the following:— 'Finding that the amount annually estimated for the Aborigines,' Establishment at Flinders' Island, has been always insufficient to meet the actual expenditure, I have caused £1,000 to be added to last years estimate, for food and clothing for the Establishment making the proposed estimate amount to £3,518 10s.'

We are willing to give His Excellency credit for his humanity, which, however, we should like to see judiciously exercised. In the present case, the people's pockets are taxed to a very considerable amount, to support an establishment, the nature of which requires not only immediate but minutely scrupulous enquiry. Originally upwards of four hundred natives were congregated on Flinders' Island, under the superintendence of Mr. Robinson and the rest of their maintenance was very considerably less than it is said to be at this time, when their number does not amount to one hundred.

Instead, therefore, for their being a necessity to increase the estimate for the support of this establishment £1,000 this year, common sense tells us the propriety of reducing it by £2,000!!! We believe we are in possession of correct information relative to it's Establishment and for that reason repeat our conviction of the positive necessity for an investigation into the management of it and of every matter connected with it. Certain it is, that in a very short space of time, three-fourths of the Aboriginal Natives have died!

If they are British subjects, their fellow subjects are privileged to be made acquainted with the cause of the extraordinary loss of life. It does not follow, that because these poor creatures have been forcibly transported to a desert Island, they should die off like rotten sheep, without receiving even the common sympathy of their fellow men. It is true that they are of a different complexion to the invaders of their country—it is true, that being goaded on by cruelties to self-defence, they sometimes retaliated upon their oppressors; and, perhaps, humane policy it was on the part of their oppressors, to remove them away from their native land. The policy of the measure, nevertheless, does not constitute it a just measure; the rightful inheritors of this land have been forcibly transported to a desert Island, where, under the deceptive colour of humanity, they are forcibly detained— are forcibly subjected to a restraint and discipline, that will only terminate in their annihilation.

What could Colonists have to fear from these poor, abused creatures, were they permitted to enjoy their native air in an undisturbed freedom?

Has our population of nearly fifty thousand Englishmen, to fear injury from less than one hundred harmless and unoffending natives, enjoying that liberty which is no less their right, than necessary for their existence? Away with such worse than childish fears. The act of detaining the rightful possessors of this land in captivity at Flinder's Island, is an act of political *atrocity, that is disgraceful to ourselves and our country and has but one parallel in the annals of civilized nations*— that of Colonel Arthur inhumanly butchering, by the hands of the common hangman, some of this same race of native blacks."*

1838

HOBART TOWN COURIER (TAS: 1827 - 1839), FRIDAY 30 MARCH 1838, PAGE 2

THE GERMAN MISSION TO THE ABORIGINES.

WE have before us a mass of papers connected with transactions which have occurred in this colony; regarding the Aboriginal tribes of this island. In our annual of this year will be found a rapid sketch of the conciliation which was effected between the colonists and the native tribes, through the instrumentality of Sir George ARTHUR and Mr. G. A. Robinson, together with the assistance of the Aboriginal committee, composed of gentlemen of ability and enlarged views, Mr. Roderic O'Connor, Mr. P. A. Mulgrave and the Rev. Mr. Bedford. A publication is also in progress, which will, ere long, make its appearance; furnishing a more detailed narrative of the history of the aborigines of Van Diemen's Land.

We have offered the above preliminary observations, because we remark in the Sydney Colonist some very curious lucubrations on the subject of the German mission, combined with confident assertions, by no means warranted by facts and experience. It is generally under stood that Dr. Lang is the soul and mover of all which appears in the Sydney Colonist and it is not unnatural that he should write approvingly of himself, by extolling a scheme of which the Colonist boasts that he is the promoter. As relates to the mission itself, a vein of pious anxiousness pervades the whole article; and it is more particularly on that ac-count that we cannot applaud that portion, where the name of Mr. Edward Smith Hall is dragged in, apparently for the sole purpose of bespattering that gentle-man with abuse, without any proof what-ever of his having acted in an unbecoming manner. We regret to see this species of warfare in the Colonist-and in this instance the more so, as the shafts are thrown by a minister of the gospel.

In perusing the elaborate article with care and attention, we cannot help observing that the premises are generally unfounded and where they are not so, that deductions arc made directly opposed to the premises. We are informed that the British Parliament has made a recognition of the important principle, that the land in these colonies belongs of right to its Aboriginal inhabitants and that it is only to be held by the British Government as trustees for their benefit. Whether such principle has, or has not, been recognised by the British Parliament does not affect the real question.

In all cases where we enter upon discussions connected with subjects of an abstruse nature, we should go to the root we should always enter on a first series of propositions and not commence with a second or third series, otherwise all will be confusion and obscurity. This globe ought to be considered as the property of all its inhabitants and no exclusiveness tolerated. In civilized states much murmuring and discontent have arisen from an unequal distribution of land; but what can be more absurd than to suppose that the bountiful Creator has given exclusively to a few savages, tracts of land.

HOBART TOWN COURIER (TAS: 1827 - 1839), FRIDAY 30 MARCH 1838, PAGE 2

We cannot, however, conclude our present remarks, without observing that the article in the Colonist appears to us to be a very lame production, a jumble of words and erroneous conclusions, drawn from false premises - in some part ejaculating pious sentiments, in others attacking a private individual, wholly unconnected with the subject. Does it follow, because two companies succeeded in obtaining exorbitant grants of land, that it must be of more profit to dispose of the waste lands to a few individuals of large capital, than to make an equitable distribution among many, won by industry would much more beneficially promote the interests of the "mother country," and the colonies ? The whole affair wears very much the aspect of a job, with Dr. Lang at the head of it. As may be expected, what has transpired in this colony, with respect to the aborigines, is carefully kept out of sight as extensive as all Europe.

The Colonist avails itself of scriptural phrases to support its assertions and we shall do the same. In the first part of the Holy Volume, we find that the Creator placed originally a single pair, male and female, on earth and from this stem has sprung all the nations of the earth. Hence it follows that all are equally entitled to a participation in the vast inheritance; and hence, also, it follows that where there is a redundancy of population, the country has an unquestionable right to take possession of waste lands in other portions of the globe.

The Colonist, as it proceeds, affords a practical illustration of the character of the "recognition on the part of the British Parliament," which is completely at variance with the premises set forth. It says, "these measures on behalf of the aborigines, form a most appropriate appendage to the great whig measure of 1831 - we mean the transition from the old feudal system of granting land in the colonies, to that of selling it to the highest bidder and devoting the proceeds to the encouragement of emigration." Here, then, we have a rare specimen of parliamentary recognition that august body, as trustees for the aborigines of New South Wales, orders their land to be sold-and for what? To promote further immigration and missions, under the superintendence of the Synod of New South Wales; that is, as Dr. Lang conceives, under his own superintendence.

But the misfortune is, that at least one-half of the Presbyterian Church of New South Wales and the entire Church of Van Diemen's Land, are totally opposed to Dr. Lang's pretensions. A question also arises by what right does the British Parliament nominate itself as trustees to the aborigines of New South Wales? Surely, in all similar cases, there are two parties to the contract - and the Colonist affords practical proofs that no such trusteeship is desired on the part of the aborigines, nor even any connection with us; for he mentions the melancholy loss of the Stirling Castle and a number of ships wrecked on the eastern coast, with the wretched fate of the mariners who fell into the merciless hands of the ferocious.

CORNWALL CHRONICLE (LAUNCESTON, TAS: 1835 - 1880),
SATURDAY 7 APRIL 1838, PAGE 2

The aborigines imprisoned on Flinder's Island continue to die at the rate of 20 percent, without any births to supply their loss. Ninety are now the sum total that remain of all the various and large Aboriginal tribes of Van Diemen's Land; to that the utter extinction of the race is hastily approaching.

Can anything be done for these injured being? All that has been done by the Colonial Government for them, up to the present time, has been to exile them and to order their confinement in a prison out of which it is impossible for them to escape and, in fact, to do for them what has been done for prisoners of another colour— appointing a Superintendent or Commandant, to see they did not escape and to enforce the Government orders and a Store keeper to serve out their clothes and rations and a Catechist or Chaplain to instruct them; so that the Government has just done as much for the aborigines at it has done for British convicts. What does Sir John Franklin purpose after having personally inspected the aborigines' prison?

Is his Excellency still deliberating with the Government that sent them there?— a short time remains and death will decide what Sir John and his Government cannot. And when; is Captain Maconochie, who gratuitously philosophizes on the amelioration of the aborigines of other colonies and wholly over looks the original natives of this? Will he not bend his lively imagination and fruitful genius to concoct some benevolent plan, in order to ameliorate the pitiable condition of the remnant of this much injured race? It wilt lie seen by a Gazette notice in our back page, that the transfer system is to be dis continued and, for the future, masters having no further occasion far assigned servants, will be permitted to return them to the Government. The plan of transferring assigned Servants was good; it was generally appreciated and the abandonment of it is injudicious.

TASMANIAN (HOBART TOWN, TAS: 1827 - 1839), FRIDAY 13 APRIL 1838, PAGE 7

TO THE EDITOR OF THE TASMANIAN AND REVIEW.

SIR,—Two of your contemporaries have concurred this week in inviting public attention to the continued mortality said to exist among the Aborigines of this Colony, shut up in Flinders' Island; and I am persuaded that you will willingly contribute your might to such a cause. It will be in your recollection that when the subject was averted to some months back in our Legislative Council, the medicament prescribed—the only one and therefore we presume, considered an adequate one and proposed as such by the relative and namesake of a celebrated Scotch doctor,—was the substitution of a Chaplain for a Catechist, that these poor creatures might be canonically married.

The community was at a loss at the time to conceive the rationale of such treatment and it is only lately that it has been enlightened by the publication in—I think your own paper— of the result of certain Statistical Returns, from which it appears that the chance of life is in some minute ratio better in the married, than in the unmarried state. But the disease being acute, this tonic application does not appear to have been equal to the emergency, Hymen has been unable to play the part of Aesclepius; and I would earnestly intreat therefore, a reconsideration of the symptoms:

The subject at the same time, is far too serious to be slightly treated. Twenty per cent, is said to be the annual ratio of decrease and ninety the entire number of individuals now left. If this statement be correct, from four to five years will extirpate the race; and what will posterity say of such a consummation?—or, when too late, perhaps even our own consciences?

Two or three reasons may be assigned as causing the catastrophe without involving much personal censure. The situation of Flinders Island may be unhealthy — or the change of habits imposed at it may be too violent — or wearied and discouraged by a long captivity, its victims may have become dejected and ready to give way on the slightest appearance of sickness —or all these causes may be combined. But what are the real facts and is there no remedy for them? Surely the voice of humanity is not clamorous. when it asks answers to these questions.

I see that the representations made on this subject Captain Maconochie's name is alluded to. I cannot know what his specific opinions may be regarding, it, but judging from his writings, I do not believe that; he is without any. And he seems to me to owe it to his own character and consistency to declare them, LAS CASAS. (our correspondent's letter receives insertion by the withdrawal of matter in type previous its being received. But, the condition of the Aborigines is exciting so very general attention and commiseration at present, that we could not delay in its insertion. He will perceive that we had anticipated his call upon us, to direct attention to the question.— ED. TAS.)

Aesclepius[xxi]

CORNWALL CHRONICLE (LAUNCESTON, TAS: 1835 - 1880),
SATURDAY 12 MAY 1838, PAGE 77

THE ABORIGINES OF VAN DIEMEN'S LAND.

A remarkably pitiless article in the Hobart Town Courier of the 30th March last, under the title of THE GERMAN MISSION TO THE ABORIGINES and of course intended as a sort of comment on our recent article under the same title, concludes in the following style:— ' The whole affair wears very much the appearance of a job, with Dr. Lang at the head of it. As may be expected, what has transpired in this colony with respect to the Aborigines, is carefully kept out of sight.' Now, we are by no meant surprised that Mr. Timothy Jackbrains, the Editor of the Hobart Town Courier, should be unable to see anything but a job in the German Mission to the Aborigines and we must be candid in acknowledging, that we would be sorry to put ourselves to the slightest trouble for the purpose of showing him that there is anything else in it.

But as to our concealing "what has transpired" in regard to the Aborigines of Van Diemen's Land and our sinister intentions in doing so, Mr. L. may rest assured, that he is for once completely mistaken. We had no wish to conceal the fact, so peculiarly creditable to the white colonists of Van Diemen's Land, than in the course of not more than thirty years from the first settlement of that island, they had actually exterminated its comparatively numerous Aboriginal population; reducing the miserable remnant of four distinct tribes or nations to a hundred and fifty individuals, whom they now take credit to themselves, forsooth, for banishing to an island in the Straits!

What possible interest could we have in concealing such a fact— the most disgraceful without exception in the whole history of British colonization and the only parallel to which is to be found in the history of the colony and island of Hispaniola, where it took the Spaniards exactly the same period to exterminate the unfortunate Caribs, the Aborigines of the Island? No! it was impossible that we could have had any private ends to serve in not mentioning, what the truly judicious Editor of the HOBART TOWN COURIER reflects upon us for intentionally keeping out of sight, viz.:— That the blood of the wretched Aborigines of his adopted country, of whom hundreds were shot like native dogs by the white colonists, still cries for vengeance to heaven against the European inhabitants of Van Die men's Land. We were actually shown a retired spot on the River Clyde in that island, where no fewer than seventeen of its miserable black natives were one day shot in cold blood by some of the settlers!

Our own blood runs cold and curdles at the very thought of it ! Oh, no, Mr. Lackbrains, we were not the people to conceal facts like these from any envious wish to keep your good deeds out of the sight of the public! You are right welcome to all the credit they are likely to bring you. Chargeable as a few of the older hands in this colony undoubtedly are with much which it were difficult to answer for, in regard to their con duct towards the Aborigines, one fact, which is notorious and cannot be controverted, speaks volumes as to the totally different measure which has been dealt out to the Aborigines of this colony, as compared with the measure of extermination pursued towards the Aborigines of Van Diemen's Land, viz. :— that whereas every district in New South Wales is quite studded with native names, which are well known as the Aboriginal names of localities, whether in general use among Europeans or not, we could not find, after diligent enquiry, that a single locality in all Van Diemen's Land is known to the colonists by its ancient native name, or is even known to have had a native name at all !

The ancient Celts and Britons left ten thousand Aboriginal names of places in England and Scotland, when they were nearly exterminated in the low countries and driven to the mountains of Scotland and Wales by our forefathers, the Saxons. But so complete has been the process of extermination in Van Diemen's Land, that the Aborigines of that island have left not a single wreck behind them— not even NOMINIS UMBRA, the shadow of a name - THE COLONIST.

CORNWALL CHRONICLE (LAUNCESTON, TAS: 1835 - 1880), SATURDAY 2 JUNE 1838, PAGE 90

DEAR EDITOR,

Sir,— I perceive in the Van Diemen's Land Almanack for the present year, which has at length made its appearance when nearly half the year is expired, (edited by Mr. Win. Gore Elliston, or, as the Editor of the Sydney Colonist calls him, ' Timothy Lackbrains, a long, verbose, trashy account of what is familiarly called the black war, appears therein. From what I can collect from the writer, he appears to be a foreign convict. He lauds the military genius of Colonel Arthur to the skies, for having in the course of two months, with a military force of two thousand men and at an expense of thirty-six thousand pounds, captured one black native. This may be one cause why the Treasurer has a complaint in the chest and is obliged to draw on the Commissary for the current expenses of the year. If the gallant Colonel proceeds in this style, in the Canadas, he will soon tranquilize the country.

The following piece of adulation is unparalleled in its kind and is a perfect climax of absurdity. It is a fine close to this successful campaign, during which the indomitable Colonel proclaimed martial law against the poor Aboriginal natives and gathered such unfading laurels as procured him the honour of Knighthood, the advancement to the rank of Major General and the Governorship of one of the finest Colonies annexed to the British Crown ; is it any wonder that one of your contemporaries exclaims— ' Are the people of Downing-street mad ?' If they are not, they have at least taken leave of their senses for some time. I fear I shall disgust your readers by quoting this abominable trash; and that you will not have patience to publish it, for the amusement of your humorous readers.

I hope you will — here it is -"It fell to the rare lot of Sir George Arthur, to achieve an object which most despaired of seeing accomplished; the fact is on record and cannot be blotted out by the ingenious inventions of malice or detraction. Had Colonel Arthur done nothing else this act would stand alone as an honourable memorial of his administration or this Colony. The honour of the transaction will remain when his enemies shall be laid low in the dust.' ' Praise undeserved is censure in disguise.'

The Almanack abounds with other falsehoods and absurdities; among the rest Timothy compares Robinson, the native black catcher, to Christopher Columbus. Is such trash worth ten shillings? I think not. I am credibly informed, that the writer of the Itinerary, which is stuffed into this miserable catch-penny, was drunk in a hut on the Clyde, during the time he was supposed to be traversing the country which he attempts to describe and never saw a foot of it, except in 'the mind's eye' of his be sotted imagination; but this and the eight hundred men 'in buckram,' satellites of the clique, who were going to drive their opponents into the sea, will be believed by credulous John Bull, fur whose appetite this precious trash was concocted. — Your's, &c. &c. A FRIEND TO TRUTH.
Ross, 18th May, 1838.

CORNWALL CHRONICLE (LAUNCESTON, TAS: 1835 - 1880),
SATURDAY 9 JUNE 1838, PAGE 2

THE CORNWALL CHRONICLE, LAUNCESTON, V. D. LAND, SATURDAY, JUNE 9, 1838.

"Liberty with danger is lo be preferred to slavery with security." Sallust.

THE ABORIGINAL PRISON. In the last week's Gazette, the public is invited to Tender for the supply of one Hundred and eighty tons or stores, for the use of the imprisoned natives at Flinder's Island. With a revenue scarcely sufficient to meet the salaries of the swarms of persons thrust upon the public purse, under the denomination of Government Officers, we protest

*most determinedly against any further draft upon the Treasury Chest,
for the support of the now, mere remnant of the original inhabitants of
this Colony— so long as they are kept under a forced and cruel control
—as it would appear to be, merely for the sake of affording a yield for
the employment of patronage. We do not pretend to be quite correct in
stating, that the original number of the legitimate proprietors of the soil of
this Island, two or three years ago— upon the forming the Flinder's Island
Bastille, exceeded 400, -- the number might have been at that time, a few
more or less. It is enough for us to know that we are correct in stating. that
their numbers now, do not amount to 90 — and, that it is decreasing very
rapidly, in consequence of a disease prevalent among the poor kidnapped
blacks, vulgarly called a broken heart. We have heard much said of Colonel
Arthur's humane disposition and the formation of the Bastille on Flinder's
Island has been brought forward as a proof or his humanity.*

*The kidnapping a race of human beings, for the express purpose of
subjecting them to ignominious and cowardly imprisonment, does not,
according to our way of thinking, saviour much of the spirit of humanity—
yet it is adduced as a proof of Colonel Arthur's humanity. Supposing it to
be possible and that a body of blacks, or whites, invaded this Island—now
claimed as the property of the British Government and the Settlers and
forcibly seized the inhabitants, habitants, indiscriminately and transported
them to Flinder's Island, or, any other Island— and obliged them to
acknowledge the authority— of men placed over them by the invaders,
who locked them up in Barracks each night and obliged them to partake of
food— provided for them according to the inclination of their invaders and
to eat and drink and go to sleep and wake —just when and where and how
the said invaders pleased. Would so great violence to all laws, human and
divine, bear the appellation of humanity? and what would be the effects
of the transportation on our settlers — presuming it occurred— why,
precisely what it is upon the native blacks— they would feel their degrading
captivity— their compulsory treatment— and die off rapidly— broken
hearted. But, putting the humanity of the transportation system out of the*

question, what does the country gain by it ? It gains everlasting disgrace: and it loses some six or seven thousand pounds annually — to deserve it. But again, the establishment affords a few luscious sops.

The natives must be governed, consequently a Governor is provided; they happen to die very frequently and disease is very prevalent among them and they require a medical gentleman; they must eat and a purveyor of stores obtains a berth; they have souls to be saved and a Parson is necessary to instruct them; he being a great man must have an assistant to do the drudgery for him and so on, until we discover that to keep these poor captives healthy, religious and under due subjection. there is maintained at the public expense, a little army of patronage hunters. We learn that independent of the conveyance of the 180 tons or stores, tendered for, the cost of them will exceed £44000 and that a further draft upon the public purse will be made for stores within twelve months. Really, this is out of all character: it is a Tax that should not be imposed upon the public, because it is not a necessary Tax — The Natives are kept in unconstitutional control, on Flinders Island, when their free services might be rendered valuable if put into operation under judicious management, in this Colony. These Natives might be made very useful to the country and to the Government, even were they divided among the police stations.

The number of men we understand, does not exceed fifty, who, if they were agreeable, might be distributed among the Police and be considered under the especial charge and protection of the Police Magistrates. They would be found exceedingly useful in tracing bushrangers and their cost would not lie one twentieth part of what it now is, because the natives only would require support, whereas, under the present system at Flinders, a most ruinously expensive establishment must be supported. We do not, however, think, that the natives, if released from their present imprisonment, should be subjected to any restraint beyond that necessary to keep them from disobeying the established laws of the country; they are as free as ourselves and areas justly entitled to the undisturbed exercise of their freedom and it is not probable that they are ignorant of our civilized institutions, or of the necessity for their rigidly obeying them— we say, it is not probable they can lie ignorant of them, because some years ago the public was informed, by means of the Courier, that the Aboriginal natives upon Flinders, were so well instructed in the rules of civilized life and so perfectly correct in the observance of them, that they might, as a body, be submitted to the white population, as an example worthy of imitation ; and that a newspaper was established at the settlement, edited and conducted solely by the natives.'

If these people had no correct a notion of the observances of civilized life some three years back— we repeat, that it is not likely, with the expenditure of some £15,000 upon them since, — a greater portion or which, is said, to have been expended in providing the means of instruction, that they can make now dangerous citizen : and we call upon the local Government to abandon the establishment at Flinders and to restore the illegally transported natives to their own lands and to the enjoyment or their liberty -- their liberty, which is their right by nature— the gift of nature's God, which no earthly power can or could righteously deprive them of. These poor men have never forfeited their right to freedom— they were disturbed in their quiet possession of the land of their birth by unlawful invaders and by unlawful means. The might of the invader was his excuse for forcibly possessing himself of the right of the poor native. Might upon most occasions conquers right. The civilized English conquered by their might the right of the uncivilized Aboriginals and finished their noble conquest by transporting to a barren island, the few poor wretches who escaped the sword's edge and the bullet. This is a specimen of Colonel Arthur's humanity! If the administration of the present day is of a different calibre to that of Colonel Arthur, it will relieve itself from the disgrace of continuing the Flinder's Island establishment one moment longer than it is necessary to arrange for the disposal and the comfort of the remaining few natives who are entitled to the liberal support and protection of this country, having been forcibly deprived of the land— their birth-right— by us and consequently their means of support; and although we urge that it is our duty to support them, we deny the necessity for taxing the country, to the immense amount it is taxed, to support an army of patronage sprigs, to constitute the 'Establishment'— a Gaol and an unconstitutional Gaol.

If there can exist a doubt of the peaceable conduct of the few Aborigines upon being restored to their Native Land and a fear that they would disturb the peace of the present Settlers— the Government possess the means to prevent it. A very large tract of land at the Westward of this Colony, is yet unoccupied and many years must elapse before it can be made available to the necessities of Emigrants or established settlers; let that land be apportioned to the Natives; there,— they will breathe their native atmosphere; there — they can procure kangaroo and wholesome water; which, by the bye, it seems, is a necessary that Flinder's Island does not possess— there they can enjoy existence in all its enchanting wildness— and after the manner of their forefathers.

The diseases entailed upon them by the merciless rigour of their gaolers— will, in a very short time, perfect their annihilation, let them be continued in, or be relieved from their imprisonment; the latter course, however, would probably soften their afflictions. We believe that the Sydney Government never found occasion to adopt the humanity of Colonel Arthur, relative to the native of that Colony. The gallant Colonel has all the honour of the humane act.

COLONIAL TIMES (HOBART, TAS: 1828 - 1857),
TUESDAY 20 NOVEMBER 1838, PAGE 5

THE ABORIGINES.

We mentioned last week, that Mr Robinson, now enjoying the grand title of Chief Protector of the Blacks, had delivered himself of a somewhat lengthy and pompous account of the manner in which he succeeded in capturing these poor creatures; and we promised to favour our readers with the same. We do so, now and shall have a few words to say on this affair very shortly.

After describing the atrocities committed by the Aborigines, previous to his embarking in the black mission and the measures adopted by the government to subdue the blacks by a military force, Mr. Robinson proceeded to relate the manner, in which he had formed the project of conciliating the natives and persuading them to place themselves under the protection of the government. He had long thought of the subject and as he had come to the conclusion, that their subjugation, by force of arms; was impracticable, on account of the peculiar formation of the country, he began to consider the probabilities of their being won over by fair means. He considered that although they might, in their savage notions, oppose violent measures to their subjugation, yet if he could but get them to listen to remonstrance, they might be civilized and rendered useful members of society.

With these views, he proposed the plan to the local government, to set out on an experimental visit to the natives at Port Davey, which was acceded to by Governor Arthur. He was furnished with a long boat, to carry his supplies round the coast to Port Davey and in the very outset obstacles presented themselves which almost prevented him from proceeding. He lost the whole of his supplies and was unable to procure more; and for the first time he was afraid of the enterprise. He was not however afraid of the danger, nor of the blacks; but he was afraid to return for more supplies, for fear the government should refuse to let him proceed. Accordingly, he pursued his journey over land to Port Davey; fell in with a party of blacks and made an appointment to meet them at a particular mount on the following day.

He repaired to the appointed spot, taking with him two out of the five natives from Brune Island, who accompanied him. The tribe he fell in with were very suspicious, having been fired at by the Europeans; and although he carried no arms - nothing, in fact, but a knapsack, containing bread they left on this occasion without any sign of desiring to repose trust in him. He then determined to bring them to an understanding; as he found that, if he wasted much time unsuccessfully, his tour of the island, instead of occupying twelve months (the time allotted), would last seven years.

Accordingly, he assembled them together and told the chiefs that he did not like their proceedings and should leave them. He requested that they would furnish him with guides across the country and he set off at 12 o'clock at night and was guided by some of the tribe to a distance from their camp, where he bivouacked. On the following morning the whole tribe joined him and he thus led them on and conciliated them, until they were joined by his own people at Macquarie Harbour. In 1830, he succeeded in establishing thirty-four of the natives on Swan Island ; and he then proceeded to explore the islands, crossing Bank's Straits, in a whale-boat and succeeded in emancipating several native women, who were kept by the whalers and sealers on the coast and conveyed them also to Swan Island.

The Government then furnished a schooner and boats for a second trip amongst the islands and offered high rewards to any other person who would join in the undertaking. No person, however, offered to go on the service and the sole duty again devolved upon him and he finally effected the removal of the most ferocious tribes that were known - the Oyster Bay and the Big River tribes. At the time that he went to endeavour to conciliate these tribes, Captain Thomas and a Mr Parker had been inhumanly murdered and a general panic was spread through that part of the country and armed forces were talked about. He had a conference with Colonel Arthur, to whom he expressed an opinion that no armed force would be able to subdue them and offered to go and subject them to reason; and he was enabled to lodge them with their own free will on Gun Carriage Island in six weeks from his interview with Colonel Arthur.

People could have but a faint idea of the toil and privations he had endured, but some persons might know that the climate was intensely cold and humid, the rains falling generally for six or eight months in the year; and when he assured them that he had been for weeks without a dry rag to his back, subsisting on fern roots and the pith of the shrub, the meeting might have some idea that his undertaking was none of the easiest. Had he been intent on the survey of the country only, his condition would not have been so bad, as he could have halted at leisure and he would have had the company of his countrymen and been provided with dogs and fire-arms to contribute to his subsistence; but in his undertaking, he was forced to submit to the greatest deprivations, if he had any hope of succeeding.

Dogs would have frequently prevented him communicating with the natives and fire-arms would have prevented their trusting him, when he did obtain interviews with them. Frequently had he lain down at night without a hope of awaking in the morning and had been surrounded by savage blacks with their spears presented at him and had been spared, when all hope had fled. He then had his hand on the place in the chart of the colony where he had a narrow escape; one evening he discovered some fires of the natives at a great distance and accompanied by some of the natives of his party, he set out and travelled during the night through swamps, up to his middle in water and arrived near to where a tribe was encamped. In the morning, he went down to the camp and the natives immediately began collecting their spears and evinced hostile intentions, which probably would have terminated fatally but for his decision. The blacks belonging to his escort, who saw that the tribe were unfriendly, immediately possessed them-selves of some of the spears and a fight seemed inevitable. He stepped forward between them, took the spears from his own men, returned them to their owners, sent his escort to a distance and stood in the middle of the tribe unarmed and ready to meet death, the result was, that they became pacified and after a short intercourse with them, put them-selves under his protection and followed him quietly.

In the subjection of the Oyster Bay and Big River tribes, the dangers were far greater. They were known to be furious and blood-thirsty people and in this matter also, it seemed, that Providence interposed between him and the savages. On approaching the place where they were encamped, they rushed down the hill, their spears pointed and shouting their war cry. The blacks who were with him, (Mr. R.) amongst whom were Eumarah and another Chieftain, fled; the women began to cry and the yells of the hostile tribe became dreadful. He knew it was little use to run, had he been disposed, as the blacks would have soon caught him; so he confronted them and awaited their arrival, looking calmly on. A parley ensued and they very shortly placed themselves under his direction. Mr. R. begged to explain that they had heard of him, that he was the blacks' friend, from other tribes and so were prepared in a manner to treat him kindly.

He accompanied them to their camp and spent the evening with them, making himself understood, as well as he could and acquainting them with his intentions - and a more pleasant evening he never remembered to have spent in his life, from the consideration that this savage tribe had also yielded to his persuasions. Montipreata, the Chief of the Big River Tribe, then shewed him the wounds which had been inflicted on his people by the white men and they appeared to have been produced by musket balls and slugs. The whole of these tribes followed Mr. R. into the town of Bothwell, where they threw down their spears and bivouacked opposite to the barracks, so great was the confidence he had gained with them and there they remained quiet and friendly to the people, until they finally accompanied him to Hobart Town, to the astonishment of all. After he had succeeded with these tribes, he felt that his work was done and told Colonel Arthur that there were no more blacks abroad, who might be dreaded, these tribes being those which had committed all the depredations.

After he had effected the removal of these tribes, he started to the Arthur River, where it was reported that a tribe was out - and here he had another miraculous escape from being killed. It appeared that the blacks had meditated his destruction and had laid their plans for preventing his escape by placing sentinels all around him. He was with them, when he observed an unusual excitement amongst them; they were agitated and employed sharpening their spears and other instruments of war. They began to encircle him, when for the first time, since he had undertaken the mission, he fled from them. He over- took a black woman, at a river which he must cross to escape from his pursuers and as he could not swim, he hardly knew what to do.

The woman advised him to hide himself in the bushes, but he knew too well the keenness with which the blacks tracked the smallest object to trust to that; and as his only hope, he launched a log of wood on which he leaned and the kind-hearted woman jumped into the water and swam across, drawing the log with her. He could truly say, that in all his troubles the poor black natives had consoled, fed him and con-tributed, in all they could to his comfort, diving for cray-fish and bringing them to sustain him; and had it not been for their attention, he must often have starved, or wandered and lost him-self in the bush - and here he begged to observe that the country through which he travelled, bore no resemblance to the fine open country of New Holland.

The entire country was a dense forest, the trees in some places being 60 feet in circumference and 250 feet high, interwoven with an almost impenetrable brush at the bottom; and for a long time, in traversing this wild, he was dependent for sustenance solely on the blacks who accompanied him, who caught badgers, porcupines and he not unfrequently had to live upon grubs. He also begged to correct an erroneous conception which had been formed with regard to the Sydney blacks who were forwarded to Van Diemen's Land, to assist in the capture of the Van Diemen's Land natives. He had never received any assistance from them and had from the first set his face against their being employed, because they knew nothing of the language or habits of the Van Diemen's Land blacks and would consequently have been a burthen, rather than any assistance in the expedition.

He would now proceed to the result of his undertaking. The aborigines of Van Diemen's Land had been represented as the lowest in the scale of humanity differing little from the brutes; but it had devolved upon him to discover and lead them forward in the scale of civilization and he had met with flattering success. He would, as the time was short, briefly touch on the measures he had taken to bring them to their present state of moral improvement at Flinder's Island, where the remnant of the whole black population were now located. He had established three schools on the settlement - a day school for boys, a day school for girls and women, an evening school and a Sunday school, which was generally attended. The civil officers, their wives and his own family, acted as teachers and they found the natives willing and anxious to receive instruction, by which they improved rapidly. In the schools, they had been taught various handiworks, such as knitting in worsted, sewing and they proved to be apt and industrious scholars.

COLONIAL TIMES (HOBART, TAS: 1828 - 1857),
TUESDAY 11 DECEMBER 1838, PAGE 4

MR. ROBINSON - THE ABORIGINAL.

When we published, two or three weeks ago, the report of a speech, of which Mr. Robinson was delivered at a meeting at Sydney and in which he detailed, with a modesty and bashfulness, peculiarly his own, the clever manner, in which he captured the Natives of this Colony, we were remonstrated with by some of our best friends for devoting so much space to the proceedings of this incomparable gentleman: but we knew what we were about; and, having in view, the exposure of one of the most gross jobs ever perpetuated, we adopted our old plan of "beginning at the beginning," and thought we could not do better, than judge this meritorious Protector "out of his own mouth."

The sole burden of Mr Robinson's speech is - "T'was I that did it!" "I, with the blessing of Providence and with my well known engaging and captivating manner of persuasion,-I! I! I! took all the 'Natives: and, having done so, see what a big man I am !" Now, we will, in that stern and undeviating spirit of independence, which is our leading star, concede to Mr Robinson all the merit, that is due to him, which is, we truly believe; by no means trivial : but we cannot go the whole hog of awarding to him that credit, which is due, more correctly, to others. Mr. Robinson states, broadly and peremptorily, that he, alone, (that is alone as a European) accomplished the capture, or whatever it may be called, of the Aboriginal Natives of Van Diemen's Land and he stated this in the face of what he must know, would ensue,- the most decided contradiction. But our Aboriginal Protector, puffed up as all ignorant, illiterate and conceited men always will be, with the astounding sound of his new title (by the way is there not, like Captain Cheyne's a "General", tacked to it?) resolves to mystify, the Sydney folks a bit and magnifies his especial vocation accordingly. What a rich treat it would have been, for some of our Hobart Town people to have listened to Mr. Robinson's grand "speech" at the Sydney meeting! How delighted would they, have been at his blushes and, bashful ness; and how copious would have been their gratitude for the extraordinary services which Mr. Robinson, like Coriolanus "alone" performed!

Now, we happen to have in our possession the voluminous, but straightforward statement of a most active individual, who was as beneficially engaged, as the Chief Protector himself and who shows most incontrovertibly that not only was he, but that others were also, actively instrumental in the work performance of which Mr. Robinson claims, exclusively, for himself We are under no bonds of secrecy in the case and we mention, at once that the person is McGeary, who with "Sandy McKay," travelled the island over and over again, employed in the Native-catching and who has furnished a simple narrative of his wanderings, infinitely more authentic, than any we have seen and which com-prises statements, not the most complimentary to our Chief Protector.

Having thus detracted somewhat from the pompous pretensions of Mr. Robinson, we have a word or two to say, respecting these protecting appointments, Mr. Robinson, it seems, is the Chief Protector, with a snug little salary of £500 per annum, while he is to be aided in his Protectorship by four assistants - the expense of the whole concern to be defrayed, in certain pro- portions by this Colony and New South Wales. Now, as the object of this formidable establishment is to conciliate the Blacks at Port Philip and other parts of New Holland, we do not see, why this Colony should contribute towards any portion of the expense; and we wonder, what His Excellency, Sir John Franklin, did not embrace the opportunity, which this new fangled scheme afforded and effect a saving in the expenditure of our decaying revenue, by saddling all the charges upon the Colony, most interested in the matter. But Sir John, we suppose, likes a more round about and elaborate process of retrenchment and prefers its accomplishment by the enactment of prohibitory laws, rather than by discouraging unnecessary and ex pensive employments.

The work produced to the meeting, was the sort of work they were chiefly employed in and in making shirts, trousers and other articles of comfort, which they coveted and enjoyed highly. [A quantity of caps, braces and stockings, of good workmanship, was presented to the meeting, as the work of the natives at Flinder's Island, which was highly approved.] They had neat cottages with gardens, cooking utensils and they conformed in every respect to European habits and were particularly careful in copying every domestic arrangement which they observed with the Europeans. He had established an Aboriginal Fund, which was raised from the proceeds of their work, which was appropriated for general purposes ; an Aboriginal police to preserve order amongst themselves and to decide all disagreements which might arise amongst them.

At first, he had appointed three of the Chiefs, who were sworn in as constables and who, with himself, formed a court before which all their differences were brought and to the decisions of which they all acceded. He had also established a circulating medium amongst them, which had been attended with the happiest effects, as it gave them a knowledge of the right of property ; and lastly, the consequent upon the latter, he had established a market, to which they brought their produce and disposed of it to each other and to the officers of the settlement. They thus acquired the habits of civilized life and felt an interest in the acquisition of property, which rendered them industrious and cleanly.

Independent of their other employments, the men had, in three years, cleared the forest and made a good road nine miles in length into the interior of the island, which was thus thrown open to enterprise. The only drawback on the establishment, was the great mortality amongst them, but those who did survive, were now happy contented and useful members of society.

1839

THE AUSTRAL-ASIATIC REVIEW,
Tasmanian and Australian Advertiser.

OPEN TO ALL PARTIES—INFLUENCED BY NONE.

Vol. XI.]   TUESDAY EVENING, JANUARY 15, 1839, HOBART TOWN.   [No. 49

CORNWALL CHRONICLE (LAUNCESTON, TAS: 1835 - 1880),
SATURDAY 2 FEBRUARY 1839, PAGE 1

BLACKS AND WHITES. COMPARATIVE VALUE OF THEIR LIVES Colonial Secretary's Office, Sydney, Jan. 2. 1839.

TWENTY POUNDS REWARD OR A CONDITIONAL PARDON. Whereas it has been represented to His Excellency the Governor, that two Prisoners of the Crown, named Charles Walthall, per Susan and John Davis, per Strathfield say, employed as shepherds at the station of Mr. J. Cobb, on the Big River, were, at the early part of last month , murdered by a tribe of Aboriginal Natives in that neighbourhood; Notice is hereby given, that a Reward of Twenty Pounds will be paid to any free person who may give such information as will lead to the apprehension and conviction or the Parties by whom the said murders were committed ; or if the informant be a Prisoner of the Crown, application will be made to Her Majesty for her approbation end allowance of a Conditional Pardon to the said Prisoner of the Crown. By His Excellency's Command, E. Deas Thomson

The above notice appears in the Government Gazette, of Wednesday week. It gives occasion for an interesting inquiry — namely, the comparative value of the life of a black man and the life of a white man. It is worthy of attention, also, in so far as it will remind the native youth of the colony, that when the government entered upon its laudable endeavour to bring to trial and, if guilty to hang, one or their countrymen, named Flemming for the alleged killing or a black native-the reward offered for the capture of this native-born colonist was [pounds] 50 and a free pardon. Away with cant! We are here presented with an instance or its hollowness.

We have here an exemplification of the animus of the government as regards the white population, European and native. For the apprehension or black savages, guilty of the well-ascertained murder of white men, a reward or £20, or a conditional pardon is offered ; whereas, (or the apprehension of a while native colonist, suspected of slaying a black, a reward of more than double the amount in money, with the addition of a free pardon, is offered : And this we presume, is a specimen of the boasted equality in the administration tof justice between the blacks and the whites in New South Wales'. This munificent reward, too, is to be given to anyone who may give such information as will lead to the "apprehension and conviction. &c." of the black murderers! Ha! ha! ha! Where are you to catch them? Where are the vagrant block murderers to be laid hold of? But this is no trifling matter.

We earnestly call upon the European colonists and upon the native born, to watch this proceeding, with respect to black marauders, who have committed murders of the most barbarous description and destroyed property to an immense amount throughout the colony. If the savages be caught and hanged —why well! But if not, where is the conscientious colonist, sitting as a juror, who could convict a white man and consign him to the gibbet, whilst the blacks may murder the whites with impunity? No; no; there must be an equality in the law — so far as the government can make it equal, or (and it is as well to speak out) the settlers will take the law into their own hands. They will protect themselves, their servants and their property— they will not be threatened, nor preached into passiveness.

CORNWALL CHRONICLE (LAUNCESTON, TAS: 1835 - 1880),
SATURDAY 26 JANUARY 1839, PAGE 2

TO THE EDITOR.

Sir,— A report is in circulation at Port Phi-lip, that Mr. Robinson who has lately been created Protector General of the Aboriginal natives of New Holland, is directed to proceed to Port Philip, with the Aborigines of our colony now on Flinders Island, for the purpose or joining, or rather leading an army of Protectors, Missionaries and Military with their families, who are awaiting the arrival or their Generallissimo, at Port Philip, to lead them into the interior, for the purpose of attempting the reconciliation and finally the settlement of the native tribes in the vicinity of that place.

The design is most laudable and philanthropic, but Mr. Robinson has a solemn charge in taking, without the consent of the government of New South Wales; the Aborigines of this colony after they have escaped the murdering shot of our stockman and bushrangers and the wasting disease of Flinders, now to be either dragged or cheated away amongst the fierce cannibals of New South Wales is an act of cruelty that deserves severe reprobation. Europeans can judge of the peril to which they may be exposed and they venture their lives in hope of reward of one kind or other, but our Aborigines have no means of judging of the situation in which they will be placed and the natives of our colony can receive no reward but to which they are justly entitled in this colony without adventuring their lives in New South Wales - if one of their lives be lost in this hazardous expedition someone will have to account for it, but— who ? Mr. Robinson passed through this town on the 9th inst., to join the Shamrock, at George Town and bound for Flinders Island with sup-plies for the settlement. –

*I remain, your's, &c., *****

AUSTRAL-ASIATIC REVIEW, TASMANIAN AND AUSTRALIAN ADVERTISER
(HOBART TOWN, TAS: 1837 - 1844), TUESDAY 2 APRIL 1839, PAGE 7

FLINDERS' ISLAND.

*It is far from improbable that the few remaining Aborigines at. Flinders'
Island will be swept away by disease, so as that race will have become
entirely extinct. The influenza rages there so severely, that Dr. Seccombe,
the Government Surgeon at Launceston, has proceeded to that Island, to
render every possible medical assistance. Is the Colony still encumbered with
the expense of an Aboriginal Establishment?*

COLONIAL TIMES (HOBART, TAS: 1828 - 1857), TUESDAY 12 MARCH 1839, PAGE 3

THE GAZETTE

*TENDERS.- Tenders will, be received at the Colonial Secretary's. office, until
Thursday the 14th instant, for the supply of the following articles of clothing
required for the Aborigines:- 68 cloth, coats, of strong materials, of sizes,
to fit from 5 feet 4 inch, to 6 feet; 68 pairs duck trousers to correspond.
Tenders accompanied by samples, will be received at the Commissariat-
office, Launceston, until Mon-day the 18th instant, for the undermentioned
supplies, required, immediately for the Aborigines' Establishment at Flinder's
Island: - 18,000lbs. 12 per cent, flour; 1000lbs. 20 per cent. flour; 1600lbs
sugar; 15 gallons vinegar; 230lbs. tobacco; 120lbs. tea; 120lbs candles.*

*These articles are to be delivered in sound casks or packages, included
in the cost price, at the Commissariat Stores in Launceston, where they
will be examined by a board of survey and if approved, the contractor
will be furnished by the officer in charge with a receipt for them, which
must be forwarded to me in order that the accounts may be prepared, for
transmission, to the Colonial Treasurer, by whom payment will be made for
the supplies.*

E. J. MANLEY, Accountant of Stores.

COLONIAL RECORD (LAUNCESTON TAS: 1839), MONDAY 24 JUNE 1839, PAGE 2

REPORT OF THE PARLIAMENTARY SELECT COMMITTEE ON ABORIGINAL TRIBES.

We trust that the little volume, bearing the above name, will not he passed over as a merely official document of dry statistics, or tedious cross-examination. It is replete with matter of the most interesting character and appears in its present form and with the addition of a valuable preface and comments, through the exertions of a society recently formed, but well deserving the warm support and co-operation, not only of the Benevolent, but also of the Christian public. No one, whose judgement is not blinded by interest can have read with any attention the history of our colonial possessions—no one can ponder over the failures averted to in the report now published, without feeling a blush of shame, as well as a burst of indignation, while he remembers that he is a Briton. The means pursued for the accomplishment of our purposes have, indeed, varied with times and circumstances, but the system has been everywhere the same. Fraud, violence and cruelty, has ever marked our conduct towards the native possessors of the soil we have coveted.

The brandy-cask and musket have gone hand in hand in the work of dispossession and depopulation and the system has accomplished a twofold evil, brutalising the oppressor, while it destroyed the oppressed. The histories of Canada, Australia, British Guiana and South Africa, repeat the same sad tale—a tale which has impressed on our national escutcheon a blot never to be effaced. While we have gloried ill the proud recollection that the sun never sets on our dominions—while we have rejoiced in those missionary heralds whom we have sent forth to preach to the heathen the unsearchable riches of Christ,"—we have forgotten, or never known, that the British power of which we boasted, was being employed in the dark and dreadful work of extermination and that the exertions of our agents were cramped and weakened by the oppression under which the helpless Aborigines were harassed and destroyed.

This is a people robbed and spoiled; they are all of them snared in holes and they are hid in prison-houses; they are for prey and none delivereth; for a spoil and none saith, Restore." Too long have the feelings of the British public slumbered on this subject; let the startling facts now brought to light speak with a voice which shall rouse to instant and energetic exertion. The evils to be remedied are great, urgent and immediate. We hail the tendency shown by the present Administration to a more mild and just system of colonial policy as a bright omen for the future; but we repeat, that it is the powerful and combined expression of' public feeling alone which can insure, extend and support a system whose introduction and establishment will meet with strong and interested opposition, both at home and abroad. We believe that ignorance must, in great measure, account for the apathy which has hitherto existed on the subject. Let not this be again pleaded ill excuse. Let this report be widely circulated and carefully read; let the proceedings of the society, under whose sanction it now appears, be watched and its exertions supported; and let every man and woman awake to a deep conviction of .his present responsibility on this subject, not only as a Briton, but as a Christian.

The above is extracted from a recent English periodical. In these colonies, where the truth of the above is more plainly read, from the personal experience of most of us, in reference to the native tribes of these lands, the exertions of the British philanthropist will be duly estimated by every right thinking man. As regards either of the colonies already established much may indeed yet be done, for the aborigines, in the amelioration of their sad condition and in their protection from future wrong. But in each of these colonies the day has past when the foundation of permanent, universal and mutual advantages to native and emigrant, should have been secured. Individuals having at heart the promotion of this great object should precede emigration. Their mission of peace and love should be well established with the native tribes, previously to the landing of emigrants on their shores, wherever, British colonization is contemplated; otherwise, the great objects proposed by the British Government to be secured to the aborigines in the appointment of protectors and their assistants cannot fully be attained.

Once let the British settler take possession of the land and who can be responsible for the result to the natives and emigrants? In the absence of the master this servants maltreat the aborigines—abuse their women—perhaps murder their infants; and, notwithstanding the humanity of the master and his constant care and kindness of these poor people, they have not the discrimination which is necessary to lead to the distinction between the innocent and the guilty; their savage" retaliation is of course, indiscriminate; and the innocent and perhaps Christian master is sacrificed to their revenge, with the reckless and wicked servant who has been the aggressor. In the contemplated establishment of new colonies, the British Government must have active agents, well supported and supplied with clothing and food in abundance, first taking possession of the locality intended to be colonized. The British nation now awakened to their duty as a Christian people, will assuredly not rest until all that is necessary is accomplished

I was wrong. I thought I was strong enough to return to this island but I was not. Shortly after arriving the nightmares resumed, the sweats, night waking and the temptation to obliterate the demons with drink.

I had hoped I would be able to face the dangers of my work, what I had seen and the moral guilt I felt; this was not to be. I realised at long last that to know your weaknesses is a strength. With this awareness I decided it was time to leave and for good this time. No one was left for me; my scarce friends, my beloved Pakana people whose few remaining were exiled and I forbidden to meet with them and the island filling so rapidly with strangers to me.

I boarded a bark of only 301 tons called the *Mary Ann* on June 24th 1839 under the command of Captain Marshall and with just 29 passengers and headed for Home so very far away, never to return.

Chapter Eight

Reporting from Afar
1840 to 1856

My remaining interest in the plight of the Pakana people and how the papers reported these events was from afar. My dear friend Andrew Bent, despite his personal difficulties, continued to post me bundles of newspapers and other writings during this time. I wondered where to stop, how to stop. My circumstances too were now becoming increasingly challenging. A life of languidity and excesses was taking its toll and increasingly I desired to search beyond my love of literature. I began to dwell on and appreciate the beauty of small things; butterflies, my young nieces and nephews and without sounding too trite, sunsets and wintry scenes.

My greatest pleasure was the mysteries of fly fishing. It may seem incredibly mindnumbing for anyone outside the world of the 'green highlander', 'black dog', 'rusty rat', et alia, but for me it was a wonderful escape: observing the insect life, painstakingly creating the fly and then simply being alone with Bent and the soothing sound of the stream. You will be pleased to know on occasions I actually did catch a fish!

I felt it best to remember the untroubled times, the people I met who showed me how vital life can be and, naturally, my glimpses of love and the sheer ecstasy that it can bring to one's physical being, but most of all my exquisite times with Lowana.

These are just a few of the articles and press clippings I have to share with you.

1840

Stories upon stories until the truth is painted over hidden from all eyes.

LAUNCESTON ADVERTISER (TAS: 1829 - 1846),
THURSDAY 5 NOVEMBER 1840, PAGE 3

....

VAN DIEMEN'S LAND.

(Continued from our last)

Although discord had arisen even at an early age of the colony, the aborigines, notwithstanding, for many years were regular in their periodical visits to Hobart Town, where they were invariably well received and obtained food and blankets. Their sable hue has afforded a theme for naturalists and philosophers. It is certainly a remarkable feature, that in a latitude so considerably within the temperate zone as Van Diemen's Land, a negro population should be found. They may have been a fragment of a world strangely riven from the coast of Africa. They may - but whilst the origin of the aborigines of New Holland is unknown, it would be futile to speculate upon that of the minor island. Here a continued and systematic hostility had arisen between the races— ere their hand was against every man and every man's hand against them - In their first stage, as it were, of war to the knife, their mode of circumventing the settlers' dwelling was characteristic:- the women were sent in the van, entering the premises with that confidence which the absence of a dread of molestation imparts; their usual demands were bread and tobacco, those were generally complied with., if the women found the inmates few, or incapable of defence, a signal was given and the barren mountain, like the hills of Rhoderic Dhu, instantly teemed with black assassins, who sped the work of rapine and murder with lightning-like celerity It must be observed, that the country is peculiarly favourable for their stealthy approach.

The fires which they have long been in the habit of making, has strewed the ground with fallen timber and blackened slumps; from these they are barely distinguishable, until all at once they start erect, the demon ministers of doom and death. At a subsequent date, when some outrages had rendered the Whites alert, if the tribes were discovered, they would assume a pacific attitude and supplicating gesture, gradually approaching their foe, who frequently, when loo late, found that they had dragged the fated spear securely and artfully fixed between their toes. The difference between a single and double-barrelled gun was well known to them and they would do their utmost to provoke the European to throw away his fire; if he were rash enough to do so, they would then, in the emphatic phrase of colonial description, rush him - the issue of such a conflict bring all but certain.

Upon one occasion, they attacked a stockkeeper's hut on the river Shannon; the roof being shingled, prevented their attempts to set it on fire; inside were three men, unarmed; the assailants in vain endeavoured to force an entrance; one, more courageous than the rest, descended the chimney, but having been greeted with a pot-full of scalding water, he made a rapid and a howling retreat. At this juncture, Dunne, a bushranger, armed to the teeth, having several loaded guns in his possession, presented himself; he at once opened a fire upon them and their flight followed as a matter of course. When Dunne quilted the hut, at the earnest request of the stock-keeper he left one of his guns and several charges of ammunition behind him. Not many days after, the natives again appeared; at that time the hut had but one solitary occupant, of which the blacks were perfectly aware. They were warned off with a threat of being fired at, should they refuse: upon this, the following reply is said to have been given, "you damn convict - you damn white - you shoot a me - gubberns hang you." Upon this, with a loud yell the blacks fearlessly and exultingly approached. The convict, however deeming the possible risk of after exaltation preferable to the immediate certainty of a dreadful death took a steady aim and drove a bullet through the savage, who fell and (according to custom) was carried off by the survivors, rending the air with their howls and shrieks as they fled. Their excited antagonist reloaded with the utmost expedition, pursuing their track and destroying, as was said, a second, - a perilous attempt for one man to make and which, not long afterwards, cost this individual his life. Whilst thus pursuing the flying blacks, some of their number entered the vacant cabin, from which they bore everything moveable: amongst the rest was a quantity of arsenic, used for the destruction of vermin. The poison had either lost its virtue, or else the blacks had not swallowed it as was supposed, none having ever been ascertained to have perished thereby, although they were seen drinking at the river in a most extraordinary manner a circumstance which was attributed to the burning heat, caused by the deadly mineral.

Another illustration of the Aboriginal hostility and this portion of the subject is at an end. A shepherd, well known to the writer, was confined by illness to his hut; a female, the wife of one of his comrades, was in attendance upon him. Suddenly the fearful native yell burst upon their appalled senses; to secure the door and window was their instant aim— a hopeless alternative, for, alas the cabin was a thatched one and the fiery spear instantly set it in a blaze. Could any position be more horrific? The old man bore his fate with constancy: 'Stir not.' said he to his female companion, 'The blaze will he seen and help may arrive.'

For a while she endured the showers of fire and flame, until her dress became ignited. 'Let me go, Clarke,' she then exclaimed; 'Better to perish at once by their spears, than thus consume piecemeal.' So saying, she sped to the door: the instant she presented herself, every spear was poised— a loud and piercing scream broke from her lips and she threw herself in agony at the feet of one of the savages. He gazed at her for a moment —that scream had touched his heart,— he motioned his brethren to desist, tore the burning embers from her neck and hair— then rapidly uttering, ' Parawa— parawa!" pointed that she should make her escape, a hint that required no repetition to enforce it, — and which is the solitary instance of mercy ever shown.

At this moment a female convict, in the charge of a constable, was passing near the spot. The constable perceiving the savages, whispered his companion to speed on with him in silence. Terror, however completely mastered the poor creature and she broke out into loud and fatal shrieks. Finding all his endeavours to silence her vain and seeing the blacks pressing towards them, the constable fled and was hotly pursued The unhappy was speedily pierced with their vengeful spears. The hut was burnt to the ground and the unfortunate shepherd reduced to a cinder, the trunk being the sole portion that remained to distinguish what once had been a piece of humanity. He and the girl were interred side by side, a male convict acquainted with her in England and who had become attached to her in Van Diemen's Land, officiating as chief mourner.

The PAKANA *Voice*

1845

THE OBSERVER:
A Van Diemen's Land Journal of Politics, Agriculture, Commerce, and General Intelligence.

Vol. I., No. 1.]   THURSDAY, JUNE 5, 1845.   [Price 6d.

COURIER (HOBART, TAS: 1840 - 1859), TUESDAY 25 FEBRUARY 1845, PAGE 3

THE BLACK QUESTION.

To the Editor of the Hobart Town Courier.

SIR,-Public attention having been recently directed to the remnant of the once numerous Aborigines of this colony by the recommendation of the Finance Committee, as stated in one of your late papers, a few remarks on the subject, from one formerly well acquainted with the people and their peculiarities, may not at this juncture be altogether unacceptable.

The epistle of your learned correspondent, Dr. Jeanneret, does credit to his benevolent sympathy with a race too generally regarded with apathy 'almost unfeeling'. But while I honour the motives which impel his chivalrous advocacy of his late charge, I can by no means concur in his general views.

The people in question are understood to have surrendered themselves on a treaty and it is indisputably our duty to observe good faith towards them and to make suitable provision for their necessities and comforts, whether at Flinders or elsewhere; but if this end can be attained at a less expense at a time when the revenue is deficient and every mode of retrenchment commendable, no argument can be adduced for keeping up an expensive establishment, where the salaries of the officers alone exceed the amount required for the comfortable support of the Aborigines, to say nothing of the many inevitable expenses inseparable from so remote and, in every way, so inconvenient a locality.

The unhealthiness of Flinders has been so generally conceded by its former medical officers and others, that Dr. Jeanneret's isolated belief in its salubrity is a matter of surprise; not to dwell on its want of wholesome water, the simple fact of the Aborigines having dwindled away from some hundreds to about forty during their abode there, satisfactorily establishes its degree of unhealthiness and substantiates the Doctor's somewhat equivocal praise of its being 'the place best adapted to end their days in;' and with every deference to so learned an authority, I should decidedly maintain that the dislike of the natives to Flinders is extreme and their wish to leave it unvarying. How, indeed, can they be expected to like a place already so fatal to them and where they are fast verging to extinction.

These children of the forest retain a strong attachment to the place of their birth and would rejoice in their return to it; nor does the measure afford any just grounds for apprehension ; the more formidable of them are long since dead and the fraction remaining have imbibed tastes which render them dependent on Government for the supply of their daily wants. From my knowledge of their character I would submit that they might be safely replaced in Van Diemen's Land, on either of the following plans: -They might be placed in some sufficiently large building in Hobart Town, under the charge of their present Catechist, or some other person well acquainted with their habits, whose duty it would be to see that they regularly received their clothes and rations, to instruct them and watch over their general behaviour; they might be visited by the public authorities and any respectable parties taking an interest in their welfare. The north side of the island might perhaps be preferred for its milder climate. There was a Government building at George Town, formerly used as a factory, that would contain the whole of them; their sole expense, besides clothes and rations, being the Superintendent's salary.

Or, they might be distributed in the several parts of the country they were originally taken from, under the control of the Police Magistrate and the Clergyman of the district, the former being responsible for the regular receipt of their clothes and rations: in what was once regarded as the most important object, their progress in Christianity, they might reasonably be expected to benefit by the change. I am not aware that the Aborigines can contribute to defray their own expense by labour or manufactures, though it is asserted Dr. Jeanneret formerly imported spinning-jennies for their use at the public expense. Dr. Jeanneret alludes to Mr. Robinson's ill success in his experiment at Port Phillip. His failure, however, can hardly be admitted as a fair instance. We should first be informed on what system these people were kept, on what plan their wants were supplied and what precautions were taken to prevent their trespasses -points demanding earnest attention in a new and strange country. These and some other matters connected with this people call for explanation.

In concluding these desultory remarks, which have run to too great a length, may I, Mr. Editor, be allowed to express my wonder that in recommending a Board and naming some highly-respected individuals as eligible to compose it, you should have overlooked a gentleman associated with Dr. Officer in his report on Flinder's Island, I mean Lieut. Friend, R. N., Port Officer at George Town - an officer of much colonial experience, scientific knowledge and philanthropy. I beg to subscribe myself, Mr. Editor, your constant reader,

PLATYPUS.

CORNWALL CHRONICLE (LAUNCESTON, TAS: 1835 - 1880),
SATURDAY 15 MARCH 1845, PAGE 4

RESPONSIBLE GOVERNMENT.

[FROM THE COLONIAL GAZETTE.]

There is a society, developed the 'Aborigines Protection Society,' consisting of a very amiable and philanthropic secretary and about half-a-dozen gentlemen of whom no harm is known — nor indeed anything. So often as the secretary can catch a quorum of his associates in his back parlour in

Lower Brook St., a meeting is held for the despatch of business and called a committee meeting. By dint of incessant begging, the society contrives to raise as much money annually as pays for printing occasionally three or four octavo pages of a report.

This description, which is as true as a daguerreotype[xxii], is not calculated to raise very high expectations of the society's importance ; and yet, among other anomalies of the British constitution, we find that to this insignificant and self-constituted association Lord Stanley has delegated the revision and control of the colonial policy of the empire. Out of 'mere love and affection,' for 'responsible government,' his lordship has made himself responsible to this conclave.

Of this fact no doubt can be entertained after perusing the following extract from the minute of the meeting of the 21st of August last, at which were present the unprecedented number of five members and two visitors — one of the visitors being a gentleman of whom we find it recorded that, ' Benjamin Stones having expressed his willingness to collect subscriptions, the committee have empowered him to do so.'

[the article continues in this vein with a rather cryptic ending]

If a member of Parliament asks about the management of a colony, he is flippantly given to understand that he is meddling with matters beyond his reach. But if the amiable Dr. Hodgkin, with his five or six toad-eaters, for the time being, but hint disapprobation, explanations and apologies are sought out and offered with palpitating eagerness. No wonder our colonies are so well governed, when Governors are kept in order by the Colonial Office and the Colonial Office by the sages in Dr. Hodgkin's back parlour assembled. This is indeed ' responsible government!'

This letter dripping with sarcasm really deserves a response. I just can't let it go without mentioning that the great British Empire had only recently outlawed slavery outside the UK in 1833.

Before then it was perfectly legal for a British subject to own another human being and of course the southern states of America retain that right as I put pen to paper. Once slavery had been abolished those who had worked so hard to achieve this outcome now put their attention to the plight of Aboriginal communities in numerous parts of the world under British rule and there were many of them. The Aboriginal Protection Society[xxiii] was formed in 1835 and managed to achieve some headway with a select parliamentary committee which recognised the absurdity and injustice inherent in applying British notions of law automatically to Aboriginal people. However, it still believed they should be subject to the law and suggested short and simple laws be implemented until more knowledge and civilization superseded the need for any such special laws. And so the debate continued although personally I give far more credence to the society than the writer of the diatribe above.

I was asked to give a presentation to the Aboriginal Protection Society at the Beaufort Buildings, The Strand, London in November 1840 on my experiences with the Pakana people. I agreed; perhaps my ego took hold, but I also wanted to share my experiences with others. Tell them of the Pakana people, their lives, the land which united them and their desperate fight for survival against the might of the British Empire. That evening in a large auditorium I was greeted by ladies and gentlemen dressed in their finery and whose universe extended little further than Brighton for the summer. The atmosphere encompassed high ceilings, paintings of a very young Queen Victoria and motifs of angels and past battles with all the glory the Empire could muster adorning the walls and alcoves.

I was charming and erudite. My voice, manners and knowledge enticed my listeners into another world so far away that few could ever have imagined the small island of Lutruwita. I told of how the Moomairremener clan lived, their customs, laws of marriage, how they lit fires, speared and killed animals. I told stories, slightly embellished, of adventure and excitement, of singing and dancing and sleeping in bark huts.

I talked easily and fluently for an hour watching as people appeared entranced by my every word. They were spellbound and I had them in my grasp, but behind this façade of a seasoned journalist was another voice. It was deep and penetrating from my soul. It burned with challenges and antagonized my persona as I relished the attention and bumptiousness.

Was this really me? Am I just like any other *rytia* exploiting and using the Pakana for my own purposes? Was I betraying the trust they had bestowed on me all those years ago? Most importantly, what would Lowana have thought? These feelings were whirling through my mind while I was talking leaving me unnerved and my composure splintering. The saying, 'Take care thoughts do not entangle your heart' sprang to mind.

I shared nothing personal; I was the epitome of a benevolent English gentleman who had bravely spent time observing a tribe of primitive natives, taking notes and acquiring information for scientific and nature journals so civilized people could improve their intellect. It would never have occurred to anyone in the room that I would have sunk so low as to be involved with these people, let alone allowing intimacy into my life.

My lecture finished to muted applause; very British. Mr Frederick Innes[xxiv], Secretary of the Society, thanked me for my thought-provoking talk and invited me to stay for tea and sandwiches (and, yes, cucumber was on the menu). I politely declined and slid into the bleakness of a wintery, smog engulfed London night with only my thoughts for company and Lowana with her deep black eyes looking into mine as her finger ever so gently traced the side of my face. God, how I missed her.

COURIER (HOBART, TAS: 1840 - 1859), TUESDAY 13 MAY 1845, PAGE 3

TO THE EDITOR OF THE HOBART TOWN COURIER.

" The Aborigines were treated like beasts and the Prisoners as beings without souls."

SIR, — The above is given in the Advertiser of the 9th, as an extract from a speech made by the Lord Bishop of Tasmania at the Launceston meeting of the Society for Promoting Christian Knowledge. With regard to the first part of His Lordship's statement, I have not the means of knowing how far the censure thus past on the Government be justly merited or not, but on the latter part I have a few observations to offer. "The" prisoners are treated as civilized beings without "souls," so says His Lordship; the plain inference from such statement being, that no provision is made for the religious instruction of the convicts.

I very seldom read the Advertiser. I have occasionally seen in it whole columns of invective against the Probation System, unsupported, I well knew, by a single fact; but until assertion be taken for proof, the lucubration's of that journal may very safely be permitted to pass unnoticed. The disciples of the porch are well known and the thinking people of the community are amused at the logic which assigns the ruin of the settler to the probation system. But when a Bishop and that Bishop a member of the Executive, puts forth a statement to the public seriously affecting the character of the government, both Imperial and Colonial, it becomes desirable to enquire how far such statement is borne out by facts. I have referred to the list of officers connected with the Convict Establishment and I find that there are no less than sixteen Church of England Religious

Instructors and four Roman Catholic Instructors permanently attached to the establishment, with two Church of England Chaplains and two Roman Catholic Chaplains, who receive an allowance for visiting the stations in their neighbourhood.

Of the sixteen Church of England Instructors six are ordained clergymen, five are gentlemen not in orders, but recommended for ordination and sent out under the auspices of the Societies for promoting Christian Knowledge and the remaining five were appointed here, having been each, as I am informed, favourably spoken of by the Bishop himself.

Now, Sir, I would ask, does this pro-vision for the religious instruction of the convicts, even though it may be inadequate to the existing wants of the department, look as though the Government either regarded or treated the prisoners as beings without souls? Can it be, that because Lord Stanley has refused to concede to the Bishop the full control of the Religious Instructors of the Convict Department, His Lord-ship has felt himself justified in affirming that the Government, by this non-recognition of unlimited Episcopal jurisdiction, have relinquished all care for the spiritual wants of the prisoner?

I am a plain man, Sir and know but little of theological matters, but it appears to me, that if the statement of the Bishop be true, deep indeed must be the responsibility of those who have undertaken the solemn duty of becoming spiritual guides to the convicts and whose ministrations, I believe, if faithfully exercised, may be expected to be of benefit whether sanctioned by his Lordship or not; — not that I undervalue the office of a Bishop — far from it; I regret, no one more so, that His Lordship feels himself unable to recognise in their spiritual capacity those engaged in the truly arduous field of Convict Instruction ; but I cannot deem that the absence of such recognition would render of no effect the labour of any truly Christian Teacher who brings to his duty that spirit without which he ought never to have under-taken it. — I am, Sir, yours, &c.

C. D.

WRITTEN LANGUAGE

I wonder sometimes if the use of written language by the British also had an impact on the events which occurred in Lutruwita. The Pakana used oral communication only, which by its very nature is fluid. Stories and ideas can change between the conveyors of the messages with obvious ramifications when fighting a war.

The British had written language which is constant and does not alter as it is passed from one to another. It can be disseminated widely anddoes not require the writer to be present. For administration, passing on orders, newspaper and laws or edicts, it is a powerful instrument.

The British bought with them to Lutruwita the printing press, critical for the production of the newspapers which were so effective in galvanising ideas into a mass format, not only reflecting views but actively influencing values, beliefs and outcomes.

On the other hand, the Pakana's communication using smoke signals was faster and far more efficient than anything the British had at the time. They were certainly able to organise and communicate effectively as demonstrated in their many successes during the war.

I am open to different views on this subject and throw these thoughts into the mix for discussion.

1847

LAUNCESTON EXAMINER (TAS: 1842 - 1899),
SATURDAY 18 SEPTEMBER 1847, PAGE 5

TO THE EDITOR OF THE LAUNCESTON EXAMINER. ABORIGINES.

Sir,—Can it be possible that Sir William Denison really intends to break up the Aboriginal Establishment at Flinders' Island and bring back the natives to this colony ? Has he yet to learn that for a series of years the inhabitants of this island were kept in a continual state of terror, apprehension and alarm, not by the open hostility of large bodies of the aborigines, but by the insidious and murderous attacks of small parties frequently not exceeding three or four in number?

Does he require to be told that these aborigines were in great measure under the control of a supposed civilized native of New South Wales, who had been brought to this country and suffered to remain at large; and that upon his instigation, or under his immediate direction, numerous outrages were committed of so wanton and blood-thirsty a character as to overwhelm the colony with horror and dismay?

Is Lieutenant-Governor Denison ignorant that under the government of his predecessor Sir George Arthur, so great was the consternation pervading all classes of the community, that he deemed it necessary to suspend all other official operations and to devote the whole resources of the Government to effect the capture and removal of the aborigines; and that the whole military force in the colony and the greater part of its inhabitants were called out by the Government and employed at a vast expense for many weeks in an ineffectual attempt to accomplish this object, which was at length attained by the unwearied efforts of Mr. G. A. Robinson, now Chief Protector of the aborigines of Port Phillip, who eventually succeeded in conciliating and removing, as is generally believed, the whole of the natives of this island then remaining thereon and thereby conferring, as was universally considered, an inestimable benefit upon the colony?

Is Sir William Denison aware that after the most careful investigation and mature deliberation on the part of the government, Flinders' Island was chosen as the most fit spot to carry out its intentions towards the natives; its insular position admitting of their enjoying greater freedom from any personal restraint and also furnishing them, to a certain extent, with the means of following their accustomed pursuits in the bush, whilst at the same time as much care and attention could be bestowed upon them as in a more confined position? I repeat, can Sir William Denison be aware of all this and yet dare to take upon himself the fearful responsibility of neutralizing all that has been effected by the removal of the aborigines, by bringing back the remnant of these unfortunate beings and restoring them to the scenes of their former outrages, only rendered more dangerous by those new wants and desires inseparable from their partially civilized condition? What good reason can be pleaded for breaking up the establishment at Flinders' Island?

If that establishment is larger and more expensive than is necessary for the due management, control and instruction of the natives, cannot it be forthwith reduced to its proper limit without involving the necessity of breaking it up and forming a new one elsewhere; an operation on which heavy expenses must inevitably be attendant? For my own part, I cannot discover that the safe custody and due management of the aborigines at Flinders' Island should cost the Government more than the attainment of that object would, if they were removed to this colony, except it may be in the cost of transport; but this charge would be nothing in comparison with the expense of forming new establishment and carrying out those additional measures for their safe custody which a removal from their present insular position would render imperatively necessary, but which measures it would be extremely difficult to render in any degree effectual. I trust that my fellow-colonists will immediately take such steps as the importance of this subject demands: let those more especially bestir themselves who were resident here during that period of terror, when we were under continual apprehension of the outrages of the aborigines and who must for ever remember those spectacles of horror too often presented to our view, in the mutilated and disfigured remains of those unfortunate beings, men, women and children, who had fallen unoffending victims to their insidious and wanton attacks.

Let me instance the treacherous and cold-blooded murders of Captain B. B. Thomas and his overseer, within a short distance of Port Sorell. Let us remember the poor, but hospitable, Gildas, of the West Bank of the Tamar, who, after several hair-breadth escapes, at last fell a sacrifice to their savage barbarity in his own garden. Let us remember poor old Fitzgerald, who lived where Mr. Coulson now resides on the East Bank of the Tamar and who was surprised and murdered by a native woman whilst standing at the door of his cottage, leaving his numerous and interesting family to the mercy of the world. Where, alas, are they now? I say get the heart-rending remembrance of these and the long list of still more barbarous outrages, arouse the colonists and induce them to do all in their power to avert even the possibility of their recurrence, which the restoration of the natives to these shores would entail upon us.

And let Sir William Denison pause and beware how he trifles with the safety of the community, over whose interests our gracious Sovereign has appointed him to watch. Let him beware how he entails upon himself the fearful responsibility of giving directions for the return of the natives to this island; but should he unhappily proceed to this length, let the colonists avail themselves of every lawful means in their power to prevent such instructions being carried into effect. In order to give some idea of the feelings of the community on this side of the island, upon the capture and removal of the aborigines, I forward you a copy of the letter addressed to Lieutenant, Governor Arthur bringing under his notice certain resolutions passed at a public meeting held at Launceston, to take into consideration the best mode of testifying our gratitude to Mr. Robinson for the deliverance he had effected in our behalf.

You may observe the letter has reference to the "special reason" the inhabitants of Launceston and its vicinity had to rejoice at the removal of the natives: it may throw some light upon this, if I tell you that some time previous to the meeting, within the short space of one week, the mangled remains of no less than seven persons destroyed by the natives had been interred at the burial ground in Launceston. I would conclude by again urging upon the notice of my fellow-colonists, that it is not because the natives are so few in number that their return to this island should be viewed without apprehension or alarm: I conceive that all who were acquainted with their former insidious mode of warfare, will bear me out in the assertion that a dozen ill-disposed natives would be quite sufficient to carry out such a system of bloodshed and plunder as would spread terror and dismay throughout the length and breadth of the colony.-I remain, Mr. Editor, yours obediently, REMINISCOR. Launceston, September 12. [Memorial.]

We, the undersigned, inhabitants of the district of Launceston and its vicinity, beg leave to forward to your Excellency the accompanying series of " Resolutions" passed at a public meeting lately held in Launceston, to take into consideration the best mode in which to testify-our deep sense of the benefit conferred by Mr. G. A. Robinson in conciliating and removing the aborigines of this island. We beg more particularly to call your Excellency's attention to the 3rd resolution-"' That the meeting "should earnestly and respectfully memorialize your "Excellency to bestow upon Mr Robinson a hand "some extent of land in the best situation now to be "obtained, to be settled upon him and his heirs for "ever, with honourable mention in the grant of those "services for which it was given".

In furtherance of this, we beg most respectfully to assure your Excellency that we are of opinion that there is no person in the colony who entertains a deeper sense of the obligations due by the colonists to Mr. Robinson than does your Excellency, as uniformly evinced by the kind and liberal treatment shewn to that gentleman; and under this impression we trust that your Excellency will favourably receive the respectful and-earnest request of those who, having specially benefitted by the labours of Mr. Robinson, are sensible that it is out of their power as individuals to testify their gratitude by any permanent and suitable token and therefore call upon your Excellency-in whom we believe such power exists-to reward Mr. Robinson on behalf of us and our fellow-colonists in such a manner as to bear a lasting testimony both of his unwearied and successful exertions and of our consequent gratitude.

And it has appeared to us that the best mode in which to carry these our wishes into effect is to solicit your Excellency to bestow upon Mr. Robinson a grant of land to be settled upon him and his children and where-his arduous labours being now ended (the last of the hostile blacks, as we believe, having been brought in)-he might retire with his family; and where, with the willing contributions of his fellow colonists and the liberal assistance of the government, he might (as we conceive he certainly ought) pass the remainder of his days in comparative ease and independence.

We would beg respectfully to remind your Excellency that in acceding to our request your Excellency would but follow in the course so frequently pursued by the parent government by rewarding those whom the public voice has held up as benefactors with landed estates as well as honours; and if those only have been esteemed benefactors who have achieved great victories over the enemies of their country, we would respectfully urge that Mr. Robinson may well be rewarded in a similar manner, as he has gained a complete though a BLOODLESS victory over our hitherto implacable and insidious enemies, by whom a continual state of terror and alarm was kept up amongst us and the lives and properties of all classes rendered insecure and has brought them from a state of the most abject degradation and wretchedness to one of comparative comfort and placed them within the pale of moral and religious improvement.

LAUNCESTON EXAMINER (TAS: 1842 - 1899),
SATURDAY 25 SEPTEMBER 1847, PAGE 4

TO THE EDITOR OF THE LAUNCESTON EXAMINER. ABORIGINES.

Sir,-Lieutenant-Governor Denison, in his Minute to the late Council announcing his intention to remove the natives from Flinders' Island and to restore them to this colony, speaks of them with commiseration as "the unfortunate beings who have been delivered over to the caprice of a single individual," at such a distance from the seat of government as to render impossible " any effective inspection or control over him." I question if the present condition of the free colonists of Van Diemen's Land could be more accurately or graphically described than in the terms of this Minute. Does not the announcement of the restoration of the natives contained therein and the grave expression of his Excellency's opinion that " they might be allowed to reassume their old habits of life without risk to the colonists" too clearly indicate that our best interests-yea, even our lives and properties are subject to the caprice, to call it by the mildest name, of a single individual, who is too far removed from the parent government to be subject to that immediate inspection and control which his actions too clearly show he so much requires.

*It is impossible that the wildest freaks of the deposed Commandant at Flinders' Island can bear comparison with this experiment of our ruler, who, of his own will, sets himself to neutralize and render abortive the greatest benefit ever conferred upon the colony ;and in contemptuous defiance of all past experience on the subject, **arranges for the restoration of a horde of savages to their former haunts now occupied by the colonists and coolly tells us "he thinks these savages may be allowed to reassume their old habits of life without risk to those colonists."** Would it not be naturally imagined by any one unacquainted with the subject, that their former habits of life had been perfectly inoffensive in their character whereas the dearly bought experience of the colonists too clearly proved, that, for some years previous to the removal of the natives, their habits of life could only be described as a system of bloodshed and plunder. Our condition as a community at the present moment is indeed specially deserving the commiseration of the parent government and of our fellow countrymen in Great Britain, threatened, as we are, with the importation of the polluted mass of convicts from Norfolk Island. The individual who has been appointed by our gracious Sovereign to watch over our interests intimates his resolution to fill up the cup of our calamities by the restoration of a horde of savages to these shores from whence it was naturally hoped they had been for ever most providentially removed.*

I rejoice to see that a public meeting is about to be held, to petition the home government upon this momentous subject and to forward to the local government a protest against its taking any measure for the return of the natives until an answer to that petition can be obtained; and I trust that such protest will forcibly and plainly set before his Excellency the heavy responsibility which will thenceforward devolve exclusively upon him should he unhappily carry out his intentions, whilst it faithfully warns him to beware how he incurs that responsibility.-

I remain, Mr. Editor, yours' obediently,
A COLONIST. Launceston, Launceston, September 20.

LAUNCESTON EXAMINER (TAS: 1842 - 1899),
WEDNESDAY 6 OCTOBER 1847, PAGE 4

THE ABORIGINES.

*Since the public meeting the following letter from the Colonial Secretary
has been handed to us for publication; Colonial Secretary's Office, 28th
September, 1847. Sir,-I am directed to acknowledge your communication of
the 23rd instant, it which you state that a public meeting will be held on the
30th, for the purpose of considering the necessity of addressing his Excellency
upon the subject of the removal of the aborigines from Flinder's Island to
the main land. In reply I am to acquaint you that the Lieutenant Governor
has acted in this matter in conformity with the advice and opinions of all
the persons who from having visited, or had charge of the natives, might be
expected to be able to form a judgment of their habits and character; and
also in compliance with the expressed opinions of the Secretary of State. His
Excellency cannot, therefore, suspend a measure which he thinks likely to be
productive of great benefit to all parties concerned.*

*His Excellency has no objection to forward any memorandum you may
wish to send to the Secretary of State; but he cannot delay acting upon
the conviction he at present entertains.- I have the honour to be, sir, your
very obedient servant, J E. Bicheno. J. H. Wedge, Esq, Christ's College,
Bishopsbourne. We now subjoin the following letter from Mr. Bartley, with
the extracts read by that gentleman and referred to in our report of the
proceedings: Kerry Lodge, Oct. 1, 1847.*

*SIR,-The publication in the columns of your widely circulating Journal, of
the accompanying extracts from the files of the Launceston Advertiser for
1829 to 183(2), inclusive, containing some of the recorded outrages of the
aborigines during that period, being immediately previous to their removal
to Flinder's will bring before the public some of the data upon which the
assertion contained in the Colonial Secretary's answer to Mr. Wedge's letter
is founded, "that if all the natives (now at Flinder's, 52 in number,) were to
return to the Bush, the damage they COULD effect would be but trifling"!!!*

Bearing in mind that the whole number of natives who were removed to Flinder's in the first instance was, 122, the question naturally arises:-if 122 natives did commit the outrages above referred to: how many could 52 commit.-

I remain Sir, yours obediently, THEODORE BARTLEY.

TO THE EDITOR OF THE LAUNCESTON EXAMINER.

[Extracts.] On Saturday the 31st ultimo, as the shepherd of Mr. William Smith, of the river Tamar, was attending his sheep, a spear was discharged through his hat, by some one of a party of aborigines, which were concealed in an adjoining scrub; the man happily escaped from them unhurt.

(Launceston Advertiser, February 9, 1829.)

LAUNCESTON EXAMINER (TAS. : 1842 - 1899),
SATURDAY 9 OCTOBER 1847, PAGE 3

TO CHARLES HINDLEY, ESQ., M.P., LONDON.

Sir,--I am induced to address you by the connection of your name with a society formed for the protection of the aboriginal inhabitants of countries subjected to the British Crown. I propose to put you in possession of facts, which may prove the impolicy of a measure fraught with peril to the aborigines of this island, now contemplated by the local Government. I cannot doubt that you will invoke the attention of Parliament, and thus avert, if possible, the threatened destruction of an unfortunate race. Its melancholy history is probably largely known to yourself and your coadjutors. From a multitude of instances, the fortunes of the Tasmanian native have been often quoted, to illustrate the fatal consequences of European contact. It may be desirable, however, to give the chief incidents of their miserable story. They will prove that the fears entertained by the colonists are not fantastic; and that the policy of the Government justifies the remonstrance of the philanthropist and the christian.

The concurrent testimony of their first visitors, assigns to the aborigines the character of a harmless race. Cook, Flinders, and Bass, unite to state that they exhibited no ferocity and offered no violence. Labillerre, the French naturalist, whose pursuits often placed him in their power, praises their gentleness and affability. These observations, founded on a cursory inspection of their habits and temper, might not have been corroborated by more extended intercourse; but they strikingly contrast with the estimate formed by the same navigators of several other tribes of the southern seas. In 1803, the authorities of New South Wales dispatched an expedition to. this island. The new colony consisted chiefly of convicts, and the military who had them in charge. A few months after their arrival, five hundred natives were seen approaching the camp. The officer in command ordered his men to fire, and from thirty to fifty of the natives fell. They are supposed to have entertained no hostile intention: they are said to have been unarmed: they were accompanied by their women and children; but a result so severe could not fail to awaken distrust and revenge; and to this catastrophe many colonists attribute the inextinguishable hatred they afterwards displayed.

But looking at the character of the colony, it was impossible that the native race could be protected from wanton aggression: a brutal contempt for uncivilised men has ever been conjoined with moral inferiority. The British Government does not appear to have foreseen the effect of letting loose in a distant country a band of lawless persons, banished from their own. The laxity which prevailed permitted intercourse, without surveillance or responsibility. An early scarcity of food obliged the authorities to permit the white population to disperse in the bush, in search of game. Afterwards, parties of prisoners, illegally at large, ravaged the country, and set the Government at defiance-sometimes in temporary alliance with the natives- but often oppressing them with incredible cruelty.

The abduction and abuse of their women, as well as other acts of outrage, were the natural effects of the then social state of the colony. The anecdotes of those times detail instances of ferocity which no mind could imagine:

probably a far greater number were hidden from the knowledge of all but the perpetrators; and, however melancholy the results to the whites, the retaliation suffered could not surpass the wrongs inflicted on the miserable natives. The Government interposed ineffectual expostulation and unavailing threatenings. The murder of an aborigine was declared a capital crime. But the testimony of a savage was inadmissible: To distinguish between a wanton attack and self-defence was no easy task. No white was ever brought to justice; and when a catalogue of reprisals of enormous length and sickening uniformity compelled the Government to treat as a crime the approach of natives within limits-to them unintelligible it became in the eyes of many a public service to destroy them.

The exasperation of the white was almost justified by the cruelty, treachery, and personal ingratitude of the blacks. It was not to be expected that their sufferings in early years, or the causes which had formed them, from an inoffensive race into a band of fiends, should be regarded in this strife. They butchered the benefactor who fed them, and the infant in its cradle: the settler saw his family lie slaughtered on his hearth: the stockman was speared by an invisible and unprovoked assailant: the colonists, when crossing the country, passed every gully and projecting rock with feelings of terror; and they were often compelled to suspend the most necessary occupations to protect their homes. It is utterly impossible to transfer to paper the scenes of consternation, anger, and grief, which were frequent at this melancholy era.

The notices of Government -the paragraphs of newspapers only faintly represent the alarm which agitated all classes of society. In one month, fourteen inquests were held over the victims of the blacks: in one graveyard fourteen out of fifteen of the dead had fallen in the strife. The advantage of fire-arms enabled the whites to retaliate with terrible effect. They surprised the encampments of the hunted savages, and poured in upon them a murderous fire. The sentiments of humanity were silent in a warfare in which no choice existed but to destroy or be destroyed. It was at length resolved by Col. Arthur to call out all able to bear arms, and by one effort to stop for ever the course of these calamities. At the expense of not less than £30,000, a military cordon was extended across the country, intended to drive the natives into Tasman's Peninsula; but they, evaded their pursuers, and only one was taken. Several were destroyed, and probably all were intimidated, and thus prepared to yield to persuasion when other measures were adopted for their capture.

These were intrusted to Mr. Robinson, a gentleman. whose courage and humanity eminently qualified him for the task. He succeeded in bringing the inconsiderable remnant which yet remained, under the power of the Government, by which they were conveyed to Flinders' Island, where they have been since supported at the public charge. This happy event saved the aborigines from utter destruction, and removed a domestic evil of enormous magnitude. The expense was regarded as trivial, compared with the mental repose which was thus restored to the settlers, and their final liberation from dangers which had proved the source of the worst calamities. The agents in this great deliverance received the strongest expressions of the public gratitude - a deliverance which can only be estimated by those who experienced the paralysing influence of those events which neither caution nor humanity could avert.

Such, Sir, is a rapid but faithful sketch of the relations formerly subsisting between the aboriginal and the British population of Van Diemen's Land. You will not be astonished that the first proposal for the restoration of the blacks was received with incredulity. His Excellency Sir William Denison avowed in a minute to Council that this object was contemplated. But the terms of the minute indicated such utter ignorance of the native character, and of the state of the colony, and such total oblivion of the history of both, that no person of experience imagined that on better information the proposal would be carried into effect.

"The expense of maintaining the establishment at Flinder's Island, for the support of the few original inhabitants of the colony who are still in existence, has latterly been increasing, while the numbers of the natives themselves have either decreased or, at best, remained stationary. The distance of Flinder's Island rendering any effective inspection or control over the officers employed impossible, has, in point of fact, delivered over the unfortunate beings to whom, both in justice and honor, every attention and kindness is due, to the caprice (for I can call it by no better name) of a single individual. This individual I have been obliged to remove from his charge; and in order to enable the Government and the community to exercise some control over the persons to whom the charge of the few remaining natives is entrusted. I have decided to remove the whole establishment from Flinder's Island, and to place it at a convenient spot within such a distance from Hobart Town as will bring it within reach of visit and inspection, not only of persons officially employed, but also of benevolent individuals. By so doing, it is to be hoped not only that any act of tyranny or caprice on the part of the officers will be discovered, and will then meet its proper punishment, but that means will be afforded of gradually inducing individuals, or even families amongst the natives, to submit to the restrains of civilisation. If these expectations should prove erroneous should the longing after that state of unrestricted freedom, so dear to the savage, still lead them to wish to be released from the slight restraint to which it is proposed to subject them,-I think they might be allowed to resume their old habits of life without any risk to the colonists ; this, however, will be a matter for future consideration,"--His Excellency's Minute.

It was not till lately that it came to the knowledge of the community that in neglect of earnest remonstrances the local authorities had actually arranged for the transit of the entire establishment to the main land of this country. The colonists complain with great justice that without taking the opinion of a Legislative Council, his Excellency has resolved to hazard the public tranquillity. The political changes which we have reason to anticipate would soon have enabled the Executive to resort to the sense of the people in a constitutional form. It cannot, however, be doubted now, that Sir William Denison will persevere, and that the protest of the whole inhabitants will have no other effect than to devolve on their rulers the sole responsibility of the but too certain issue.

Two reasons only are alleged for the removal of the aborigines to this island: the expense they occasion, and the oppression to which they are liable. The first, though doubtless not insignificant, is in this case unfit to compete with the least interest of the native. We are not, As A NATION, guileless; as a colony, we are not without sentiments of remorse. Compunction, not less than commiseration, is proper when surveying the fate of this injured people. The expense, even were it greater, would not surpass their claims. They are wasting away, and we have been the instruments of their destruction. It is some satisfaction to know that all their wants are now supplied: that they are no longer liable to persecution. In all our complaints of extravagant outlay-and they are many-none of the people have touched on this branch of colonial expense. It will, however, afford you gratification to know that the better protection of the natives is the alleged chief reason for their restoration. It cannot be doubted that the distance, of Flinders Island is inconvenient. Experience will not permit us to assert that the remoteness of a subordinate ruler from control may not tempt him sometimes to play the tyrant: but there is no conceivable motive for the oppression of the natives. Their stores are found in kind: they have no taxes to pay: their labour is voluntary: no hostile interest exists to invade their tranquillity: civil officers are employed in their superintendence.

The island is often visited: concurrent reports describe them as possessing comforts in advance of their powers of appreciation; and if any acts of wrong are committed against them, the Governor of this island has authority to apply the remedy. I now proceed to point out the consequences apprehended as the result of the intended change. The gentlemen who have predicted them, are at least entitled to deference. They form a large proportion of the most opulent and intelligent inhabitants of the colony.

Many of them are settlers of long standing, familiar with the native mind, and conversant with the feelings of the lower ranks of British Society. Their past experience demands for their opinions a weight which cannot be due to mere official deliberations. The views of his Excellency are necessarily theoretical: HE HAS NEVER SEEN A NATIVE; and although his claim to exercise a dispassionate judgment will not be rudely disputed, it is not usual to attribute greater authority to mere abstract calculations than to conclusions based on personal knowledge. The remonstrant are by no means reconciled to the measure by the strong assurances of a stranger, however respectable, that their fears are morbid, and that they are moved by an excited imagination. It is proper to remark that the gentleman who leads the opposition in this measure is among the last who would embarrass the representative of the Queen. Parties, if such exist on this colony, have united their efforts in this question. The alarm expressed is real and not factitious, and the appeal to the Crown has resulted from the failure of private interference. You will easily understand the importance of these explanations. They will fully answer any reproach which might be cast on the agitation, and relieve the remonstrants from the charge of wilful exaggeration. Nor is the welfare of the white, population the sole or even the chief concern of these gentlemen. They believe, whether justly or not, that after a rapid series of calamities the blacks will perish. They are therefore anxious to retain them in security, to preserve them from premature extinction, and to avert from the colony additional guilt and dishonour.'

Without assuming extraordinary humanity, it may be admitted that any people would view with horror the approaching extermination of the fragments of a race our preserved only by their careful sequestration. It is the opinion of all who are familiar with the natives of Van Diemen's Land, that their partial acquiescence in the modes of civilised life is the result, not of preference, but of constraint. The efforts to impress on their minds the objects and value of European customs have generally failed. Whenever an opportunity has occurred they have gladly cast off their clothing, and renewed with great enthusiasm the habits of barbarism. Whether it may be possible under favourable circumstances to train their youth to the sentiments of civilised man, is yet a speculation but slightly encouraged by past experience. It is not doubted, however, by any practical person, that their arrival in this colony will be followed by the readoption without delay of their vagrant way of life. Many of them were of mature age at the period of their capture. They are well acquainted with the country; possess great skill in traversing the bush, and in obtaining the casual means of subsistence. Their strong attachment to their former places of abode will prove a powerful obstruction to regulations for their safety. The native country of a savage is bounded by narrow limits: it is the district in which he was reared ; and a short remove from that spot is not less banishment than location in another land.

The remnants of various tribes belong to slips of territory which had no political or social relations, and thus, instead of being held together by their restoration, the impulses of patriotism which it is intended to satisfy, will only in proportion to their power insure their dispersion. To the Tasmanian black a region two hundred miles from his early home has no greater attraction than any other portion of the earth. Englishmen are apt to impart the same colouring to subjects only kindred in name, and it is therefore right that what constitutes the native country of the aborigines should be correctly delineated. But if his supposed feelings of patriotism are gratified they will lead him at once to districts often thinly inhabited by whites, and sheep stations now private property. It is needless to insist on the dangers which such a position would entail.

The black, however harmless, could not be regarded but with feelings of suspicion. The low valuation of life is but too clearly proved by late incidents in the neighbouring colonies, and the past history of this. The very fears of the lower classes of whites would induce them to interpret the movements of the black as hostile when his intention was innocent. Shepherds with arms in their hands, and impressed with the tales which have been repeated in their hearing, would scarcely hesitate to use their weapons on the first alarm. It is quite useless to urge the barbarity of such premature resistance. Were the reasons for apprehension less cogent it cannot be supposed that deliberation or humanity would correct the suggestions of terror.

The harmless native on his first appearance would be shot down; and the homicide, if he ever considered the sufferer as belonging to the human species-which certainly many do not would acquit his conscience under the plea of necessity and the right of self-preservation. If the result I have indicated would be probable in any country, I think you will be justified in taking into special account the peculiar state of our European population. The education, past life, and present condition of the many must certainly increase the danger of the experiment. The women would be liable to the repetition of those abuses which of themselves insure collision; and surely no philanthropist can reconcile his feelings to the inevitable diffusion of maladies which are fast extirpating the Australian blacks, and must in a few years, even without any other cause, extinguish the whole nation. I am not wondering amongst conjectures and probabilities. The justice of these expectations is confessedly favoured by the past. It is from the supposed reformation that has transpired that the Governor contemplates a different issue. His Excellency expects to be able to restrain the blacks. He may certainly do so by confining them; but this must be done by walls and chains. The first attempt at personal coercion would throw them into hostility. Their notions of law are connected solely with the presence of a magistrate. But would it not be irksome to tie them down or to restrain them within such limits as an overseer would choose to range.

They are now only bounded by the ocean: they possess a breadth of country fully equal to the extent of their former ordinary migrations. In this island they could not be retained under the eye of a British functionary except by prison discipline. It follows that from their landing they will at intervals acquire the same personal liberty as formerly, and be exposed to sinister influences without effectual control or I protection. However fair tile intentions of the Government, the state of our laws generally excludes the aborigines from the protection of public justice. They could not be received as sole witnesses: the difficulties of admitting their evidence in cases of life and death have never been surmounted; and yet it is clear that in the majority of instances where wrong is done, none but themselves can know the precise merits of the aggressions.

Who perpetrated, or by which party the first signal of hostility was given, would be the I real point in a criminal trial, and few English jurors would be disposed to trust to the I equity of a savage seeking revenge; nor t would they convict a fellow-countryman on such testimony." Against all these evils the present sequestration of the natives defends them; and they have nothing to fear beyond the caprice of a commandant, which would rather amuse than offend them--who would be unlikely to injure seriously his little empire. Hitherto I have allowed the supposition that the literature of the natives would be simply perilous to themselves; but I do not the less believe that the measure will occasion a considerable amount of European suffering.

His Excellency has suggested that the return of the blacks to their former habits in this colony would be of little moment. Had he reflected after proper enquiry he would have differently estimated the consequences. He doubtless fancies that they will return to the place, and subsist on the indigenous productions of the island. But the out-stations of the flock masters would be inevitably exposed to their depredation. Base-minded men would even stimulate them to crime. These actions must lead to resistance; and when the first blood is drawn it is not difficult to perceive that revenge and retaliation will end only when there are no more to avenge. The now surviving natives are not unaccustomed to violence: there are among them men who in former times were the terror of the settlers. The most absurd inattention to the savage character alone could induce the supposition that submission and even mildness in captivity are inconsistent with a latent fierceness and thirst for blood. Brought back to old scenes, and liable to insult and oppression, the black would exhibit again the propensities of his nature.

Aborigines, far superior in their mental and physical constitution, after conforming to the demeanour and almost imbibing the tastes of polished life, have generally, on regaining the licence of their savage state, remembered only the arts of destruction. It is impossible to imagine a wider departure from the law of probabilities than to suppose that men reared amongst the excitement of constant personal warfare, and trained to cunning and unrelenting ferocity, may be safely allowed to slip off the restraints which it cost infinite labour to impose. His Excellency relies on the diminished numbers of the blacks as a proof that danger is chimerical. Is this inference sustained by past experience? When twice their present number they sufficed to fill the Government with alarm, and to arrest the entire business of the colony., Thousands of white men were deemed necessary to hunt them down. Their powers of. destruction were then found sufficient to fill the interior with mourning. A white, even if a murderer,-is unwilling to shed blood without necessity, and he is restrained and haunted by remorse.

But a savage is insensible to these emotions: he slays without trepidation, and strikes with an unerring aim. Even his colour assists him; and lie is able to conceal himself from pursuit with incredible dexterity. Against such foes the valour of the soldier is unavailing. If his Excellency had compared the numbers captured, with the deeds they performed on the eve of their apprehension, lie would not have thought the present population too insignificant for dread; and even he might have felt that if instead of a weekly outrage they should murder at longer intervals, they might still last long enough to complete a sad catalogue of woe. A demonstration that these people are terrible even in their weakness, closed the black war. One family alone evaded capture, burit remained a family of foes. Three men on one establishment fell by their spears! Can it be wise to calculate on the impotence of fifty savages, and among them possibly these very murderers?

But let it be supposed that the colonists are needlessly excited, and that the care of the Government could prevent a recurrence of disaster, is it prudent to disturb the public repose by a measure so formidable ? The people have

still fresh in their memory some of the most appalling incidents of colonial
his story. All were exposed to these calamities, and they are remembered
now as men reflect on the ravages of a tempest or a plague. What right has
a government to renew the anxiety of those afflicting visitations, even if they
are never to return? But should the expectations of the colonists be realised,
and should they be destined again to hear of murders and outrage, with
what sentiments of abhorrence will the reckless contempt of warnings be
reviewed? The christian, in estimating character, may allow to motives what
he cannot concede to actions; but the politician is bound to pass over such
niceties, and to declare that the statesman who countenances the sacrifice
of men's lives must answer for their blood! To you, sir, I appeal as to a
christian and philanthropist; and in the earnest hope that neither my appeal
nor your exertions may prove too late. JUSTINIAN.

The article then goes on describing many attacks by aborigines
during the 20s and 30s.

Human emotions, I have decided, must be located on the far
side of our brain, or perhaps even in our left toe, but far away from the
source of rational thinking. Here we have perhaps 50 Pakana people,
mostly elderly and dispirited, whose only wish is to return to their
homeland now populated with close to 65,000 *rytia* and yet the fear is
palpable. Letters and articles are rife and vitriolic in their expression
and devoid of sensible commentary. Of course the war and loss of
life was still painfully close to the hearts of many and hence their
emotional reaction is at least fathomable and should not be too
lightly dismissed.

LAUNCESTON EXAMINER (TAS: 1842 - 1899),
SATURDAY 9 OCTOBER 1847, PAGE 5

TO THE EDITOR OF THE LAUNCESTON EXAMINER. THE NATIVE BLACKS.

Sir,--This is new trouble to me: we have obtained that great blessing of putting a stop to the transportation; now letting the blacks at liberty is bringing on us a greater curse. The reason that I did not stop and send for my family and friends to Sydney was the disagreeable appearance of the blacks. You well know, Sir, that a few months back I went to London, Liverpool, New York and the Canadas; at all those places I recommended this island in preference to other colonies to my friends and others.

When mentioning the many advantages the other colonies had over this, I could say that the blacks were troublesome and very disagreeable there, but that there were none here. When the news gets abroad that the blacks are let loose, my friends will blame me for bringing them. We still have one consolation: the misguided Governor cannot move the island from the healthiest climate that I have met with yet.

Sir, I remain a well-wisher to the colony. J. R.

COURIER (HOBART, TAS: 1840 - 1859), SATURDAY 9 OCTOBER 1847, PAGE 4

THE TASMANIAN ABORIGINES LAMENT AND REMONSTRANCE WHEN IN SIGHT OF HIS NATIVE LAND, FROM FLINDERS ISLAND.

Fair Island of my birth, thy distant rocks
Call forth the tenderest feelings of my heart;
Although the sight of thee my yearning mocks.
For cruel waves thee from thy children part.

Ah I white man, why—Oh! why thy childhood's home
Did'st thou abandon, to drive us from ours?
Why, unprovoked, with terrors did'st thou come,
To cloud with woe a people's once glad hours?

Thou can'st not tell with what a fond desire
We cling to thoughts of what was once so dear;
When sadly gaze the children, wife and sire,
On those loved cliffs, so distant—yet so near.

Not ours to cultivate the teeming ground.
And with luxurious dwellings stud the soil;
Not ours to pore upon the page profound,
And reap the rich rewards of mental toil:

Far other are our labours and our joys;
Nature, to us and ours, is all in all;
No implements of art our race employs,
For nature heart and answers every call.

She taught us to transfix the kangaroo.
And the swift emu, with the quivering spear;
She showed us where the hidden ground-bread grew.
And many a root, to swell our frugal cheer:

'Twas she instructed us the honied flower
To steep in water and to roast the seed;
And she endued us with the magic power
To call forth hidden fire, in time of need.

Thou, white man, with thy ever-growing store
Of learning, mak'st a home in every land;
For thee all countries forth their treasures pour,
And nature waits, the servant of thine hand.

Not so with us; linked with our native earth
Are all our pleasures and is all our care:
The state our fathers lived in at our birth,
Is but the lot that we are born to bear.

Let us return to our loved land again!
Ah! white man, wherefore dost thou keep us here?
Thou dost not know the exil'd bosom's pain,
Nor wear'st away thy life with many a tear.

Our race is fast decaying;—far and wide
Extend thy riches and increase thine heirs;
Oh! let us die where our forefathers died,
That we may mix our wretched dust with theirs.

October 6, 1847. AUSTER. [pseudonym for Mary Leman Grimstone]

It won't surprise you to know I have gout. I'm telling you this because that's what old blokes do; they always want to offer a long, boring and unedifying narrative about their decaying bodies. I am no exception and as there is no one else to listen except Bent, who just turns over and goes back to sleep, you are it! So, my advice is never ask a gentleman of maturing years how they are feeling unless you are prepared for an excruciating monologue.

However, there is some relevance to my ongoing story. Having gout means seemingly endless periods of being confined to my study with one leg resting on a stool and without the solace of a decent drink! It gives one plenty of thinking time and often random thoughts lead to some semblance of inventiveness. It began a few weeks ago, when walking, or if truth be known, limping with stick in hand through my local village only to have a child run past me as other little beasts yelled a series of unpleasant names at the poor wretch.

As he stopped to catch his breath I heard him mutter:

"Sticks and stones will break my bones but names will never hurt me". Then vanish behind the church cloisters. I wondered just how true this old saying really was. Why was he running away unless the name calling hurt? Names and language do matter.

Here I was grumpy, impatient and altogether out of sorts and needing something to occupy my mind. I began to think about the language and names used to describe the Pakana people during the years I was reporting from Lutruwita. I picked out the words used in the press and ticked them off by date; it was fascinating. Keep in mind this is the work of an amateur and one poorly equipped to apply scientific rigour, but it does make the point well. You will see that some words are repeated which indicates how often I spotted them during the period in question. Naturally it is beyond my character and disposition to contemplate how to present this information in a sensible way. Before you ask, it was not I who penned the graphics below but my niece. She has a natural aptitude for numbers and concepts which are way beyond her mathematically illiterate uncle!

I won't insult your intelligence with my attempts at interpretation and give my blustering opinions about these two depictions. But a couple of thoughts I do have are fairly obvious. The most used term for the Pakana people was 'Black Native' or 'native', in the early period, often without malice, dropping off just before the intensity of the Black War from about 1827 to '32. It sharply rose during that period but with negative connotations. 'Aborigine' rose steadily throughout the period while 'savage' rose sharply in the first part of the war.

The other interesting factor is in the latter period when writings become more sympathetic toward the Pakana and adjectives such as 'poor', 'degraded', 'miserable', 'unoffending'; and are more prevalent.

There was a whole gamut of words which came in and out of currency depending on the press' particular stance during each period. I have simply allowed the words to float and flutter with time and these are the ones which drifted onto my page:

Hostile natives, Black fellow, murderous, depredations, untutored, unenlightened savages, poor Aborigines, atrocious race, merciless savages, Black wretches, harmless creatures, happy, unhappy and benighted people, poor native, unhappy savages, poor men, imprisoned natives, kidnapping a race of human beings, poor people, inoffensive tribes, unfortunate beings, insidious, poor wanderers of the woods, children of nature.

As I sat back and looked at such an eclectic selection of words it occurred to me that on no occasion did the press apply the actual name the people living in Lutruwita used to refer to themselves: Pakana or any derivation. There is the occasional mention of the British name of a nation such as Big River but certainly not the Aboriginal name nor the clans living within. I leave this for you to contemplate at your leisure.

USE OF LANGUAGE BY PRESS DURING THE LUTRUWITA WAR 1814–1856

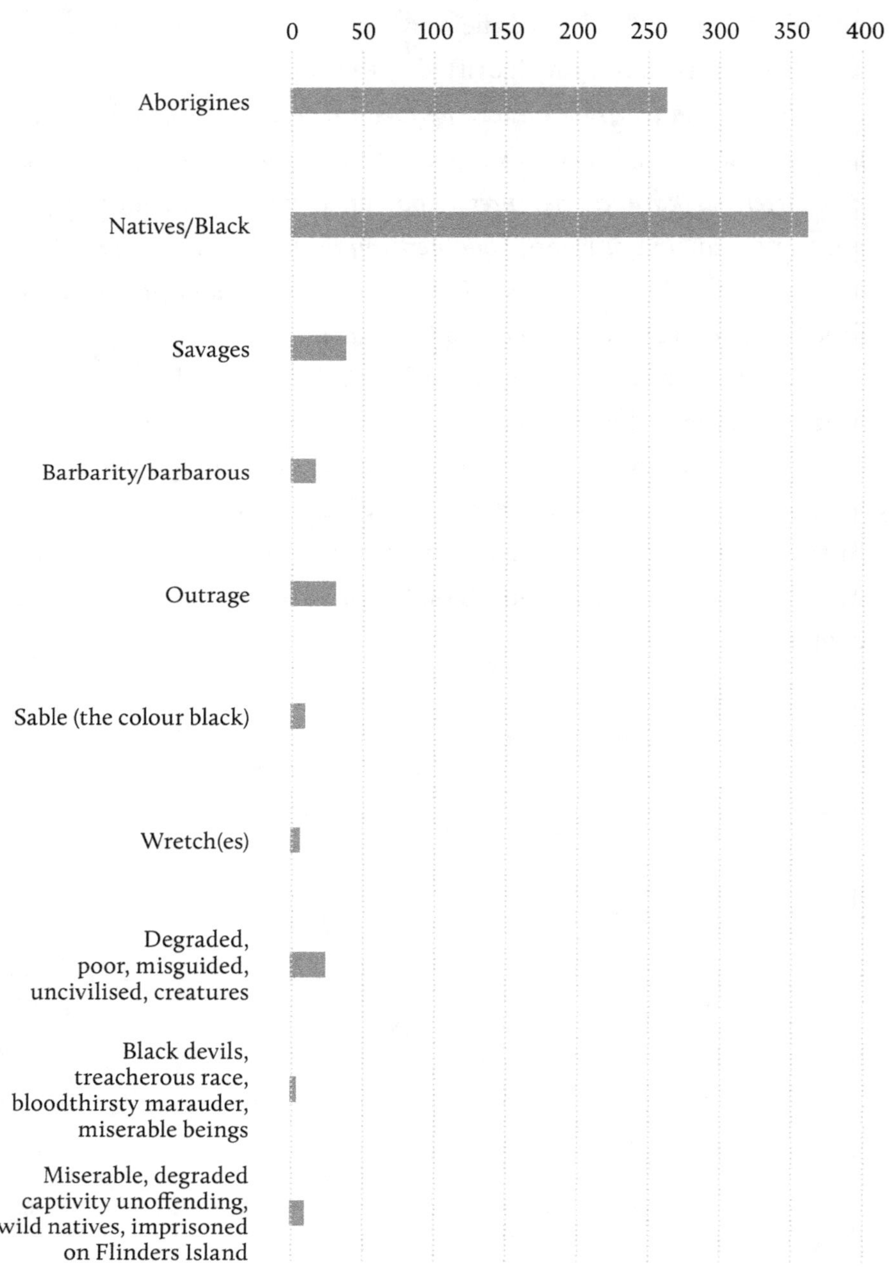

USE OF LANGUAGE BY PRESS DURING THE LUTRUWITA WAR PERCENTAGE BY YEAR CLUSTERS

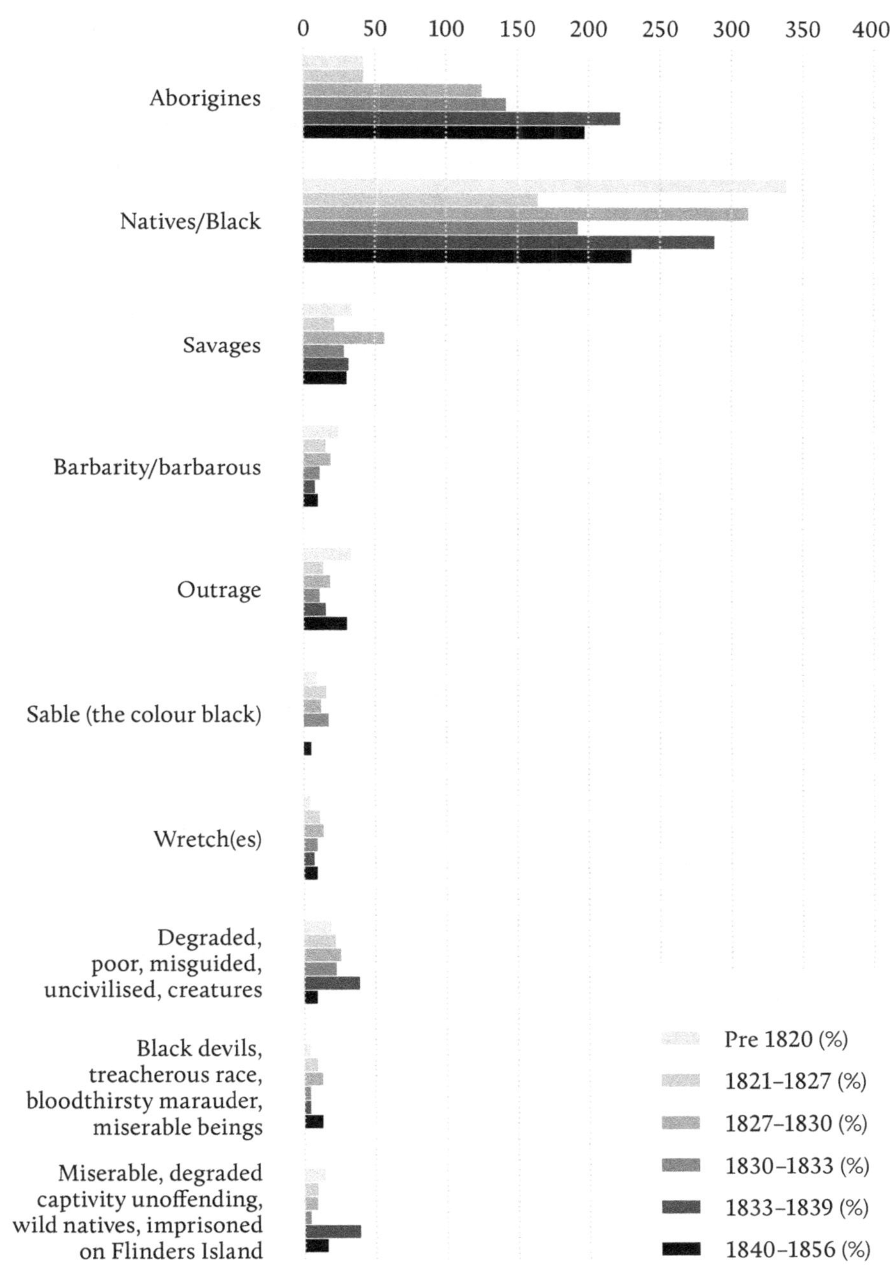

LAUNCESTON EXAMINER (TAS: 1842 - 1899),
WEDNESDAY 13 OCTOBER 1847, PAGE 4

TO THE EDITOR OF THE LAUNCESTON. EXAMINER. ABORIGINES

Sir,--I see by your paper, that the Governor of this colony has sent a vessel to Flinder's Island for the purpose of conveying the blacks back to this colony, to re-establish them. I would ask two questions.

First has the Governor power, without the sanction of a Council, to re-establish them: Secondly: what will be the result of such proceedings? As far as his power extends, I know not but the result I do know--this would be it. First when the Home Government hear of his proceeding, they will recall him (and no great loss, either) That would not be the worst. If the Governor's anticipations are not fully realised, this race will be turned upon the inhabitants. I think Sir, if the Governor were to ask himself the question: How should I like to have these savages (if I were a farmer) come to my house with their spears and perhaps be the death of me or my wife, or any part of my family? I think he would not do it then

Sir; then let him do as he would be done by. Secondly of course, people will leave the colony; they will not stop to be tormented by them; nor to be imposed upon by the Governor no Britons, nor the descendants of Britons, will be treated in this way. It is painful to them to think of the past,- how much blood has been shed- how much trouble Sir George Arthur took to re move them and now they are all coming back again. What can be more sickening, or more heart-breaking, than to think that we are to have our children killed, ourselves turned out of in habitation, to leave the labours of our hands, to go to another country for the safety of our lives?

CORNWALL CHRONICLE (LAUNCESTON, TAS: 1835 - 1880),
SATURDAY 30 OCTOBER 1847, PAGE 4

TO HIS EXCELLENCY SIR WILLIAM DENISON. KNT., LIEUT-GOVERNOR OF VAN DIEMEN'S LAND

Sir,— I have the honour to address your Excellency as I understand it to be your intention to remove the aborigines, from Flinder's Island and to bring them back to the Island, — a measure which I believe will be fraught with danger to the lives of her Majesty's subjects here, to the aborigines and to the peace and welfare of this colony. While I earnestly insist every care, without regard to expense which humanity can possibly suggest, should be given to this unfortunate people;

I maintain this must be accomplished with a due regard to the safety of your Excellency's colonists and without risking a repetition of the fearful scenes, the horrible murders committed by the natives and which ruined the peace and will never be effaced from the memories of but too many of the old colonists. I have heard with deep pain how the aborigines were treated in olden times by some of the unfeeling stockmen of those times and in later days have seen the heart-sickening massacres of innocent persons by the blacks, — of persons whose feelings and station rendered them incapable of unkindness to any and whose only feeling towards the natives was kindness and sympathy and I naturally dread any step likely to lead to a repetition of such occurrences.

The aborigine, unfortunately, never discriminated between those who had and those who had not, injured him — the friend, the foe, the pregnant woman, the child, the man, fell in his treacherous attacks, beneath his murderous blows — mercy he was never known to shew — and so subtle, active and clever was he in the bush that there was no eluding him — a spear through your own, or the body of your companion, at a moment when you imagined yourself perfectly safe, or a spear, with blazing bark lashed to it and sent into the thatch of your home, were generally the first warning of his merciless attacks — the house reduced to ashes, its peaceful inhabitants massacred— the results, broken into bands of from eight to twenty- five and spread over the whole island, their attacks were carried to an extent so alarming, that many colonists seriously thought of abandoning their farms; and so pressing had the danger become, as to induce our eminent Governor, Sir George Arthur, to direct, at an expense of nearly £30,000, the whole energies of the colony to attempt their capture.

The colonists rose in a body, about 6000 men *scoured the country for two months without success and so superior aid the black feel himself to them in the bush, that one of them stole down, speared a white man through the loins while on duty upon the main line and escaped with impunity. Murders, accompanied by mutilation, were of almost daily occurrence; in one month, I believe, fourteen look place; but it is painful to repeat the scenes which happened after the blood and treasure expended, both for the sake of the aborigines and of your colonists. I trust your Excellency will afford no chance of repetition by bringing the natives again upon this main land ; the sight of their old haunts would recall old recollections — man's nature does not easily change— and if the native wishes to escape, all the vigilance of your officers could not prevent him: and retake him you cannot; £30,000 was fruitlessly expended in the attempt before : by force he would not be taken; he was, by what all regarded at the time, as a providential interposition and as the greatest blessing ever conferred upon the colony, a feeling still cherished by numbers of those who knew what the natives were to contend against. Another fact I would particularly press:*

This is a peculiarly circumstanced colony; suppose the lawless runaway convict join the black, — we had not this to dread formerly every white man who had the misfortune to fall in his way was murdered without distinction. Now the black knows our language —our customs; he may not so strongly object to the white man joining him; the consequences of such a junction demand your Excellency's gravest consideration.

The recollection of what has occurred is too painfully impressed upon my memory to allow me to remain silent. The natives might remain peaceable and quiet, but I believe they would not; and should they return to their old haunts and habits, the most serious results must follow their return to this island. Had your Excellency witnessed the misery they once caused — had you seen the wives, children and faithful servants of your colonists murdered, mutilated in the most revolting manner, with every circumstance of cruelly and their homes reduced to a heap of ashes (as, alas! too frequently was the case)— then I feel assured your Excellency would take no step which could, by the most remote possibility, ever lead again to scenes so dreadful. I beg of you not to risk their recurrence by bringing the aborigines again upon this main land, for against this measure I respectfully but solemnly protest ; that your Excellency has been actuated by the best intentions in considering this subject, I am convinced, but I believe the step cannot be taken without endangering the lives and wellbeing of a great number of persons who are equally entitled to and I feel persuaded will receive, an equal share of your Excellency's humane consideration.—

I have the honour to be, your Excellency's obedient servant, W. Race Allison. Macquarie River, Sept. 27th, 1847.

Oh, how facts become fiction ever so quickly!

CORNWALL CHRONICLE (LAUNCESTON, TAS: 1835 - 1880), SATURDAY 30 OCTOBER 1847, PAGE 4

COLONIAL SECRETARY'S OFFICE, 8TH OCTOBER, 1847.

SIR, I have the honour to acknowledge, the receipt of your communication to the Lieutenant Governor, in which you protest against the removal of the aborigines from Flinder's Island to like main land. His Excellency desires me to acquaint you that the measure has been decided upon, not without the most serious and careful consideration; and has received the sanction of the Secretary of State.

The Finance Committee of 1844 whose report was laid before the Legislative Council, were the first to recommend its adoption, partly as, a matter of economy, but certainly after taking the opinion of all those who were best capable of judging, of the nature and habits of the existing aborigines; and the three years that the arrangement has been in contemplation has been allowed to pass away without a single objection being stated to it.

The land on which they will be located, being situated at Oyster Cove in D'Entrecastraux Channel, where every attention will be paid to their safekeeping as well as to their comfort, is sufficiently remote to guarantee the security of the settlers generally ; and to prevent any evils, the anticipation of which His Excellency cannot bt feel is to a very great ex tent unfounded. Could he believe for a moment that your apprehensions were based on fact, or that anything like past outrages would be committed by the aborigines on their return to the mainland, he would even now when the vessel is daily expected with the establishment, withhold from carrying out his arrangements.

The united testimony, however, of all those who have visited, or had the care of them, leads to an opposite conclusion and His Excellency cannot defer any longer to take the steps which he deems to be imperatively necessary to put an end to mismanagement and to secure the protection and proper treatment of the remaining few of the original inhabitants of this island. —

I have the honour to be, Sir, your very obedient servant,

J. E. BICHENO. To W. Race Allison, Esq., Macquarie River.

HOBARTON GUARDIAN, OR, TRUE FRIEND OF TASMANIA
(HOBART, TAS: 1847 - 1854), SATURDAY 6 NOVEMBER 1847, PAGE 3

ABORIGINES OF VAN DIEMEN'S LAND.

The remaining portion of the original inhabitants of this Island, who have been so long in exile in Bass's Straits, have at last been returned to their native country and are now located at Oyster Cove, in D'Entrecasteaux Channel.

For some short period, after arrival there, these people seemed to entertain fear; but that feeling has now gone off and they now venture to roam about in diligent search of their favourite food—the kangaroo and opossum.

They have succeeded in capturing several of the former animal—and seem quite delighted to have an opportunity of once more enjoying the chase on their native soil. They occasionally visit the houses of the neighbouring settlers and, as they now understand the English language —remove any unfavourable impression, which a recollection of their former atrocities might have raised. We hope that the Mechanics' Institute, will procure a grouped drawing of these people, so that our descendants may be able to form correct ideas as to the personal appearance of the original inhabitants of Van Diemen's Land;

COURIER (HOBART, TAS: 1840 - 1859),
WEDNESDAY 10 NOVEMBER 1847, PAGE 2

THE GAZETTE.
GOVERNMENT NOTICE. NO. 109.
COLONIAL SECRETARY'S OFFICE, 4TH NOVEMBER, 1847.

The Lieutenant-Governor directs it to be notified for the information of the public and of those persons interested in the return of the Aboriginal inhabitants of Van Diemen's Land to their native country, that they consist of 13 Adult Men, 5 Boys and 22 Adult Women, 5 Girls.

That, of the thirteen men two have been reared from boyhood amongst Europeans, three have been educated at the Queen's Orphan Schools, one has been reared on the establishment of a settler (now deceased) and is a good bullock driver and farm servant, one is nearly blind, one is imbecile : that, of the remaining five four are from 45 to 55 years of age, two of them having been pretty regularly employed as boatmen and one having for years done the duty of cowherd, with a steadiness which would have been praiseworthy in a man bred to labour.

They have all lived about fifteen years in civilized habits; several of them can read and write; and they are almost all addicted to gardening. They raised at Flinder's Island, in gardens fenced by themselves, peas, beans, turnips, cabbages, carrots, onions, parsnips and pumpkin, betides cultivating fruit trees.

The Aboriginal women have lived in the practices of civilized life for even a longer period than the men.

The children are to be educated and trained in a manner to fit them to mingle with and to be ultimately absorbed into, the community.

The adult Aborigines are now located at Oyster Cove. Respectable persons may visit the establishment; and, on doing so, they will be required to write their names in a Visitors' Book kept there.

The Lieutenant-Governor sees in the insignificant number of the Aboriginal men few who have ever been at large in the Colony; and His Excellency possesses, in the fact of these men having acquired a taste for settled habits and industrial pursuits and in their appreciation of the comforts and advantages of domestic life, a sufficient guarantee for their future good behaviour.

By His Excellency's Command,

J. E. Bicheno.

BRITANNIA AND TRADES' ADVOCATE (HOBART TOWN, TAS: 1846 - 1851), THURSDAY 18 NOVEMBER 1847, PAGE 2

ORIGINAL CORRESPONDENCE.

We do not on all occasions identify our opinions with those of our Correspondents.

To the Editor of the Britannia. New Town, November 6. 1847.

Sir, — In the course of my perambulations a few days since, I visited the Aborigines, now resident at the Oyster Cove Station and a more deplorable set of creatures I never beheld ; they are suffering under the baneful disease (the influenza,) which I believe to be induced by the miserable and unhealthy quarters in which they reside. In a conversation I had with one of them he said, " Massa Guhncr all very well, he bring us from Flinder's very warm there, here very cold and wet, all soon die,"- and it is my firm conviction, that in the course of a few months, his prediction will be verified.

The Government promised to make the Station comfortable for their reception, (it having been uninhabited for some time past), but as it is With all their promises, " it ended in smoke ;" however, it will be a satisfaction for the Government to know that the Revenue is daily increasing as the Natives are decreasing. There is a medical man appointed to visit them, but I fear he is too much engaged elsewhere to waste his valuable time in so thankless a task as that of saving the life of a native, (due regard being paid to the Revenue,) but from a feeling of humanity he sends the medicine, which is distributed on Squeer's brimstone and treacle system, first come first served. I am no advocate for their being brought again to this Island, but as the Government has done so, It is bound to provide them with a comfortable home.

I am, Sir, yours obediently,

Mullagain.

Reading between the lines of the brief and poignant correspondence I now received from Andrew I realised that he was in dire straits both financially and in his personal health. The gods had not been kind to him in the last decade or so. The 1840s depression was merciless in its severity seriously affecting the family as it did for many others. Andrew's ventures became progressively far-fetched, ending predicably in increasing debt and poverty. As much as I considered him to be a friend, I imagine his disparate and erratic temperament may have been a hindrance to his business partnerships. The loss of Mary in 1846 was devastating and left him bereft of meaning and with several young children.

It was time, I decided, to part with my jottings and muses before it was too late. I wished so much to share with him my work not only to deflect his state of mind but because he had been so much part of my story. This is a copy of the last letter, accompanied by my manuscript, that I sent to my dear friend Andrew Bent in the far flung and now thriving colony of New South Wales.

Mr Andrew Bent Esq
C/- Sydney Benevolent Society Asylum,
Sydney, NSW

1st January 1850

My Dearest Friend,

I have no more tears to shed. My eyes are dry and sore from sensing the many words I lay before you. With my ink well close to empty, the time has come to put down my quill and let history move on without me.

After so many years of reporting, standing apart from events around me, I am now part of life again. I give you the little I have to offer with these jottings which are about nothing in particular but everything of importance to me. I have seen too much for one lifetime and you have felt it too and expressed it so enigmatically from behind your desk and with words in print.

The last few weeks have allowed me to unburden, release and cry out as I laboured and drew blood on so many pages. I feel at ease now. It is as though this writing has encapsulated my life and may now be released to the wind and shared only with the spirits I wish to join.

I penned it from the heart for Lowana, my only true love. A love so brief but so pressing, forever within my being. We are now drawn together through the intricate cobwebs of time and love. You know of whom I speak. We were so young. She a warrior and I a scribbler, so naively leaving her and her people to their fate. The thought torments me to this day. Perhaps she knew I could do more by telling her story than by staying with her. She also knew I was no warrior and would have been hopeless as a fighter!

I entrust this script to you. My desire is to see its ashes flung out to her spirit with the powerful winds of kunanyi so she will know I have tried to tell the world of her fate and that of a free people. My fear is that no one was listening during the time it mattered, but maybe one day in the distant future someone will catch the scent of my words on the breeze and begin to listen.

I wish you well.

W.C.

Catherine Bent, Andrew's second eldest, wrote and informed me of his passing. I received the letter in late January 1852 some months after the event and was deeply saddened by not only the loss of a dear friend but for one who had done so much for our right to read and write as we choose. He suffered greatly for his beliefs and much to my shame I could never claim such strength in character and principles. I was also shocked to hear his last few years had been so materially shattering.

I had always felt closer to Catherine than the other children perhaps because she seemed to relish in my stories of adventure with the Pakana people and my encounters with the Vedda in Ceylon. By now though she had a family of her own and married to Thomas Hall, a surgeon-dentist of all things. It makes me shudder just thinking about it! Although she too had her own hardships to bear. With her mother's death, her father's endless succession of business failures, emotional turbulence and eventual destitution she was responsible for not only her own children but I would imagine her younger siblings as well. Added to this her older siblings were spread far and wide with Elizabeth now married in New Zealand. Their brothers and Catherine's erstwhile husband had deserted her tempted by the ever-elusive lure of gold. It is little wonder that Andrew ended his days in the asylum.

Catherine kindly continued to send me many of the articles, letters and odds and sods from newspapers I relished so much. I am truly indebted to her.

The following are some of those she sent for me to learn of the remaining story to the point where Van Diemen's Land became formally known as Tasmania. These I pasted into a scrap book with a few brief notes although without Andrew my heart was no longer in my work. However, I do believe they do illustrate the changing values and attitudes presented in the newspapers toward Aborigines during this period.

1853

LAUNCESTON EXAMINER, Commercial and Agricultural Advertiser. (WITH WHICH IS INCORPORATED THE "LAUNCESTON ADVERTISER.")

COLONIAL TIMES (HOBART, TAS: 1828 - 1857),
TUESDAY 6 DECEMBER 1853, PAGE 2

LOCAL INTELLIGENCE
PLEASURE TRIP TO OYSTER COVE AND THE CHANNEL.
THE ABORIGINES.

THE second pleasure trip by the steamer Culloden took place on Saturday afternoon. The day was beautifully fine and the number of pleasure seekers unusually large: so much so, that many were unable to obtain a passage. At the time appointed, three o'clock, orders were issued to "haul from the wharf;" but as the tide was very low and the number of people on board very great, she could not be got off till most of the passengers went ashore to lighten her. This caused a delay of nearly forty minutes. Once fairly on her way, she steamed off right gallantly. Passing Mount Nelson, the city with its cares and anxieties was soon left far behind. Presently our attention was drawn to, a vessel with stunsails set, gallantly sailing through the water with fine wind right aft. She proved to be the Australasia, from London.

When passing she was greeted with hearty cheers which were responded to by those on board. When in the vicinity of Brown's River, the water became rather rough, causing a slight rolling of the vessel. Several of the gentlemen turned deadly pale, but putting on a most determined air, walked briskly from stem to stern. Others in mute silence resigned themselves to the inevitable. The ladies at once became silent, no doubt they were lost to silent admiration at the grandeur of the surrounding scenery. But this did not last long. We were soon in smooth water. Leaving the Iron Pot to our left we soon entered South West Passage, obtaining a beautiful glance at Bruni Island --After proceeding along the channel a few miles, a most magnificent view of mountain scenery was obtained. We stopped a short time to allow a party of gentlemen an opportunity to visit the aborigines settlement in Oyster Cove. Some dozen got into the boat and as the tide was very low a difficulty occurred in landing. This it was proposed to obviate by the rowers carrying the passengers ashore. The first gentleman was rather unfortunate, his bearer being a little man, while he was tall and weighty.

The consequence was that the bearer stuck fast in the mud, retaining hold of his charge, who was almost precipitated into the water, but managed to reach the landing place by only going knee deep. Some ten minutes walking brought us to the settlement, a quadrangle with a range of wooden buildings on three sides. The first person we saw was " Mary Ann," the Queen, a fine, portly, smiling lady about thirty years of age. The King stood close by. He is stoutly built and about five feet and a half high.

Only four men were visible. We saw some half dozen ladies, but with the exception of Her Majesty they had all passed their prime. Some youngsters we caught taking a survey of us through a partly opened door, but when our eyes were turned that way they beat a retreat. The men were all neatly dressed. The women wore a sort of sack made from thick blue woollen? Only one wore a printed dress. One of them wore a very neat sort of woollen dress, fastened round her waist by a bright leather strap. Most of them had for their head-dress a tall conical woollen red cap. One lady had a silk handkerchief bound round her head inside of which, above her left ear, was stuck the well-worn pipe ready in case of need. They asked for tobacco - cigars they would not smoke -and complained of their own tobacco being bad. Mary Ann, it appears can read with fluency and asked for books.

She wanted "some-thing lively" She had read "Uncle Tom's Cabin" and pronounced it "very much true." Books were promised her. Our stay was cut short by hearing the "bell pealing" and after many bows and shaking of hands with the ladies we finally took ourselves off accompanied by his Majesty. These singular beings are fast dying out; only nineteen are now left of a race who once competed with the white man. Regaining the vessel we steamed home In rapid style. The greatest good humor and hilarity prevailed, many regretting that the pleasant trip had so soon come to an end. We came alongside the wharf at half, past eight.

Well it's pleasing to hear the 'pleasure seekers' all had a jolly good time!

1854

The PUBLISHED DAILY. Courier.

HOBART TOWN, SATURDAY AFTERNOON, JANUARY 21, 1854.

And now it is was time for reminiscing as newspapers began to fill their columns with memories of the not so distant past.

COURIER (HOBART, TAS: 1840 - 1859), MONDAY 10 APRIL 1854, PAGE 2

GENERAL INTELLIGENCE.
SOME UNRECORDED PASSAGES IN THE HISTORY OF VAN DIEMEN·S LAND.

(From a Very Old Stager.)

NO. V. (Continued from last Friday's Courier.)

It appears from the subsequent portion of the Journal of the Expedition that Mr. Kelly's party land among the aborigines and some curious particulars will be gathered as to the habits and customs of a race now almost extinct.

Continuation of the Log, - Land at Ringarooma. - Minanbunganah. - Aboriginal Press Gang. - The Treaty. - Sealing - Tolobunganah.

13th January. - Launched at daylight with a fine breeze from the westward and clear weather and ran along the shore to the eastward. At noon landed on Ringarooma Point; here we suddenly fell in with a large "mob" of natives, who, upon their first appearance, seemed hostile, - but on seeing Briggs, whom they knew particularly well, the chief, whose name was Lamabunganah, seemed delighted at the interview and told him he was at war with his own brother Tolobunganah, a most powerful chief and then on the Coast near Eddystone Point.

Tolobunganah was also one of Brigg's acquaintances. Briggs had left two wives and five children upon the islands during his absence at Hobart Town and had taken this trip round the West Coast thinking he might fall in with some of his black relations near Cape Portland. One of his wives was a daughter of the chief Lamanbungaah, whom we had just fallen in with and he generally called his father-in-law "Laman" for shortness. The chief made enquiry after his daughter and was told that she and her children were safe over at Cape Barren. Laman said he knew that, for he saw her smokes every day. After some further discourse Laman asked Briggs if he had any firearms in the boat Briggs replied that we were well armed. Laman said he was glad of that, as he had heard that five or six white men well-armed were with his brother Tolohunganah at Eddystone Point and that they intended to come and attack his (Laman's) tribe and kill them all.

He intreated Briggs to join him, so that they could go and meet them and fight it out. Briggs, of course, declined, telling him that he had no control over the boat and that Mr. Kelly could not agree to any such proposal. At this Laman seemed greatly dissatisfied and told Briggs in a very hostile tone that he had often before gone with him to fight other tribes when he (Briggs) wanted women. Laman gave a loud "cooee," and in two minutes we were surrounded by above fifty natives. Laman said to Briggs, "Now we will force you to go with us and fight Tolo," meaning the chief his brother.

We suspected, as a matter of course, that the white men spoken of were Howe and his party and upon Briggs asking whether they had a boat, Laman said "No."

We now got very much alarmed at the dangerous situation we were in and as an excuse, Briggs told Laman that we would go over to Cape Barren and fetch Briggs's wife, that we would also get five or six of the sealers to join us with plenty of firearms and come over and fight Tolohunganah. Laman was much pleased at this assurance and enquired when we would go? Briggs replied that we would start directly - sleep the night at Swan Island and go on the following morning to Cape Barren and return in three days. Laman and all his men were well satisfied with this arrangement and the boat was launched. We pulled to Swan Island highly gratified at an escape from Lamanbunganah's impressment. Had we stoutly refused his proposal to aid him in his campaign, he would have killed every man of us, as it was impossible we could have stood against such a number of natives.

Briggs had been employed as a sealer in the Islands in Bass's Straits for many years previously and had acquired the native language of the north east coast of Van Diemen's Land fluently, in consequence of his often having gone over from the island to Cape Portland to barter for kangaroo-skins with the natives, as also to purchase the young grown up native females to keep them as their wives, whom they employed, as they were wonderfully dexterous in hunting kangaroo and catching seals.

The custom of the "sealers" in the Straits was that every man should have from two to five of these native women for their own use and benefit and to select any of them they thought proper to cohabit with as their wives and a large number of children had been born as a consequence of these unions - a fine, active, hardy race. The males were good boatmen, kangaroo hunters and sealers; the women extraordinarily clever assistants to them. They were generally very good-looking and of a light copper colour.

14th January. - Launched from Swan Island with a moderate breeze at north-west and steered along shore to the south-east. Soon after leaving the island we saw smokes on the shore and saw natives walking along the beach, whom we supposed to be our friend Laman and his tribe. They shouted and made signals to us to come on shore, but we took no heed of them, having had such a narrow escape the day before. Just before sunset we hauled up on King George's Island or Rocks on a small sandy beach, not wishing to give a chance to Mr. Tolobunganah to serve us as Mr. Lamambunganah had done the day before and while we were on the island we were safe from their attacks. Here we found a number of seals lying on the rocks basking in the sun, but having no salt with us to cure the skins we thought it useless to kill them.

On the following day, the 15th January, the wind set in at south-east and fine weather. We thought it needless to lie idle with a foul wind and being provided with knives, steels and clubs and being all old hands at scaling into the bargain, we commenced killing and "flinching" flensing? the skins from the bodies, stretching them out upon the grass with wooden pegs. They were dried in the sun and in one day became perfectly cured. This day we killed and pegged out thirty skins.

The following day, 16th January, we killed, flinched and pegged out 25 sealskins. Wind southerly and fine weather. Several smokes on the shore opposite the island and a large number of natives on the beach.

Caught this day ten young Cape Barren geese, which, afforded us fresh meat and, with a little of Major Stuart's fine pork, we fared sumptuously.

17th January. - Wind south-east and fine weather. Found the seals getting shy of coming up on this rocks - we therefore gave them a rest, as it would not do to storm them only at low water. At noon launched the boat and went over to see the natives and took with us four seals' carcases which had been skinned and four young "pups," about three weeks old, alive.

We did not go closer to the beach than musket shot for fear of being surprised by a shot from Howe's party. Briggs stood up in the boat and called out to the natives in their own language to come to the water side. They seemed shy until he told them who he was, when an old man rushed up to his middle in the water. Briggs called to him to swim to the boat, which he did and we hauled him in. It turned out to be the old chief, Tolobunganah.

** We have already stated that the Tasmanian aborigines seemed to have a means of telegraphic communication by smokes.*

(To be continued.)

COURIER (HOBART, TAS: 1840 - 1859), WEDNESDAY 12 APRIL 1854, PAGE 2

SOME UNRECORDED PASSAGES IN THE HISTORY OF VAN DIEMEN'S LAND.

(From a Very Old Stager.)

NO. VI.
(Continued from Monday's Courier.)
Tolobunganah - Trading with the Aborigines - Lady Passengers - Sealing.

Tolobunganah was overjoyed at seeing Briggs and enquired if he had seen his brother Laman, which Briggs denied. "Tolo" asked where we came from and was told from Cape Barren, by way of Swan Island. Tolo said he knew that, for he had seen us come from there. We then pulled a little distance along the beach to a small rock that lay off about fifty yards from the shore. Tolobunganah stood up in the boat and called to the natives. About twenty of them came down to the waterside; they all knew Briggs and seemed glad to see him.

We made Tolo a present of the four dead seals and the live pups, at which he seemed highly gratified. Immediately after they had obtained the seals six women came down, each with a dead kangaroo on their shoulders. Tolo ordered them to be brought to the boat and said we must receive them in exchange for the seals, we had given unto them, - that they had no more kangaroo, but to-morrow they would catch plenty. Tolo seemed anxious that we should come on shore, but we declined, telling the natives that we did not wish to come in contact with the six white men they had seen. Tolo asked if we were afraid of them. Briggs replied in the negative, that they were bad men, but we wanted to know whereabouts they were.

We felt obliged to make use of these equivocations, to extract all the friendly information we could from the aborigines relative to Howe and his party, as we were still of opinion, more especially as the information we had received from Lamanbunganah led us to expect, that they were close at hand, but the natives assured us that they were gone a long distance to the southward, towards St. Patrick's Head. We took leave of Tolo and his followers in the evening, telling them that we should come over next day and bring them a further supply of seals, a promise which seemed to delight them very much. They informed us in return that if we brought them plenty of seals, they would supply us with plenty of kangaroo and skins in barter. The wind being fair, we ran over to the island, hauled the boat up and had a good kangaroo steamer for supper, the first which we had been able to cook during our voyage.

16th January, 1816. - At daylight, being low water, there were a good number of seal on the rocks; we stormed them and killed twenty, which we skinned and pegged out to dry. The weather was very fine, wind from the south-east. Found the fresh water on the island getting short and very brackish. Launched the boat and put our three water-kegs into her, with a view of getting the natives to fill them with fresh water. We also put into the boat twenty of the seal's carcases, to barter for kangaroo-skins and took six young pups alive, as presents. Early in the morning smokes were made on the beach, inviting us to come over according to promise.

On arriving at the beach did not see one native, which made us suspect something was the matter. We waited about half an hour, when Tolobunganah made his appearance on the beach: we called to him to come to the rock where he had been the day previous and he complied with our request. We asked him why he did not join us when we first arrived and he informed us that all the tribe were in the bush hunting kangaroo and getting skins, but they would return shortly.

We still entertained a suspicion that Howe was with them, but Tolo assured us he was not. We told him that we wanted our kegs filled with fresh water and that we would buy all the kangaroo skins he had. In about twenty minutes the whole tribe came down on the beach: there were about two hundred men, women and children and at least fifty dogs. On seeing them approach we pulled the boat out a little distance from the shore, leaving Tolo on the rock. We got out our arms and examined them, to see if they were in firing order and afterwards held up three or four seal's carcases and acquainted the natives we wished to trade for kangaroo skins. Tolo ordered ten women to go into the water, each loaded with kangaroo skins and flesh. We gave them in return the carcases and they carried them to their tribe, returning immediately to the boat with more skins as payment. We then requested Tolo to fill our kegs with fresh water, which he did; but we would not let them take more than one keg at a time, for fear they would not bring them all back. Tolo seemed much displeased at this evident want of confidence.

The natives asked if we would bring over more seals on the following day. Briggs informed them that they were getting scarce and shy of being caught. Tolo considered that we had better take some women over to the island to assist in catching them, as they were very dexterous at sealing. This course being agreed on, Tolo ordered six stout women into the boat. They obeyed with alacrity, evidently delighted with the prospects of the trip. The wind being fair, we ran over to the island, hauled the boat up and pegged the kangaroo skins out to dry. The women perceiving some seals upon the outer rocks were anxious to commence operations.

Briggs having been on the Islands in Bass' Straits a long time, was perfectly acquainted with their mode of sealing. A very singular mode it is and it is thus described.

1855

LAUNCESTON EXAMINER (TAS: 1842 - 1899),
SATURDAY 15 DECEMBER 1855, PAGE 2

STATISTICS OF TASMANIA FOR 1854.

The collection of returns laid upon the council table by the Colonial Secretary and printed by order of the house, is interesting; but they supply little that was not known before, a great deal having been extracted from the last census (1851). There are fifty-two returns, relating to subjects of almost every imaginable kind, - social, commercial, industrial, judicial, meteorological and religious, - indiscriminately mingled. We propose, if possible, to condense and arrange the information contained in the-twenty-seven pages now before us. The first return professes to show the population of the colony on 31st Dec., 1854, exclusive of the troops and their families. This is given as follows, 'although in the absence of a more recent census we doubt the correctness of the figures: -

Free--males 14,263, females 13,208, children 25,695; convicts -males 8408, females 3310; total males 22,661, females 16,518, children 25,695: total population, 64,874, or about 5000 less than in 1851. The military in the colony were, - one staff-officer, 10 officers and 365 rank and file of 99th Regt. 75 women and 161 children; deaths in the year, men 7, women 1, children 19.

We come next to the aborigines-the miserable remnant of Tasmania's native population maintained at the Oyster Cove Station and we beg to draw the attention of honourable members to this return:- Men 3, women 11, boys 2 - total 16. There are two officers on the establishment and the expense £2006 8s. 8d, or a yearly cost of £126 10s. 6d. for each man, woman and child, a sum in itself almost sufficient to support the whole. What are the duties of the "officers" it is not easy to divine, but they cannot be excessive, seeing that each would have to look after 1 1/2 men, 5 1/2 women and one boy; besides which there appears to be a general superintendent, whose salary we suppose has to be added to the above.

The next three returns are interesting:-Births registered during the year,-males, 1339 ; females, 1264; total, 2603. Deaths,-males, 1149 ; females 779 ; total, 1928 : of these 976 were under two years of ago, Marriages,-Church of England 731, Rome 317, Scotland 122, independent 113, Wesleyan 47, Jews 3, Baptist 1, deputy registrars 9 ; total, 1343. Returns 8, 9 and 10 are extracted from the census and it would therefore be unnecessary to repeat them; but they are rendered valueless by the palpable contradictions which they contain.

Thus, No 8 showing the strength of the different religious denominations and No. 9, distinguishing between the married and single inhabitants, each gives a total population of 68,609, whilst return No.,1 declares the entire population of the colony to be only 64,874. No. 10 refers to the number of houses, the material of which construct-ed and the number inhabited in 1851, manifestly useless now. Next we have a return of the immigrants who arrived in the colony in 1854. Immigrants at the public expense - men 1750, women 1576, children 846; total 4172. Immigrants at their own expense - men 3847, women 1307, children 199; total 5353 : total in 1854, 9525. Total expense £23,133 8s. 3d. In return 12, which shows the ports from which the immigrants sailed, the number who arrived is set down at 9524, whilst those who left numbered 11,280.

The imports amounted in value to £2,604,680, of which £95,295 were from foreign states, £36,078 from the United States; the exports during the same period were £1,433,021. Vessels engaged in the fisheries: - Colonial, 5-tonnage, 1247; British, 1-tonnage, 375; foreign, 2-tonnage, 737. Vessels entered in:-1057, of 198,612 tons.; cleared out-1028 vessels, of 200,398 tons; Vessels built, 10-tonnage, 401; registered, 90 - tonnage, 10,344. Number of steam vessels registered at the ports of Hobart Town and Launceston :-2 of wood, 9 of iron ; 1766 tons, 744 horse-power.

PEOPLE'S ADVOCATE OR TRUE FRIEND OF TASMANIA
(LAUNCESTON, TAS: 1855 - 1856), THURSDAY 27 DECEMBER 1855, PAGE 2

ABORIGINES

In our last issue we promised to offer a few remarks upon the Return included in the Tasmanian Statistics for 1854 of the Aboriginal Inhabitants confined at Oyster Cove Station and the expenditure incurred thereon and we now proceed to do so We cannot take a retrospective view of the past and glance at the statement before us, without feeling the blush of shame arise and spread to our very finger nails as we note the fearful extent to [?] MIGHT has been carried against? MIGHT the oppression, captivity and nearly completed work of destruction of the hapless Aborigines of Van Diemen's Land Tasmania, however, in the history of her primitive children, affords not an isolated instance of the effect upon them, of what we call civilization. ?? other countries reveal: the same truth. It is equally strange and true, that when the white man seizes upon a territory, its earliest inhabitants fall into misery ruin and annihilation.

They lose any of the innate good they once possessed; whilst they readily acquire the vices and because they do so, the persecution of their usurpers. We do not intend, however, to moralize upon the question of where justice for the white man begins, or where it ceases to exist, when claimed by his dusky brother; did we desire to do so, it is now too late ; the deed is done, no, not quite done yet : Van Diemen's Land can still, yes, still exhibit SIXTEEN descendants of what a short half century ago, was a numerous and happy People. Three men, eleven women and two boys still remain, proud trophies of our merciful, Christian and "civilized" power; remain to drag out a miserable existence in that salubrious retreat Oyster Cove! And for the twelve months ending, 31st December, 1854, the public have been saddled with an expense of £2006 8s 8d for the maintenance of these sixteen remnants! By the shade of "Cocker" what for?

Are they clothed in purple and fine linen and fair sumptuously every day? "We rather calculate not." Allowing them to have the fullest rations, say 2 lbs. bread, I lb. meat, tea, sugar, soap, starch, blue and caudles candles &s &c. each per diem and charge the same at the market rates, we cannot make our calculation come within many hundred pounds of the sum we have quoted. Oh, but stop; we are too fast; there are two officers attached to the establishment. What do they filch in this common robbery from the People? The cost per head of man, woman and child, is £125 /8/- per annum. And if this is not monstrous we know what will ever become so. These statistical returns are of course in the hands of honourable members and they cannot surely allow such an evidence of reckless expenditure to pass unnoticed. They cannot recall what is gone, but they can at least prevent its being perpetuated; and we shall anxiously watch what steps, if any, are taken in the matter.

1856

Remember this? It seems so long ago.

PEOPLE'S ADVOCATE OR TRUE FRIEND OF TASMANIA
(LAUNCESTON, TAS: 1855 - 1856), MONDAY 11 AUGUST 1856, PAGE 2

1814.

Prices at New Town established. Aborigines fed as paupers by Reverend R. Knopwood. Price of Wheat taken into store, 10s, a bushel - Exportation of Grain prohibited.

LOCAL INTELLIGENCE
THE ABORIGINES

Sir Henry Young and Mr Maule A D C went to Oyster Cove on Saturday last, proceeding from Brown's River in Mr Kirwan's whale boat, accompanied by the Reverend Mr Freeman. Mr Kirwan, the Magistrate, was unable to attend the Governor from the effects of a fall from his horse in July last when enroute to visit the natives. His Excellency found the natives in good health and contentment.

Their dwellings and that of Mr and Mrs Dandridge, the resident Superintendent, have recently been re-shingled and repaired, but the contractor had withdrawn the workmen without opening a drain at the back of Natives houses, which is required to prevent decay and damp to the floors. Mr Dandridge promised that this should be remedied. Walter the chief Native complained that a road long in use to the land had been stopped off by a Mr Carpenter and that the correspondence between the Colonial Secretary and the Road Trustees had not yet resulted in Mr Carpenter's re-opening the road.

Chapter Nine

The Ambiguity of being
a War Correspondent

It is usual at this juncture in a volume such as this for the author to make his own profound and eloquent pontifications on matters he now regard as his own. Once again I will disappoint. As I have reiterated many times within these pages, I am not an historian nor anthropologist and although I claim some familiarity with the quirks, quandaries and idiosyncrasies of the press, I am a mere reporter.

However, in point of fact this just an excuse I use to avoid facing the truth. That is after all this time I can still draw no conclusions nor understanding of the events which occurred in the four decades following the arrival of the *rytia* (white man) and *numeraredia luna* (white woman) in Lutruwita and the anguish inflicted on the Pakana people. Which begs the question: what perspective should I take? As you can see from my writing I could with ease reinterpret almost any of the articles so that they may be read from a different angle. Indeed, whilst my modesty forbids it, had I the inclination, it would be possible to present several points of view relating to a single incident.

Which brings us to the universal question of what is truth? Is there only a single truth, as the Protestants insist, or are there many truths depending on where you are standing at the time. Among the killers or the killed? Black or white? Child, man or woman; we all see the world only from our own eyes. Even if we try to walk in another's footsteps we are only pretending. In the end we give them back their moccasins and continue along our own path.

I do feel qualified to comment on the English press of the day as it existed in Lutruwita and to emphasize how fortunate it was for a man like Andrew Bent to be present and willing to go to prison and forfeit so much because of his commitment to the freedom of the press. We have been left a legacy of extraordinarily diverse opinions and beliefs about these occurrences which would never have been the case without Bent winning his battle for a free press. Australasia and indeed the world, are greatly indebted to his and him fellow libertarians for their strength of purpose and driving passion.

My hope is simply to enable you to read, think and ponder on what you see before you and not be distracted by the inconsequential jottings of a crusty old reporter. In my more blasé abstruse moments, I think this frowzy manuscript should be thrown from a great mountain to allow its pages to fly with the wind along with the spirits of the Pakana.

As for Lowana, she remains an enigma to me. I recall vividly those cavernous black eyes staring so intently into mine as though she could read my very soul. Alas this was not the case for me; to this day I have no insight into her thoughts or feelings. Was it love, infatuation or merely an intimate escapade? I often wonder what she really thought of me, this lumbering, inept *rytia* whose only evident attribute was scribbling words onto paper, which must have been baffling and alien to her. Our lives could not have been further apart in terms of culture, way of life, language and so on and yet her very presence had a profound effect on me. I will never be certain but I do know deep in my desolate heart, that I have never loved anyone since with such hunger and unforgiving passion.

Rialim too remains deep in my being. Our parting moments left me in awe of this man, his impenetrable eyes reading me, understanding more than I ever will and then vanishing from my life forever. I fear though the boy never became the man; I remain in an unsettling limbo betwixt the two.

And as for Bent and me, we've gone fishing!

EDITOR'S NOTE

There is no way of knowing if Andrew Bent ever read W.C.'s scribblings or if indeed he actually received the manuscript. Its ashes were never to be cast to the winds of kunanyi or any other mountain crest as W.C. had requested in his final letter to Andrew. By the time the tattered, misshaped tin box arrived, Bent was confronting his own troubles. Now bankrupt and decrepit he died as a pauper in the Sydney Benevolent Society Asylum on the 27th August 1851.

The rusty old case disappeared and was lost from sight until it was discovered in a box of junk, part of an insignificant auction of a family estate in Launceston, Tasmania in 2010; coincidentally 200 years after the first British paper was published in Lutruwita.

On the day of the auction Lot twenty-six was listed as, 'Box containing books, hairbrush, assorted tins and containers and miscellaneous items. No Reserve.'

The purchaser was an amateur history buff who wanted the hairbrush for her granddaughter and paid $17.50 plus commission for the contents of the box. You can imagine her delight when she found a long forgotten tin box at the bottom waiting to be opened!

Its former owner, W.C., had died at home on the 9th January 1856 after a short illness, eight days after Tasmania was adopted as the official name for his beloved Island. His grave is marked by a small headstone discreetly sheltering under the Yew tree in the grounds of the Church of All Saints, next to his home in Martock. Long neglected and covered in moss and ivy the epitaph can only be read at a slight angle to collect light and shadows. Slithering diagonally across the stone is a snake leaving in its wake a chiselled indentation as though to split the surface apart. Its symbolism is unambiguous.

The local curate notes that it is often mistaken for a sign pointing the way to the conveniences, a witticism which I am sure W.C. would have appreciated. His final notes compiled after Andrew's death were kept safe and passed onto the Martock Heritage and Historical Society along with the sketch of W.C.'s grave by his great niece Kathleen in 1950. The family folklore of W.C.'s adventures in far flung lands and their fondness for him were passed down for generations.

W.C.
15 MAR 1795 — 9 JAN 1856
LOVED BROTHER OF SOPHIA
"I fear the old adage that
we learn from history
is indeed a misnomer."
K
1950

Author's notes

I have great empathy for W.C. even though he is of my own creation. We met when I was searching my mind to discover a way to make sense of the myriad colonial newspaper reports, letters to the editor and articles related to the Aborigines during the first fifty years of British settlement in Tasmania. I needed a way to entice you, my readers, into this time and world which had such a profound effect on an entire race of people in a very short period of time. I wanted to examine different perspectives being presented by the Press and especially what was not being said.

Eventually W.C. emerged, reluctantly, from the recesses of my mind. He was ideal, a war correspondent who had seen firsthand what had occurred and, better still, with luck and encouragement might be persuaded to write his own interpretation of events as they occurred. I only ever envisaged W.C. in his attic library which he characteristically called The Bridge. While I could see him, smell his pipe tobacco, step over his lazy dog and feel the heat of the fire, neither he nor Bent were aware of my presence. How could they? I had imagined them and they existed only in my mind. W.C. was not in a position to image the imaginer and his creator.

We sat together for hours during the many weeks and months it took to write this narrative. I watching, listening and waiting while he, blissfully unaware, gradually revealed his story. It was not easy. I only met him in the latter part of his life, alone, despondent and burdened with a broken heart. Sometimes I had to wait days or even weeks before he would reveal some of the events in his past. I couldn't communicate with him or he would have known of my existence, so I had to be patient, an uneasy attribute for me.

We started with many late nights, drinking, smoking, reading and thinking. I am not sure what he was thinking, but I could sometimes read his expressions and try to interpret what was in his mind. We walked together across the fields and lanes around his house with Bent running in all directions at once and organising W.C. to throw endless sticks. I would sometimes wait for a long time while he slept and see him fight off demons in his dreams and wake drowning in perspiration. I knew then that he was contending with post traumatic stress disorder sometimes experienced by journalists who are ridden with a sense of moral guilt for seeing and recording terrible events but not being able to help. I needed to know what he had been through.

Other times I would see him with a barely noticeable smile, mouthing the word 'Lowana' over and over again. Who was Lowana and why had she remained with him for so long through his close to three score years?

Gradually, I did manage to plant in his mind the idea of writing a journal or diary of sorts. With that I could at least glean his thoughts and experiences from his text. However that is as far as I could go and the rest was up to him. This is my first experience of writing fiction and in my naivety I thought I was in control. Soon the reality set in. While I may have created the character, he was very much in charge of his own destiny. For example, I had in mind a nice neat journal with dates, order and legible hand writing. However, as you realise after reading his text and learning a little of W.C.'s personality and disposition, the notion of him producing such an orderly and neat artefact was fanciful.

So it began, slowly at first. I would gaze on impatiently as he sorted through piles of old newspapers, bound with brown string or pink ribbon in some vague semblance of order, mainly by years, but at times in a random collection of cut or torn articles. But once W.C. started to write he was unstoppable. He wrote using the most delicate 'Copperplate' writing which flowed from his quill like silk from a silkworm. It was after all his craft, revealing the talent he was born with and his natural flare with words and phrases. This is who he was.

I stayed with him to the end. In fact, I was there as he died in his favourite chair, deep into the night and quietly slipped away. And no, W.C. did not call out Lowana in his dying breath, but I am sure she was not too far from his being.

Bent knew of course and gently rested his head on W.C.'s lap, letting out the most mournful cry. He stayed there until Sophia found them both in the morning. Curiously ever since Bent appeared, I had been anxious about what would happen to him should W.C. die first. I need not have worried and was comforted as I watched Sophia ever so gently entice him away from his master and help him down the attic stairs to the warmth of the kitchen for breakfast, his ablutions and lots of TLC. I knew then he would be well cared for.

I looked around the room one last time noticing so many things which I wanted to keep as fond memories of my time with W.C. His well-thumbed pipe aged with time and contemplation, the still to be drunk Malt beside his comfy brown leather chair complete with holes, horse's hair protruding and stacks of books, papers and so many more bundles of newspapers still tied with string. Forever elusive to me now that W.C. is no longer there to pull the bow and reveal the secrets from within. I looked through the dirty, cracked attic window to the town square and St James Church for one last time and heard the melancholy toning of a solitary bell ring out telling the world. Soon after I too slipped away, hoping W.C. had found peace at last.

This text is the result. I hope it worked for you, that W.C. was able to lead you into these extraordinary times and that you found the press articles as fascinating to read as I did.

The actual newspaper articles are copied verbatim with mistakes and oddities as published and were extracted from TROVE. It is an amazing resource of old newspapers and other related documents from Australia produced by the National Library. I am truly indebted to all those who were responsible for its creation and maintenance. The methodology I adopted was to randomly select clippings from each year in order not to allow my biases and values to creep into the book.

Names and dates of the ships and people such as the brig *Jupiter* and Andrew Bent, John Batman, Henry Melville and so on were all taken from history and are based on fact. Places are also as accurate as possible, including the location of Bent's printing shop, the Hope and Anchor Tavern which still operates, as well as names for rivers and mountains.

One of the many quandaries of this book was whether or not to use a capital for Aborigine. The choice by the newspapers of the day seems to be random so I have chosen to use a capital letter both in W.C.'s manuscript and the additional notes.

Lowana's language is derived from James Fenton's 1884 book, *A History of Tasmania from its discovery in 1642 to the present time*. In the appendix he lists many words recorded by both the early French and English settlers. They are attributed to 'Tribes from Oyster Bay to Pittwater' which is where her tribe lived. The Pakana words are deliberately placed before the English translation out of respect and in keeping with W.C.'s sense of propriety. Fenton also describes the voices of the people as being softly spoken, song-like and melodious, hence its portrayal in my description of their meeting. I have taken some artistic licence by using the word rytia to mean white man as recorded by Thomas Scott from the Oyster Bay Tribe in September 1821 although it may not strictly relate to the southern region.[xxv]

In my view there remains an association of this language interpretation to Lowana and her people. I could see in my mind's eye two people worlds apart sitting together two hundred years ago somewhere in Lutruwita; one Pakana and the other European. Perched on logs around a fire, one with a parchment and pen, the other with knowledge of words they are willing to share. Words are written, they talk some more, perhaps sit in stillness and eventually part. The words though remain beyond their lives and are passed through time until I become entranced with their timeless, imperfect beauty. They are a link, tenuous as it may be, to the people I wanted to recreate in W.C.'s adventure. To me it is a precious connection and one which I treasure.

Information about the culture practices of her people are scant. However, I have based my writing on research although some of it will remain contentious. For example, I have Lowana using a spear which is supported by the Robert Neil's 1828 sketch '*Savages of Van Diemen's Land Hunting*' in which a woman is depicted using a spear to kill an animal. The main intent was to set the scene for the remainder of the book and present her people as a cultured, well-functioning society in stark contrast to the predominant depictions associated with the press during that period.

Lowana's character is derived from *Tarenorerer* (1800-1831) also known as Wayler, an Aboriginal leader and warrior from the Tommeginne people whose life was dramatic, eventful and full of drama. Known as Amazon, she banded together remaining men from various tribes to lead a tenacious and brave campaign against the British. More information is readily available on her remarkable life.

My thanks go especially to Jim Everett-Puralia Meenamatta whose generosity of spirit and willingness to share his knowledge has added immensely to this book and for which I am greatly indebted.

I must also thank Terry Whitebeach whose editing skills challenged me to think and develop my writing, leading to a much higher standard than I could have achieved alone. Sue Kennedy was my final, meticulous and excellent proof reader to whom I am truly indebted.

Thanks also to Annie Rushton, whose encouragement and interest in my work kept me going through challenging and difficult times. Sally Bloomfield, a descendent of Andrew Bent through Catherine for her meticulous editing and feedback as well as Damien Bester from *The Hobart Mercury* for his incredible knowledge about Andrew Bent and the early days of printing in VDL.

Finally I am indebted to Sally Sara, an ABC foreign correspondent for sharing her experiences with PTSD after tours in war zones throughout the world and increasing our awareness of the impact such trauma can have on reporters emotional and physical wellbeing. W.C. suffered alone and isolated as many others have in the past and still do today.

I hope this book will help in some small way to improve our understanding in this subject just a little more.

Naturally I have tried to research the material to the best of my ability and I apologise in advance for any errors although I am yet to find a history book, especially historical novels, without any mistakes.

Finally I hope you find my book of some interest and that it at least disturbs your thinking a little. I am after all a teacher at heart!

REFERENCES

Andrew Bent: Father of the Free Press in Australia Authors: Sally Bloomfield and Craig Collins
url: https://wordpress.com/view/andrew-bent.life

Bonyhady, T., & Lehman, G,. (2018) *The National Picture: The Art of Tasmania's Black War* NGA

Boyce, J. (2018). *Van Diemen's land*. Black Inc..

Fenton, J. (1884). History of Tasmania. *Walch & Sons, Hobart.*

Johnson, M., & McFarlane, I. (2015). *Van Diemen's Land: An Aboriginal History.* UNSW Press.

Ryan, L. (2012). *Tasmanian Aborigines: a history since 1803* (p.14). Sydney: Allen & Unwin.

The complete poetical works of William Collins, Thomas Gray, and Oliver Goldsmith. With biographical sketches and notes. Ed. by Epes Sargent. Collins, William, 1721-1759., Gray, Thomas, 1716-1771., Goldsmith, Oliver, 1728-1774., Sargent, Epes, ed. 1813-1880.

ENDNOTES

i   W.C. was probably experiencing phenomenon known as moral guilt or moral injury which is often felt by journalists with PTSD. It is where 'the damage done to one's conscience or moral compass when that person perpetrates, witnesses, or fails to prevent acts that transgress their own moral and ethical values or codes of conduct.' The Moral Injury Project Syracuse University Website NY

ii   Henry Crabb Robinson (1775–1867) was an English lawyer known as a diarist. Born in Bury St. Edmunds, England, he was youngest son of a tanner who died in 1781. In 1796 he entered the office of a solicitor in Chancery Lane, London, but in 1798 a relative died, leaving Robinson a sum yielding a considerable yearly income. Proud of his independence and eager for travel, he went abroad in 1800. Between 1800 and 1805 he studied at various places in Germany, meeting men of letters there, including Goethe, Schiller, Johann Gottfried Herder and Christoph Martin Wieland. He then became correspondent for *The Times* in Altona in 1807. Later on he was sent to Galicia, in Spain, as a war correspondent in the Peninsular War.
https://www.revolvy.com/page/Henry-Crabb-Robinson

iii   In the early newspapers The long Gothic ſ was used in the place of 's' in certain places until the early 1820s. However here Bent is using 'f' instead. He may not have had a type set for ſ. These have been changed for ease of reading. In the first paragraph above the text has been left verbatim for the purposes of illustration.

iv   For more information see Boyce, J. (2018). *Van Diemen's Land.* Black Inc.

v   This is a useful reference for more information about Musquito. Naomi Parry, 'Musquito (1780–1825)', Australian Dictionary of Biography, National Centre of Biography, Australian National University, http://adb.anu.edu.au/biography/musquito-13124/text23749, published first in hardcopy 2005, accessed online 11 September 2018

vi   Adapted from talk presented by Jim Everett-Puralia Meenamatta at UTAS in September 2018

vii   Clayton E Aristotle Politics *Internet Encyclopedia of Philosophy* sited 15.01.19

viii   Reference for this incident may be located using Colonial Frontier Massacres in Central and Eastern Australia 1788-1930 Newcastle University

ix   The population history of Tasmania to Federation Rebecca Kippen, Centre for Health Equity Melbourne School of Population and Global Health University of Melbourne 3 December 2014

x   Meyer Eidelson, *The Melbourne Dreaming: A Guide to the Aboriginal Places of Melbourne*, Canberra, Aboriginal Studies Press, 1997, p26

xi   Christie, M. F *Aborigines in colonial Victoria*, 1835-86 /.[Sydney] : Sydney University Press, 1979

xii   *The last of the Tasmanians*; or, *The black war of Van Diemen's Land* by Bonwick, James, 1817-1906 Publication date 1870

xiii   The unabridged article may be located using Trove with the national library of Australia.

xiv   W.C. probably did not know the full extent of the massacres which were occurring at the time. A massacre is defined as the killing of over six people at one time. There were in fact 42 massacres of the Pakana people in Lutruwita comprising 632 individuals. No white people died in a massacre in VDL. Full details, including map locations, are now available from the Centre of 21st Century Humanities at Newcastle University NSW Australia.

xv   Henry Melville (1799-1873), journalist, publisher and author, purchased the *Colonial Times* from Andrew Bent in 1830. Like most pressmen of his time, Melville fell foul of Governor Arthur and spent time in prison. Quite a character.

xvi   *the Ægis*: The protection, backing, or support of a particular person or organization. Oxford English Dictionary Oxford University Press 2018

xvii   *Junius*, the pseudonym of the still unidentified author of a series of letters contributed to Henry Sampson Woodfall's *Public Advertiser*, a popular English newspaper of the day, between Jan. 21, 1769, and Jan. 21, 1772.

xviii W.C. presents the conventional version of the Black Line.
However more recent interpretations are now being espoused.
For example, Lyndal Ryan contends that 'far from being an
aberration on Arthur's part, the line was a strategy widely used
in other parts of the Empire to forcibly remove indigenous
insurgents from their homelands and there was not just one
but three lines in operation over the fifteen months in 1830 and
1832, which ended in the forced surrender of the Tasmanian
Aborigines.' Ryan Lyndal, Introduction, 'The Black Line in Van
Diemen's Land (Tasmania) 1830', *Journal of Australian Studies*,
2013 Vol 37 No 1, 1-2 .

xix W.C. has presented a conventional view of the experiences and
lives of luna who were involved one way or another with the
sealers at the time. As with all aspects of history there are a
multitude of views, and in this case, it may be worth reading
more recent studies on the island communities. Suggested
reading: Cameron, P. (2011). *Grease and ochre: the blending of two
cultures at the colonial sea frontier.* Fullers Publishing.

xx Read more about Eumarrah in Michael Roe, Eumarrah
(1798–1832), Australian Dictionary of Biography, National
Centre of Biography, Australian National University, http://adb.
anu.edu.au/biography/eumarrah-12905/text23313, published
first in hardcopy 2005, accessed online 18 September 2018

xxi Asclepious In Greek mythology Asclepius (or Asklepios) was
a demi-god hero as he was the son of divine Apollo, and
his mother was the mortal Koronis from Thessaly. In some
accounts Koronis abandoned her child near Epidaurus in shame
for his illegitimacy and left the baby to be looked after by a goat
and a dog. Ancient History Encyclopedia

xxii The daguerreotype was the first commercially successful photographic process (1839-1860) in the history of photography. Named after the inventor, Louis Jacques Mandé Daguerre, each daguerreotype is a unique image on a silvered copper plate.

xxiii It is worth reading more about the Aboriginal Protection Society which information is readily available.

xxiv Frederick Maitland Innes visited Tasmania as a youthful adventurer and married Sarah Elizabeth Grey at Avoca in 1838. He was eventually to became Premier of Tasmania in 1872.

xxv Calder J E Aborigines of Tasmania 1821 – 1827 Notebook available from Mitchell Library NSW

'I fear the old adage that we learn from history is indeed a misnomer'

— W.C.

www.ingramcontent.com/pod-product-compliance
Lightning Source LLC
Chambersburg PA
CBHW070731120726
47910CB00001B/60